The Light Warrior

This book is a work of fiction. Names, characters, businesses, organizations, places, events, and incidents either are the product of the author's imagina- tion or are used fictitiously. Any resemblance to actual persons, living or dead, or actual events is entirely coincidental.

ISBN: 0-6154-6902-7
ISBN-13: 9780615469027

# The Light Warrior

## Cynthia Robbins

2011

# Acknowledgements

First to Joan Adamak, I could not have written this story without your wisdom and coaching. You are such a dear friend and teacher.

To my husband Tom—you are my rock.

To both my children Christiana and Noah—thank you for putting up with my time spent on the computer lost in my imaginations. You are my inspiration for all that I do.

To my parents for supporting me no matter how crazy my ideas might have been through the years. Thank you, my light shines more brightly from your love.

To my best friend Crystal, thank you for your straightforward advice and support.

My deepest gratitude to my friends and colleagues for being such an incredible support.

To the GAPSTERS—your stories and experiences inspired me!

# Prologue

Every night for many years, the mother patiently waited until she knew for certain that her precious little one had fallen deeply asleep before she blew out the bedside candle. Routinely during the hours of darkness, the child awakened shrieking and once again when she woke up, it was pitch black and she found herself alone, calling for the comfort of her mother's arms. One night, the girl waits to cry out for her mother. Like the other nights, the unknown of what can appear out of the dark mass surrounding the bed panics her. This night she stifles wailing for her mother as she reminds herself that she is no longer a child, but a young lady. She reaches out for the matches and lights the candle on her own. The young woman realizes that she need never be afraid of the dark again as she had found the strength to light her own candle. The next night the young lady loses the matches to light this candle and has to force herself to conquer the darkness alone. Shutting her eyes and huddling like a frightened child, she has to prove to herself that the dark mystery was powerless. When she opens her eyes, a Light shining from inside her soul illuminates the entire room.

# Chapter 1
# Restless Rumbling

"Lucy, are you okay in there?"

My friends are playing with that frightening Ouija board again. Sonya's probably the only one who noticed I slipped out and locked myself inside the bathroom. It's safe in this brightly lit, enclosed room. I unfold myself from my tight huddle on top of the toilet seat. "I'm okay, just really tired." I can't let on that the board scares me. Actually it isn't the board at all, but the ghostlike chattering. Alex and Jess thinks it funny how that little wooden planchette flew across the room. They didn't hear the scratching or feel the coldness of the room. When the ominous voice hummed, thinking it was Brad, I hit him in the chest for scaring me on purpose.

He said, "Wha, what! I didn't do anything." I had to leave that room.

I've got to find the courage to open the bathroom door and conceal my terror from my friends. I hate to appear weak. Fearing the unknown and the invisible things that lurk in the dark always leaves me anxious. I feel silly for acting so scared.

*What's wrong with me?*

The irrational idea of a ghost or demon sends chills down my spine. Sneaking to view scary movies at an early age programmed me for years of sleepless nights. My deepest fears remain unexpressed for I worry about speaking of things that aren't supposed to exist. Such visits from shadows and orbs of light haunt my earliest memories. Mother always said there wasn't anything there, but I think she was more scared than I of the unknown. She never let on if she was afraid.

Her most recent comment, "Shouldn't talk about things like this. Don't draw attention to yourself and what makes you more special to have such abilities?"

I splash water on my face to shock me out of my terror and shut off the crazy images that I had conjured up. I must forget what I just witnessed. "It's only a game," I say to myself.

"Hey, where'd you go?" Michaela asks. "It's your turn."

"Just to the bathroom, but no, I'm gonna chill on the couch a while. Go ahead."

I sit, observing the usual nonsense emanating from the boys who are joking about the unexplained movement. Believing the planchette was actually swept from the board by one of the players allows them to deny that any supernatural force is actually moving it while I feel the heavy glacial air filtering from it.

Alex shouts, "What's wrong with Jess? He's blue. Is he breathing?" Everyone stares at Jess. Since I know CPR, I step over to see if he'd swallowed something. He doesn't clasp his throat like he's choking. I can't see anything, but sense a darkness sucking the air from his lungs as he was the loudest mocker of the powerful presence in the room.

One of the girls yells out, "Oh my God!"

I start chanting in my head, "Please God, make Jess alright. Please." Within seconds his breathing resumes and his once blue face regains its usual peachy color.

"What just happened?" Alex asks the board, now holding the wooden piece, the planchette.

I can't help myself from watching Alex hold this innocent looking piece of wood, which moves swiftly around the board spelling out, "He pissed me off."

Alex asks another question, "Why'd you stop?" It pauses and my nails dig into my palms, creating little dents and pain.

He asks the question again. Then it moves once more to spell out, "Because of that bitch!" The planchette flew off of the board again, but this time it landed at my feet.

Everyone laughs nervously and Sonja scolds Alex, "Why did you play such a mean trick on Lucy?"

I stand frozen, gritting my teeth and gasping because I am the only one in the room who realizes the meaning behind this unnatural occurrence. Trusting an outside divine force to swoop in and stop this madness, I asked for spiritual help. Perhaps Jess knows something that he's not saying because he just sits there, quietly sipping his beer and rubbing his sore throat. He's like me; afraid to admit that something out of the ordinary just happened.

There's no way I can spend the night at Sonya's tonight. I have to get home, away from this board usually used in séances to communicate with the spirits of the dead. The mile to my house in the dark seems less frightening than staying here another moment. Quickly I get my bag. At the back door, I quietly tell Sonya, "I think I drank too much soda tonight. I have an upset stomach. I'm gonna walk home. Hope you don't mind."

I dart out, rushing down the street. My body is tense and thoughts flood me like someone turned a fire hose on in my brain. The screech owls sound like looming wraiths following me. I jog even faster until my heart flutters so fast I think I might pass out. Hopefully nobody is looking out their windows as I must look rather foolish. Fortunately they cannot see my fright.

Only a few steps until I'm safely at my front door. I hope Mother doesn't ask why I came home early. She'd think I was nuts or a baby if I told her the reason.

I try to keep the squeaking screen door from banging. I drop my bag and keys inside and hear the television blaring in the back room. I turn off the TV and cover Mother, who is asleep on the couch, with a blanket. I then tip toe upstairs and get in bed. I don't even undress and put on my pajamas. More than anything I seek the security and safe feeling my bed gives me, especially when I pull the covers over my head, to hide from the unknown.

*Oh yeah!*

The night air breezing through my bedroom window causes the curtain sheers to billow out. My heart quickens and thumps as I sense a shadow lurking at the foot of my bed. I pull the sheets over my uncovered feet and tightly grip the blanket over my head. Every other night, I gather enough confidence to turn my bedside lamp off and sleep in the dark. Tonight there is no way I'll turn it off and overcome this hysterical fear.

*Or is it hysterical?*

I ponder about how it's undeniable that an invisible world exists.

*Please be only a figment of my imagination. Go away!*

I don't want to feel this ridiculous hysteria. It's illogical to assume that something creeps around in the darkness of my bedroom. Instinctively I know that I'm not alone, but I have to believe that I'm safe and sound. The most enlightening lesson gained from tonight is that whatever evil lurked and controlled that board was forced to mysteriously stop. The power of good has to overcome the forces of evil, at least that's what I hope.

I struggle with myself to overcome this ridiculousness and push the button on the clock radio, hoping the music will drown out any childish deep-seated fears. At least Mother sleeps nearby if I actually see or hear something terrifying.

With the covers still pulled completely over my head like a small child, my panting absorbs all of the oxygen under the blanket. As I struggle to regain my stability, my entire body tightens. No matter how hard I try to convince myself nothing lingers in the room, uncertainty undermines my bravado. Some would say its immaturity, but I know what I feel.

Another sleepless night awaits me until I discover how to banish these fantasies, if that is what they truly are. Where does this fear stem from? I must solve this mystery if I'm to out grow such foolishness.

The clock chimes twelve o'clock, a reminder to close my eyes soon before an early rise tomorrow morning. I grab my night robe and thrust my arms through the sleeves, heading downstairs to Mother's office and a bookcase filled with her favorite classics. I need to find a good read that will bore me to sleep. To elude any possible repeat of my bedroom imaginations, I turn on every light as I move from room to room until reaching the bookcase.

Standing in front of the books, I decide to grab the oldest and most tattered for it would probably prove to be the dreariest, but a hunch pushes me to keep looking until the right one is found. Without warning, a book tumbles off the tallest shelf so forcefully that for a second, I think someone is attempting to strike me.

I inspect the bookcase thoroughly to dismiss any possible supernatural causes, but find nothing to trigger this book, apparently on its own, to pop off the shelf and land at my feet. This is the very thing I'm afraid to face every night. It's truly remarkable I haven't run back upstairs to hide in my bed. This feels different; oddly, harmless. Instead, this unexpected occurrence ignites a courage previously hidden within me.

*This is truly interesting. Is someone trying to get my attention?*

Curiosity overcomes my anxiety and I pick it up. The title reads "Inanna, Goddess of the Overworld and Underworld." I've never seen Mother read this book. It looks a little dusty, probably from being so high in the bookcase and hidden from view. Who in heavens name is Inanna? I flip through the pages and on the front facing page, in ink I find a drawn heart with the name "Eli" written in the middle. The scribble looks eerily similar to my bubbly writing, but I've never seen this book and I don't know any person named Eli.

I turn on the computer and google the name "Inanna" seeking an answer. My research of any facts or myths about her reveal: The heroine Inanna is recorded in the timeless, ancient Sumerian cuneiform tablets, written long before the existent ancient texts.

*This book sounds so intriguing. It overcomes my original quest to find a dull read.*

I continue searching the internet and find more amazing information: "Inanna was a more renowned Goddess of the heavens, being intelligent, beautiful and powerful. It's a story of spiritual initiation in order to understand the polarity of good and evil. She had to follow the restless rumbling inside to discover something veiled from her sight. She descended from the heavens to marry a man on Earth, who became King. With only the experience of knowing humankind at their finest, she desired more understanding and chose to visit her sister of darkness in the Underworld."

The title captivates me more than how it mysteriously fell off the shelf. I take the book with me back to my bedroom to scan through the pages of my intriguing discovery. I turn directly to the chapter of Inanna's descent into the Underworld as this story stirs some kind of unknown restlessness within me.

Inanna blindly descended into the Underworld to embrace humanity at its worst. In order to know their best, she had to know their most evil. The veils of illusion were stripped from her sight as she endured humility at the hands of her sister of darkness, who commanded Inanna to disrobe and further, to surrender the possessions of her illusions, one by one, through each of the seven gates descending into the Underworld. As she stood naked and bowed low, the Annuna judges pronounced her guilty, struck her dead and ordered that she be hung on a nail in the public square until the body became a rotting corpse. After three nights, she was rescued and ascended back to her seven cities of Earth and heaven with more wisdom and compassion for humankind.

She was aware of a great responsibility as she challenged herself to know more by letting go of fears, old ideas and beliefs and with strength, rise anew by overcoming her vulnerabilities.

This mysterious book certainly has my attention now. I lie in bed musing over its many twists and turns, after having read only the short portion of Inanna's penetrating the Underworld. Spending three hours with my nose in this book still finds me alert as the sun is dawning.

*Will I ever discover why this book appeared so suddenly in my life without any effort on my part?*

I realize, of course, that the few pages I read has inspired a tremendous yearning to discover what it symbolizes to me. Sleepy, I turn my bedside lamp off.

# Chapter 2
# Lighting a Candle in the Dark

*There has to be more to life!*

I silently scream as I sit on Shane's couch inside his family's basement.

For the first time, I've finally found the right words to explain my restlessness. Yesterday I remembered thinking my life couldn't get any better. But today as I watch the end of summer, I slip into a depression. In recent days, I've been fighting increasing mood swings and unease as something unidentifiable shifts inside my usually complacent state of mind. I should be happy as starting on Monday a whole new life at college lies ahead. It's Saturday night, and my last weekend before chucking aside my various excuses to grow up. This last party with all my high school buddies is supposed to be a cheery sendoff as we head off in our separate directions. Instead, agitation preoccupies me.

Caleb Ryder, my most recent crush, flops down beside me asking, "What's wrong, Lucy? Chill out and have fun tonight. I won't be seeing you for a long time." Caleb's irresistible smile spreads across his face, but I ignore his attempt to change my mood. I don't understand the urge to push him away. Apparently distress shows on my face.

He's leaving for basic training at San Antonio's Lacklund Air Force base on Thursday. He'll be gone for the next eight weeks. After that, who knows where he'll be stationed. On top of that, last month my best friend since grade school moved to live with her family in England. I'm reluctantly happy for Jenna's dad and his promotion, but I hate the fact that I will meet this first day of college by myself. Without my best friend and shield from loneliness, I fear college. Once it was decided that her family was moving to England, easily Jenna was accepted into the University of Oxford.

Jenna saved me from a miserable seclusion and bolstered my self-confidence through the gawky years once I reached past the braces, greasy unwashed hair and shiny, pimply-skin stages as we both struggled through this awkward phase together. My senior year I came out of my shell after discovering that I had blossoming good looks and a curvaceous shape. I was fine with being second to the most beautiful girl in school as Jenna helped me to not feel like the ugly duckling anymore.

Caleb's impulse to join the military gnaws in the pit of my stomach. Robert, my father, was a prominent military man so I understand the difficulties and stress associated with being a war hero. He went missing from his undisclosed job in Afghanistan shortly after my twelfth birthday.

One day two officers of the military showed up at our door and announced that he was missing in action and believed to possibly have been killed by a road-side bomb. Because the bodies in the vehicle were so terribly mutilated after the explosion and couldn't be identified, I choose to believe he's only missing. My heart doesn't feel his absence from this world.

The haze from the smoke lingers in the daylight basement of Shane's home and the music blares. Shane's parents don't really care what we do downstairs as they're more consumed with their own addictions. I never ask Shane how he always has a range of booze and weed. It's like a playground for teens with a pool table, swimming pool and trampoline. Even being at another party with an assortment of high school friends, I still feel isolated and cut off from them. Naturally, my gullibility tolerates the brunt of their teasing and jokes. I usually laugh it off when they make fun of my belief in the paranormal as I once made the mistake to openly share my strange ideas. But tonight I feel differently. I can't shake off this inner pressure to be doing something else.

I get up from the edge of the couch, thinking to myself, *I'm done.* Finally insight prods me to realize and accept that my old life is ending. It's not fun anymore to party and stay awake all hours of the night. I can't tolerate anymore midnight runs to Bagby Hot Springs when Caleb and the rest have an impulse to hike a few miles just to sit nude soaking in a tub. I opt out on the whole skinny-dipping sequence encouraged by the guys just so they can gawk at us girls. Alcohol now tastes disgusting. My body has become allergic to even taking a sip. My eyes are swollen and red from the smoke hanging in this blazing hot room. Not able to breathe, I rush outside through the sliding glass door. I leap, alarmed because one of my so-called friends wearing an alien mask jumps out from behind a bush scaring me. "Asshole!" I yell in response to his infantile ambush.

Caleb catches me just before I reach my parked car. "Where you going? Don't let Brad get to you like that. He's an ass."

"It's not about the prank, Caleb. I'm done with this."

"Come again?" Caleb asks, confused.

"This! The parties. Never knowing what's going to happen next, you leaving and Jenna gone. I'm not sure what's happening to me, but my gut tells me the life I want isn't here."

I gently inform Caleb that I'm not going to pass time waiting for him to return on military leave. I softly kiss his cheek and say, "Goodbye. Please email and keep me informed wherever the military sends you."

He looks frustrated. I get into my car holding back the tears, but at the same time I feel liberated and free.

My shattering, piercing alarm clock jerks me out of my dreams of Inanna and her adventures. I knock the clock off the bedside table, attempting to silence that screaming buzzer. The worst sound to hear. Staying up late another night unable to sleep has caused me to wait until the last minute to start the day. I dread the monotonous morning routine. If only I were a genie, I'd snap my fingers and instantly arrive fully groomed. Today is my first day of college. I've only given myself fifteen minutes to shower, dress, apply makeup, grab breakfast and run out the door.

The charcoal black eyeliner pencil scratches the bottom of my eye as I paint the line in place, causing both my eyes to shut with sympathetic tears. I stare into the mirror above the bathroom sink, but it appears that my eye is okay. I fumble around looking for something suitable to wear. My bedroom's organized in unsystematic chaos. I have a method of knowing where to find what I am looking for, but certainly it wouldn't make sense to someone else.

I hear Mother downstairs calling, "Lucinda Marie Hayes. Get yourself out the front door! You're running late!" The frustration in her voice jerks me out of my musings. She continues, "Do I have to pull you out of that room and take you to school myself?"

I holler back, "I'm eighteen. I can do this. Don't worry." Despite her doubt, I hope to restore her confidence in my blossoming maturity, regardless of my usual chaotic morning schedules.

Racing the clock with only minutes to spare, I claw through my closet searching for something acceptable to wear the first day.

*Should I wear a professional outfit that doesn't flash "incoming" freshman? Will it matter? How many people will actually look at me?*

Not knowing how to dress doesn't help my anxiety.

*Be more prepared in the future!*

I throw on a pair of well-worn jeans, white tee and my chucks. Facing the unknown with my regular attire seems more relaxing than an uncomfortable new appearance. At least I had done one thing right by preparing a brand new backpack with all the essentials I would need to get through the day.

I stare into my mirror for a quick glance to make certain the outfit agrees with the confidence needed for today. This simple look pleases me. Small amounts of eye shadow bring the green out in my big round eyes. My favorite headband pulls my long and full auburn hair away from my face. Feeling satisfied and comfortable with my decisions makes me proud of my appearance.

*Not too bad for a kick off to college.*

Anna, my mother, standing at the bottom of the wooden staircase, now appearing calmer, lovingly says, "Good morning, sunshine." Childish embarrassment floods my face, but I make sure she doesn't see it as I admire her and cringe when she raises a disapproving eyebrow. Rushing, my feet clop forcefully down the stairs.

Willamette is only a neighboring University and I can drive it in about thirty minutes on a high-traffic day. When selecting an institution of higher learning, I didn't have the heart to leave Mother and attend an out-of-state-college after Father went missing. To reside at home in Silverton remains my only choice.

The community inside this small Oregon rural town provides encouragement to Mother, but isn't the fix she desperately needs to heal her ruptured heart. Each day, frayed emotions and depression lessens as she faces the reality of her life without Robert. Peaceful and beautiful, she never appears too overly stressed as she meditates every morning in her favorite room of the 1930's bungalow that she acquired at age seventeen when her parents passed away.

I feel cheated in never having known my grandparents, especially my grandfather, a Native American from the Osage tribe of Pawhuska, Oklahoma. I'm dismayed at knowing little of the tribal traditions. I truly desire someone to educate me about the culture of my heritage that modern society isn't capable of teaching. Mother isn't good at passing down this knowledge. As earthy as she may appear, she isn't very connected to teach me the Indian ways that I long for. I just don't think she's interested. Often she rejects my deepest thoughts and ideas by concluding I haven't lived long enough to make a rational opinion about the philosophy of life or the latest political sham. I miss my father as he always validated my ideas even if they did seem irrational and far-out. He was just like me, but as a stoic, staunch, military man, was unable to express his beliefs.

I really love my mom but we're so different. Lately, she focuses more on her new vegan diet and sipping wine with her closest friends at their favorite venues. I can't complain. She's making progress in overcoming her grief.

I admire my mother's most favorable attributes; her big eyes and poise. Today she wears a cream shawl thrown over her shoulders and her feet are bare. Her natural appearance and confident voice soothes me as I clumsily run down the stairs.

"Thanks, Mom, but gotta go!"

"Haven't you learned your lesson by now? Allowing more time to get ready in the mornings?" I knew she spoke wisely, but presently I'm not ready to take the advice. I know that when the time comes, I will be forced to be more responsible.

The screen door squeaks and slams against its frame as I dash down the covered front porch steps. Digging through my purse, I grab my car keys and jump into the blue sedan I purchased with hard earned summer money working at Lily's Deli & Grill. The car isn't in the best shape, but it had a decent paint job once and an observer would glance over the small sporadic dents. It gets me to where I need to go with minimal problems. Panic strikes when I realize I may not have enough gas left in the tank from yesterday's errands to pick up school supplies and map the newly assigned classes.

"Yes!" I state loudly when I find that the gas gauge shows a fourth of a tank. Just enough to make it to the campus parking lot. I'll have more time after school to stop at the nearest Quickie Mart for gas and a soda.

Music from the car radio changes to the local weather report announcing temperatures in the low 80's and clear skies. Knowing the sun will not be hidden by clouds soothes the tension in the pit of my stomach. If I need a reprieve from the uncertainty of the day's schedule, a grassy knoll and a pair of sunglasses are all that are required. I sporadically hear the news when the report catches my attention that earthquakes are mounting.

Earthquakes, volcanoes, hurricanes, tornadoes, floods, disasters that all rattle my sense of security. I'd say my overly protective life in Silverton has been a decent sanctuary from most uncertainties of impending doom. I'd rather view the world in rosy colored shades even as Caleb and his friends try to scare me. They think the world's going to end soon, but not me. I won't consider the possibility.

The repetitive drive through the windy country roads for once does not draw my attention to the surreal beauty of the recently cultivated fields. Instead, my restless thoughts wander to what I will do after college. I haven't started my first day and already I concern myself about the unknown after I've earned my degree, let alone the uncertainties if the world will just fall apart and prove my theory wrong. I'm often laughed at for wanting to save the world. I'm completely misunderstood when I argue my point that there has to be more to reality than meets the eye.

I really haven't put it all together as to what kind of career I want for the rest of my hard-working life. It would be so easy to take the easy way out and skip college altogether. I could become a beautician or work additional hours at the Deli and share an apartment with a roommate. That way I'd be close to Mother and still have my own personal freedom.

*What an incredible feeling. Freedom to come and go as I wish!*

As independence and free will attractively tug at my impulsiveness, there exists a bottomless craving inside, a nameless mystery just waiting to be discovered. The not knowing motivates my purpose to meet new people and attend college. Yet, I know that graduation day isn't necessarily the answer to my disquietude. The unidentified emotions that unleash my curiosity are enough to drag me to class week after week, year after year.

These unknown aspirations from childhood haunt me. Though I've never been able to unveil this enigma, there isn't anything else I can do but press onward. Everything happens in its own time. I suppose maturity will come in fleeting moments because of my unsettled thinking. The lack of clarity about these important conundrums actually pressures me to evade the wayward path. I want more to life than worrying about who's throwing the next party and how wasted and stupid we can get.

The parking lot at the campus is full of activity. Students, such as me, rush to get to their class. Tomorrow will be the first day of forcing myself to arrive earlier so I won't panic about making it to class before the lecture begins. It's time to grow up and openly embrace the prime of life and learn how to shine my own light in the dark.

*Crap!*

My watch shows I'm three minutes late. Remembering past times in high school when the teacher focused on me for being late, I sprint in the direction of my first class.

I enter through the doors and see the only available desk situated at the front of the room. My heart quickens and my stomach churns. I walk staring at the floor in fear avoiding any eye contact. Hopefully the action will make me invisible. My plan foils as the professor says some kind of clever remark that I didn't understand while everyone laughs. I missed the wisecrack since my mind races on and although appearing outwardly confident, I quiver within.

I just smile, coping with this stressful first experience as a college student. The guy sitting next to me says, "Don't worry. Professor Biel takes jabs at all of us. Word of advice: just laugh along with his rude jokes if you want a good grade."

I whisper back, "Thanks." I sure hope the rest of the day doesn't go like this. I'm about to fall apart.

# Chapter 3
# The Nature of Evil

Prior apprehensions vanish as the day progresses. Whatever happened earlier isn't any concern at this very moment. The
last scheduled class has finally arrived with a potential opportunity to find like-minded people such as myself.

The "Introduction to Philosophy" class precisely satiates
my ever-seeking mind, stimulating me after my inattention to
the prerequisite math course. In my opinion, school curricula
requiring math as a necessity to earning a document that states
"Lucy Hayes has attended Willamette University and graduated
with a Bachelors Degree," simply annoys me. I loathe math with
its concrete concepts. Appreciation of a creative quality suits my
restless mind. The wonder of the adventure into this unexplored
world at college remains hidden and I know I'm about to uncover
something of value from this course.

Feeling bolder than usual, I walk into my last class feeling
more confident. The room actually would be perfectly suitable as
a large lecture theater. Finding a seat close to the front presents
no difficulty and I sit relaxed in the chair. I've pushed myself
throughout the day attempting to locate my way around this
unfamiliar structure.

The many introductions from fellow students in each class
leave me feeling uneasy. Usually my shyness betrays my initial
fear of meeting new people. Today, smiling and greeting other
students doesn't feel so uncomfortable. I'm beginning to understand the appropriate conduct for this new environment. Yet,

I'm still incredibly bashful. It appears safe to remain withdrawn, thereby avoiding a frivolous exchange of words with other students or even the instructor.

I notice the growing arrival of beginner scholars like me. Chatting comes to a gradual halt and silence spreads throughout the room when our instructor, Professor Callahan, steps forth through a cracked door on the side of the room. He appears to be in his early sixties with deeply creased skin and long grey hair pulled back in a braid. I judge from his rough appearance and wrinkles that his life experiences have helped to develop his wisdom. He's dressed comfortably in a sweater vest and slacks, but shows a possible rebelliousness as he flaunts the dress code by wearing socks and Tevas. On the surface, he comes across as a pleasant man.

"Welcome, class, to the 'Introduction to Philosophy.' I'm Professor Callahan." Pausing to clear his throat, he continues. "As many of you here are expecting to learn of such famous ancient philosophers as Aristotle, Socrates or Plato, I look forward to directing your ingenious minds to think for yourself and develop a personal philosophy.

"The conventional philosophy course typically begins with a presentation of the five branches of study. For instance, Epistemology: study of knowledge and how we comprehend what we know. Metaphysics: study of the unknown. Politics: structure of government and law. Aesthetics: perception of the five senses in regards to beauty, art and pleasure. Finally, the study of Ethics: personal behavior and choices in how to live a moral and just life.

"Developing your personal, moral philosophy should be a goal of all humans, although each individual perceives morality through different eyes, based on personal present social and cultural conditions, customs and lifestyle norms."

Professor Callahan stops pacing after presenting his opening remarks. It looks as if he's considering his next statement. "But today, I will begin this course by introducing and centering on the problem of evil from a philosophical aspect."

Professor Callahan catches my full attention as my ever present intellectual hunger lures me to endure one more lecture. I ignore signs of hunger, causing a certain rumbling in my stomach and my usual persistent craving of a Dr. Pepper, which triggers recalling my car's empty gas tank.

I become impatient with Professor Callahan's pausing after each careful statement as he continues to ramble on about historical references to the subject of evil and why he feels it so important to start the course on this topic. Perspiration beads on his forehead, which I assume is caused by mulling over the best way to convey his ideas.

*Might there be more behind his switching to a different subject matter?*

As I sit listening, I mentally wander off the subject to my own most central, endless questions as to why there's unspeakable pain in this world: the problematic quest to solve the deepest tragedy on this planet; the problem of evil. Questions race through my mind. In which direction is this lecture leading?

Preoccupied with my impatience, I smother my intense restlessness and refocus on Professor Callahan's words. "Evil is the construction of the human moral mind. Humans define the meaning of good and evil and have recognized that good feels different from evil. Yet, if good feels better, then what is the motivation behind acts of evil?"

A smug sounding, confident male voice from behind me answers. "Man is innately evil. It's part of the fall from grace, retold in numerous old sacred texts."

A new voice from off the side questions, "If man's evil, then why any motivation to be good?"

"Simply to manipulate a given situation to gain pleasure," the first male sullenly mutters.

A young woman reacts, "Babies are not evil."

Another voice adds, "Evil is a learned behavior and people are naturally morally weak. Can't the power of situations influence individual behavior such as the German Nazis torturing and killing during WWII? Each one of those soldiers who held a gun to a Jewish child was once a child himself. That soldier had to endure psychological torment in order to be motivated enough to kill; convincingly brainwashed by his superiors to believe that Jewish blood was tainted. Couldn't that have been the motivation?"

Quickly reflecting on these statements and scanning my brain for an appropriate comment to expand the debate further, my mind goes blank. I find that I'm exerting too much energy to discover my own reasoning. If only my emotions could speak for my brain right now.

The clock ticks closer to the last minutes of class. The debate moves forward with more offerings on whether humans are born good or bad, but the opportunity to voice my own viewpoint is slipping away. It's difficult to access an opening to slide in a comment. I wait for an appropriate time until a sudden pause interrupts the increasing emotional ranting.

I state, "Ordinary people are capable of infinite cruelty, but we are all equally capable of great good." I realize that I passionately spoke based on my own convictions. It feels like a shocked silence pervades the audience. The reactions on their faces seem to imply, "How can a young girl with such a mousey appearance produce such a thunderous voice expressing her convictions?" I have kept silent all day, simply observing and listening and then suddenly erupt like a dormant volcano when the pull of the topic overcomes my reticence.

I have to say something else as all eyes center on me, some curious, some antagonistic and some disinterested. "Humanity is good! I know I am good at heart! I might make some bad choices, but I do not believe my soul could ever become corrupt. I cannot believe the current system in which we reside is a natural human environment!"

A male sluggishly says, "Are you kidding me? Even a saint has the capability to be corrupt under the right circumstances!"

I don't like his tone. I consider his reaction to be a personal attack on my inexperience in the world. I grimace. The rest of the class appears to support his opinion. I pursue my emotional reasoning. "I am sure that under the right circumstances, anyone would kill to protect their people. I am certain that I would save a family member at the risk of my own life. I would have done this with the right information and tools to save my own father when he disappeared in Afghanistan. On top of fighting a war that I do not believe in, I not only would rescue my father, but lift from my mother her pain as a result of the absence and possible loss of her husband."

Professor Callahan turns his attention to me and asks, "Is your motivation to avoid pain the actual cause of your evil activities? How far are you willing to cause pain for someone else to avoid the pain in yourself, including the loss of your parent?"

Panic seizes me after exposing even more about my life. "Evil is nothing more than a disease on this planet and everyone is too lazy to heal their bloody asses!"

*Crap!*

My spontaneous outburst brings out a hidden radical side of me who always has been an activist for peace, a side of me that I don't want to leave as a first impression. I know I can't return to class, especially after being upset because I lost my composure.

When I arrive home, different aromas emanating from the oven titillate my nose. I can smell onions, probably chopped for dinner; the sweet smell of yeast in homemade bread and a cinnamon candle my mother almost always has burning in the house. She likes to heighten her natural senses through smell, sight, taste and sound.

These aromas divert my uncomfortable shame of having exposed a rare discernible part of me to the class. Only a few close friends and relatives whom I can trust know my vulnerability when it comes to revealing the overpowering strength of my principles. I feel like fire is rising from my feet to my head. Inhaling deeply, I welcome myself home and walk into the kitchen where Mother holds a prepared casserole. My childhood home is a refuge, the one sanctuary I can always rely on away from the daily stress of fitting into society's mold.

My favorite comforting tool, a hammock, hangs directly between two shade trees, secluded in the back yard. Before my retreat to the backyard, Mother inquires, "How did your day go?" I know she seeks a rundown of the events.

I conceal my frustrating experiences and simply respond, "It was interesting and a lot different from high school."

After a quick dinner, I swiftly head towards the hammock with my new textbooks and a glass of lemonade. The sun continues to hang over the tops of the shade trees before its descent for the night and a slight amount of humidity still lingers in the air, creating a nice warmth.

Lying on my back, I watch humming birds flying around, sucking the nectar from the last pink blooms of the crape myrtle trees. I hear birds chirping and the trickling of Mill creek behind our enclosed fence. Closing my eyes, staying in this one moment, I allow nothing to affect my recollection as I rehash the thought-provoking discussion of the philosophy class.

I've always had a deep fervent desire to uncover the great mysteries to the meaning of life: Who am I in this vast universe? Is happiness possible? Why is there so much suffering in the world? How do all the pieces fit together? There's nothing more important to me than to unveil these great conundrums.

I'm an optimist in a cynical world while I cannot deny that evil exists. What's to laugh about for wanting the world to live in peace? I'd like to believe in the stories of perfect Utopian societies, but my fellow classmates are wrong to assume that the human condition is naturally prone to evil. My momentous expectations have to exist in the abyss of knowledge somewhere.

Regardless of my personal reluctance to share my innermost wondering, because of a fear of being looked at as being different, I know there must be others like me out there in the world. I cannot be alone in feeling that I'm an odd ball because I intellectually think deeply, even at my age.

*I feel like such an alien on this planet.*

Even with my new found moment of courage to confront the challenges of college, I still have many fears to wrestle with. Besides my embarrassing fear of the dark on the top of my list, over which I have no control, is the disappearance of my father. Will he return? Can he really be dead? The agony of this possibility hurts too deeply. Can my mother repair her unexpected loss? How will the war in Afghanistan end? Not only in the Middle East, but world-wide? It takes great effort to contemplate such horrors.

*Life is such a struggle. Why does it have to be so hard?*

The pains of this world weigh me down. I have this unexplained willingness to stand up and fight, but for what? I do not know. It's just a restlessness that pushes me to accomplish some obscure task. I feel completely helpless as how to end so much global, seemingly endless misery. Aware that most of these horrors are not my personal hell, when does this nightmare stop? The worst of all these very real nightmares is to feel incapable to express my innermost thoughts and ideas and, yet, aching to accomplish something. I cannot even begin to understand what that something may possibly be. Reflecting on my ruminations, I question the accuracy of my comments today in class. I've hit a boiling point and feel extremely miniscule to the sizable problems this world faces, even if I do have a crazy belief to try and save it.

Pondering over my ideals and questions is suddenly stopped by the stinging bites of mosquitoes. Darkness indicates that it must be about nine o'clock. Lowering, breezy temperatures chill my exposed skin. After grabbing and hauling all the books and drinking glass back inside the house, I proceed straight to bed.

Besides enduring the absence of my father, I now have to cope with my best friend Jenna and Caleb moving on. My life is changing markedly fast. The transition from high school is more depressing when I have no one who understands me and now I must face another day of college after exposing my private thoughts to strangers.

Mercifully, no fear of the darkness catches my attention tonight as uncontrollable crying on my pillow overcomes me. I can barely catch my breath for my heart has a hole in it. There has to be something to give me hope in this crazy, nonsensical world.

Maybe, the book on Inanna can help me discover the meaning and purpose of my life. Inanna loses everything in the Underworld, but transcends obstacles while carrying the flame of hope. I clutch the book against my chest as a sign to myself that I will find the answers to my anguish.

# Chapter 4

# Eli

I feel different, lighter from the burdens of last night's worries. Blinking my eyes, I see an orb of light moving swiftly from over my bed into my bathroom. Struggling out of my sheets to follow the amazing thing, I run towards it, but it's gone. The craziest and most staggering supernatural incidence since the mysterious book fell off the shelf has just occurred and I'm not scared.

Procrastinating, I delay my inevitable morning routine and jump back onto my bed. I let my imagination run wild, dreaming that the day will be filled with enchanting fortune, possibly unearthing a great passionate love. I haven't found anyone that irresistible in my short life. Caleb was fun, but not the "take your breath away" kind of guy. Maybe staying in this magical flow of bliss will attract some kind of dreamy romance.

I could really use some adventure in my dreary, boring life. Now that I'm an official college student, there are even greater demands besides the many obstacles that I had to overcome to get here: Good grades; SAT's; applications; tuition money, endless adult responsibilities. I remember the words of wisdom my father imparted before leaving on his last tour of duty. "There are no easy routes in life, Lucy. You have to work hard now to lay the foundation for the rest of your life. No one else is going to do it for you, only you!"

I contemplate Jenna's new experience and lifestyle in England, plus her many new adventures on the continent and the ugly beast of jealousy rises in me. I don't like these kinds of emotions. I truly want to be happy for her with this opportunity to attend Oxford.

No one's going to find the adventure for me, so I'm on my own to find an exciting activity if I want to overcome the monotony of just studying and doing the same old unchanging routine every day.

I pick up the book on Inanna and read a few more pages to gather some inspiration for the day. Inanna learns to let go of her fears and desires to ascend into the radiance asleep within her, retaining a resourceful, all-embracing ambition while searching for her home and personal power of uniting heaven and earth together, matter into spirit.

I'm most fascinated with the interesting account of Inanna's descent into the Underworld. There's something important for me to realize in this story. Before she left on her journey, Inanna had instructed and pleaded to her servant, Ninshubur, and to the gods to save her if anything goes wrong because most everyone never returns from the Underworld.

It's like her tale represents a symbol of empowerment, independence and determination, which inspires me. I really like her sense of style as this story has magically appeared to me under perfect timing.

I perform my usual morning rituals with more hope. A rhythmic favorite song blaring forth from my radio entices me to dance around the bathroom. I dismiss any idea of sulking and refuse to feel miserable today. Suddenly loud static interrupts, spoiling the sound, irritating me to become angry. I shut off the radio, resisting my impulse to slam the top of it, hoping it would effectively erase the static.

Walking back into my bedroom, I see my sheer curtains fluttering out from the window as I search for my backpack. Yet, when I go to shut my window, I cannot feel a draft from either the wind or an air vent. I don't have time to think about it any further and rush to the bedroom door.

*Oh my God, the handle is stuck. It was okay last night, but now the knob won't twist so I can get the door open.*

Total frustration sweeps over me as I feel like a victim being subjected to some unknown forces delaying me to be on time for classes today.

"What the freak? Let me through this door!" I loudly demand, whereupon to my surprise, the handle effortlessly turns and I run down the stairs to the car.

*Damn it, now the car won't start after three attempts so what's going on? This has always been a dependable car.*

I still manage to get to class with fifteen minutes to spare and outside of the building, I gratefully relax on a conveniently placed bench. Essentially I need to find a moment to clearly analyze the past bizarre patterns of events. It feels as if I've invoked some kind of paranormal activity with my desire for new adventures.

The sight of nature in its glory of trees, sweet smelling grasses, sunshine and fresh air cleanses me before my entering this old institution of higher learning. I enjoy watching the people walk past. I'm curious about their life stories. Unconsciously I draw a psychological profile as each person passes, which entertains me while waiting for class. Reflecting on yesterday's introduction lecture on the problem of evil, I speculate about what sort of people these bystanders might be? Do they have kids? A boy or girlfriend? I conclude that nobody can know for sure if any certain person is capable of acting maliciously simply by looking at him.

But an uneasiness invades my musings. There's something about the abnormal events that occurred in Mother's office library and then what transpired in my bedroom this morning that unsettles me.

*Is there any explanation for the peculiar phenomena?*

I mull over these weird events. The way the curtains moved, making it appear that something other than wind was moving them and then for no reason, I couldn't get the door to open, but then suddenly the knob turned inside my palm, and that strange orb of light flew through my bedroom. These actions were not natural.

*Wow, do I ever have a wild imagination!*

I could get lost in my own fantasies and waste an entire day. I really doubt any of this to be more than a coincidence because it's not normal to believe that paranormal activity can exist, except for the shadowy figments of my imagination.

Regardless of my ruminations, I make it to class without the aid of a watch. I seem to possess a special gift of instinctively knowing when it's the right moment to take action, especially since managing sequential time is not my forte.

I find a seat in the back, thereby observing the discussions instead of participating. A list of growing homework assignments await me this weekend, spoiling any expectations of having any fun time. Fortunately, at the close of my last class, Professor Nielson allows us a reprieve from more assignments. Immersed in gathering my notebooks together with pens falling on the floor, I am startled by a tap on my shoulder and the sound of a man clearing his throat. Regaining an upright position, I find myself looking right in the eyes of a mysterious stranger. Restraining my immediate reaction to flee, I focus and look into eyes the color of the ocean that gaze at no one but me.

He doesn't appear to be much older than myself, but gives off an aura of maturity. At the same time, I'm drawn to his striking features and athletic body. His first impression reveals excitement and complexity. My intuition tells me that there's a sense of danger that comes with knowing him. I examine him more closely, taking note of his thick flowing brown hair and a forgotten morning shave. His plaid shirt with the sleeves rolled up reveal broad muscular shoulders. His posh style indicates that he must be of the affluent social class and his retrosexual flair ignores traditional fashion.

His demeanor reveals his confidence when he says, "Hello. May I introduce myself?"

His asking me for permission to introduce himself certainly is different than what the ordinary college student says. They'd say something like, "Hey, uh, what's up?"

"Yes. Sure. Go ahead." Incoherent, I attempt to camouflage my bewilderment and shyness. I can sense he knows that I find him most attractive. Obviously he's experienced in flirtatious encounters. He remains expressionless as if he chooses not to notice my obvious staring. Suddenly his approving grin and a wink erases any consternation or shyness I am experiencing. In a split second, I know without a doubt that we are going to become more than simply acquaintances.

"My name is Eli. I overheard the remarks you made yesterday in the philosophy class. I want you to know that I like your ideas."

"My ideas? Can you be more specific?" I am uncomfortable, not knowing his intent behind the comment.

"What I really mean is the way you stood up to your classmates and disagreed with their ordinary responses to the problems of evil."

*What did he mean by my classmates?*

I had assumed that he's also a student.

"You give the impression that people can be liberated from unseen forces."

"Well, I never said unseen forces."

"No. You did not, but it is the passion behind your words. You suggest that there is hope in an impossible future for human-kind. You spoke from your heart, unlike most people I meet."

"What are most people like?"

*What is he implying?*

"Hopeless and distracted," Eli states, passionately. He pauses, waiting for a response from me. His words overpower me and I desire to know more of the depth of his reasoning. Then like a big neon sign flashing in my mind, I see the words "cau-tion," a caveat which I choose to squash. This surprising infatua-tion gives way to my curiosity as it overcomes all common sense and I've already decided, for once in my life, to live a little dan-gerously.

*I hope I can keep him interested in me, although it probably will be just a lame attempt.*

But apparently I have no worries as he continues, "I would like to discuss this subject more with you. At the moment I'm rushing for an appointment. Let us get together at the "Apollo Café" on Monday after class."

"Do you need my number?" I enthusiastically ask and then am a little abashed for my eagerness betrays me.

"No," he responds. "See you at five o'clock?"

"Sounds great. See you there." After being so eager, I find that I'm a little unnerved. I now have second thoughts; a little apprehension. I'll be meeting with a stranger after all, off campus and alone. Since middle school I've usually only hung out with familiar people; pretty much isolated from the outside world. I suppose this is my fortuitous opportunity for adventure, meeting an eccentric, gorgeous and mysterious stranger. As long as he doesn't turn into *the creature from the black lagoon.*

Leaning closer, he offers me a book and softly says, "I'd like you to read this story." As he hands me the book, his warm fingers lightly brush mine, sending an electric charge through me. A scent of cedar and fields of lavender wafts under my nose as he shifts his position closer to me. The fragrance causes an exotic energy to run up my spine and I gasp as if exploding inside. Arousing erotic images flash in my mind. This imagery frightens me and, yet, his attractiveness fascinates and hypnotizes me.

I'm truly confused now. My runaway emotions first pull me one way and then another: common sense vs. perhaps a dangerous adventure; immature teenage romantic notions vs. more mature sentiments. I cannot ignore the invitation to meet him again. His presence doesn't compare to anyone I've ever known.

Before I can respond, obviously in a hurry he bolts down the stairs and I keep him in sight until he turns suddenly on the landing, grins and winks once again. His charm leaves me breathless and it takes me a moment to gather myself. At this moment I'm bewildered by my reactions for this guy is a man, not just a boy. His sophistication is new for me. Without taking my eyes off him, I barely manage to place the book into my backpack along with other items still in my arms.

As I emotionally settle down, a swoosh of fresh air like a swift kick hits me. I glance around, but nothing presents itself and I stand alone. Static electricity causes my hair to rise.

*What's this strange energy following me around today?*

I quickly shake this off as another misperception and proceed to leave another day of college, but with a promising and exciting new interest having caught my full attention.

With no plans for the evening, I spend it at home in the solitude of my bedroom. Mother's out with friends for the evening. Classical music plays as I finish several homework assignments. I spot my cello standing in the corner of the room. It looks as if it needs to be played as I stopped expressing myself musically when Father was declared missing. At the time, my talent and developing musical abilities impressed him greatly to see his little girl play the strings. It hurt too much to play the instrument after his disappearance and I decided to not open the case again until he returns.

I finally close my books and quit frying my brain on Algebra and wonder about this mysterious Eli. I analyze the conversations over and over again like a broken record, reliving the startling events of the day. It's interesting how he thinks my comments in class yesterday were intelligent. This aspect of our meeting shakes my world. Most guys are not interested in my ideas, but only on my curves.

*Wait a minute! It's not everyday I'm introduced to a guy named Eli. Could the book I found in Mother's library with the scribbled name "Eli" inside a heart be another mystical sign?*

I dig out the book he handed me from my backpack. I'm astonished, almost frightened. This can be no coincidence. It's the book I have been pouring over, *Inanna, Queen of the Overworld and Underworld.*

*What's the significance of an attractive and very manly guy handing me a book about a goddess who discovers self-empowerment?*

His random approach out of nowhere adds another facet to the mystery of the odd events commencing earlier this morning. There has to be more to all of it. Flipping to the last page, I find a handwritten note, "Killing evil doesn't solve the problem. Evil can only be redeemed." Below that is another note, which reads, "We are here to know the game by looking for a light in a dark world."

The door bell rings and quickly I place the book on my bedside table. I don't know who it can be and I'm a little apprehensive. Upon cracking the door open, I see two strangers dressed in business attire. Instantly, I assume they are religious missionaries trying to save themselves by convincing me to accept their premises. Today I'm not in the mood and intend to be abrupt and short. They look out of place. There are two more strangers in a black SUV with Washington plates sitting in my driveway.

*Are they a secret branch of the government about to tell me they found my Father?*

"Hello, do you have a minute?" the thin, out-of-place lady modestly asks.

Feeling a little excited and longing to hear good news, I respond, "Yes."

"We are wondering if anyone hearing impaired lives at your residence?"

In a flash, disappointment spreads through me as if betrayed by my wishes of good news. The tone in my voice reveals my disappointment. "No. There isn't anyone at my home that cannot hear."

The young man in his early twenties asks, "Do you know of any neighbors that might be?"

"No, I'm sorry." I stand there, waiting for them to give me the usual sales pitch, but they don't. I'm so depressed because of my disappointment that I don't even think to ask them why they came to my door, but their presence does seem peculiar.

"Thank you, miss." Both of the strangers leave and I close the door behind them, locking it while peering out the glass window. The black SUV drives down my street without visiting any other neighbors, which discomforts me. I cannot explain why it makes me anxious except they didn't act like the ordinary sales people knocking at one's door.

I shake it off the instant my phone rings and I'm pleasantly surprised. It's Jenna! "Oh my God! I'm so excited you called me! How are you? How's England and the guys, I might add?"

She sounds just as excited and we chat for an hour. Jenna informs me of all the fine points to campus living at Oxford and the new people she's getting to know. She's just as sad as I am about being far away from me. I miss her greatly after hearing her voice. She was equally excited about my new adventure next Monday with the mysterious Eli. It has been too long since our last phone call, but it satisfies me, at least for a while.

# Chapter 5
# Apollo's

This morning another strange orb flickers as I awaken to this same occurrence as yesterday. Instead of wishing the intruder away, I attempt to touch this white wispy sphere suspended in mid air over the center of my bed. When my hand tries to grab it, the orb is gone in a flash. After the initial shock, I erupt laughing, wondering how much stranger these recent paranormal events will become!

It's Saturday morning shortly before noon. It feels like I ran a marathon in my dreams last night. The sun peeking through the cracks of my window shades begs me to get moving. Instead, I savor the moment of not having to rush to school.

Stretching one muscle at a time, I yawn, recalling the odd chatter in my dreams last night. My gut senses a connection of my dream to the orb of light. And yet, there remains a small trace of doubt.

*That couldn't have been real, maybe a lucid dream.*

I wander into the bathroom and splash water over my face to shake off sleepiness. Eli fills my every thought since his introduction. He fascinates me with his exciting personality, enticing me to explore this newly found adventure further. I must discover what makes me quiver when in his presence and why his lure makes him so different than others I have met, regardless of any sense of caution that lingers.

He simply doesn't behave like any boys that I have known and he's plainly not the run-of-the mill college student either. At least this book presents a good excuse for another encounter as I have many questions to ask him. The note he left in his copy mystifies me further. I wish to know the rules of this so-called game of life, how close can it get? It's like he's reading my mind.

I need a distraction from my rambling thoughts so I meander downstairs to see how Mother is occupying her time. She sits at a round pedestal table next to the bay window, reading the newspaper.

"So what's the latest news story?" I ask, although knowing she's reading the lifestyle section.

Mother answers, "Well stocks are down slightly, a new garden show opens next weekend and a local dance studio is presenting swing dance lessons next month.

"There's cranberry muffins on the counter. Too bad you didn't get a taste of one when they came out of the oven this morning."

Obviously this is her way of implying that she's not pleased with my staying up late and sleeping till noon. "Um, thanks." I grab two muffins and sit on the other side of the table with a glass of orange juice. I read a small headline on the front page "Space Debris Falls from the Sky."

*How uncanny that meteors burning up and rocks hitting the earth can pose such a problem.*

It never entered my mind until now that manmade objects can fall back to earth and possibly strike a house. I can picture myself driving to school and a burning space object strikes my car. "Ridiculous!" I say aloud.

"What's ridiculous, honey?"

"Oh, I was just thinking what if space junk hit me as I drove to school. Silly thought, right?"

I hope she will humorously respond.

Scoffing at the comment, "That's a strange thought and not likely."

"Look at this article. It shows an increase of space debris striking Earth more often. A farm in Texas took a hit in a grassy field and caught on fire!"

"That's interesting. Maybe that's why more meteor showers are appearing lately. Just last night while getting into the car, I caught sight of what I assumed to be a meteor shower lighting up the sky with a lime green color. It was really quite remarkable."

Quietly sitting, I reflect on how many people have actually seen space debris burning instead of a meteor. I consider sitting outside on the roof tonight wrapped in a blanket. I'd like to spot a burning falling object. I wonder if there's an obvious difference.

Taking this moment to be the perfect opportunity to ask Mother what she knows of this book on Inanna, I place it on the table. "I found this book on the shelf in the office. What do you know about it? Have you read this story?"

Shrugging her shoulders as if she doesn't have a clue, "I've never seen that book. You found it in my office?"

"Yeah, it was up high on the book shelf behind your desk. It literally fell off, landing right at my feet."

"That's silly. I'm sure it barely rested on the shelf and your movement caused it to fall."

I don't respond, knowing that she would have some sarcastic comeback to erase any mystical conception. I'd like to continue believing there's a purpose behind the book manifesting right before me as much as the idea causes some unease within me.

The day passes uneventfully. After night falls and watching TV, I head upstairs to finish some homework. The boredom gets to me so I decide to call Caleb. I wonder how his packing is coming along since he leaves for the Air Force soon. Unfortunately, he isn't home, but away with some out-of-town friends. If I didn't have Eli to look forward to on Monday, I would seriously fall into a deep depression. Pushing Caleb away too many times has taken its toll. It's just as well we missed each other tonight since our last goodbye was hard enough to do the first time. I actually don't have the strength to do it all over again.

Peering out my bedroom window, I see a clear night sky and the stars shining brightly. Climbing out of the window and onto the roof, I find a safe position and make myself comfortable wrapped in a blanket and a pillow for my head. The air's perfect with no moisture or breeze. The crescent moon receding allows the stars to appear more vividly. Just myself and the night sky. As my eyes slowly close, I drift off to sleep lulled by the chirping crickets, never having glimpsed a falling object.

Monday arrives at last. My heart quickens as I enter Apollo's at the time Eli suggested we meet. I look around to see if I managed to arrive ahead of him, desiring to not appear eager and nervous. I appreciate finding the trendy hang out to be particularly busy today, which can cover my nervousness.

I distract myself by counting to five and discover that he's sitting in a secluded curved booth in a back corner of the restaurant. He's concentrating so intently on something in his hands that he isn't aware of me approaching the booth. A circus of emotions swirls through me like a merry-go-round out of control. The intensity is almost too much to bear.

I feel like fainting as I can't breathe when standing directly above him. He must sense my presence for he looks up from the object he holds. Unable to identify the item, his beaming smile diverts me.

Eli stands up and says, "Please have a seat."

Shaken, I sit. "Thanks."

Eli's composure is admirable as he casually chats. Since I struggle to converse intelligently, I just listen and nod when appropriate. Finally, he speaks a familiar word; Inanna.

Overcoming my silly trance, I ask, "Can you repeat that question?"

Politely he says, "What did you think about the tales of Inanna? Have you been reading them?"

Now we are on ground where I feel more confident. "First of all, I'm perplexed why you asked me to read this particular book. This is a story about a goddess and I do not know any boys. Um sorry, men, who would offer a woman such a feminist writing."

Eli shifts a little in his seat before answering. "There is a significant point in one of the stories. Can you guess which one I am referring to?"

Taking a second to insightfully reply, the answer instantly surfaces. "Inanna descending into the Underworld."

"And why this story?" Eli poses.

Taking a second, I reflect on the point of his question. "I suppose it's because she's brave and willing to face death to uncover the mysteries of humankind."

"Remember last week when I mentioned how your passion and deviation from the rest of the class inspired me?"

"Yeesss." He needs to be more forthcoming. I'm impatient with the way he speaks.

*Just say it!*

His reaction is strange, but we're interrupted by the waitress approaching to take our order. Agitated, I can't wait until the waitress leaves.

"Well, that is not the main reason I want to talk with you, but your outlook on the philosophical problem of Evil. I mean, you stood practically alone in your class."

"And you like that?"

Eli emphasizes his reply, "Absolutely! It's refreshing to find someone who shares the same sentiments as myself."

He speaks like Jenna and her family, the same mannerisms. Obviously Eli has lived an urbane lifestyle.

Curious, I ask, "Where did you go to high school?" His answer may provide a clue to his background.

He responds, politely. "An academy in Massachusetts."

"Oh!" I'm pleasantly surprised that he answers so honestly. "Is your family from Massachusetts?"

"No, I do not have a family, just my three brothers."

Noting his reluctance, I know that he would like to change the subject. "Sorry the topic shifted." I glance at his facial expressions, but Eli just smiles and nods. I can't stop myself and continue with questioning. "Aren't your brothers family?"

"Yes. They are my close friends. Lucy, you are persistent. My parents died when I was three years old. I was raised by Uncles as guardians and trustees for an inheritance we received. So to satisfy your curiosity, I am not here to get a degree from Willamette."

That answers my question from last week when he said "your" classmates. "So what are you doing here? And why did you happen to attend the first day of that philosophy class?"

Eli states, "Looking for a likeness to Inanna." I know his intent behind this bold statement, but conversely, his answer only confuses me more. I allow him to continue.

"Inanna believed that humankind should be given a chance to choose whether to ascend or descend. She was the divine link to the other worlds that has been almost suppressed by violent patriarchy."

Barely without a sigh, he continues, "One cannot destroy evil by inflicting more violence. The very act of doing this refuels the evil that is drawn by destruction in the first place. It is like a vampire sucking blood from a struggling victim so it can survive. By existing, it must take life energy through death and destruction. There is another way to destroy evil that very few believe to be successful."

Without realizing she was approaching, the waitress has returned with our food and eyes us strangely. I'm too absorbed assimilating Eli's statements to eat. Immersed in the subject matter, we continue our dialogue.

He says, "Transforming evil by supplying the unaware with knowledge and wisdom allows a choice, a genuine option. Lucy, your idea that evil is like a virus is right on the mark. Humans are at war within themselves, struggling to overcome this malady. Too many on this planet are doomed to failure having forgotten what it means to be human. They forget the true record of Earth's history.

"Do you know of the story written by Plato, *Allegory of the Cave?*"

"I'm only familiar with his name and that he lived in 4 B.C."

I listen intently as he explains, "The parable commences with a few humans chained and imprisoned in a cave with only a fire burning behind them, reflecting shadows on the wall while the humans sitting in darkness believe the shadows to be real. Never knowing anything else, there are no complaints until one releases the prisoners. Some react with fright and want to return to their bondage and step back into their familiar dark existence. Others liberate themselves from the charade and look at the sun, understanding the shadows had only been a deception.

"After the light of the sun enlightens some of the free prisoners, they become upset because their friends are still in the dark cave. Ridiculed and mocked, the enlightened ones try everything to convince them that their current existence is artificial. The shadows are only a reflection of a more authentic world. Therefore, legitimate truth must be experienced as words lack the ability to light the fire within, no matter how hard the facts may offend or sting."

I sit motionless listening to his astute observations, breathing slowly so as not to miss a single word and yet, sensing an imperceptible emotional sphere encasing us.

His dedication to the subject matter continues. "Furthermore, stepping outside of what you think is real and comfortable by means of releasing material attachments, you begin the ascension back out of the Underworld or, in the case of Plato, out of the cave."

I ask, "Eli, what do you mean by material attachments? You have a trust fund and didn't come here tonight dressed like a Franciscan monk."

"Yes, I know what you mean, but I am speaking of illusions: the convictions that hold back the possibility to transform. The definition of ignorance is the lack of knowledge. How can you not be polluted if the whole story has been nothing more than shadows on the cave wall? Having the bravery to gain knowledge without manipulation and secrecy is the cure, even when it shakes the foundation of everything you've ever known."

"How does Inanna relate to my quest to seek answers as to where we come from? Why we are here? The meaning of life? And an absolutely unquestionable in-your-face truth!" I tire of feeling so alone in my quest. "Eli, most people I come in contact with lack the ability to deeply analyze anything; simply repeating speeches and words they have been taught like a spellbound zombie. Frustrated, I cringe when they go on and on about immaterial issues while real problems in this world desperately need attention. Imagine if everyone on this planet could see the importance of standing united for a cause in the same way they get together for their tribal ritual such as Super Bowl Sunday? But, I don't even know how to take action."

Leaning in closer across the table, Eli says, "What if I were to share that this alleged Evil acts as a spotlight, deliberately creating distractions to masses of people so that they remain ignorant of a small, elite, underground brotherhood? The real deal actually occurs while the masses watch shadows appearing on a cave wall."

"I would say you were crazy!" Completely startled and shocked, I question his sanity instead of my own. But his description ignites my repressed exasperation.

"Now stay with me. The only way out of the rabbit hole, like *Alice in Wonderland*, is to keep digging deeper until you are stripped of what you believe to be truth. Like Inanna, she disrobed her material items the further she went into the dark underground to die, then to resurrect. Only by surrendering her illusions, could she return with clarity and awareness. A part of herself had to die in order to gain wisdom."

"In order to make any sense of your statements, I have to assume that this alleged Evil is not human? Last week I was presuming the problem of evil to be as a virus. Are you saying?"

Eli cuts me off. "I wanted this meeting because you are ready. I mean, you are about to ascend to higher levels of conscious awareness, but not as fast as it needs to be. Tonight I cannot tell you everything as you have already called me crazy. I will have to show you. Words are meaningless for this kind of disclosure. Are you willing to take this next step?"

The invitation sounds like a con or a real adventure. I cannot decide. My wish for answers to fall into my lap can actually be sitting across from me. There's a saying, "When the student is ready, the master appears." How do I discern without falling for a gullible line? Mother has always thought I was too trusting. I need to prove my maturity by protecting myself. Eli's a stranger to me.

If I say "No," this one-shot opportunity can be lost forever. I have insisted on a new direction and yet I still remain afraid of change and prefer staying in the comforts of small town living, merely dreaming and seeking small bursts of information. If I take his offer, will I regret it? Maybe he's hideously insane, even though Eli shares much valuable information. He's wise beyond his years. I wonder how and when he reasoned this all out. Can this come from education only available in elite prep schools? Father taught me to trust my gut feeling. I sometimes cloud my rational mind with emotions. Panic ensues as Eli awaits my answer, right now!

Quietly I sigh, "Yes," at the same time watching for his reaction. "So what does this mean? How does it work? You showing me, um, whatever it is you need me to see."

His face remains expressionless, "Next Friday night, meet me here after your last class. Wear hiking shoes or something comfortable."

As if the comment about me ascending to higher levels, out of caves and a possible malicious brotherhood lurking and then ask me to wear hiking shoes, throws me completely off balance. It isn't enough to possibly end any further contact with him. Perhaps there's safety in ignorance.

*Nope!*

There's no way I can refuse the invitation. I'm deciding for adventure and will pull bravery out of the closet.

Barely eating the food on the plate, time passes too quickly. I know our conversation will resume again another day. Silly optimism for another close encounter pursues me. The ambiance carries on buzzing sensations. Gathering my bag and looking inside the deep crevices of my purse, I find change to leave a tip.

Eli refuses to let me pay, even the tip. "I got it. Remember, the Trust Fund." He raises his left eyebrow as he says, "Before you go, I have something to give you."

Surprised, I ask, "What is it?"

He pulls out what looks to be a deck of cards from his pocket. The mysterious object he was looking at when I arrived. They appear to be worn and tattered from overuse. "These are pictograms. The goal of the cards is to open memories that have been lost or veiled from your current sight. Here are the instructions: look at each symbol without allowing your own interpretation. It is like emptying your mind of any thoughts. If performed correctly, an image or scene will appear, which will feel like your imagination. It is not and you will know the difference because the sequence of images will appear just like a motion picture. Do you understand?"

"Really?" I reply, feeling definitely inadequate.

"Trust yourself. Oh, and write down descriptions of what you experience. One more thing. Before Friday tell me the first item you choose to disrobe. Metaphorically speaking, of course. No need for nudity."

His humorous comment relaxes me.

*I wouldn't mind seeing what exists under his garments.*

I whirl around to catch another stare at Eli while we walk in opposite directions to our cars. Eli turns at the same second and I modestly entice flirtation while retreating into my car. Inanna was also known as an honorable sexual love Goddess and so I send a persuasive smile to test these new waters as he's more than I had asked for to solve the problem of my boring life.

# Chapter 6
# Rescue from the Underworld

The antique clock chimes ten o'clock when I return home from Apollo's. It's not exceptionally late. I consider eighteen as old enough to no longer necessitate a curfew, but I creep past Mother's bedroom to avoid any explanation as to why I'm late on a school night, according to her standards.

She likes to keep a short leash on my whereabouts. I cannot explain my lack of consideration to just dial her cell phone; a quick check-in most often allays any worry she might have for my wellbeing.

As I stealthily move across the old wooden floor, it squeaks beneath my feet. I stop and hold my breath, listening for any sound from Mother's room. When I hear none, I resume breathing and slip past her door.

*Phew!*

I've escaped her usual lectures about the rules of the house as she must be sound asleep.

Tonight, I ignore my commitment to acquire good grades. I use the last hours of the day to investigate these mystery cards. My responsibility to complete the assignments from school ends up in second place. Uncovering the meaning behind them wins my attention at the moment. The possible memories stored inside the gap between my conscious and unconscious mind motivates me to discover the answers.

Eli's unexpected homework assignment makes him more like a teacher than a potential date. He speaks in symbols and I have to read between the lines to get a clearer picture of what he's suggesting. I sincerely hope I understood his instructions for interpreting the cards.

I pull them out and notice another note he left. "What are humans really capable of? Trust yourself." Is he implying that humanity can grow wings and glow in the dark? Buried sixth sense abilities seem more probable.

The backs of the cards are covered by an assortment of symbols, similar to previous primitive cultures consisting of simple geometric shapes drawn as black lines on contrasting white parchment. The first card displays a perfect circle with four identical dividing lines like a pie divided into four equal slices. I take this card between my fingers and thumb, concentrating and focusing on the design. I anticipate that my slow purposeful movement might add the magic necessary to bring out the answer from the sleeping part of my mind. I wait for an image to form, but all I see is darkness. Nothing.

*This process isn't as easy as Eli explained it.*

One more time I hold the card out to stimulate a vision. I close my eyes again and slowly inhale and exhale long deep breathes, bringing myself into a state of self-hypnosis. Continuing to retain the image on the first card in my mind, like being fed information, a mental image flickers into a shape. Specks of light begin shining and twinkling. As the vision becomes more solid, I see images of stars, moons, comets and solar systems.

My attention is drawn to a gigantic, pulsating illumination analogous to a star. Blinding light disrupts my inner sight until I realize that there is no harm in a simple vision. No words can adequately express the beauty of this luminary pulsing like a beating heart. I concentrate more deeply to refine the vision. I see the outline of what looks to be the Milky Way galaxy. This mega collection of light synchronizes with the corresponding pulse within the earth's core, known as a hertz rhythm. The vision depicts Earth struggling to maintain its heart beat. Great sadness fills me as it appears the planet is crying out for help. The beats are irregular and constrained within a tightly woven web, like a spider's silky web.

Our rotating solar system borders the edge of this enormous galaxy. I see rotating gears and a systematic galactic clock. The geometric pie with four equal slices awakens life within our great galactic star system. The symbolically divided circle indicates the four consecutive ages of time, like a clock about to strike midnight before the dawn of a new day, but instead, it's designating the beginning of a new epoch.

*Could this be the calculation of the great Mayan Calendar that everyone is discussing? Can this actually mean the end of our world?*

Telepathically, I hear the words, "No! It's not the end, but is known as the Great Shift: the beginning of a cyclical time when everything on Earth, as well as your entire solar system, emerges anew to restart a cosmic galactic year."

"How and why does this happen?"

The telepathic voice becomes stronger. "There's nothing to fear. Embrace change and become aligned with Source." The vision shows the Galaxy's center emitting a vibration sending radiating Light in the direction of our solar system. I sense nowhere to escape or hide as it floods every planet. Even though the facets of this vision seem overwhelming, instead peace erases any fear as the Earth becomes encased within a streaming supernova-like wave.

*Wow!*

This technique works just like my mind flashing lucid dreams. The downloaded information operates as if I were in a virtual reality computer with new software.

When I open my eyes and focus on the familiar objects in my bedroom I begin to doubt that any of what I just witnessed is valid. It was probably just a repressed memory from a documentary seen in the last month or so. I'll have to ask Eli the meaning of this symbol when I see him next. It certainly is a fascinating enigma. Deeply engrained, these sequential impressions weigh too heavy on my weary mind and I fall into a deep slumber.

Before I know it, I am startled from what I think is an earthquake. I struggle to become fully awake out of my deep, coma-like sleep. Clammy moisture covers my body. I utter, "Whoa!" What is this strange feeling? My inner trembling imitates seismic activity. I scan my room to determine if any objects are moving or being shaken off the shelves, but its calm with not a shuffle of a single figurine. The clock shows the time as shortly after five a.m. "Ugh." I slam my head back into my pillow and again fall asleep.

The week slowly passes. I wait in anticipation of meeting Eli again and learning the mystery behind the hiking boots as well as finding out how to accurately read the images on those cards. I anxiously long for a chance encounter at school, but I get a feeling it's not going to happen since he's not a student.

In just a short time, I've met several people whom I can see myself hanging out with. Kari and Eliza asked me during algebra class if I want to go clubbing with them tonight.

"Yeah, sounds fun! When you leaving and who's driving?" I ask. My first instinct is that I should just stay home. It seems irresponsible when classes resume tomorrow, but I justify my decision to go with them as my first class on Thursday starts late in the morning. I'm a little suspicious of their intentions, but then I need to get out and meet new people. This becomes my first priority.

Kari responds, "I have my Dad's beamer for the week so I'm driving. I'm excited you're going out with us, Lucy!"

Eliza squeals, "We're gonna have *so* much fun!" Eliza addresses Kari, "We should have her meet Jose. They would totally hit it off!"

*Who's Jose? I don't want to be set up with anyone right now.*

I respond, "I think I'll pass on the whole blind-date thing. Okay?" I do appreciate them bringing me into their social circle, but I have no idea what kind of taste they have in regards to the dating scene. I don't like uncomfortable situations. I'm the odd one out since they both share a history together from attending Salem high schools.

Kari says, "Sure, we don't want to pressure you."

I change the subject. "Where's the club?" I'm curious as most clubs in Salem have been shut down because of too many fights and unscrupulous activity. The clubbing crowds have migrated up toward Portland.

"Can't tell you. It's a secret, but it's here in Salem. The guy who's putting it on is a real playa'. Discretion's advised," Kari says.

"Don't want to piss off Pacho," Eliza adds.

This sounds like a hot mess to find myself in. I'm having a hard time saying no, especially now that I wonder what kind of club this might be. "How about meeting here at the campus? I'll leave my car in the parking lot."

Kari agrees, "Let's say eight-thirty tonight?"

"See ya tonight." Just enough time to go home, have dinner and maybe avoid a million questions from Mother as to my whereabouts for the evening. Maybe I'll luck out and she'll be gone for the night.

Fortunately, when I arrive home I find a note stating that Mother is out at another dance class. It's easy to text, "Out with some new girl friends. Will call before midnight." I don't think she'll be upset despite her excessive worrying as she often comments that I need to make new friends. I have my cell phone on me just in case.

Kari and Eliza are not on time and I sit twenty minutes in the car waiting. I see headlights arriving as dusk turns into night. I get out of my shabby car as a black BMW pulls up next to me. Kari leans over as Eliza opens the passenger door and says, "Wahoo! Get in the car, girl! We're gonna have some fun!" I ignore my gut feeling cautioning me and get in the back seat. A new adventure liberates me from keeping safe all of the time.

Sliding across the seat, a boy about my age says, "Hi, I'm Jose."

*Damn it! They set me up after all.*

I don't want to be rude so I adopt a friendly manner. "Hi, my name is Lucy." During the entire ride to this secret location, Jose and I remain quiet. We both listen while they blare the music. Only shouting would work under these confined conditions.

We step out of the car, parked in a large lot next to an old warehouse in the industrial section of Salem. A variety of cars pack the parking lot. Someone has to be pulling strings to keep this one under wraps. As we approach, I feel the thumping vibrations of music blaring from the open doors. My confidence blossoms as I wore a satin dress and heels. My hair flows down my back, moving gracefully as I walk.

Boom...boom...boom...the sound system blasts from the floor. Kari and Eliza take off without me and head to a bar serving alcoholic drinks to under-aged kids. Obviously this isn't put on for the public and the need for secrecy. Taking in the scene, I discover that I stick out like a sore thumb. I see bandanas, rosaries hanging off the neck and old English tattoos as the boys expose their sweaty chests from the humidity and hip hop dancing. Some were popping and giggin, others posed slightly bouncing to the rhythm.

I feel out of place in this unfamiliar atmosphere. I quickly scan the room for Kari and Eliza. Both of them are off to the side, feverishly dancing while holding drinks in their hands. I circle around the outside of the dance floor, scrutinizing the place I was sucked into.

*I should have listened to my gut. I really feel uncomfortable.*

Plastic seats line the back of the wall. I find a place to sit and wait patiently as I contrive a way to get back to my car only a few miles away.

While I sit, a group passes around a pipe and a bag of a white substance being held by one of the young participants adds to this mayhem. I glance down, hoping they didn't observe me staring. Getting up to find the restroom, I hear some derogatory comments directed toward me. Pretending to not hear them, I continue toward the restroom when an arm out of nowhere pulls me into a dark corner. Adrenaline floods my system and I start fighting with all my strength, which is a puny force. I am shocked when the arm turns out to be attached to a familiar face.

I scream with relief, "Eli! What, wait, why are you here?" He doesn't belong here any more than I do. "Did you follow me?"

"I did, along with my brothers," he responds. I look around searching for them. At that moment they slip out from the shadows in the room, but I have little time to actually see their faces. Eli directs me toward the back of the building with his three brothers walking behind me like my personal body guards. At the back door, a guy named Sumo and another guy looking like his gangster friend, stand abreast with arms crossed as if to block our exit.

Sumo asks, "Is this guy with you, sweetheart?"

Under the circumstances I can understand why it might appear that I'm being kidnapped. "Yes, I'm fine. He's my boyfriend." I hold myself together as this actually does feel like a kidnapping. He lets us pass and my mind races to various possibilities as far as my survival. Eli is still holding my arm tightly and walking toward a car when two men dressed in out-of-place dark suits fall into step behind, moving rapidly towards us. Air swooshes past me causing my hair to blow around my face. Eli's brothers immediately attack the anonymous men. Eli forces me into a car and slams his feet on the accelerator, causing the wheels to shriek, which momentum flings my body against the passenger door. I become more frightened when Eli tromps down hard on the brakes, stopping the car so his brothers can jump into the back. I close my eyes to avoid seeing any possible aftermath of Eli's action as the car speeds away.

Calming my nerves, I look around to the rear seat and examine the three brothers. The largest one says, "I'm Zeke. Nice to officially meet you, Lucy."

The one in the middle identifies himself next, "I'm Marcus. This here is our brother Ki'el. We call him Ki. He doesn't speak much, so don't think he's ignoring you. He converses only when he needs too."

*I don't know if I was rescued or abducted!*

I can sense these guys are good, but my agitation increases as I have no idea what just happened. "What the *hell* is going on?" I look at Eli for an explanation as he drives down the road. Emotional shock overwhelms me. "Give me a clue as to what just happened."

He continues to drive calmly, but Zeke yells at Eli, "Go ahead. Tell her! She's gonna figure it out soon anyway."

"Tell me what?" Although I continue to eye Eli, Zeke' continuing spiel strikes me as being fairly obnoxious.

Zeke says, "He's nervous. He doesn't like frightening folks by telling them too much too quickly and he thinks it's gonna ruin the schedule."

"What schedule are we talking about?" I'm now disquieted by the vague clarification. "Well, ya gonna start talking, Eli?"

"Yeah, Eli, it's a little too late for a civilized awakening party," Marcus scoffs.

Speeding down the road to an unknown destination, Marcus and Zeke continue to jokingly harass Eli while I impatiently wait for an answer. He doesn't talk and I'm beginning to wonder if it was less harmful back at the club with Kari and Eliza.

Eli pulls off onto a back country road and then takes a right turn onto a faintly tracked dirt road. Large fir trees line the road like large dark sentinels when suddenly a big white barn looms up, which would be hidden from sight if it wasn't for dimly lit windows. The barn hides a small farm house sitting further back and a pudgy looking woman clad in a dress and rain boots, stands on the front porch waving. A rocky hillside backs the farm house like the walls of a fort and a few pines cover the hillside. I wonder if the clearing around the barn, house and garden acts as a protection so that no one can sneak up to the house or barn.

By the direction we went, I am guessing that we are some-where near the foothills of the Cascades, a place I know well, except that I don't recognize this exact location. As we all climb out of the car, I ask, "Where are we, Zeke?"

"We're at Mama Jane's house."

"And where exactly is that?"

"About thirty minutes east of your place," he replies.

I become more irritated with Eli as the seconds pass be-cause of his continuing silence. I have no other choice, but to just go with the flow and see what transpires. I've been taken too far into this puzzle to turn back and head home right now, as if I have the ability to do so. Plus, I must determine if those men were there to hurt Eli and his brothers.

We walk toward the house and Mama Jane reaches for my hands and, to my surprise, nonchalantly kisses my right check. Such a warm and gentle soul. Her hands are soft but cold. She says, "We've been waiting for you, honey. Come in. Let me get you something warmer to wear. That dress barely covers your bottom." I giggle because I appreciate her kindheartedness and sense of modesty. "Come have some warm tea that I just brewed while I find something suitable in your size to wear."

I'm too nervous to sip on tea at the moment and instead I sit down on a rocking chair in a living room, staring down the three boys, as they sit motionless on the couch, staring back at me. Eli stands to the side, leaning on the door frame between the dining and living rooms. He looks like he has the world on his shoulders.

I'm a little scared as I ask, "Are you ready to start talking, Eli or do I have to start asking a million questions to your brothers?"

Eli answers, "No. Start asking."

"Who and why did those men attack?" Frustration heats my face.

"Next question. I cannot tell you at this moment," he responds.

"Fine. Then tell me why you were there watching me at the nightclub. Let alone, how did you even know I was there?" I demand.

"I had prior knowledge after our second meeting that you were in danger."

"Wait a second. I'm in danger?" My voice cracks when I spill out the word danger.

"Yes, I knew the minute I started talking to you that this likely could happen so we have been keeping an eye on you."

"Spying on me?" I am not sure how I feel about any of this. I just want to return home and forget I ever went out. "I never should have gone to that club."

Eli mutters, "It started before the club. Those men started tracking you the minute we began speaking. It set off an alarm that their actions were to prevent us from meeting any more."

"But how is that even possible? How could anyone know when and where to spy on us and we didn't do anything wrong."

"Lucy, there is something stirring inside you about to be awakened. When I asked if you were ready to wake up, I didn't realize that these words ripped through the airwaves. I believed that I had taken the steps to be discrete in our meeting. This changes the next chess move. Meeting and sharing this information has increased the stakes. We need to make this happen as fast as we can."

"How did they hear our words?" I'm stuck on this quandary, feeling rather violated at the invasion of my privacy, brushing over an even bigger question and then I shout, "Make what happen?"

"There are mystical things in this world that you are just about to discover and it will blow your mind. There is danger in telling you too much too soon. This information you desire must wait until I take you to that spot we planned for Friday, except that we need to go a day early. It is imminently important that we do this tomorrow."

"I need to go home tonight so I can make arrangements. Oh crap! I have to call my mother. Where's my cell phone?"

"Uh, that cell phone won't work up here, Lucy," Marcus speaks up. "We set a block to all electromagnetic air waves entering this zone. You won't get service. But you can use the old dial phone Mama Jane has in the kitchen."

*What am I to say?*

"Who's going to take me home tonight to get my car?" I demand. Mama Jane comes out from the back with a handful of clothes, making me aware that perhaps I have to stay the night.

"Deary, you will have to stay here tonight. You don't understand what's happening quite yet. You're too important to place in any more harm's way. Let's tell your mother you're spending the night with your friend. I'll tell her I'm chaperoning to lessen her worry. Okay?"

Something about her reassures and calms me. I stay the night on a farm in a location, I am not exactly sure where, with a crush on a guy I barely know, including his three brothers, who are also strangers to me. Not only am I in a new possible form of danger, but I'm about to be told tomorrow some kind of enigma of a brand new hidden world. How can I ever sleep tonight with all this on my mind?

# Chapter 7
# The Ascent into the Unknown

The smell of fresh brewing coffee wafts through the cracks of the door in the spare bedroom at Mama Jane's farm house. I hear chatting coming from the kitchen along with clanging utensils and clinking dishes. The tantalizing aroma of bacon and eggs causes my hungry stomach to rumble.

I rub my eyes and look into the mirror to see if I will pass inspection, but actually I look so ludicrous, I can hardly recognize myself. Mascara smears and tangled hair adds to my unsightly appearance. Sweats and an oversize t-shirt drape my curvy shape. Mama Jane left a fresh comb, toothbrush and paste out on the counter.

*What a sweet lady as she understands the needs of a woman.*

Mother didn't have a problem with me staying the night with whom she assumes to be a new girl friend and it doesn't feel right misleading her. I suppose it won't hurt this time as it would have made my situation worse if she knew that I had gone to a shady club, hanging out with girls who demonstrated that they were not looking out for my best interests and to top it all off, four young men posing as my personal body guards because of some possible impending danger looming around the corner.

As I enter the kitchen, I am met with the sound of breakfast in the offing and the deep voices of Zeke and Ki laughing and poking fun at each other. Marcus is fixing some kind of mechanical item in the adjacent living room. Mama Jane turns from the stove and says, "Good morning, sweetie. Grab a plate and start digging in before all the food is gobbled up by these boys." I smile and gratefully accept the invitation. The food tastes amazing and I try not to wolf it down.

I ask her, "Where's Eli?"

"He's outside gathering the gear for your hike, honey," she replies.

"Mama Jane, why this major concern to take me out in the woods. It appears to be a lot of work when right now everyone can share what they already know."

She sets the wooden spoon down on the counter, turns off the stove and eases herself in a chair at the rustic table. I get the impression that she's using up time in order to decide what she can or will say. The fact that Zeke and Ki continue their rough-housing in the other room confirms my suspicion that they sense Mama Jane needs a moment of silence to collect herself before she speaks.

"Lucy, have you heard about the colony of bees dying because they couldn't find their way back to the hive?"

I reply, "I have only heard the news say that bees are disappearing, but no one seems to know the exact cause."

Mama Jane continues. "Instinctive navigational skills the worker bees require to return back to the hive are being interrupted by electromagnetic waves synthetically pulsing out from towers, thereby emitting a radiation. This energy blocks the bees' capacity to zone in and return from where they came, thereby disrupting their natural homing ability because they are thrown off course.

"Different forms of light can have the same effect. The bees simply get lost and the Queen is left with her eggs, no workers and the colony collapses."

"That's really sad. How can we fix the problem as bees are necessary for pollinating our food supply? Without them, there would be no plant life where there are flower buds that need to be fertilized."

"There's a plan and you're an important actor in it. Eli's taking you to this spot because it provides access to something very profound. This site breaks down the synthetic electromagnetic interference, returning you back home, like the manner of conditions that are destroying the bees and, subsequently, the hives. Marcus has done a good job blocking most of it here on the farm, but we still have problems. However, the grove best suits for clarifying your questions and breaking you out of your shell."

She points to the center of my forehead and says, "You have to see it to be able to open this, which is commonly known as the third eye. This inner sight stimulates sensory structure capable of light reception and strengthens the pineal gland located in the center of your brain, much like what can be done to return a bee to the colony. So let's leave it at that and wait to talk more after the excursion. Okay?"

I actually feel impatient and weary from all of these "wait till later" admonitions. But I smile as if in agreement as Mama Jane has a way of looking right through me like an x-ray machine. She speaks gently and strongly. Confidence emanates from her honest soul. This story about the bees restores my belief to trust all of their motivations. I do know I'm safer within their protection from the two strangely dressed men outside the club.

At last Eli comes in from outside. I help Mama Jane in the kitchen, cleaning up the breakfast mess. It's the least I can do after her preparing my breakfast and offering me a place to sleep. This morning Eli has a different air about him. He seems less tense and smiling like the first day we met last week. Something glimmers in his eyes like a child in anticipation of opening a present. He must be looking forward to the hike.

"Here, Lucy, take this backpack. It has a few supplies like water, snacks, a flashlight and first aid kit. We can stop by your place before driving up the canyon so you can get some fresh clothes and suitable shoes."

"You're really taking me home before we leave again? How am I going to explain you to my mother? Or where I'm heading off next when I'm supposed to be at school?"

"We can figure that out on the way there. Let's go before time runs out," Eli asserts.

Walking toward me from the living room, Marcus holds out my cell phone. "Here, it's untraceable after a few adjustments. I also added all four of our cell phone numbers for contact purposes. We'll be seeing a lot more of each other from here on out."

Apart from just meeting them, I like the idea as Eli has pierced my heart unpredictably with a tenderness that cannot be denied and, in addition, his brothers and Mama Jane also have a place there.

"Thank you, Marcus. Is there something wrong with my cell phone?" I ask.

"Nothings wrong with it, but for today just keep it turned off."

Eli turns and says, "We do not need it where we are going. It would be a distraction to our purpose."

Following Eli to his hatchback and thinking how it looks smaller in the daylight, I remember his Trust Fund and ask, "So why a hatchback and not a Hummer?"

He chuckles softly and says, "We need to drive incognito and not stick out like an elk on opening day."

"Oh, I catch your drift." We get inside and I check the mirror above the visor to make sure my face is in place.

*Ugh! I keep Eli from looking directly at my face and hair as I feel gross without a shower.*

"Is there time for me to shower before we head up the canyon," I request.

"Hum, just make it quick." He looks at me and I turn my head away and stare out the window, absorbing the topography attempting to get a sense of direction and hoping he doesn't get a close shot at my unsightly morning appearance.

While driving home, I wonder if I will have to live in fear of returning home forever. As if he can read my mind, Eli says, "Sorry to place you in this dangerous position. I waited too long to get you to the grove. I was naïve to believe all of this could be done effortlessly."

My body language must betray my private thoughts. Desiring to ease his mind, as there is no sense in both of us worrying, I say, "No. I'm okay, just a lot to take in right now."

We pull into my driveway and Mother's car isn't parked at home.

*What luck!*

She was out again. Must be running errands or at the grocery store. Eli follows me up the porch stairs. Having him at my house alone awakens all of my fantasies. However I promised to hurry and shower.

On my walk about examining the house for signs of Mother or possibly worse, I find a note in the usual spot on the kitchen counter. She persists in leaving notes as much as she likes the security of tracking me by cellular. *"Lucy, sorry I missed you after school today. See you after dinner tonight. Grab the leftovers in the fridge. Love you, baby."* I leave another note for her as she will see it and assume my departure took place after school.

I quickly shower and daydream about spending an entire day with Eli, which animates my mood and lightens me like a bright ray of sunshine. Gathering my things, we hustle to his car and speed away.

My happy thoughts together with the bright skies buoy me up into the clouds and fill the car. I cannot help but broadly smile while listening to Eli as he's also lively. Every worry from making sure Mother isn't upset, missing school and to panic from strange stalkers following us, fade completely away. I almost forget the reason for our trip as we listen to music, effortlessly share opinions and most importantly, live for the moment.

Reaching Eli's destination at the end of a winding dirt road up in the forested hills, we unpack the gear from the car. "How long is this walk?" I ask.

"It will take about an hour to reach the clearing and another thirty minutes to get across and walk down the ravine. We can rest awhile and eat the meal Mama Jane packed for us when we get closer."

I sure hope that Eli realizes how good natured I am because ordinarily, I whine and complain if I walk too far. The only real hiking that I've done is the loop around Silver Creek Falls Park. But I'm going to suck it up and pretend to enjoy the climb as I'd like to avoid the appearance of a complainer.

We follow an animal trail through a wooded area at the beginning of our hike. This is a perfect opportunity to ask him, relative to his homework assignment, the meaning of the first card envisioned. "So I did what you wanted me to do. I chose my first card, but nothing came to me. After the second time I deeply contemplated on the card, I saw an image, which I decided had to be translated into a meaning. Is that what was supposed to occur?"

Eli slows his pace as his interest peaks. "Which card did you gaze at?"

"It was the circle that has four even slices like a pie. What does this mean?"

"No, what does it mean to you?" I'm taken back by his question as he demands my answer.

"I think the image represents a big wheel turning and measuring a cosmic year, but I'm clueless to what that means." I look to see if he's satisfied with my answer.

"You are better at this than you give yourself credit. Didn't I say to stop doubting yourself?"

"I suppose you did. Isn't doubt the best way to collect information to make sure the data is correct?"

"When listening to another's opinion or that of the public to decide whether a person is lying or not, you have to rely on your inner sight, whether it feels comfortable and if not, then naturally mistrust the answer. Often when using your extra-sensory abilities, which is what you are doing when scanning the cards, there can be interference from an unhelpful energy and that is why, if you don't feel comfortable, stop. Mentally see yourself surrounded with a shield and know that there can be no interruption.

"Your mind is not your brain. It is composed of multiple layers of consciousness. The goal is to have direct connection to the universal web of information, transmitted naturally through electromagnetic energy, making a connection to the Universal internet via mind connection. The body vibrates with EM energy as does Earth and everything else."

"So I have the right answer to the pictogram?" Eli frowns as if I did something wrong. "Oh, I did it again? It's the right answer?" His glowing smile confirms my accuracy.

"Mistrusting yourself is the only thing holding you back right now. Your super-conscious connection to this universal web has been impaired and today we are to begin restoring the union."

He speaks cleverly but I add, "I'm searching to understand the meaning behind your words."

"Okay, let me make this simpler. Your mind has been running on a dial-up mode internet connection. Today we are upgrading you to a faster speed."

"What a strange analogy," I say.

"Just wait. There are even stranger things to come."

I restrain my nervous giggle as I don't know whether to be excited or weirded-out. "So is this the awakening party Marcus mentioned in the car last night?"

"It's only the beginning. From here on out, there is no turning back. Once you cross this threshold, you cannot return to living an average life. You are about to see the world as it is, not the way you want it to be. You may parallel your pathway now to that of Inanna's to the Underworld and back. Once she started her seeking to know everything, she could not turn back."

Like only drops in a bucket for a person dying of thirst, these little tidbits of clues from Eli frustrate me and I increase my pace to reach whatever it is that we are seeking to find. I feel like a pirate searching for lost gold or the stupid girl in a horror flick about to walk into the hands of a murderous slaughter. Sweat pours off my temples and I quench my thirst from the bottle of water in my backpack. I shake off the creepy vibes as I sense Eli and his family as the good guys while the villains lurk far away from us today.

"What if those men from last night are following our path, Eli?"

He stops for a moment, facially expressing reassurance, "There is a fleet of protectors surrounding us today. You are very important, Lucy."

Slowly I look over my shoulders, surveying what he could possibly mean by this statement, but of course only the two of us are visible. Re-collecting myself after feeling an electric current move down my spine, I ask, "Eli did you feel a tremor the other morning."

"Can you explain the word 'tremor' because there were no reports of an earthquake?"

"I woke up sweaty and my body was shaking. I know that the Pacific Northwest has had a few small quakes."

Talking to himself, Eli mumbles, "It's quickening faster than I calculated."

"Speak English. I'm still learning the definitions of your terminology!"

"Alright, sorry. Continuing to explain your vision about the cosmic year, the center of the galaxy emits a large magnetic energy that even secular scientists are publishing as 'magnetic filaments.' Earth and the other planets in our solar system are all actually moving into alignment with this magnetic energy. Old myths tell of this grand cosmic year occurring every

26,000 years, but only now being confirmed by astro-scientists who identify the phenomenon as 'higher light' frequencies. This alignment causes the sun to react in unusual ways, which also directly affects Earth and all life on it because of this magnetic pulse, thereby activating star codes. The quaking you felt directly relates to your body responding to this initial activation.

"At the crossing of each quadrant during this most recent grand cycle, civilizations have fallen in the past to rise, again struggling for power. There are pictograms and messages written on stone, which have become myths in most of the world, describing the events as catastrophic. These are believed to have been left as warnings to future mankind. This grand cycle naturally revolves as a galactic cosmic regulator. Unfortunately, there are a few elite groups who want to keep this knowledge to themselves for personal gain. These few are misled as they are still serving the age of the old parasite."

Eli slows his stride for he is talking too much and becomes winded. He turns and says, "Oh, and by the way, Global Warming is such an example of being misled. The magnetic fields are becoming weaker on the Earth and the sun becomes stronger in the process, which causes the ice to melt at the poles and rising oceans are the result as the weather patterns change. Cover-up of the data reveals that all the planets in our solar system are heating up, creating storms and even the spot on Jupiter is almost gone from the intense changes."

"There actually isn't anything wrong with the Earth right now?"

Eli elaborates. "Except for the idiotic pollution from toxic chemicals being let forth in the atmosphere, our oceans and throughout the veins of this planet!" He stiffens and shakes his arms as to throw some kind of invisible ooze from them like the mane rising up on a lion about to attack.

"The few that hoarded this knowledge several years ago disseminated misleading proof and mislead the evidence. Only when the planet is under stress created by the inhabitants, then earthquakes, flooding, hurricanes, tsunamis, fatal diseases, famine and flames engulfing large land masses are all part of this natural birthing process. Fighting over natural resources and fear from shortages and destruction overcame the most recent civilizations until they collapsed, wiping away all human memory and leaving the surviving inhabitants to restore any existing remnants."

"Eli, is there any possibility the bulk of our current civilization will take this seriously? Too many dark and disturbing actions plague this planet. I see a lot wrong with our world."

Eli roars, "But there is a lot right about this world too! Time, as we know it, is at the end. No soul can see past the transitioning from this era to the next as we are in the middle of no time, walking between two realms. People of Earth collectively decide the future in the present moment through their thoughts, emotions and actions. The portals open for a small period of time before the Great Shift closes a window of opportunity to either make it or break it for the entire planet. Do we continue living a lie or can a mystical magic of enchantment return to this once perfect planet? It is up to all of us to rise above the limits and decide the outcome.

"We are the ones we have been waiting for! For instance, a child does not learn to take responsibility if a parent enables the child's mistakes. We are down to the wire and its time to wake up to find our way out of this darkness, known as the path of enlightenment or more precisely, "Ascension from the Underworld."

I question, "Wisdom has a cost? Until we strip the personal objects of this world, we can't move through this Great Galactic Shift? Is it appropriate to consider these personal objects to money, cars and property?"

"Take it a little further."

I assemble my thoughts and attempt to utilize the same mental concentration I used with the card exercise, except there is no symbol to trigger my mind. "It's not about simple material items that make life more pleasurable. It's our attitudes, beliefs and ideas that keep humanity clinging and grasping because we are afraid to lose pieces of our self-worth. The story of Inanna explains her standing naked to face death; or the release of her previous self-identity; to resurrect more beauty in a new era and world."

"Lucy, I have seen from Wall Street Brokers to diehard criminals reach their rock bottom, lose everything and only when their blinders release, do they ascend to a higher place than ever before. There is nothing to fear when the old buildings and paradigms start crumbling around you. As long as there is air to breathe, food and water to drink and the ability to make shelter, we are all right."

"Yes, but I still like my car and big screen TV."

"Like I said, there is no need to suffer as long as those items do not own you and feed the ego. I have not given away all of my Trust Fund. That would be foolish."

*That's a relief.*

"Relative to your original question of a quaking the other morning: rising magnetic fields within your body are causing vibrations inside it. As the sun, because of its position in the galaxy, emits this massive energy, Earth also undergoes the same change. As above so below. Your atomic and cellular structure is adjusting and tuning into more energetic wavelengths.

"Here's another analogy. It is like changing your radio from AM to FM. Your tuner only gets about one or two stations and pretty soon you will be able to tune into more channels as you get an upgrade."

"This is all amazing and it feels right. Don't get me wrong as I need to digest the information that you have just thrown at me, particularly the claim about a group of few that you call parasites."

Our attentions turn to a creek bed and we find sturdy rocks to cross over to the other side. Beyond the trickling water, we enter a grassy meadow surrounded by giant fir trees. We welcome the silence after our busy discussion. The piercing beauty of this natural world answers the question as to why anyone from the urban areas would not choose to live in close proximity. My reverence for these trees, mountains and view causes my heart to expand in love, sending electrical pulses throughout my body. In this one moment, all sense of time has vanished and the connections to everything above, below and in-between converge.

# Chapter 8
# New Sight

"Quiet yourself and listen to the voice of your heart," Eli instructs as our meal settles. Feeling sluggish, we just sit observing the surrounding scenery. On the horizon, crimson and orange beams of sun stream out from behind the clouds as it sets. Hawks in search of their dinner fly above screeching. The captivating splendor creates snapshots inside my mind. My instincts tell me I'm exactly where I need to be, walking along the path with Eli as my guide, crossing an invisible threshold to enter a new adventure.

He continues teaching, "We are about to be hooked into the greatest power source that exists, which courses through every cell of our being. Entangled personal thoughts and beliefs can overpower our senses and then the magic becomes just a shadow so don't limit yourself. This next step requires a radical process of transformation. It can only be seen with eyes of a newborn. Fear cannot enter your body.

"Within your biological structure are seven seals. The Sanskrit word means 'spinning wheels' as they are meridians forming energy spirals. Some mystics have described them as vortices. When the seals harmoniously spin, energy moves up and down the body, bringing about a powerful life force. The story of Inanna illustrates her entering seven gates to reach the throne room of the Underworld. On her return, she ascends through these seven gates and Inanna lifts the veils and gains more wisdom and sight."

I push for more information. "I read somewhere from ancient writings on the internet that the number seven symbolizes completion or enlightenment. How does this relate?"

"Activating the seven seals is nothing more than opening the *Book of Knowledge* or unveiling that which has been hidden. It is like stepping up each stair and gaining a little more wisdom each time a seal is unlocked. Acquiring knowledge has a cost and only by reaching a state of humbleness and letting go of the superficial image of self, can one then open the seals, which hold humanity in bondage, and thus, unable to reach their full potential."

"What is that full potential?" I have learned more walking with Eli than most possibly discover within a lifetime, but my instincts hint that something incredibly different is about to happen to me tonight. My body cools with the breeze, and I reach for my sweater in the backpack.

"Lucy, you promised me something. Do you remember what that was?"

His stare fixates on me and I ask, "Come again?"

"Tell me the first item you would choose to disrobe, like in the story of Inanna?"

Shamefaced, I respond, "Aw! I forgot! Letting go of any doubt in myself." I inhale and then slowly sigh, betraying my present feeling of inadequacy.

"Now that we are in the right state of mind, are you ready to move forward?" he asks with an idyllic grin.

Assuming he refers to the peace surrounding us in this moment, I say, "Of course. This is what you've been mysteriously keeping from me the entire week that we've known each other."

With no effort Eli jumps to his feet, catches my hand and pulls me up. I like his hand touching mine even if it only lasts a second or two. Anticipation causes surging vitality to revive my stupor. Today he is my guiding star leading me to my destiny.

Keeping up with his vigorous descent almost causes me to drop my backpack, but nothing can break my grip holding his hand. Excited, I laugh racing down the hill and thousands of pine cones crunch under our shoes. The trees here are enormous and their tops reach up to the sky.

I gasp for air, lean over and attempt to recover from the run, when Eli says, "Come on, this way." He sees something, but whatever it is, I see nothing as I follow him into the thick undergrowth. In the middle of a ring of more pine trees posturing upright like soldiers watching guard, a large boulder sticks halfway out of the ground. The rock must be the essential heart of this sacred grove, like the focal point inside a circle. The waxing, gibbous moon appears boldly behind the branches as if greeting the Fall night sky.

Eli's head bounces up left to right, following some kind of invisible firefly. More than ever do I question his sanity. Our previous twenty-four hours together dissolves any such thinking as his genuine kindness attracts him to me. He motions with his hand, indicating that he wants me closer. His right hand holds an apparatus of some sort close to his side. "Now please, stay in the right frame of mind."

*Wonder if he suspects this experiment will backfire.*

I remember his previous advice and like a newborn babe free of opinions or judgment, only observe since I am about to participate in something inconceivable.

*Can I ever prepare for a moment like this?*

"Do not let fear take over your mind, Lucy."

Anxious, I answer as calmly as possible, "I'm ready."

"Take these goggles carefully in both of your hands. This technology does not come cheap and I do not want them thrown on the ground!"

"Technology? What is this?" I stammer, although willing to assume any risk that would not cause me to freak out.

Before lifting the goggles to my eyes, he says, "To believe that we are the most advanced and intelligent race in the Universe is a deadly mistake."

Wild thoughts cause me to pause while slipping the goggles on. I will never know the answer without looking through the lens. They are malleable and cold against my cheeks as the device presses down into place. My eyes still closed, I wait for a cue to go for it.

"Open your eyes, Lucy."

My eye lids flutter open and although unfocused, orbs of white light float in the air like gracefully hovering dandelion fluff. Gently lowering the goggles below my nose, I look to see if the fluff can be seen without them.

*Of course not. Why would I think such?*

Almost immediately in the same position, a larger orb floats across my sight and I instinctively move to avoid contact, but there is only a feathery tickle on my arm. Another glides to me as if it wants to make contact with me too. My eyes lock onto the orb to examine its features. It resembles a ball of static electricity taking flight like a ball of lightening.

Approaching me is a yellowish orb, which stops directly in front of the goggles, stationing in one spot like it's waiting to act and it begins to form the features of a face, clearly indicating an intelligent presence. It is a feminine vision of innocent beauty appearing in a scintillating light form who watches me observe her. I wait to hear from her either orally or mentally, but receive nothing. My mind races back to the years of my childhood and folklore about angels and fairies and, yet, they can't possibly exist. I tremble because of her delightful radiance, unable to classify her essence.

I try to count these elegant spheres moving all around, but more of them increasingly appear out of nowhere and I cannot keep up. With my goggles still on, I look in the direction of the stone and see a cluster of light beaming out from the center. Rainbow colored sparks like darting fireflies zoom out of a crystalline geyser bubbling forth from this large hunk of mineral.

An obscure movement behind this illumination materializes as Eli. He steps onto the core of the stone with palms down, perceiving the flying orbs without the aid of the goggles. The light embraces him and he stands there with his arms outstretched as if bathing in the cascading luminescence. The orbs also surround him, wrapping him in a circle as he stands motionless absorbing this precious light stream. As I focus the goggles on him, radiant love flows toward me from his beautiful and unusual blue eyes as if his soul shines forth. His skin reflects a whitish flame, but I cannot tear my eyes away from him, even though he seems more a vision than a human man.

An exquisite love rises within me and merges with his essence. Eli jumps from the stone in front of me and because of my overwhelming desire to consume him; I stifle my impetuous urge to reach out for him.

Before I can replace the goggles on my face to seek more orbs, Eli takes them and turns me in the direction of the stone and I intuit that he wants me to stand on the same spot on the stone. By looking into his eyes, I seek reassurance that the light will not devour me. His gaze encourages me and without the goggles, I step onto the stone where the light had been seen.

He gazes at me from below and I close my eyes, attempting to glimpse this beam from memory. I shut my mind to all thoughts and let this warm sensation of Love flow through me from my toes, up my legs, thighs and hips to my heart and forehead. It's like pleasurable electricity streaming through my entire body. This new phenomenon almost instills a little fear, but I stomp it out. I'm receiving some type of blessing and perhaps even an initiation as I stand on this same spot that Eli had. I glance toward him, inundated in the powerful love vibrations connecting us as if we are linking together as one. I am lifted slightly off of the stone by surging waves and my body trembles. On my forehead between my eyebrows, a pulse like a heartbeat stimulates me to become fully alive. Weakness and blackness overcome me, the only firing wave active in my brain.

Eli's voice calls, "Lucy, Lucy, are you okay?" and I finally regain consciousness. The cold wet grass beneath my body helps to revive awareness. Vaguely I realize he's gently shaking me, although his image remains cloudy.

"What just happened?"

"I suppose assimilating the energy from the stone was too shocking to your physical nature this first time. I caught you falling off of the rock."

Struggling to recover, blood flows back into my face, erasing its pallor. I can scarcely speak. "I feel woozy and spinning. There's throbbing between my eyebrows." I recall the conversation with Mama Jane earlier today. Could this be the pineal gland throbbing? I feel nauseous as if I were on a fast rollercoaster. Attempting to rise from the ground and regain my strength with the help of Eli, I vomit. I'm so embarrassed and attempt to stop the convulsions. When it finally subsides, I take a minute to clean up and teary-eyed because this is not the image I want to leave with Eli tonight. He consoles me as he senses my entire state of being; the great soothing love, fainting and then retching.

"Don't worry about this, Lucy. You have taken in so much all at once. Becoming sick does not take away your beauty."

*He called me beautiful!*

This word erases away the last few moments of embarrassment. I almost forget the goggles are not covering my gaze as I glimpse the same glowing lights. Mystery and awe reflect on my face and Eli says, "Can you see traces of light now?"

"Is that what it is?" I've only seen momentary flashes, but now circles of light faintly glow without completely fading away.

"Your field of perception is broadening into higher light spectrums. There are things in this world that most humans do not perceive. It does not mean they don't exist, but the eyes of the ordinary individual cannot see this energy because it vibrates at a faster frequency, something like a radio wave." As if to reassure me, he says, "Don't be too startled for as the days progress, you will be able to see more and more."

His statement should make me nervous, but I'm too off balance and feeling woozy while adjusting to flashes of light halos. What happened to my clear sight? I cannot focus. Closing my eyes again helps to force some of my old sight back and cope with this new reality. Yet, I feel overly blessed with my new sight.

It's apparent why Eli had to bring me to this special location instead of telling me about it as there are no words to explain my experience. Only observation and participation make me realize the depth of it. I need to know more. "What is this mystical place?"

He folds his arms while explaining its significance. "To put this bluntly, it is one of several entrances from other worlds or what we might call realms; an entry, doorway, threshold, gateway, portal or even a stargate. So contemplate about it to your heart's desire. There is no denying what you saw. It will always be regardless of the label or name you place on it. The stone is an old and ancient site where different star races and beings of Light can enter through to help this planet heal and maintain a balance between the light and dark energies."

"Just like the yin-yang symbol!" I proclaim.

"Yes, that is correct. I promise not to ignore your inquisitiveness, but this topic needs to be addressed another day. There is one more thing I still want to show you before it gets any later." Eli nods his head in the direction he wants me to go.

I lean down to fetch my backpack. "Yikes!" I jump backwards as a creature slithering side to side comes into focus. I scream "What is that?"

"Ethereal life forms can now be seen with your new sight," he wisely replies.

I want to determine if I can hold the vision so I refocus and see it slithering on the ground. "The woodland creature moves just like a centipede. It's about two feet long by a half foot in width; round, green arching back and silky like an inch worm. The face has a round opening for a mouth with two tentacles atop the beady eyeballs." Truly concentrating on this living being, I see it with fresh eyes, which gives me a sense of awe as it now looks more attractive. I laugh at myself as this is a harmless new critter I found in the woods.

Stepping back to take in the new sight, the towering pine trees come alive in a florescent glow, unknown to me before standing on the ancient stone. The invisible fireflies or orbs Eli chased only moments ago are now manifesting form as I follow him back up the hill walking in a glittering dark. He takes my hand, helping me along the path with my new sight. After this newly-found discovery, I am filled with absolute happiness as I stride higher up the moon-lit mountain, about to uncover more of this magical world.

# Chapter 9
# Spider in the Web

Because of my new sight, the night sky lacks the luster of twinkling stars compared to the land showcased. It's getting crispy colder as the hours progress. Eli pulls me the last few feet to the tip of the peak. I mull over the hike back down the winding trail, not to mention the drive back home. Exhaustion will settle into my muscles for sure by morning. I don't want to return home too late, given that Mother will demand an answer because I have classes tomorrow.

"Do not worry about your Mother" Eli interjects.

*How can he know my thoughts?*

He interrupts my deliberations by saying, "I cannot read your mind, but feel strong emotions, which can be translated into words, another skillful ability you will foster. You have always had the capacity, but did not realize your potential."

"Yeah, well, you don't know my Mother."

He turns and with his usual confident smile, says, "The very act of your worrying will create the expected outcome. Instead, focus on a welcoming return home. We have good intentions for our coming to this ancient site. Awakening from your deep slumber points to where the journey begins. Focus your emotions and thoughts on your mother understanding." Eli turns his back on me, gazing up at something in the darkness.

His words make complete sense, as foreign as they seem, but as to the actual effect it can have on the outcome is unknown. However, I will try to practice what he's preaching. Traces and flashes of pristine lights continue to affect my new vision and it makes me a little dizzy. I find a mossy boulder to lean against.

Eli approaches and hands me the goggles, which I accept, carefully.

"Gaze high in the sky and look." This feels like a case of de je vu from my previous experience. I place the gadget to my eyes once again with a degree of confidence and wait as the darkness now has a greenish cast. I see movement of hovering shapes soaring around and flying in and out of some type of spacecraft. The shapes appear anchored in the above space like boats in a harbor.

Frozen in disbelief, I burst out, "Incomprehensible! No way!" I remove the lenses and ask, "Why can't I see the outlines of what looks like ships without the goggles? This doesn't make any sense."

"What is logical about any of this? Get out of your brain and into your higher mind. That is where the stream of infinite higher consciousness resides."

"Okay, once again you are schooling me," and I raise the goggles to my eyes, scrutinizing the moving shapes. I have read accounts and legends about the existence of the objects now appearing before me, but nothing can prepare me for actually revealing them.

"You sure know how to shock the hell outta me! This whole undertaking proved to not be the ordinary sightseeing trip or hike I expected. This is difficult to conceive, let alone to validate! There are no lights in the sky or glowing spheres to prove our bona fide testimony to the average man on the street. I can't deny the realism of what I've been experiencing, even though I hold this bizarre and expensive technology in my hands."

"Lucy, are you telling me that it is easier to accept seeing the Light beings from another world around the stone? You want to remain skeptical because if you were to tell others, you fear humiliation. What is the first reaction when a person reveals that they saw a UFO?"

Coyly, I look directly at him, "They are made fun of and told they're nuts and to check into the nearest mental institution." After all my years of yearning to know more, yet a certain annoyance prickles me and a deep voice rumbles within my subconscious. I trust my new found instincts as they honestly confirm that there are things in this world that have been deliberately hidden. Anger shoots through me like an arrow.

"Why must this remain secret from the people on the planet? I don't get it."

"In order to understand the purpose of the Light, you must understand the darkest of the dark. Your struggle to fully comprehend the problem of evil is not a new quest as this same wondering has stirred in the unknowing for thousands of years. Although, gaining access of forbidden knowledge about the roots of evil may turn out to be dangerous.

"The two men the other night are agents who helped create this malady. They saw an opportunity to make contact with you and prevent your unveiling. Their goal is to unnerve a target and intimidate the victim so that she or he discontinues digging deeper into the rabbit's hole."

"Ugh, am I still a target?"

"No. You are safe for now. We will not let anything happen to you and our protecting Watchers assist to dismantle Dark Brotherhood agents' attempts, an empowerment that you will soon learn to consciously do yourself."

"Watchers? This sounds more like a cheesy movie than an actual truth"

"When the time is right, you will commence seeing them too, Lucy."

Although I am a little amused, yet deep within undesired hysterics threaten to surface, which I prefer to remain hidden from Eli since he has a gift to sense any of my emotions. Observing and attempting to stifle any judgments are the only keys to unlocking Eli's world of reality. Thankfully he's patient with me.

"By the way, I'm too weak physically to fight off grown men."

"Physicality is only one form of strength. In the coming weeks, we will teach how to develop your intrinsic defensive abilities. Moving forward rapidly to empower them is the key to your staying power. Standing on the stone unplugged you from a shadowy instrument planted to override the core of Earth's natural pulse, but a signal was received by those in the ethereal realms that you now shine more brightly. It is like you have become a lantern to light the way for others."

I just remember something significant. "After meeting you the first time, a few days ago I had a mysterious visit by some strangely dressed people ringing my doorbell. They were inquiring about the hearing impaired. Their black SUV had out-of-state plates and they had only come to my door, not to any of my neighbors. Out of suspicion, I watched their vehicle leave. They weren't there to sell me something, right? Were they agents that wish to keep me in the dark?"

His face betrays his concern. "I think they were checking out to see how much you actually are a threat to them. Could you see others in the vehicle?"

"Yes, there was a driver and a shape of someone sitting in the backseat."

Eli pauses as if he's waiting for an answer to pop into his head. "Uh, they have scanners to read energy fields. They did not get anything from you. That is why they left. There was no threat at that time. We will have to develop your shield to block their continued tracking. In the meantime, the strong presence of Watchers surrounding you is a safety measure that you can rely on."

"What?"

"Guardian races act as body guards to those who need them, as life on Earth has become so dangerous. Like I said, you will start to see them too.

"Some time ago, dark energies ensnarled this planet in a network of electromagnetic, vibrating strings, resembling a spider web. When humans become entangled in this mess, they become the prey. They have poisoned us with ignorance, using technology and mind control to accomplish this mission. Once we begin to see the truth, we can start weaving the pieces together. You want answers? Then, it is time to look at the darkness to understand how to take your power back."

I make the connection and answer, "Frequency waves can change behavior in the human brain, just like Mama Jane said about the colony of bees not able to find their way back to the hive; essentially the human brain is an electrical operating system."

Eli continues, "Yes, you understand this. The majority of humans have been induced into a trance, watching shadows on the cave wall. You see those ships up there? Only through the help of these goggles are you able to detect higher Light frequencies. The hardest message for anyone to swallow is finding out that reality is not what we have been led to believe. A whole other world exists while the shadow watchers merely are slaves in servitude to this masked leadership: keeping us addicted and trapped into laboring in their companies to pay for items that begin to own us. This destroys our freedom to express ourselves. Those who choose to be masters of their own fate in the commercial world only succeed as long as they play by the rules of these hidden puppeteers. Resources are dispersed in small amounts to the masses while these few masters of deceit continue to stockpile enormous wealth for themselves and their hidden agendas. Consequently, history continues to repeat itself time and time again."

After deeply considering Eli's observations, I add, "I believe that every human is seeking answers as to who we are, despite the varying degrees and interests. But why are we walking blind with no Light to see the way?"

He answers, "You want a hardliner? Just look at the detached pyramid with the all-seeing eye on the dollar bill. The same symbol shows up in churches, artwork, logos, architecture, government, fraternal organizations. Should I go on?"

"No, I get the point. It represents a hierarchy of power," I respond.

He continues. "This ancient occult symbolism represents an invisible ruler not of this world. Obscured leaders appease the people enough to keep them distracted while they do their bidding behind closed doors as the system is set up to deter a rebellion since nobody knows who sits on the throne.

"In our media, we are warned of alien invasions. The hard truth that I want you to understand is that Earth was already invaded thousands of years ago and we are living remnants within the structure of our interrupted destiny. Our culture and sciences have been interfered with and we do not even know who we are anymore."

Raising my voice I ask, "Is that the greatest cover-up in history? That history books are wrong!"

He explains, "Let me set the first piece of the puzzle in place for you. Every human being on this planet is made of the stars."

"Although I totally believe what you are saying, but it's hard to conceive."

"Yes, of course, this will take some time to assimilate."

"Explain the dark energies. Our first encounter was the result of my speaking out against the instinctive nature of evil in human existence." I nearly wish to take back the last question, not sure if I'm ready for the answers.

"Darkness is notably referred to as the absence of light. Scientifically, it is only possible to have a diminutive amount of light. As an analogy, it is like a candle flame. Everything is energy and nothing is absent of Light. Nevertheless the dark has Light, but it shines exceedingly dimmer. To make this simple, even the darkness has an abiding quality as the Light never disappears."

"Like the note you left in the book. Right? Evil cannot be killed or destroyed."

"Energy never disappears. It only changes to other forms and that is a proven fact. Your electromagnetic field yesterday was bright, but today it could blind a destructive force."

I look down at my arms and legs, attempting to catch a glimpse of reflecting Light, but with no luck. "How? I don't see anything."

"Believe me, your physical eyes do not want to see all of the Light spectrums in this world as they exist. You would walk around needing a special pair of sunglasses to get through the day. There is a way of seeing without physical vision. By the way, is your forehead still throbbing?"

"Yes. How'd you know?"

"Just a hunch. It is because of you reclaiming your new sight." He shrugs. "These dark energies are similar to black holes devouring light. The disagreeable human-looking parasites consume Light from others. Most people are not aware of their power and become credulous victims as their energy fields are drained often without their suspecting. I am sure you have been around someone of this nature and had no knowledge other than to feel exhausted or abnormally fatigued.

"In the days to come, we will work on developing your shield against these attacks. The darker the spirit, the more successful at instilling such confusion as to lead the victim into be-lieving they are crazy."

"Come again. Whaa, are you implying these parasites are in fact Vampires?"

"It is true; they are among the Dark Brotherhood."

"What a sick concept," I say, shocked at his claim.

"Until enough of us can move against them sufficiently, they will continue to move invisibly on this planet, possessing human hosts to be the puppets to carry out their wicked deeds."

Eli cringes, becoming uncomfortable with this subject. I should halt my increasing curiosity and ask no more questions at this time. There must be more to his outward expression of emotional pain. Maybe having a first hand experience with some-thing of a wrathful nature?

Then Eli seems to recover and continues, "Regardless of your surprise that such denizens exist, the only way to destroy their agendas and banish them from Earth is to expose them. It would be like shining a light on cockroaches causing them to scurry for dark, hidden recesses. It is time to fight and take back the planet. That is our destiny; to resist the Dark agenda's plans to fully take over the planet, modify our DNA and cripple us in such ways that the current human genetic lineage would be liquidated forever. Thus interfering with our future timelines."

"Is there any mystery left? You are alluding to timelines?"

"Yes, dinosaurs did exist at the same time as humans on this planet." Determined to resolve the many questions that he knows are bouncing around in my brain, Eli passionately ex-plains. "Time control technology is real. It is my personal forte. Rumor is that I am the most advanced traveler able to move in and out of other timelines, disrupting little when visiting them. I can also read probable future events with a device Marcus calls

"Maggie." It acts as a magnifying glass, which is designed to pick up invisible wavelengths of Light. It would look like a circle of mirrors.

"Every creation in the Universe has sound vibrating a wavelength signature, rather like the vibrations that resonate when striking a gong. It matters not whether the creation is as large a planet or as small as a nanosecond. Calculations can be entered into this device and presto! I am describing this instrument as simply as possible. It truly is more complex than my description."

"To be able to look through time and space, this kind of ability must come with extreme responsibility," I answer slowly, almost overwhelmed by all of this new information.

"Absolutely! Often the outcome is changed by time travelers without anyone even knowing about it. The only clue that a timeline has been altered is an inner feeling one gets that something is off. The scary part of all this is how items or information disappear without anyone ever knowing about them in the first place. How can a solar powered car exist when the design for it disappears before manufacturing it? Right?"

"Wow. I never thought about it that way. Left to the public domain, this knowledge can wreak havoc without ethics or values supporting it."

"Remember this. You can time travel without the assistance of a time control device. Your mind has that technology naturally. Humans place more focus on shortcomings and nearly not enough in seeking their perfect design. By controlling the influence and action of this darkness, humanity can discover their greatness and be guided to restore it."

"Many have reached a point in life where they believe that humanity and the planet are doomed to failure. But you make it sound so hopeful, like there is a way out of this dilemma. I'm tired of witnessing the horrific global pain and suffering of the masses and waiting for a miracle."

Eli points out, "That is precisely what the Dark agenda is betting on: our lack of determination to protect ourselves as we are swallowed up into this, metaphorically speaking, giant black abyss."

"Did you use Maggie to find me at the club the other night? And how about our meeting the first time? Could these so-called Dark agents, for all intents and purposes, have found me before you did? And, what were they going to do to me?"

"Yes, after our meeting at Apollo's I used Maggie to follow the trail of the Dark Brotherhood. I had been instructed by a Watcher to walk into that classroom on that day to give you that specific book and to bring you to the ancient stone to activate something seeded within you, but this Watcher would not tell me more."

Surprisingly, I'm not unnerved as he explains that a foreign thing has been inside me. Possibly my entire life. Eli's entire body exudes a pale, iridescent glow, exposing his excitement. "There needs to be a counterbalance of power before the end of the Great shift, which is approaching soon. We already are in the middle of this transition period. Currently two timelines exist creating parallel realities and one is very destructive. The individual can choose which side to serve, but Earth needs assistance to release any entangling webs of deceit and restore her brilliance."

He continues explaining the dark side, "There are hidden wars on this planet, not the wars in the Middle East or the jungles of Africa. It is a space and time war being fought by brothers and sisters of the Galactic Council of Light, which consists of many planetary beings, including those of ascended humans.

Lack of knowledge and secrecy suppress hope for real change. Playing small and remaining ill-informed does nothing to help.

"The nameless and most destructive darkness on this planet are the *Naki*." Eli's consternation shows as he speaks their name. It is like when Genghis Khan and his golden horde were approaching a city. Just speaking his name caused panic in the people. I assume the same applies for those who are knowledgeable of the Naki. It dredges up the same response.

Shifting gears, Eli announces, "We need to get you back home. Thinking positively can only have a small effect before your Mother truly becomes angry!"

This reminder will, indeed, make the walk back seem more taxing as I can imagine Mother trying to reach me by cell phone while waiting impatiently on the porch.

At the end of this mind-bending sojourn in the mountains, I take one last look through the goggles at the extraordinary discoveries. I see a circular space ship discharge a shaft of Light, which strikes an oncoming triangular shape and an enormous explosion occurs. In disbelief, I now witness a glowing neon green object falling like a meteor, which must be space junk falling from the sky, the result of this undetectable war.

# Chapter 10
# Legend of Far Away Lands

My sore muscles already cramp after falling asleep on the way home. I wipe away the drool on my chin and sit up. The car slows down when reaching the familiar turn onto my street. I had slept so deeply that an indent from the window sill leaves its mark on my right temple. I regret falling asleep as I don't want to miss a minute alone with Eli.

"We are back. Made it before twelve-thirty. Let me get your things out from the trunk. I want to meet your mother."

"Right now? It's late and really I've never."

Eli cuts me off. "You are too anxious. Just relax and think positively." Eli sounds overconfident.

I'd forgotten his previous advice to always think and feel positive outcomes. I walk up the steps chanting to myself, "positive outcomes, happy Mother." At least she's not sitting on the front porch swing.

Walking inside I hear the late night news blaring from the family room. I stroll in nonchalantly, saying, "Mom I'm home. I have a friend here with me to explain why I'm so late tonight." I hesitate and look at Eli seeking a little reassurance.

Mother is wrapped in a cotton blanket lying on the loveseat and after my entering the room, at the sound of my voice, she groggily responds, "Hello, Lucy baby. I must've fallen asleep while watching the television waiting up for you." She turns the noisy TV off.

Nervous, I respond, "Yeah, I know, Mom. I should've called or texted. We were in the woods and no service was available. I fell asleep during the car ride home. I'm really sorry."

Eli moves forward and reaches out to shake her hand before she can react negatively. "I'm Eli Sinclair. It is nice to meet you. Sorry about bringing Lucy back this late. Not good for first impressions."

His charm seems to work. Eli irresistibly grins and Mother lights up, obviously flattered to receive such gracious attention from an attractive, young man. He cleverly crafts attentive comments, keeping her attention focused on him, continuing to talk in his low masculine voice. She has forgotten about the time. For the next fifteen minutes, I am left out of their conversation and neither glances in my direction.

Wide awake now, Mother says, "You should come over for dinner sometime soon. Lucy and I would love to have your company."

"Yes that would be great, Mrs. Hayes." Eli acts as if this is the most delightful dinner invitation that he has ever received.

I gape at the two of them. Mother appears to be entranced and Eli gives me his "I told you so look." I'm stunned to see her giddy reaction as she hasn't flinched a bit regarding my late arrival.

"Well I'm tired. Eli, I will see you tomorrow, right?" I ask because he didn't express what the next step in this unveiling process would be. There are numerous answers I must pry out of him. I could spend an entire week isolated with him, discussing the nature of the Universe as his voice is absolutely seductive.

"Tomorrow, yes, after school. I must be off, ladies and have a good night. Again, Mrs. Hayes, it has been exceptionally nice meeting you."

Mother emphatically says, "Please call me Anna. It's been my pleasure."

I walk Eli to the front door alone, whispering. "Show-off. She usually isn't that sweet at this time of hour. You put some kind of spell on her, didn't you?"

Mother vibrantly calls out, a tone that I have never heard before. "Thank you for bringing Lucy home."

Eli softly replies, "It was not just me." He reaches over and gently sweeps a strand of hair behind my ear. I'm sure he can hear my heart throbbing in my chest.

*Oh mercy!*

Even though I wish he'd kiss me, I restrain myself and hold back so he'll retain an interest in me and we say "goodnight" at the same time. From the look on his face, I do believe he wants to, but he's too much of a gentleman to force any move. I float on wings to my bed and the sweetness in the air seems to magnify and enliven me. I lose myself dreaming of Eli Sinclair.

"Good morning, my little lady." Mother stations herself at the side of my bed.

Glancing at my clock, I beg her, "The alarm hasn't rung yet. I still have thirty minutes!"

"I couldn't sleep much last night and you'd fallen asleep right after Eli left. I'm curious. How'd you two meet?"

"Why, does it matter?"

"He's different from most of the other boys from this area and unusually sophisticated. Can this be a potential boyfriend? I like him and I get a good vibe from my first impression."

"No, Mother! We're just friends for now and we met at school."

She says, "Oh, by the way, don't make it a habit of walking in that late without telling me first that you've been tramping through the woods. At least, tell me who you're with, where and what you're doing, regardless of your barely legal age. Got it!"

I lay motionless as I wait for her to leave my refuge, my personal room. The enchantment must've worn off as she seems to be snarling. From her attitude, I've been given the okay to spend more time with Eli and his unconventional family. As I prolong my dreaded morning ritual, thoughts of yesterday ramble around in my head as to the various subjects he might teach. Will I learn how to move objects with my mind or maybe alchemy; the art of turning iron and lead into gold! Of course, these additional responsibilities crown the homework.

In retrospect, the day effortlessly progressed with limited dysfunction. I hadn't spotted a single, strange agent clothed in designer suits sporting celebrity style sunglasses. I almost forget about my latest new sight as the bright new day dims the glowing halos around objects. I try to ignore any uncomfortable conversation with Kari and Eliza in Algebra class, but the two of them make eye contact with me.

Kari assails me first. "Lucy, whatever happened to you the other night? You weren't here yesterday, plus I tried calling your cell with no luck!"

Eliza perked up at her opportunity to question me, "Yeah, I saw you leave with a bunch of guys. That really freaked me out!"

I feel apologetic, "I was fine. No need to worry. I didn't have time to find you as I was being rushed out of there. My friends found me and, well, I'm just sorry I didn't say anything to either of you."

The fast moving events that night erased my good manners, even though an opportunity to say goodbye could not possibly have happened under the circumstances. Nice, that they considered my welfare in spite of their taste for clubbing. The conversation sharply cuts off and I sense their harsh feelings causing little pricks on my skin, contradicting their previous claim of concern. A stream of images like an instant telepathic vision whooshes through my mind.

*Can this be how Eli reads emotions?*

I'm okay with disappointing them as I have new intriguing friends. Eli has opened a new portal into another world to explore and today I have a stronger sense of self. We go our separate ways inside the classroom, understanding that we hold opposing views on the definition of "fun."

My attention during the last half of the Algebra lesson focuses solely on the clock reaching the end of the hour. At least I accomplish writing down the page numbers and lessons before class next Monday. Mooning over Eli and what our next meeting will be like buzzes through my brain like a swarms of bees. Finally, the signal to meet up with him arrives with the last closing remark by the Professor. I bolt out the doorway and race as far away from Kari and Eliza as possible, searching for him.

Eli, appearing particularly relaxed dangling his tinkling keys, stands outside of the Library where we agreed to meet. He steps over in front of me and gives me a tender squeeze. Aware of my intense daily scholastic schedule, he's thoughtful enough to ask, "How was your day?"

I respond, "Nothing exciting like yesterday. Where are we going today?

"Would you like to hang out at Mama Jane's place and kick back with my brothers?"

"It sounds like a blast." I'm elated to spend a casual evening relaxing with friends. I follow him in my car, focusing on every road and turn to find the farm on my own again if such necessity arises. Driving past the barn, I catch sight of the brothers nestling in lawn chairs around a smoldering fire pit and Mama Jane carries out a platter of food, placing it on the picnic table. The table overflows with food and drinks. Fit for a celebration, candles and strings of pearly lights twinkle. The waning sunlight reflects the approaching twilight. It's the end of the day and I'm exactly where I want to be.

Staying at Eli's side as we walk towards the family, I ask, "What's the party for?"

"It's for you. Mama Jane likes to pamper all of us whenever something special happens."

"Special?" I'm confused, although I suspect it has something to do with my journey to the grove and recent new sight.

"We just want to welcome you into our family circle. Our home can be your new hideaway and you are welcome to come and go as you wish. For all of us here, this is our safe house. I am not suggesting that you uproot, pack your bags and move in with all of us. You are a new member of our extended family, if you so choose."

I'm flattered and sincerely jubilant by their extreme kindness, but a little taken aback by this quick invitation since we just met last week. I look at the ground to hide the kaleidoscope of emotions flitting across my face and ponder his intentions. Perhaps he knows that I truly like him. "Certainly, of course I would love to be a member of your extended family, but what does that mean?"

Zeke stands up from his lawn chair, approaches and wraps his arms around me as if I am a long lost sister. "Glad you came back. We were all betting you'd freak at the Grove."

Eli, endorsing his faith in me, quickly interjects, "Not all of us felt that way."

Mama Jane brings out the last of the goodies for dinner. She motions us to leave the fire and gather around the table. "Grab, root and holler, boys!" Zeke, clowning, attempts to wrangle a reaction from Ki, horsing around and battling for first position. Marcus slowly moves intent on examining some type of device in his hands. He's the more studious of the bunch while Eli appears more serious. I'm not sure about Ki as he remains cloaked in a kind of anonymity.

Mama Jane sure knows how to cook; fried chicken, corn on the cob, fresh garden peas, homemade rolls and strawberry shortcake. I'll gain a lot of weight if I share many meals with this family.

Sparks popping from the bonfire float off into the air. We all sit quietly after enjoying the meal, although Zeke and Marcus are still hogging down food. Mama Jane pats her hand on the bench next to her, signaling me to join her. "Come now, Lucy, have a seat here. I have something to give you." She opens her hand and in it lays a pendant attached to a thin leather cord. "I'm giving you a very special and sacred stone that has been passed down through countless generations within my family. Stories told to me by my great grandmother say that this stone has been worn by the reigning royal class from the past times of mythical goddesses; the long forgotten rulers from the land of Mu. They referred their motherland as Lemuria."

The feast has satiated everyone's appetite and quiet ensues so that Mama Jane can continue her story and I sense the seriousness and importance of the moment.

"These great leaders did not have to rule the people as the citizens were effortlessly peaceful and diplomatic. They were not interested in gaining power or dominion over others. They were highly evolved, spiritual people, hundreds of years old, living free of stress and disease while dwelling in the natural elements. They were not as physical as we are today. Their beingness was more ethereal, allowing them to be in tune with the natural flows, rhythms and cycles of the Earth.

Lemurians had no desire to become immersed in the physicality of the planet and develop mechanical objects as they had the natural ability to mentally transport themselves wherever they chose. All they had to do was to envision themselves wherever they chose to be and it happened. Likewise, their minds could provide any of their physical necessities in a nanosecond. They communicated telepathically, mostly in pictures rather than words, which made their meanings more clear. Their extrasensory perceptions were highly superior to others existing on Earth at the same time. They saw life born of women and, consequently, honored the divine feminine gifts of protection and creation."

I look to see any reaction from the boys as Mama Jane retells this tale of centuries-old wisdom and knowledge. Matriarchal societies living in peace and prosperity threatened the foundation of the current, male-dominated patriarchal social order. The boys cannot hide their admiration for her, as they sit quiet, motionless, listening to every word Mama Jane shares. I know this is not a virgin tale to them. They must have been told these stories many times before.

"The people of Lemuria were a very old civilization privy to Universal truths. Their knowing of the countless cycles of the Great Central Sun prepared them for the natural ebb and flow of moving through the galactic day and night of awakening and sleeping. This Great Sun sits in the middle of our galaxy, emitting an eternal flame to pierce our Third Eye, releasing valuable wisdom, connecting us all to the cosmic web. This undervalued little gland inside the center of the brain is the receptor in the human body that allows humankind to see and know beyond what is physical. But it takes a certain amount of spiritual, mental and physical exercising to awaken this sight. Which has been asleep.

"Our location in this processional 26,000 year passage is the cusp between the astrological sign of Pisces and Aquarius. Each zodiac sign moving through the equinoxes takes 2,160 years. Furthermore, the Cosmic Year is like a cross separated in four quadrants, each taking 6,500 years completely passing through each quadrant. Moving from the Golden Age to the Silver Age, to the Bronze Age and to the Iron Age.

"Due to an alignment of this central rift, our planet has an opportunity to tear down the synthetically crafted shields of the Dark Brotherhood and to unleash the divine energies, thus alchemically shifting our biological structures. The point between the Iron and Golden Age transforms the physicality of all species from heavy ionic alkali carbon atoms into a crystalline based expression, which consists of new atoms carrying vibratory light. The movement in the heavens changes the vibratory levels from gold to silver to bronze to iron. We are now entering the Golden Age again, which accounts for the tales of using alchemy to change iron into gold. Crystalline forerunners are being born on the Earth as we speak, but unable to fully evolve into their capacity until more of the darkness can be expelled.

"Mama Jane, is the entire planet going to move into this Golden Age?"

"The land of Lemuria is once again rising and in time, will become a land of enchantment. It isn't a sunken island, but a rising luminous spark throughout the entire world. The Dark Brotherhood plagues the planet, as they fight within themselves desperately attempting to find ways to halt this awakening. The last 13,000 years has been the acme point of their dark night to reign.

"Lucy, at the end of the recent Silver Age, the Lemurians faced a new challenge. A small percentage of malevolent Star races from other planets came and left, awaiting and planning ways to take the Earth's many rich resources and become the dominating race on the planet. Wars and destruction on the ground and in the skies caused rains to flood and vast areas of Lemuria sank because of inhuman, stealthy Atlantean incursions. The statues of Easter Island, huge erected stones sticking in the ground, and other mysterious relics on the Polynesian islands, Hawaii, Fiji Island, Europe and the west coast of the Americas are all that remain of those grand and glorious times.

"The very tall scientists of Atlantis were not spiritually evolved, but advanced in technology. For eons of time, the Atlanteans subjected humans to terrible scientific experiments, including blending their DNA with animals, thereby creating monsters. Traces of these creatures are pictured in existent hieroglyphs in various parts of the world. The lands were ravaged by great beasts pillaging and Atlantis built walls to keep them out. The small remnant of the Lemurians, who survived all of this chaos, had to resort to living underground or caves in higher elevations in order to be safe from these carnivorous beasts. Lemuria no longer existed, but left vestiges of their influence in the Indus Valley in India and through shamans of some indigenous cultures keeping the sacred records throughout time."

Mama Jane covers her eyes and tears seep through her fingers. I take her hand and hold it as the story touches me deeply.

Her voice cracks as she continues. "Lucy, seek the mysteries without fear. This stone pendant survives as a remnant of this lost knowledge and will provide you with courage and shelter from the darkened hearts of negative forces. It's the stone of cosmic Truth and this etching in gold symbolizes the Great Cosmic Cross.

I see that the etching has the same pictogram as on the cards Eli gave me. It's also the image of the Great Year. I understand more clearly how these teachings are coming full circle now. Eli rises from his chair and approaches me.

"Here let me help you tie it." Eli places the stone around my neck and it lies perfectly between my heart and throat. The gemstone is a deep blue Lapis with specs of gold that shimmer like stars.

"Thank you, Mama Jane. This is the most beautiful gift. I'm thrilled with your confidence in me, plus your wonderful hospitality."

"You make us proud, Lucy. Shine your light where there is darkness and never forget what it's like to be human. As a great spiritual leader once said, 'Be as innocent as doves and as wise as serpents.'

"Good night, boys. Good night, Lucy. It's time for me to hit the sack."

I thank Mama Jane once again as she heads towards the house. The boys help with the clean up. When our labors are ended, Eli catches my hand and leads me toward the barn.

*Could this be an ideal moment, given the pleasant events of the evening, to receive a kiss?*

Still holding my hand, Eli takes me into what looks to be a bachelor pad. Instead of a barn for stowing animals, it houses four boys. The bottom of the two tiers of the usual barn stores the tools and farming implements and an open wooden staircase leads up to the second story. I discern through the opening, beddings and items appropriate for a bedroom. This barn uncharacteristically appears dirt free from its usual purposes.

"So, you live in here?"

"Yes, cool, huh?" Eli says.

Actually the barn has a tasteful quality. Leather seating and rugs are set aesthetically about with their beds nestled in this hay loft.

"I have to say, you boys have good taste, considering you live in a barn!" I giggle.

Eli shares in my comical moment and laughs. "Do you like it here?"

I respond, "Obviously, silly! Mama Jane and all of you make me feel at home and the food is delectable."

He says, "Good!"

"To be truthful, somehow I've always felt like an outsider, never blending in, but here with your family, I fit in. You are just as bit strange as I am." My head lowers and I peek upwards to see if he reacts.

Eli nudges me. "Nice. I am glad that we fit to your standards."

Walking around looking at the antiquities and art appears like I'm inside a museum. Countless tall bookcases extending to the ceiling of this loft are filled with endless shelves of books. Standing in the corner catching my attention, is a towering statue at least seven feet tall. The unusual upper bare torso is that of a man and from the hips downward, his body is a snake. Examining it closely, I find this fine sculpture has been artfully carved from wood. The face radiates the artist's portrayal of a half-man, half-snake morphing from a human into a creature. At the crown of the head, rays emerge like celestial sunbeams; perhaps a symbol of illumination.

"I like all the art you've collected. Did you buy all of these?"

"No, they were handed down to me from um, ancestors. As you may have guessed, this is my corner of the barn."

"Is this statue a family heirloom?"

"You might say that. It has been around a long time, one item reminding me of my parents."

Looking at my cell phone, my time has run out. The phone was on vibrate and I forgot to check in with Mother. Three missed calls display on the screen. Quickly, I send her a text reporting that I'm on my way home.

"Well, gotta go. It's too bad I don't have more time as I'd love to delve deeper into all your books and antiquities, which look like ancient artifacts."

"Another time soon, I hope," he says.

He walks me to my car and in his expression I see no hope for a kiss. I look through my rear view mirror and he continues to stand in the middle of the gravel driveway until finally the house, barn and the outlying structures vanish from my view. I clasp the ancient gemstone with its protective symbol and possible magical powers passed down from a faraway land.

*It has come home!*

# Chapter 11
# Speaking of Snakes

"Crimany!" My mind won't shut off images going around and around. I turn on the bedside lamp and drink from the glass of water beside me. I'm not consumed by lingering shadows in my bedroom, but of Eli. My room actually sparkles from some kind of static electricity, but the diffused artificial light lessens the shine.

I spot the pictogram cards on my bedside table. What a great way to distract my musings! Perhaps I can solve another great enigma. One card almost leaps out at me. I am impressed by the picture on the card of a man and woman embracing with the lower half of their bodies interweaving into snakes. This is far more than just a fluke correlation with the fascinating statue in Eli's barn.

I close my eyes, concentrating, but my mind containing so much trash conceals any answers. Again, I try to blank out. Nothing! My shoulders droop in defeat when I tried so hard. Despite the setback, I focus on the card once more. "Oh success be with me," I cry out loud, straining to release this answer. Psyched out and disgusted, I pull the bed covers up and snuggle into my pillows as my eyelids feel heavy.

Suddenly, floating images appear, resembling those strange people with snake bodies pictured on those cards. Part of me slumbers. The other remains with the card image. I don't budge for fear that any small movement might erase the impressions.

My mind can hardly catch and retain the information. It's like a movie rapidly flashing scenes or transferring important impressions inside my mind as the processor. Words bubble up: medicine, DNA, genetic manipulation, two types. Narrowing the images, I see two totally opposite gene codes, although unyielding, finally blending into one.

*What do these two forms integrating as one represent?*

Then the picture of a rotting apple falls to the ground beneath a tree. Opening my eyes, I bolt up! I can't believe it. This cannot be the canonical creation story told to me as a child. Retelling of this myth always caused a deeply heated debate on whether it should be taken literally or symbolically to represent origins of the human race.

In spite of an urge to share with Eli, doubt rises in my throat. I don't want to humiliate myself if I'm found to be in error. I'd feel like the kid in the back of class afraid to raise their hand, terrified of having the wrong answer.

*He firmly persisted that I should trust myself.*

I jot my impressions down on paper. "The apple and tree represent the forbidden fruit. The woman and man's snake tails intertwining illustrate two different forms blending together like a chimera; the mixing of cells from two or more different species." I learned of this little known phenomenon last year in Biology class.

The new revelation excites me and I race to the office computer to google the word "chimera." The search engine pulls up definitions from online dictionaries and encyclopedias. On one link, it reads, "A chimera is a mythological, monstrous, fire-breathing creature of *Lycia* in *Asia Minor*. A creature with accumulated parts from multiple animals integrated." Yet, another site references medieval art exposing embodiments of dark forces of the unrefined world with a human face and scaly tail.

I found a plethora of information describing real life forms in areas of botany, genetics and molecular biology that were created previously as separate entities. Mama Jane's story mentioned the Atlantean scientists experimenting with different animal genetics and DNA, there by creating monsters.

*It isn't just a story. This could be for real?*

Personally, I haven't seen any chimeras roaming around, although, there are legends of chupacabras. I've always considered this story as some rogue geneticist cloning various species in their basements and the thing broke out and was seen by a few farmers while it was sucking the blood of animals; maybe a combination of a mosquito, bat and something else? This idea shared with my biology class caused them to judge me foolish and weird. I have a dark feeling that perhaps cloning and the symbolic forbidden fruit are one and the same.

*There has to be more to this disturbing image.*

If the apple represents knowledge from the Tree of Good and Evil, then one can conclude that the intertwining human snake tails symbolize genetic manipulation, the end of paradise.

*But why a snake?*

The term chimera also can mean hard to believe or difficult to understand. All of this analyzing makes my head ache. Yet, I can't leave it alone and relax back in my chair as I mull over my recent discovery and reasoning.

*These ideas clearly make me stranger then any eighteen year old girl starting college.*

I need more clarification relating this Evil experiment as a possible chimera-like human. If this is correct, then what creature has been genetically manipulated with human DNA?

Previous misgivings regarding Eli's words relative to hidden and protected

Dark societies abounding with the ability to keep human-ity controlled and subject to their whims, now appear more real to me. The very speculation sends chills up and down my spine. This amazing quest to uncover the mysteries of life has to be more relevant to me than waking up, showering, brushing my teeth, running to school and earning a degree just to subsist on this controlled planet. My ramblings will all have to wait until tomorrow. This bottomless questioning finally fatigues me.

Pulling up to Mama Jane's, Eli approaches my car with his usual welcoming smile etching his attractive face. There must be a security camera alert system since he came to greet me almost as suddenly as I arrived. Marcus would have constructed such a technology as it seems to be his talent.

My excitement ignites. Never in my life have I been so drawn like a magnet to any man or boy and no words can de-scribe the connection I feel with Eli. Like a gentleman, as usual he opens the car door for me. "Glad you decided to swing by. We have much to discuss relative to your training and instructions as we need to pick up the pace."

"What kind of training? Is it going to be strenuous?" I'll endure any amount of knotty sweat and suffer any tireless prepa-ration so long as Eli's my instructor.

"No need to strain. Zeke and Ki will coach a variety of martial arts to physically strengthen your form of defense. Mar-cus will teach a little about the technological devices you might utilize. He's a genius with his knowledge and skills. Thus you cannot always rely on us to safe-guard as we may not always be around."

"Seriously? I have puny muscles."

"Just give me a chance to show what you are capable of. You have more potential than ever imagined. It is more about the strength of your mind and spirit than your fist. Just trust me."

Reluctantly I agree to become a superwoman. He continues, "Mama Jane always has a good shoulder to cry on and happens to be a good listener if all this gets to be too much. She has a way of bolstering me up with a few short words of wisdom and common sense. I can never repay her for all she has done and not just for me, but for my brothers also, positively a heroine on the top of my list."

"Yes, I agree. Mama Jane's a heroine. Like a sage, she's insightful when speaking to me. Has she always lived here at the farm? Where does she come from?"

Eli chuckles. "Where does Mama Jane come from? Hmm." He stops walking and turns to me, his countenance serious. "Do you mean, where was she born and where did her family raise her? Or do you really mean, where does her life force come from?"

Surprised by his rephrasing, "Well, now that you presented both questions, then answer each for me."

"Mama Jane was born and raised for most of her life in California. She says it was better in the Northwest and moved on the farm after marrying an Oregonian farm boy, who was passing through when she was a teen. She hastily rushed into marriage out of an impulse to go anywhere other than Los Angeles. As she puts it, the slower pace away from the city life appeals to her more. In regards to the other question, well, Mama Jane is like Inanna descending into the Underworld, but more like an angelic missionary here to help others find their way back to their true nature. Her precise identity and quest did not make themselves known until turning nearly thirty. She told me how alone she felt in her life until understanding her true calling as a healer and helper.

"Furthermore, she identifies herself as a "Keeper of the Light." The Keepers are an ancient order preserving the knowledge of the past and the alchemy of science. This group has been known as Gnostics, shamans, leaders, teachers, but who have been killed and persecuted by the Dark Brotherhood in the past for revealing these Truths. Beings of Light descend into this Underworld seeking ways to impart knowledge and, according to her exact words, 'awaken the masses of humanity from their deep slumber.' One by one she found us like a shepherdess seeking her lost sheep."

Walking into the barn, we see Zeke and Ki sparring with each other in some form of martial arts. They kick and fly through the air in a magical and effortless form. If I didn't know better, I'd think they were out of this world and flying.

I whisper, "How are they doing this? I mean, move about with poise as if they were attached to some kind of invisible harness? They're moving like ballet dancers, but fighting and blocking in aggressive stances."

"This is an ancient traditional system of codified practices meant to train for combat. Not only is this a form of self-defense, it also cultivates mental discipline and fitness."

Zeke and Ki stop their grappling when becoming aware of our presence. I'm learning more about why these two are always wrestling each other. They both bow toward each other at the same time and turning in our direction, bow again. I'm not familiar with any form of martial arts other than what I've seen on television. I assume the bowing must be a sign of respect. I break the silence. "Why are you bowing to each other? Is this some new custom? I certainly am curious."

For the first time I hear Ki's voice as he answers, keeping his eyes riveted to the ground, "It's to show humility and lack of arrogance. We respect our opponent."

"Oh, thank you, Ki." I nod my head to show that I desire to be respectful also.

"Come here, Lucy." Zeke commands.

I don't know his intentions, so I remain a little aloof. I listen to his directions as I like how Zeke presents a brotherly and hilarious comical personality. "Come on, I'm not gonna hurt you. I'm gonna show you a key principle of agility to toughen your reflexes. It's just learning how to duck and move out of the way."

"Duck and move out of the way. Sounds intimidating, Zeke."

A circle has been drawn on the barn floor and I move to its center. Zeke bows at me and I return the movement since I now understand its meaning.

"The goal is not only to defeat your opponent, but to develop self-control while defending yourself from a physical threat. I'm going to approach you with a strike, but will not hit you. Practice controlling your response of fear. Relax. To win, one must be willing to accept defeat."

Zeke walks away from me as I try to anticipate what his move will be. He can't possibly hurt me, can he? I don't think Eli would allow him to go that far.

"Awggh!" I jump backwards and scream at the dreadful sound that Zeke unleashes like an animal's growl. He scared me half-to-death even though I was prepared for him to come at me.

"Oh my God! What the hell?" I react, shocked.

"See, the idea is to develop self-control as you don't want your opponent to sense any fear in you," Zeke explains.

I nod, "Okay."

He continues to hold my attention so that I'm not aware of Ki sneaking up behind me until he's only seconds away from my face with an even louder snarl. I surprise even myself as I manage to remain calm after his attempt to startle me. I did blink a lot and breathed deeply, however. It might be more like gasping for air.

"Better, Lucy. You were more prepared the second time. When we are unmindful, we let our defenses down by not being present in the moment. Pay attention to everything around you at all times. You're developing your animal instinct to always be alert and this can be developed by continually practicing mindfulness. Your effectiveness lives in the one moment and observing without any response. A human's usual instinct is to fight or flight. By practicing this technique, you will remain fearless."

"Now that you two have startled Lucy, I'll take it from here," Eli commands.

"In addition to Zeke's instructions, you will need to create an aura of impenetrable energy around you, like a coat of armor. See it in your mind's eye and do not doubt as your belief makes it effective. Try it. See a form of Light energy surrounding you. See it strong, protecting you totally."

My eyes are closed and I allow myself to relax with an intention of opening my inner sight. I envision what it might look like. Gradually, form takes shape as a sphere or globe of iridescent translucence.

"Do you see it?" Eli enthusiastically asks.

The vision is strong and I open my eyes. To my surprise, the sphere appears all around me, beaming and shining like a multihued pearl.

"Wow!" I almost fall over amazed. I can hardly believe it.

Eli displays his pleasure at my quick reaction. "This is the shield I have been telling you about. It blocks outside forces or energies and makes you invisible to them. You do not disappear physically, but the shield blocks the onlooker and they will stride right by or it can repel them away. The more you envision this, the more resilient you become.

"Zeke and Ki are showing how to be fearless while I am showing you how to block. The two techniques go together as neither works without the other. These are the first steps in learning self-protection."

Eli nods to Zeke and Ki, "Thanks for helping Lucy."

Zeke replies, "Any time, bro."

Following Eli's lead and climbing the stairs of the barn to the boys' makeshift bedroom, I'm back again where we left off last night.

*Maybe another chance moment for the kiss that I've been romanticizing about.*

"Do you want anything to drink? We have soda, tea, water," he says as he walks toward a refrigerator in the back corner of the loft behind a metal folding partition with clothes draped over it.

"How about water," I reply.

While awaiting his return, I investigate the intriguing statue that caught my attention last night. "Eli, can you tell me more about the message of a human-snake figure such as this? I have to tell you that a series of images came to me while doing the exercise with the cards last night and this statue looks almost like the same symbol as the pictogram."

"Lucy, you tell me first because I do not wish to influence your recall by any shape or form."

"Well, I drew a card at random and while staring at the picture, I recalled this statue as both the card and the sculpture have the same likeness of a half human and half snake, like this," and I point at the carving. "The images were of the epic creation story of eating the apple in the garden with the snake. Then a rotting apple and well, to put this all simply, I raced to my computer. I searched the word chimera on the internet, remembering this term in Biology class last year. The only conclusion I've come to is comparing the apple to knowledge or DNA and a genetic manipulation of human characteristics."

"That is a mouth full of information. So, we are talking about crossing species' barriers. Correct?" Eli cleverly replies, looking rather smug.

"I think that's what I'm saying, but are you implying that humans?"

"Yes! This is great you have come to me with this now. The analysis takes some unbending of the mind. Here's a story for you."

He holds out his hand and directs me to a leather seat. I wait in anticipation while he clears his throat. "We are spiritual beings having a physical experience in this realm. We are infinite and eternal, endless spirals of energy. We simply transform and change like shapeshifters; as Light beings moving from one form to another, thereby changing shape. Shadows take on physical form in this realm, creating havoc as well. Legends and writings have all pointed to a fall of mankind or some downward spiral, abandonment or kicked out of the garden, as you might say."

I find myself completely wrapped up in his speech, while at the same time, images stimulated by his words pass through my mind. Sometimes a picture portrays meanings better than words.

"The humans of our past were genetically modified by combining two other Star races during the last Silver Age. This became the most recent downward spiral and invasion on the planet, virtually wiping out the previous Lemurian culture. The genuine origins are encoded inside human DNA like a software program. The so-called missing link has never been found by mainstream scientists because humans did not evolve from apes. It is such a laughable waste of time to even argue about. I have traveled back in time at certain points to collect lost data that was in existence, but destroyed in the fire of the Library of Alexandria in Egypt at the time of Cleopatra and Anthony. Not to mention all the crazy burning of books during the inquisition."

I try not to become too angry, "That part of history infuriates me. Imagine if those books were never destroyed. Sometimes ignorance can be bliss, but wisdom is more powerful. We must not only remember all of our joys, but remember and accept all of our pain and sorrow endured or caused upon others. Now that takes a real hero to be knowledgeable of all that we have done and maintain courage by moving forward and become more brilliant."

Eli continues, "Nature repeats patterns striving to create order out of chaos. Roughly speaking, there is much occurring in the region of our other worldly friends."

"Other worldly? Now you have to tell me everything about these Star races! No beating around the bush anymore. I want answers to what you consider to be other worldly!" I sit directly across from him, waiting for his response

Giving attention to anything outside of Earth seems unreal, but a connection to the stars has always fascinated me. I frequently stare into the sparkling night skies, wondering about the vast distance between me and the unknown. Every time, I feel infinitely small and imagine the possible existence of new worlds in the limitless celestial space.

Eli responds, "There are over 100 billion stars estimated to be within the Milky Way Galaxy alone, and countless billions of other galaxies consisting of billions of stars with planets. The size and scale of the infinite Universe reveal that humans are members of a reality much larger than most can perceive. While this fact only explains the physically seen realities, the Universe is constructed in higher and lower frequencies of densities and dimensions. Higher indicates more expansive and inclusive. Densities are vibratory states ranging from shadows to light, whereas dimensions are known as realms. Presently humans of Earth are within the third dimension and, of course, Star races occupy everywhere.

"The astral realm, as postulated by esoteric philosophies, is also known as the place where earth and heaven meet. This existent veil between these realms can actually be visited consciously through astral projection, meditation, near death experiences, remote viewing, lucid dreaming and other methods."

"What are we, Eli?" I pry for more details as to how this relates to the other worldly Star races. I wait impatiently for more answers while he momentarily pauses.

# Chapter 12

# Family

"Please don't become alarmed," he says, sincerity reflecting in his voice. "Our ancestors diversely came from many various ethnic cultures. Just expand your perception further by including genetic codes of Star races."

Reminiscing over the story from last night, I comment, "Mama Jane disclosed that horrible monsters were created by Atlantean scientists!"

"We are the descendents of this calamity. These experiments were not the worst to come. The most destructive Star race were the Naki, as they became the driving force influencing the intelligent Atlantean scientists, to create a new humanoid species, consisting of genetic codes from the Atlanteans, Lemurians and what is termed the serpent race the Naki."

"Th, th, this is the reason for symbols portraying the half-human and snake!" I am so wound up that I stutter. It's almost impossible for me to accept all of this information and, yet, a part of me begs to hear more.

"The Atlantean scientists were guided by the Naki while experimenting with the Lemurian genes and manipulating them with various species. Coveting the natural abilities of the Lemurian inner technology built within their genetic material, both the Atlanteans and Naki hoped to improve their races by making some adjustments. Secretly, the Naki knew their DNA would allow them to invade the Earth. The Naki were and are aggressive and physically powerful and in the past when the Lemurian humans had been finally tainted, they continued to infect the Earth with a series of destructive and foreign programming."

"How could the Atlantean scientists be so intelligent and not see this coming?"

"The scientists needed further expertise from the Naki who were highly knowledgeable in genetic manipulation of species. They were blind to the real intention of the Naki, which was to slowly enslave all civilizations and be the master and controller on the planet.

"The Atlantean scientists were so immersed in their experiments that they could see nothing but their results, with no thought of the consequences. Due to the flattery of the Naki, they were deaf to any warnings by others. In the end, laws of nature overruled and the aberrant genetic coding infected all Star races and began to plummet into a very dark place isolated from the higher realms. Even more shadowy Dark forces were let loose to the farthest boundaries. The fruits of their labor opened Pandora's Box, thereby freeing the lower realms and unleashing a presence unknown to this world at this critical time. The Naki intended to introduce their own power structure and flourish from the Earth's natural resources, which would be available to them after enslaving the entire planet.

"The key to their success was downloading their genetic codes into the newly created species. Having now the superpower abilities of the Lemurians, intelligence of the Atlanteans and the brute strength and forces of the Naki, this was the perfect combination to guarantee that after a few generations, their race would dominate, thereby granting them access to shut off DNA codes of all supernatural abilities to those whom they deemed not worthy."

Disgusted, I reflect on the destruction. "Why, Eli? What motivation did they have to invade?"

"Their planet was devoid of and needed minerals such as yellow gold. This mineral, through the use of alchemy, could be turned into a powder substance, as it provided long lives and god-like abilities for the Naki. Only the nobility were permitted access to it. As masters, they could force their newly created species to supply these minerals by underground mining."

As he talked, I could see tension mounting in him until finally shaking his head, he declared, "I would not ingest this substance, even if forced. It can make a sane man insane. I will stick with posting myself on the ancient stone.

"Since those dark and disastrous days, these Atlantean scientists are profoundly united and by divine intervention you might say, responsible to clean up their own mess. They trespassed against the Lemurians' path, affecting their own destiny by literally ripping open a dark portal, inviting madness that spread worldwide, implanting fear, hate and cruelty, which vibrated through every living creature.

"I have something here." He walks over to a small wooden box positioned on the bookcase and grabs a hand-size metallic ball. Sitting next to me, he continues, "I found this ancient device on one of my trips. It's a visual history book as it can reflect a hologram right before us. Only bits and pieces of this record still remain on this advanced piece of technology." He presses down on the top of the device and excitedly I watch the ball hover in mid air, projecting images inside the loft.

The stories Eli and Mama Jane told manifest like an exhibit. I can see these scientists weep, begging for forgiveness as this mistake fostered a bloodbath. Then the surviving Atlanteans used all of their scientific knowledge to subdue the god-like monsters and Dark entities, but were unable to stop this maniacal rampage and so they had no choice but to leave Earth and help from a distance.

*Could I, in fact, be viewing the centaurs, satyrs, tritons, dragons, griffins, gargoyles, werewolves, vampires, demons, all from mythical lore?*

Tears fill my eyes as the fighting, killing, bloodletting and even cannibalism engulfed the planet as the last great civilization submitted to the Dark Brotherhood. Warfare between these two opposing forces in the Universe fell upon this once revered planet, now largely isolated in darkness. I then see the scientists generate a gigantic tsunami from the ocean, forcing death on these creatures. Eli reaches out for the floating device as the images stop. I want to see more.

"Where did the Atlantian scientists go to? What did they do to try and correct this mistake?"

"The only thing they could do. Destroy the creatures. When it didn't work, they had to face the Elders of this Galaxy, who form the Galactic Council of Light."

Bells and whistles go off within me and visions of the distinguished Elders flash through my mind as I now realize the mystery behind this name. I see tall saintly beings gathered around a round table, somewhere off in the farthest reaches of the galaxy. They are beings, not particularly human, but life forms in various sizes, shapes and forms! It's a heavenly vision as I can see a resemblance to human-looking faces with beautiful smiles staring, as if they recognize my presence at their table, although I am not physically in attendance. "I just had a vision of these Elders or something! The words triggered some kind of web camera in my head." I place my finger against my throbbing forehead.

"Yes, the GC, as I entitle them, were informed by a few Atlantean representatives, as they desperately ran to them for help, reporting the careless experiments. The others stayed in a ship near the sun devising ways to rectify their foolish blunders. Their instructions were to de-escalate the situation. They were told to return and stay in this realm and bring to Earth forces of Light to counteract the ravaging Dark force until the end of the Iron Age. This age is the most challenging as the Light body becomes enclosed tightly in matter, like being imprisoned inside a box, and we become heavier physically and consciously; the Iron Man."

"What allies or weapons did they have in fighting back?"

"Really it was not hard to find who would help as the Pleiadeans were already entrenched in the saga. The Lyrians are like cousins to the Lemurian race. Of course, the Atlanteans found their own members within the Sirius constellation. These beings of Light eagerly took on the challenge along with many others to restore Earth. Even members of the Naga came to serve as they are a benevolent and enlightened serpent race."

"There are actually nice serpent races that aren't wicked?"

"Yes. Every creation in the Universe has a choice to embrace the Light or Dark energies no matter what form they all undertake.

"The only solution is to magnify the dimly lit flame everywhere as this is the true path to liberation. The amount of aggression the Dark Brotherhood creates must be met with an equal force. It is not in the Keepers' hearts to kill so they do their best to subdue these situations as often as they can. The tragedy of death upsets them. We honor the soul who loses its life in such circumstances and anticipate its return back to Source eventually.

Shifting a little closer on the couch, I speak, "It's now transparent as to why humans obsess in retelling the struggle between the two opposing forces related in our myths, books and modern movies. The Light fighting the Dark carries on in almost every story. Hey, where are these Naki residing today?"

"A few live underground, dictating movements and shaping the world society by influencing high ranking members of a small elite group. Most live among the rest of us without anyone ever knowing of their presence, forcing nonconforming creatures to live behind the scenes or be killed."

"Have you had direct contact with the Naki?"

He grimaces and snickers, shaking his head "yes" to my question. "When I turned thirteen I found myself invited to special dinners and parties, gradually initiating me into an ominous inner sanctum and I learned more than I should about the ins and outs of this Dark Brotherhood. After this, I took a long-extended vacation anticipating that I may not be able to totally disappear from sight. Fleeing to the other side of the country and across the ocean, as miniscule as it sounds, set in motion my finding Mama Jane and arriving on the Hawaiian Islands. She found me alone and a complete emotional mess."

"So, did all of you boys run into Mama Jane in the same manner?"

"I suppose we all did, but we have different accounts. Marcus and I were school roommates and close friends during the many years sent away at prep schools. Feeling the same isolation and disconnection, he followed me out this way."

I lean closer to Eli on the couch, sensing more comfortable vibes flowing toward me. These embracing sensations sort of saddle my brain.

All of a sudden, an ear-piercing alarm sounds throughout the barn. I search for a sign of smoke, thinking of fire. I look to Eli for a clue as to what's happening. Panic overcomes me at the same time because his blue pupils become slits like cat eyes. In shock after witnessing this alteration, the alarm draws my attention again. Quickly shaking off this bizarre reaction, I follow him down the stairs to the bottom level of the barn. In a state of frenzy, Zeke rushes with Mama Jane from the outside into the opened barn doors en route toward us.

Now portraying an uncertainty, Eli says, "Did you spot anything, Zeke?"

"Not yet!" He replies, appearing annoyed. Mama Jane appears to be concerned, yet calm.

Within a flash, we veer from sitting cozily on his couch teaching me vast amounts of history and knowledge to sprinting down a flight of stairs. I follow them to an illuminating glow at the bottom. Eli reaches over and clasps my shoulder as if to comfort me. The underground room reveals some sort of hidden vault. Ki and Marcus are looking over something at a table. There are computers and machinery placed next to every wall of this room. Wires lead to multiple screens, the visual arms of a security system, confirming my previous assumption upon my first arrival here.

"Eli, what's all this?" I wave my hands around the room.

"This is where a little of that Trust Fund has been spent. Essentially it is Marcus' sanctuary to tinker with his tech, but also our safe room and brain to the security system."

"Look, guys!" Marcus points at the screen in front of him as a limousine drives down the long, graveled driveway. I think whoever it might be is fairly brash as there are no exits other than the access where the limo entered.

"Mama Jane, what do you want to do about this?" Eli speaks boldly in her direction.

Mama Jane commands a powering presence of leadership in her voice and her take-charge attitude. "Nothing to fear, boys and Lucy." She looks at me and continues, "Eli, Zeke come with me. Ki attend to Lucy and keep her down here and, Marcus, if there's any sign of others coming, sound the alarm." She points a finger upwards, glancing at the ceiling. I'm assuming she's referring to the GC that Eli had disclosed to me moments ago.

I watch the monitors with Ki and Marcus, like Sherlock Holmes looking for clues to discover the purpose of the mysterious visitor. The three of them walk slowly to the limo, stopping at a safe distance.

*I wonder what the term "safe" means in this circumstance.*

The door opens from the back and a well-dressed man steps out to greet my new extended family. I'm scared while patiently awaiting the outcome. I sense the tension. From the sharp appearance of this man, he looks to be about sixty years of age. Eli approaches him with a familiarity and the two embrace in a ritualistic fashion. Zeke and Mama Jane stand, positioned like soldiers in the event of a possible threat. Zeke looks like he might be growling. The man holds the partly open door as Eli stoops and steps inside the car. My heart drops in fear for him as I don't know the purpose behind any of this.

Intently watching all of the movements, I see what appears to be a poised and confident female figure sitting in the dim interior, wearing a hat that overshadows her face.

"Marcus, who's that man?" I purposely avoid asking about the woman in the car as her posture blocks my even wanting to know at this point in time. Could this be an old girlfriend returning to take Eli back to the East coast? Would he leave Mama Jane and his brothers? My stomach flip flops due to this uncertainty.

*Get a hold of yourself, Lucy.*

Marcus stares at me as if he's considering whether to tell me or not. I assume his reluctance to be a bad sign. I look at Ki for a clue, but he's not making eye contact and ignores the question. I find a chair behind the table displaying the monitors. I cross my arms to close myself off from this whole situation and submit to patience.

The waiting becomes almost unbearable because I fear the appearance of Eli's long lost girlfriend. I breathe shallowly. Ki turns around and sees my distress. He lowers himself onto his knees and places his hands on my finger tips, which are clenching my thighs.

"Lucy, it's going to be okay. This won't lead to any acts of aggression."

"Aggression? There's a woman in the limo. Who is it?"

He quietly laughs at my suspicion. "The woman in the limo is Eli's sister."

I sit straight up in the chair and draw back, "Oh!" Trying to put the pieces together, I remember Eli telling me that he doesn't have a family and his parents died.

"Ki, how? I mean, Eli told me he was raised by Uncles and didn't mention any sisters. Only you three as his brothers."

"Our apprehension is well-founded as we didn't think they'd have the gall to show up on the farm. Their kind doesn't wander this way unless there's good reason. I'll allow Eli to explain in detail all of this. It's not my place to share."

Nodding, I'm simply happy that my fear didn't transpire as a past girlfriend. Feeling more confident and taking this opportunity, I whisper in Ki's ear, "Does Eli have a girlfriend?"

Shaking his head "no" in response, he whispers back, "I think he has a crush on the student." As I lean back, I catch a smirk on his face and I can't help from beaming ear to ear after hearing this terrific news.

Eli steps out of the limo holding a box and returns to stand next to Mama Jane, his face stoic. I rise from the chair, eyeing them and waiting for more to reveal itself. The man returns to the limo, enters it and the driver backs around to exit down the driveway to the main road.

I follow Ki up to the surface while Marcus remains on guard in his favorite room. Walking outside of the barn, Eli's discussing something quietly with Zeke and Mama Jane. They stop talking when we come within hearing distance.

"Sweetie, let's have a little sit down over here under these trees." Mama Jane gently places her hand on my back shoulder guiding me to the lawn chairs. The boys follow behind us.

I look at Eli and ask, "So why didn't you tell me you had a sister?"

Looking rather apologetic, Eli says, "She is my half sister and I really do not like her much. She is not nice and I would prefer to keep a distance. We only share mothers. Catherine lived with her father in New York. Even as she persistently tracked me down to deliver this message in person, regardless of her dark side, I have to admit that she still carries a sisterly compassion for me because I am her sibling."

Eli looks stressed as if her presence has stirred up some nightmares. I sit down in the chair Mama Jane provided, waiting for Eli to reveal the meaning of his half-sister's appearance.

"Several gates are gearing up to open, bringing in an enormous amount of star codes as the alignment with the galactic core approaches. Catherine says a large stargate threatens to open in the Arabian Sea near Karachi, Pakistan. Many countries from all over the world have sent military craft, making it known this is one of the largest stargates and, therefore, instructing elite members of the Dark Brotherhood to abandon ship, in a manner of speaking."

"Wow, that's incredible!" I decide to withhold my bag of numerous questions and simply listen.

"Remember when I told you that humanity, as we know it, all share ancestry from our diverse brothers and sisters in the Universe? Correct?"

"Yeah, it's pretty mind blowing."

"Here is another bombshell." Eli looks at me and pauses as if scanning to see how I'll react. "My sister, Catherine, and I are both direct descendents of the Naki ancestry. We share a mother who is not human at all. She does not even live on the planet right now. She had to leave when I was three."

"This explains the cat eyes you flashed when the alarm sounded at Catherine's arrival. Is this the only eccentricity connected to your Naki genes?"

"No, the heavy network of synthetic EM fields and gravity mask the irregular norm, causing me to appear more human-like and enabling me to intermingle with limited dissimilarity."

Fighting to be quiet, finally I have to ask, "Then do you look like a snake-man?"

Zeke rocks with loud laughter, almost falling to the ground as he stands next to a tree trunk. I feel almost embarrassed for asking, but I think it's a legitimate question.

"No, I do not look like a scary snake-man!" Now Eli tries to hold back laughter because of this hilarious situation. At least the amusement reminds me of his more human side even if he is part Naki.

Mama Jane interrupts the laughing. "Lucy, when Eli and others like him leave Earth, there is a subtle difference in appearance. Skin pigmentation turns a slightly greenish, brown or pale white hue; ears appear smaller than they do now, and sometimes the canine teeth are elongated."

I twist around to examine Eli and see if I've missed anything unusual. Not that I would, having been studying his facial features so that I remember him when away. Nothing has changed as I still get butterflies in his presence. Whatever he looks like, I'm sure he's strikingly handsome.

Eli continues describing the visit with his sister. "She lives in the elite circles within the Dark Brotherhood and has had recent contact with our mother. I was given the message to join them as most are leaving Earth."

"Where are they going?"

"With the money and power, they have constructed spacecraft to return to an ancient underground base on Phobos. This is their safe zone away from any backlash that might erupt as the star codes release and unveil the forbidden knowledge they have desperately kept secret from the masses of humanity.

"Wait, isn't that a moon of Mars?" I ask.

Ki enters the discussion by saying, "You may have learned about it in the news as it's had minimal coverage about the monolith found by satellites on the surface."

"Imagine the news when they actually start covering the inside quarters of this resident moon," Eli discloses.

Mama Jane shares, "The Naki struggle with increasing star codes seeping through these stargates. They have had success purposely blocking them by using disharmonics, but some are becoming unstable now. Phobos has a structure that shelters some light from entering. It also lacks crustal shifting as the alignment puts a lot of pressure on all the planets in the solar system. They have quite the community setup.

Eli exclaims, "Well I feel sorry for them! Leaving and missing this great opportunity, I will not go. Catherine is not happy since promising to bring me back to Phobos with her. Anyway, we have a job to do here, attempting to keep the peace and preventing scorching violence as the fears in people remain intense with the programming agenda left in place. I assume they hope we will annihilate each other, return to brainwash the survivors and rebuild their civilization by pretending to be these great Saviors. Blah, blah, blah! I have heard too many veiled stories from my sister about their devious plans."

He faces me directly, "One more thing my sister told me. Another large stargate is trying to open. Many earthquakes are resulting in this large section of the planetary grid system."

"Well, where is it? What can we do to help?"

"The location is near Fundo Pedregal, Peru. I have been attempting to find the one missing disk as all four are required to open the obstruction. The other three are locked away down in the safe room. Catherine knew the location of the fourth all this time and has kept me from knowing about it. I suppose she does have some redeeming quality to her razor-sharp personality as she risked a lot by giving it to me."

Zeke pops into the discussion, "If this stargate doesn't unblock, more devastating earth shifting will take place in the South and Central of America, including the Caribbean Sea and Gulf of Mexico, affecting all the lands surrounding this area. Basically, the whole region will go boom!" He makes a loud explosive sound effect.

"The Keepers are already stationed in multiple locations trying to harness Light through their bodies to balance the dysfunction worldwide. Once this gate opens, the star codes will resonate through the geomancy field to activate all the ancient sites," Mama Jane adds.

"There has been infighting between members of the Dark Brotherhood competing for the control over these stargates. It will take some thinking, but we have to at least try and unseal it. If we do not, there could be a major tragedy. The people in these areas need the star codes to help ease the tension and empower the posted Light Warriors." Eli opens the box and pulls out a round disk one inch wide and having a moderate circumference. He places the disk in my hands and I examine the object. I find that it's a very heavy metal and has been notched.

He explains the etching, "Look." He points to a symbol representing the circle with a cross inside it and continues teaching, "The etching explains the Great Year, the four alchemical ages and location of the stargates. The other three all have the same etching accept one is made of pure bronze, one of pure silver and one of pure gold."

My stomach begins to growl. I try ignoring it, but it continues to rumble. I'm embarrassed since everyone can hear it.

"Sounds like you need some food, Lucy," Zeke says.

Eli announces, "Want to get something to eat in town? My treat, of course."

Zeke responding to Eli's hospitality says, "Sounds like a good idea, Sir Eli. I'll go round up Marcus and Ki."

"Mama Jane, are you coming with us?" I ask, politely.

"No, honey, you go ahead and I'll keep an eye on the fort." She's smiling at the pleasure of having some time alone.

We jump into our cars. I take my own, thinking ahead that I'll leave directly from town afterwards. Eli hitches a ride with me and gallantly proclaims, "Thanks for taking the news lightly, about my Naki bloodline. That meant a lot to me. You did not run away."

"I should be the one thanking you. I can't imagine my life without all of you in it!" We head to town with me driving. The previous fear of facing the world alone disappears now after inheriting Eli and his family. I've almost forgotten about my old friends as they previously had been my shelter and protectors from not feeling alone. Someday I'd like to visit Jenna and Caleb, but for now I'm looking toward the future and the promising endeavors ahead. The straightforward stories told by Eli and Mama Jane carry such wisdom and depict my greatest questioning relative to the Mysteries as the terrible problem of Evil has haunted me for most of my life. I have more hope and clarity than when I arrived with this afternoon. Time seems to be accelerating as the days do not appear long enough to handle all of the events that are falling before me.

# Chapter 13
# Unforeseen Forces

We stand outside waiting for a table at the locally famous *Rudy's Steakhouse*. More well-known as a sports bar than a restaurant, the locals play pool or watch a game during the evening hours. Tonight we're all extremely famished and impatiently wait our summons for the next available table. Standing still in the cool evening, my legs and lower back tire so hesitantly I lean into Eli's side.

*Amazing!*

The simple motion of intimacy feels right and I want more, but will take this slowly. I worry that he might take my gesture as being too forward, not realizing my sense of insecurity. Eli doesn't seem to mind and actually places his arm around my shoulder and embraces me as if in response.

The boys sporadically discuss recent sports games until they become more interested in acquiring new technological devices. My concentration rests solely on my close proximity to Eli and the possibilities that may await us. Traces of his clean, masculine smell exacerbate my senses. This new facet of Eli intrigues me and I intensely desire to know the sum total of this man.

"Sinclair." Finally the hostess announces an available table. We settle ourselves into our seats and I sit next to Eli, although not nearly as close as a moment ago. I miss the headiness of his masculinity and desire to scoot my chair closer to him, but I restrain myself and instead ask, "What's good to eat on the menu?"

"Lucy, you're at a steakhouse," Zeke says, raising a slanted eyebrow while he playfully smirks.

"Yes, well I think some pasta sounds good," Eli states.

I flirtatiously grin back at Eli and respond, "That sounds really good."

*I wonder if he's trying to hide from the others this pulsing energy passing between us.*

The lights are dim in the room and the noise of public chattering makes it harder to hear the discussion between Marcus and Ki. I make small talk to catch Marcus' attention. "Eli told me you two were roommates in prep school."

Marcus, nodding, responds, "Yes, I've known Eli since the fourth year in Elementary. It's been a long time, hasn't it, bro? The first day I met him he was rescuing me from a crew of school bullies down at the stables. He has that effect on people, you know, saving others."

Eli, choosing to take the attention from himself, cuts in. "Well, I could not let you be forced to eat horse crap. It is cruel and I could not just stand there and do nothing."

"Try being the recipient," Marcus lightheartedly scoffs.

"I agree!" Filling in the details for me, he shares, "I could not put up with those Barton boys. Having many siblings attending that school gave them a feeling of power and to exercise it, they pleasured themselves in harassing small, new students who could not defend themselves. You know, they never picked on others when alone, but only as a gang. Plus Marcus was just a tad geeky, which made him an easy target."

"I could've taken them on," Marcus jokingly responds. "Actually, Lucy, back then Eli was fearless because he always had a chip on his shoulder. He was angry, a loner, but with good boxing skills. Enraged, he cold-cocked the oldest Barton boy, who was taller and broader than Eli."

"So what happened to those mad skills? Oh yeah! You hate to fight." Zeke adds, poking fun at Eli.

I look for his reaction, but he no longer holds such pent-up anger and smiles, shaking his head as if to down-play their sarcasm.

"You like fighting, Zeke?" I ask, responding to his remark.

"Hell, yeah! Put me on the front line and I'll squash those shady invaders. I know. I know. Peace and forgiveness, but if given an opportunity then let the games begin!" Zeke cannot hide his sheer delight in anticipating a challenge and his eyes betray this, yet, attempting to make me laugh and, at the same time, appearing to mean serious business.

Marcus continues the story. "Eli picked up a large scoop of horse shit in one hand and tossed it at Roy Barton's face while drawing back with his fist to punch him. I jumped into the skirmish, taking up Eli's cue to plaster crap as well. After that day, we were pretty much left alone as all four Barton boys were covered with horse crap, and crying like sissies to the headmaster."

"They were more concerned with the excrement on their uniforms than winning the scrap," Eli adds.

Marcus is almost hollering, "Yeah, both of us had to clean stalls in the stable every afternoon for a month."

Sticking out his arm to fist-bump Eli, Marcus continues, "That's when we became bros sticking it out together to brace these fiends. At the time, our defense was crap throwing as they were a bunch of weak cowards!" All of us laughed at the visual images they were verbally drawing for our amusement.

"Well, Marcus, I haven't stopped being fearless. I simply do not feel the need to assault stupidity as it is a waste of my time and energy. The path of least resistance is the road for me now. Do not let these guys fool you, Lucy. They are not thugs seeking a fight as they like to flaunt themselves. Aggression depletes the Light within.

"We are reminded of a principle that we already know, which is, engaging in violence opens a bridge to forces that feed off turmoil and fear, leaving the aggressor in miserable shape. Nowadays, we take fighting seriously and only respond in such manner when there is physical threat to our survival."

"He's right, but I still look forward to a good stand-up fight. Can't help it. It's what I am, with the exception of self-control and being in the flow of Source, which reveals the most powerful energy in the whole cosmos. The greater good for Earth wins over my need to beat down a bloodsucker or Naki." Zeke offers his advice with more enlightening perspectives.

While rapt deeply into the discussion, I watch a young male walking past our table with two attractive, flashy, half-dressed girls. To exaggerate his persona, he wears gold chains, prison tattoos and swaggers like a gangster. I blink my eyes to clear the black spots floating before my pupils, but they don't dissolve and instead gather into a black mass almost covering the male and females as they strut down the walkway. The cloudy blackness continues to envelope them even after they are seated. I scan the room attempting to spot any more dark auras around other individuals and find some to be grey. Once again I blink my eyes, which clear and I see a mixture of light orbs. Eli notices that my attention is no longer with the conversation and I gather he's receiving impressions of my evolving receptivity.

"What caught your attention?"

Leaning closer to him, I mutter, "Do you see that man sitting over there?"

Before I finish my sentence, he answers softly, "You mean the dark cloud floating around the entire table?"

Eli's precise description, which coincides with my own vision, mystifies me, but my reasoning concludes that if light orbs exist, then the opposite must be real. This new ability to view or spot a possible menace will help me to distinguish when I should be more cautious.

Whispering in Eli's ear, I say, "By tuning in and reading emotions as they walked by, I sensed a good reason to avoid contact or bring any attention to myself and my new sight confirms my instincts."

Eli's warm sweet breath wafts into my face as he softly responds, "Look at the woman to your left sitting in the booth."

I see a large black fog envelope her head and face so that I cannot identify her facial features. She is tall with short blond spiky hair, wearing a trendy business suit. Clearly she appears ruthless as this harpy shouts at the waitress for not being quick enough and now unhappy with her food. The waitress spins around, returning the dinner to the cook. The woman mocks and ridicules the bustling waitress, making snide remarks to others at her table.

I am saddened because this woman lacks compassion for others and yet, I pity her for I know the type of Dark energies she draws to herself. It must be miserable and depressing to wallow in such spite.

The same waitress slowly walks by our table, obviously upset and frowning. Her day isn't flowing well. I catch her hand and say, "I'm sorry you have to put up with people like that woman who was so rude and uncaring. I wish to say that you're doing a great job. It's not easy dealing with angry people."

Shocked by my compassion to her plight, as it must be rare for her to receive such understanding, she responds, "Thank you. That was kind of you to say."

Eli squares his shoulders, staring at me intensely as if he'd like to sweep me up in his arms in a passionate embrace. He doesn't stop staring as I lock eyes with his. I lose myself in the great loving vibrations flowing between our auras and for the first time, I feel confident that I'm interpreting his emotions correctly. I think he's impressed with my natural compassion for this waitress. I detect a swelling infatuation between us. It cannot be denied and I know there must be a kiss coming as surely as the sun rises over the horizon.

Clearing his throat, Zeke mutters, "Food's here, guys. Hey!"

We unlock our connection, sensing that Eli now feels as I do because one cannot deny the magnetism drawing us closer. Fortunately, our server brings out our food restraining me from revealing to the others my obvious adoration of Eli.

Marcus speaks up, "Eli, when are you going to start planning the trip to Peru? There's a great deal to smooth over and settle. It will not be an easy mission. You do know this, right?"

"Yes, I've been reviewing the possible outcomes. Let me contact Thurston. I believe he is our key to getting inside this zone."

Concerned, Marcus articulates, "But isn't Thurston in El Salvador? How are you going to make contact as he's probably in that untamed, mountainous jungle teeming with ferocious criminals, none of which any of us would care to meet face-to-face. I'd like to keep my head intact and connected to my body, thank you very much!"

Zeke and Ki look as if they are not in agreement with Marcus. They both try to dispute Marcus. Eli overpowers the conversation.

"Remember, he's under cover trying to make a difference. Thurston has more staying power and resilience than I could ever possess in this life time. The most amazing component of his spirit is how he stays focused as a Light Warrior. We need his connections and expertise because we will not be welcomed at the heavily armed entrance."

Eli leans in closer to quietly elaborate on the situation and keep it confined to our table. "The last time I spoke with Thurston, we had mapped out the entire geomancy grid points locating the stargates. This one in Peru has been a strong hold. Each location is fortified and guarded. Despite the inside competition for control, the Keepers and members of the GC are progressively gaining control and reversing the web of disharmony. We might actually have a chance at this. With the four disks, we can open the gate and reverse the damage. Thurston indicated an alternate access point in the mountainous terrain, an ancient tunnel system. He is the only one who can get us there. I have no way of finding it without his help."

"If we have to track Thurston down in the jungles, we'd be way better off facing Peru on our own! Thurston does deserve a lot of credit for having the nads to keep exerting himself in that dark chaotic jungle." Marcus shows his obvious concern.

I tug on Eli's shirt sleeve to catch his attention, "What's in the jungles that scares Marcus so much?"

"You saw the Dark shadows around the man and woman over there, right? Imagine facing that force, but expand it tenfold. The gangs and violence in the area are feeding the darkness and it becomes more expansive and powerful by the people who terrorize others to provide a supply of fear. Too many Light Keepers born in this area become victims of the circumstances. It takes a special Light Warrior to do what Thurston does."

Zeke speaks up like a boisterous young boy, "You guys are weak, man! It'll be a train ride. Eli, before we met, I spent some time in San Salvador, mostly drinking and chillin' in the jungle, but regardless, let me handle this for you. I know a few guys in the territory who still owe me a favor. Let's just leave it at that, okay?"

"Of course, I will accept your offer. This can provide more time to plan and coach Lucy before heading to Peru. I need to get her a passport too." Eli watches my reaction.

I become zealous. A real adventure in another country! If I would be left at home, I'd be horribly worried thinking of Eli in the jungles searching for his friend and I'd probably chew my nails to the quick. If he leaves the country right now, our newly discovered romantic sparks might dwindle. Appreciating Zeke's offer, I have reservations as to why they want me to go with them. "You want me to go with you guys? Won't I get in your way?" I ask, apprehensive. The journey out of the country might lead to some real danger or maybe Mother will foil my venture to Peru before I even get a chance to place myself into jeopardy.

Zeke raises a question, "Ki, didn't you just tell me yesterday that Lucy has some supernatural, diamond-clad skills under her belt?"

"You've got to be joking, Zeke! Seeing a few orbs and reading emotions are all I've got in regards to the supernatural! Well, so far at least." I shrug my shoulders wondering what Ki might know that I'm not aware of yet. I can tell that Eli's a little baffled by Zeke's comment.

Speaking for himself, Ki explains, "Lucy's energy field is expanding almost as if she's about to burst like a rocket firecracker. Her atomic cellular structure is really electrifying. I've only heard the legends of Ascension, but not what it actually looks like. This is intense as I mean no harm in scaring you, Lucy. I only told Zeke that you're breaking out of your shell at an accelerating speed."

My panic must show for Eli reaches for my hand and squeezes it, thereby confirming his thoughtful support. He whispers in my ear again, "One of Ki's abilities is seeing the spinning vortex Light fields. I think Ki is implying that our trip to the grove and standing on the ancient stone were more effective than it had been for these guys."

"She's only been to the stone one time in just a few days, Eli! Look, it took all four of us years to get where she's at right now. Besides, that time was full of dedication and focus," Zeke asserts.

More than before, I'm absolutely shocked as to the possible side effects the ancient stone portal can endow one with. Eli was determined to take me to the grove without any warning of its hazards. My breathing increases, causing me to become lightheaded. This is the first time since meeting Eli that I'm literally frightened to the point of panic because of unknown consequences. So far, my head has been in the clouds. Now, Ki's description sounds as if I might burst into flames because of possible supernatural abilities waiting like a ticking bomb.

We're about finished dining, but Marcus and Zeke order pie for dessert. I cannot eat any pie under these new circumstances as my stomach is churning. It's getting late and I want to go home and in the privacy of my own bedroom, think over every facet of any potential dangers or at least try to make sense of it and investigate if there are any further odd implications.

After telling Eli I'm heading home, he offers to walk me to my car having parked far back under trees by a bridge. I stand up and gaining my composure, I politely say, "Good night guys. Thanks for the conversation."

The previously jam-packed parking lot at the restaurant has cleared during our meals. Eli and I nonchalantly walk side by side, stalling. I try to think of the best question as to what's happening to me.

"Is there anything I should be worried about concerning Ki's observation?"

"Never has there been an unforeseen calamity by receiving these star codes from the stone. Equivalent to a geyser, it is a small outlet relieving pressure points in the ley lines of the Earth's grid system. Multiple sites have been used as enhancement vortices for a long time."

"Ki makes it sound like I'm going to detonate or burst like a supernova or something of that nature. The other day you mentioned some kind of seed inside me and the Watcher instructed you to bring me to the stone to activate it."

He stands there with his arms crossed staring into space. "Something obviously different is having an unexpected affect on you, more than anyone else I have known. I know very little about Ascension. Not enough to discern if this is the case. This Watcher never told me why I had to take you, but that it was highly important. I didn't question the instructions because she told me I'd be given more information soon."

"Ascension? Like the story of Inanna?" I'm feeling more panicky paralleling the tale even though it sounds exciting. The unknown fascinates and terrorizes me at the same time. I fear drastic changes despite my desire for them. "What can you tell me about this enigma?"

"The key to Ascension directly links to emotional intelligence. How you process them. You see, activating the inner sight and Ascension are different intensities of the star codes. I will ask Mama Jane for her opinion about this new development and do my best to search for the answers. For now try not to worry."

I'm not convinced to not worry. There's something unsettling and unspoken in his voice.

"May I ask what emotion you were feeling at the time you stood on the stone?"

Scanning my memories, I felt intense admiration, perhaps more like Love. Personally I question the unquestionable. This cannot be love for Eli. It's too early for that to develop, but I cannot deny my falling for him even though every caution sign should have slowed it down. Regardless of the reason, my emotions erupt and I'm helpless.

I keep my thoughts to myself and respond, "I was happy and fortunate to be at the stone to see this mysterious other realm and not be afraid of it."

Only a few bystanders lounge outside near the restaurant entry and we are virtually alone. I'm only a few feet away from my car when he grabs my hand and pulls me into his chest. I feel as if my entire body is on fire. He pauses to see my reactions. I raise my lips up closer to his, inviting him and he slowly lowers his head and presses his lips against mine. His nervousness is as great as my own as I feel his heart thumping against my breast, matching the rhythm of my own beating. Passion rises within me as if a volcano is erupting. There is no sound. The earth stops and we are embraced tightly together as if we have become one.

I hear several of the boys hooting and crying Eli's name, searching for him, probably to pay the bill and jet back home. I don't want this moment to end since it's what I've been waiting and wishing for all of this time. We have been outside a considerable amount of time and fortunately, my parking far away has shielded our private moments. He steps back a bit, takes my hand and kisses it just like a gentleman suitor would do in an old time movie. Seeing that he's about to pronounce the words "Good night," a stillness surmounts his returning to an upright position. The sounds and movements of passing cars have slowed down at a snail's pace. I move my free hand side-to-side and the slow movement eerily frightens me. Nothing like this has ever happened to me and I haven't taken any psychedelics. Seconds become minutes until sluggishly lingering sounds return to normal tempo. I wait for his face to resurface.

*This is beyond strange.*

Anxiously, I wait for this lengthy moment to end so I can ask Eli about the impact of the long-drawn-out movements and sounds, but he's still set in slow motion. In an instant, time resumes its normal speed and I can distinguish the bustling of cars and hollering boys. Eli's expected good night becomes a fixated stare.

"Lucy, your feet are not planted on the ground!"

I stand speechless, unable to react. Fortunately, I don't have to always speak as he can interpret my emotions. Just a moment ago I was deeply imbedded inside my personal fantasies while savoring his lips against mine. I realize now that my heartfelt desire took place at the same time I felt as if I was hovering. Now, confirmation that my feet are not firmly placed on the ground. Indeed, I am suspended a few inches in the air!

"What the hell is happening here, Eli?"

His shock reveals itself in his voice and he sighs before saying, "I don't know, might possibly be linked to a strong emotion like our kiss. I haven't an answer for you this time."

I see his torment and want his angst to go away. Regardless of my feeling distress, at least my feet return to standing firmly on the pavement.

"I've got to get home." He stares fixedly. I say, "Eli?"

He answers, "I'll have the guys follow me to your place. Hand me your keys. I'm driving. You have no choice in the matter and do me this favor, try not to let this scare you, please! Practice the skill Zeke and Ki taught about controlling fear. I need a few days to figure this out. We will get through this." I climb into the passenger side of my car and turn on the radio, hoping that the noise will jerk me back to reality for a safe drive home, but it's all static.

# Chapter 14

# Isadora

I'm sprawled amid my scores of pillows as my head throbs like a beating drum. I wipe the drool from my chin and then chug the glass of water next to my bed thinking that the highly complex dreams during the night have manifested another crash course of lessons. I felt as if my body stayed resting on my bed while my spirit roamed the galaxy, somewhere. I can't pull into my consciousness the images as waking washes them away.

Opening my eyes wider, I lift my bed linens from my legs, but fall back onto my pillows. In the process, I bang my head against the solid wood headboard.

"Ouch! What the, who?"

The inside of my stomach feels as if it had dropped to the floor. Startling me and before I'm able to explain to myself the flowing feminine face appearing a foot away, it speaks to me. I try to distinguish the words, but they sound as if they are being filtered through water. Her face and Light body begin to take form before me. The voice telepathically rings inside my head.

I hear, "Lucy. Lucinda." Initially I think its Mother calling my name. Instead, I make out the hum echoing from this Light being standing at my bedside. In my room nonetheless! I wonder if hitting my head has caused this illusion, but I know this to be incorrect as she materialized prior to the whack.

"Lucy, can you hear me? I know you see me. Hellooo!" She waves her shimmering hand in front of my eyes. Star struck I stare as she bears a resemblance to the same light orbs at the ancient stone. I don't know how to respond or if I should respond since my mind is frozen.

*Who is this and am I having a psychological meltdown?*

Instead of giving into my usual deep seated, childish fears, I become euphoric as I realize that this is a true encounter with an intelligent Light being who is emerging in front of me. I'm surprised and excited to embrace this new life-altering encounter, plus she spoke my name.

This entire journey with Eli has changed me forever: Ki's description about the hidden mystery that my body's energy field is shifting at an intense speed, then having evidence of last night's hovering and the slowing time blip and now I can see Light beings and not just floating orbs. The only rational explanation is that my Light spectrum is expanding, giving me a broader range of options.

*Silly, it's really as simple as tuning into another channel on the radio.*

After my speedy deliberations, enthusiastically I respond, "Hello!" The Light being displays her delight by shape shifting back into an orb of light bouncing around my room like a super ball. She rematerializes back into her feminine human-looking form, thereby making it seem more natural to me to converse with a person rather than a ball. She starts chatting away so fast that I cannot keep up with the words. All I can make out are the recognizable expressions of Light, Eli, Willamette and shifting. Although her non-physical lips move, her words are transmitted directly into my mind as images.

I say, "Slow down, please." It feels abnormal to speak aloud. If Mother was near, she'd think I really went nuts. I didn't notice if she had already divulged her name. If she had, it wasn't clear as the art of interpreting images into words is still a struggle since I haven't had enough practice.

"Who are you?"

"Call me Isadora!" She speaks firmly, obviously impatiently annoyed that I still don't recognize her. "I've only been your best ally for like, eternity! You can finally see me! This pleases me greatly." Her face lights up from elation.

Although inquisitive, I'm almost fearful to ask where she comes from and why? Her features are human with long and wild russet, kinky hair and large almond shaped eyes that glow like emeralds. She wears a white dress with a ribbon tied below her breast. A sparkling diamond droplet hangs in the center of her forehead. Her beautiful features are more impressive than any physical Earth female and the perkiness of her thoughts reveal her to be highly spirited!

"Isadora, what are you?"

She gleefully laughs, but then stops and stares penetratingly, scanning me for information.

"I am your friend." She smiles as if showing her admiration. "From your point of reference, I come from a higher realm of planes in the Infinite Universe. We are ministering to the Earth realm as it spirals out from its plague of darkness. My home is one of the seven star sisters within the Pleiades constellation of Taurus. We who reside among our seven sisters strive to help bring wisdom from the higher realms to Earth. Information of your spiritual evolution is animated in the living library located on the star sister, Alcyone. Your ancestral legends tell that the ancient Lemurians and indigenous cultures who populated Earth since its beginning are, in fact, brothers and sisters from the Pleiades. Humans on Earth who choose to tune into our realm receive our wisdom and will gain knowledge that has been hidden by the Dark forces on your planet. We Pleiadeans are here to stimulate the memories of all humans who so choose this path as we are deeply involved in the life and evolution of Earth. The Elders placed a quarantine on Earth after the Atlantean scientists and Naki opened a bridge to the lower realms. All individuals entangled within this drama are challenged to not surrender to the darkness."

I hear Mother stirring downstairs. I assume she's about to leave when I hear her clinking keys. I open my bedroom door and call down, "You leaving?"

"Good morning. Yes, I have a date with a new guy I met a few weeks ago at dance class. He's taking me out in his boat on the Willamette River. I'll be home later this evening. See you. Love you!"

"Love you too, Mom." I'm glad she will be away today, making it easier to roam about the house talking to the invisible Isadora. I need some time adjusting to Isadora hovering around and press her for answers about these strange anomalies.

As I turn, she lingers as an orb next to my face. I should have known she'd be right behind me. When Mother leaves through the door, Isadora flashes back into her Light body.

Perplexed, as I'm not sure how to understand the shifting forms she assumes, I ask, "How do you do that? Shift into a ball of Light and then into a glowing Light body?"

"Higher Light vibrations and will power, using both thought and emotion. As you can see, I'm not physically in your presence right now. But watch."

She becomes more physical and I can now see a tangible fleshy body before me.

"Go ahead. Touch my arm."

I reach out, shocked to find that she is solid and as real as any human body. "Wow! Tell me how you do this."

"Lucy, I'd prefer to not descend into your realm. It's like sitting at the bottom of the ocean feeling the dense pressure of the water." She returns to her Light body in a split second.

I state, "This is so cool!"

"You have been asking about Ascension. What I just demonstrated is the ability to move in and out of higher and lower fields of Light vibrations. The word you are looking for to describe this ability is *Merkaba*. It means 'riding the chariot of living creatures'. This knowledge, explained in secret doctrines, has been withheld and hidden by the Dark Brotherhood on your planet."

"Buried secrets that humans have inner technology built inside the core structure within us, like the ancient Lemurians possessed before the last cataclysm. Is this right?"

"Yes and you, too, will be able to do this again. It's going to happen soon, but the time's not right, not yet. Be patient as it's coming sooner than expected," she announces.

"Oh great! I like the new sight and all, but what if I don't want more alterations? I'm on a fast track experiencing changes within my physical body that no ordinary doctor can explain. Let alone, I don't want to expose myself to someone that can whisk me away to a laboratory to study." I don't have a single ounce of patience left.

"You are fusing matter and spirit together like a welding patch," Isadora explains.

"Is this how you describe Ascension?" I ask, becoming more and more frantic.

"You are so beautifully divine," she says, smiling delicately.

I see rays of vibrant colors emanating from her lifeforce flowing through me, erasing away my frustration and filling me with peace. Whatever she did, it works as I'm calmer. "Eli mentioned that a Watcher told him to find me and activate a seed inside me. Do I have an alien germ?"

"Eli, ghats! I know you find him irresistible, but don't fall in love with him. There's no time anyway. I'll admit that both of you have good intentions but," she stops midstream and I wonder what she's withholding from me.

*No time for falling in love? To say such a thing worries me as I feel a loss of my life nearing if no passionate love can be experienced.*

"Isadora, we've only officially met just now. Obviously you have an advantage seeing that you are not of this world and have been following me around since."

She cuts me off and says, "Before your birth!"

"I still don't know what you are and if you're about to put Eli in a negative light, then you will have to keep a tight lip. Granted, I've just met Eli and his family, but he has imparted mysteries about this crazy reality show that."

She cuts me off again. "You can be so muddled, Lucy! I'm not trying to convince you that Eli's bad. Actually, his dedication shows expanding awareness and internal transformation for his kind. Eli's also opening star codes to the higher realms and correcting his genetic predisposition since the Naki opened the gates to the lower realms. Okay, he's a good guy as he brings Light into this world, but I don't have to like his sort."

Challenging Isadora, "I thought that all Light beings are supposed to be happy, loving and impartial!"

Isadora is sassy and reacts, "Happy, loving, yes. Neutral? Not yet in my realm because polarity between the two forces continues to be fought. Maybe in the next realm over and above my world, they are more angelic and saintly.

"There's a realm above you?"

"I thought Eli told you all about this? Well, not really above. More like vibrating at different frequencies in the same space. The Universe is constructed with infinite realms."

"I suppose he did explain, but I just can't wrap my mind around this idea."

She responds, "Many things still sleep inside your mind. Try seeing the Universe like a loaf of bread. Carving the bread into different slices would be your realms."

"Then my realm must be the heel of the bread?" I joke.

"Your curiosity about everything is moving you to ascend much faster, but you can't be frightened as fear will amplify your worst nightmares. Noticeable symptoms will increase and most notable will be your ability to manifest things instantaneously and perceive an acceleration of time, wondering where the day went. Of course, when you're feeling blissful, you float. The whole time blip was you attempting to stop time."

"I'm almost frightened of what I can create with this ability! Hey! You still didn't answer what's inside me?" I demand a response to free my worries.

"It's kind of complicated to explain from your viewpoint. For now, let's just say that you carry a blueprint that was launched by star codes at the stone. And now you act as an antenna. Basically, you're a Light Warrior with a mission, but this launch could only occur at this specific point in time and someone in your world had to get you to the site."

"What mission?" I ask, completely bewildered. But she ignores my question.

"Eli was correct by sharing that emotion is the key to human Ascension. I was there with you as you stood on the stone receiving and transmitting that overwhelming emotion of Love. Regardless of whether it's unconditional love or romantic love, it doesn't matter as long as the essence radiates purity."

"Wait. Eli knows about, are you the Watcher who told him to find me? It's kind of creepy knowing you were hanging around without me aware of it."

"Don't worry. We get vague impressions when you want space to yourself, but I do know what happened in the parking lot last night."

She's *feisty for being an ascended Light being.*

"Isadora, why are you hanging around me when you have an entire Universe to explore and discover as clearly you are not restricted."

"You don't remember now, but before volunteering, you appointed me as your personal Watcher. Safety measures had to be instituted. I've been trying to get your attention, but it's not easy when there are so many distractions on this planet. I'm also here to accentuate signs to guide you toward the target. I'm fortunate enough to have found Eli since he can see and hear me."

"Are you the orb I've seen flash by me?"

She becomes tickled and says, "Yes, but not the only Light being to grace your presence. This planet is bursting with us, watching, protecting and trying to get noticed. Evidence to our existence has been seen in what you call digital photography. This rudimentary tool has the capability to catch snippets of the higher Light frequencies."

"I have a collection of snapshots with orbs. I suppose you've solved that piece of the puzzle for me."

"As you've already grasp, this planet has become very dark. The whole point to having me by your side, as you journey, is to have a planned rescue team in place, if you get stuck. We especially spend time with you while your body sleeps. Ascension progresses while sleeping and integrates the star codes seeping in toward the Earth by transforming your atomic cell structure. Eventually you will ascend by activating the Merkaba and leaving Earth."

"Wait, I'm not leaving!"

"I'm afraid you already made the choice long before now. Besides, you have plenty of work that can be done on this side of the veil too. I told you before coming, it would be a messy clean-up job, but you wanted to be the missionary. We are not here to save them all! It's impossible! Broken and shattered ignorant young souls who are destined to be slaves in the lower realms for another few thousand years are all too happy to allow their personal power to become bogged down in hopelessness and fall into being a victim. I know it sounds completely harsh, but maybe the only way out of this mess is by fixing it."

"Wow, I'm not sure how to respond to that. Where's the compassion, Isadora?"

"Lucy, there's a lot of outpouring love energy enveloping the Earth and its life forms. It's rewarding as incredible joy exhilarates us while watching the progress. Yet, it's absolutely exhausting. For a long time, we've been working with the Galactic Council and the Keepers to bring knowledge, healing and protection to Earth. Even Light beings need a holiday to avoid becoming jaded. It's not an easy job!"

"What am I going to miss if I'm not firmly planted on the Earth when the coming Shift is in full swing?"

"If a few million on the planet begin thinking the same way, then a giant wave of change will transform the power structure. If it goes really well, then everyone will begin to see bits and pieces of my realm and gain access to the living libraries."

"What's the bad news if this doesn't happen?"

"Destructive cataclysms that have already wiped out major remnants of the previous civilizations. The Earth's north and south poles shifted when paralleled to the midway point when Virgo shifted into Leo and if the waters didn't wipe out the monuments and races, then the blood bursting inside their veins caused them to fall to their death."

"Great, thanks for the bloody details."

Amused, she replies, "Blood, wait to hear more about the bloody sacrifices the Dark Brotherhood have been performing for thousands of years. Only now it's done in the secrecy of their dark caverns. Once you hear the details, you will be more than happy to ascend back immediately as the terror is unbelievable!"

"Are you talking about death?"

"No, no, no! Ascension is completely different from leaving the body. It means you have the freedom to leave the current Earth realm and move in and out of time and space with this inner technology. Just like an inter-dimensional space ship. You hold the star codes within you to be able do this soon."

"I hold all in high esteem for having the moxy to descend on this planet as it stands. I'd rather teach and provide homecoming parties than to be encased with no knowledge and walk blindly on this planet, sharing space with the Naki and their minions."

Isadora's actually bringing back my nocturnal fears of the dark and shadowy figures. "If you're my protector and guardian, then I expect you to do a good job as this creeps me out. You do know I just recently overcame my fear of the dark?"

Her colorful smile emits calmness and love vibrations float through me. I feel peaceful again and see why I appointed her my personal, spirit bodyguard and teacher. She's fun and full of spunk.

My cell phone rings. I take a moment, stepping away from my conversation with Isadora while she hovers about like a butterfly.

"Hi, Eli, I'm excited to hear from you. Uh, I have something to tell you."

He ignores my statement. Trepidation in his voice concerns me. I don't know what the unrest might mean and I need to see him in person.

"Lucy," he pauses to clear his throat and I know there's something wrong. "I'm going to be out of town for a few days. I'm doing more research on what caused you to hover and if additional anomalies might crop up."

"Well, that's what I want to tell you about. I just met Isadora. Actually, I mean we have reacquainted ourselves, but I have no memories of her yet, but," Isadora motions me to stop revealing our conversations and I wonder why. "When can I see you again?"

"I'll call you when I get back, promise. Just in case anything drastically changes, you can contact Mama Jane. You will not be able to reach me where I'm going."

"Where's your destination?"

"Tell you all about it when I get back. You are in good hands with Isadora. Plus, Mama Jane would love to see you while I'm gone."

"Sure, I'll stop by. I have many more questions for her. By the way, did Mama Jane have anything to share about how to slow down my Ascension?"

I hear a loud gulp, "We will talk when I have more information, okay. See you soon."

I'm unsettled and don't like all the masked feelings and lack of straightforwardness. I stand in front of Isadora, look her straight in the eyes and ask, "Do you know why Eli's masking his feelings and why'd you motion me to stop?"

"He's got a meeting with a certain team, oper...Oh! I forgot about a class I'm teaching. I have to go. I'll be back." I watch her shift from her Light body to a Light orb and then vanish. Now I have to face the day alone to interpret what this all means. Every day something else transpires as time seems to be speeding up. I'll have to try and distract my worrying by taking a long, hot bath, listen to music and catch up on some tedious homework, as if I can focus on school when I'm about to break out of this cocoon and possibly fade away into some kind of Overworld!

I'm going to bombard Mama Jane with questions to get the answer as to why Eli is so reserved in telling me what I want to know. That goes for Isadora as well, when she shows up again. I hope it's not when I'm indisposed.

# Chapter 15
# Creatures of the Dark

The next morning I decide some personal downtime shopping at the mall will lessen some of the uneasiness. Besides I need to buy some new lotions. While I wait for Eli to return, I have to keep myself sidetracked. Study time at home gets pushed off to the side today even though I have an exam on Monday. My classes seem to be the least of my worries.

With a bit of luck, the strange anomalies will be held at bay while shopping in public. I don't want the front page headlines to splash "Unleashed Freak at the Mall" as my last bit of normalcy would disintegrate forever. I'd certainly be hidden away from social venues as an extraordinary, abnormal creature.

*How dramatic will this unknown transformation inside me turn out to be?*

Random thoughts possess my attention on the drive to the mall. I'm excited about Eli and his family, along with learning of a hidden, mysterious reality, but the gaining momentum of this new reality in such a miniscule amount of time is difficult to integrate. I have to look at the world from a completely different angle, including the interesting addition; Isadora.

My brain must have shifted on autopilot. The last thing I remember was pulling out of my driveway. I'm completely oblivious and thankful someone has been watching over me. I couldn't afford to get into an auto accident.

Looking in my rear view mirror, I notice a peculiar out-of-place suburban following me as I drive downtown. Even more unusual, how it's making every turn in sync to mine and slows into the same parking garage. I search for an open spot to park my car near a crowd of incomers.

My imagination runs wild as I must be going crazy to think someone could be following me.

*Ridiculous, Lucy!*

My alarm bell keeps jarring my nerves despite trying to convince myself there's nothing strange about that suburban. I glance from side-to-side to avoid a possible encounter with a member of the Dark Brotherhood. I don't see this vehicle anymore and so I just shrug it off as paranoia.

*If only Eli or any one of his brothers were here right now as my personal body guard! I wonder where the mystifying Isadora might be. I hope she's watching my back.*

I walk inside the entrance, finding the shopping center to be fairly busy. People-watching in the mall can be interestingly addictive as I find it intriguing to study human behavior. Even stranger, to have gained a new perspective after listening to the stories of an alternate history: that Earth has already been occupied by a small subversive group of space beings and we're all the forgotten remnants of that incursion. Only in the movies have I heard such a declaration. What a colossal discovery despite the strange shifting piece of information. This takes my observation to an all new level. Today I view people with a different perspective seeing that we are all relatives of Star races throughout this endless Universe.

As a result of my new sight, my eyes squint from the glare of Light orbs around the people walking down the strip. Shimmering opalescent spheres surround some while other individuals walk trailed by shadows as if energetic leeches have attached themselves.

Reaching my destination, I wander around the Soap Depot savoring every scent of assorted body sprays and fragrances. The smells permeate throughout the store and I find myself drifting around inhaling the soothing fragrances.

I notice a baby in a stroller looking up at me, her two little teeth exposing her smile and she scrunches up her nose. A massive glow of loving emotions exchange between me and her gigantic soul encased inside this little body. I've always known babies were full of purity, but this little one clearly flashes the Light being within her. I sense she can see the shining Light within me too and I return a smile, thereby acknowledging her sweetness as I say, "Hello."

I continue inhaling the various fragrances until I find the perfect delicate scent to match my blissful mood. I purchase the entire collection of lotion, soap and mists and turn to walk outside the store as a number of people walk by me and, instantly, I'm filled with anxiety for no apparent reason. I look around searching for the cause for it's like being sucked into a black abyss and extremely weary. Tracing back my movements, I detect someone in the meandering crowd like a stealthy, surreptitious Vampire sucking Light energy from me. I feel cool and clammy as if I'd given away a gallon of my own blood.

*Ugh. How do I repossess my energy? Who was it and where did it go?*

Using my new sight, I focus and walk in the direction of something, which I sense to be most ominous. Expecting the culprit to be an Emo street kid, I discover that my assumption is erroneous. The culprit is a little grey haired lady. She doesn't look at me and I'm almost standing in front of her now. She continues her conversation with what seems to be her family. I don't think she's even aware of her sinister skill to suck energy from others.

It's not like I can go up to her and say, "Hey, you've just sucked my energy from me when you touched my arm, you Vampire!" Such a statement would almost certainly make me look like a crazy fool.

I decide to get some food and a little rest in hope of recovering from this psychic violation. I grab a vacant seat situated in the food court. It feels good to eat as it seems to do the trick. Resting a bit while energizing myself, I drift off daydreaming and marvel at the interesting aspects of various people walking past me.

I'm reminded of Joan of Arc as someone fighting for truth and believing she heard voices from a divine deity. The claim was an absolute sacrilege in her day and time. It was said that she cried in the field when the messengers, Saint Michael, Catherine and Margaret, left for they were inexpressibly beautiful.

*This sounds much like the description of Isadora.*

Joan of Arc was a radical for her time, wearing men's clothing, fighting and leading the French army to unite France under King Charles. Once captured and sold to the English, she was put on trial, found to be a heretic and burned at the stake. Only later after her tortured death, she became a respected saintly heroine.

*How much am I willing to expose myself in fear of being put to trial, metaphorically speaking, and burned at the stake?*

Thankfully, our society has come a long way from burning heretics in the town square, but it will take some vision to try to piece together a grand disclosure effective enough so that the message doesn't become distorted in the media.

*We weren't ready then, but are we now ready for a mass awakening?*

Considering this mystical reality smack-dab in the face takes it to an entirely different next level. It seems completely unfair as everyone should have access to this same knowledge bestowed on me. It's never good to live a half-truth. Would present-day humans really flip out? The majority of people on the planet already believe aliens exist, but have been conditioned to perceive only little green men from Mars.

I hope to become a Light Warrior one day, fighting to release the greatest hidden mystery on the planet and to reveal truth without the public humiliation a whistleblower suffers by gaslighting: a terrible intimidation causing one to doubt one's own memory or perception. I suppose you can make people believe anything if you tell it over and over until the truth becomes twisted and bent.

I've already endured my share of being the butt of the joke and made fun of from previous debates with my friends and Mother over the years. Every time I opened my mouth I was told, "Lucy, you are so gullible. Lucy, you are such a freak. Lucy, conspiracies are not real." I suppose that's why I've kept my thoughts to myself for so long. There has to be hoards of others just like me waiting to be unleashed from their fears of contempt to uncover answers as to why the people have been purposely told a different history.

I wish Eli was here so I could ask him more questions. I feel a loss by his absence and miss him incredibly. Especially, since he isn't a phone call away. I crave his moist lips and he haunts my every thought since I awoke this morning. I'll leave soon and head out to Mama Jane's as it's a simple way to be closer to him. Besides I need to uncover exactly what he's up to and learn more of their fellow Light Warrior, Thurston. Zeke and Ki left this morning for El Salvador, but Marcus should be around to question.

My energy seems to have increased some and I leave the mall to get my car in the parking garage. Panic chills me again as I should have thought to park closer to the exit when I arrived here earlier.

*Stop being such a chicken, Lucy!*

It's time to stop all the fear and practice some of my new skills I've recently come to possess like the invisible shield I channeled that day in the barn. I walk out to my car and, at the same time, I attempt to create the force field around me, but my lagging energy and focus limits the results I expect. I hurry to my car and stick a key in between my fingers, just in case. It's my only weapon right now after having been drained of Light energy. Walking down to my car on the lower level, I see that same suburban parked within a few feet of my car. I gulp and my throat feels tight.

*Oh, no! What can I do?*

Three intimidating male figures step out from the other side of this vehicle and one approaches me. I look for any witnesses nearby. Regrettably, I am alone. This well-dressed, male stranger wears leather and gloves and is about the same age as Eli. His waxy pale skin emphasizes his sleek styled, groomed hair. He nears. I look into his eyes, seeking a sense of his nature and possible threat. The black emptiness of his eyes pierce through me revealing a monstrous pathological soul. Persistently I try to cloak myself in an invisible shroud as this creature approaches me. I can hope for a miracle while waiting to discover what this stranger wants from me. I mentally scream, *"Isadora!"*

*Isn't she supposed to be my protector right now?*

Speaking in a slithery tone and a polished accent, this foreigner says, "Lucinda, hmm, so nice to have you grace my presence."

I don't know how to react. I'm frightened that he knows my name. I stand at the rear of my car and his approach backs me up against it. My heart pounds until I feel like it will jump out of my body. He reaches out and creepily strokes a lock of my hair as he inhales my scent. I feel his power tug at my essence as if he's another energy Vampire.

*Why me, why now? Where's my rescue team? Isadora!*

These strangers do a good job of masking their darkness except from those with the sight to see them. I surmise that the darkness is firmly encased within their brutish bodies and my gut instinct detects that they are most dark and hostile; an unfamiliar kind.

"Who are you?" I demand, struggling to hide any fear in my voice.

"I'm Zeke's long time brother and comrade, Lamar. What? He never mentioned me to you. How boorish of him. So, where is my mystical brother? It has been years and every time I try to catch up on old times, he brushes me off."

"He's not here with me and I don't know what he's doing. Why are you asking me anyway? It's not my business to keep close tabs on Zeke."

Lamar snaps his tongue, "Dear Lucy, you are so unwise." Lamar's gang begins to walk toward me and a shadowy woman, whom I had not noticed before, reaches for the back door handle to open their car door. I cannot believe what I see sitting in the back seat. A tall, broad-shouldered, grossly disturbing, ashen-faced man with a protruding jaw looks at me. He emanates an almost inhuman and cold hatred. His powdery blue eyes glow. He scares me more than Lamar with his ghoul-like appearance. Positioned under this fiendish man's arm is a tiny, frail, blond-headed adolescent girl who sullenly looks at me. She doesn't look happy to be sitting next to this disturbing beast of a man. I sense a pulsing shady energy surrounding and tugging at me to enter this vehicle. Even though my fright weakens me, I fight the urge to be afraid and slow down my responses to gather the Light as if sucking it from the earth's energy field.

Lamar speaks again in his unrecognizable dialect, which sounds out of the ordinary. I know with all my heart that I must not enter that vehicle. My panic subsides and in this second, I powerfully thrust forth my invisible coat of armor. I see the pearly iridescent glow and it thrills me to know I did this on my own. Never have I felt so confident to protect myself or to help this young girl.

These shadowy creatures jump backwards as if I am covered with holy water. Before they leave, I block the car door from closing and look directly into the eye of this beast sitting next to this drugged girl. "Let her go now!" I command.

The lock on the car door pops open and the girl is released from the other side. She slides dizzily onto the ground. Without any further comments or identification from this gang, they all leap into the suburban and speed toward the exit, but not before I see Lamar arrogantly scowling at me through the car window.

I cannot explain what has just happened or the identity of these dark ones and why no one was watching my back! They scurried as soon as my Light shield recharged.

Leaning down over the young girl as she weakly attempts to rise, I ask "What's your name?"

It takes her a minute to find the words, acting as if she'd been heavily drugged, "My name is, is Sarah."

I wonder if I should call the police, take her to a hospital or Mama Jane's farm. I have no idea what kind of spell Sarah's under and to what degree of possible abuse she may have endured. I gently ask, "Sarah, do you feel okay if I assist you to my car? I'm going to get some help for you."

Sarah slumps on the seat in the passenger side while I call Mama Jane. A few shoppers walk by and pretend to either not notice this scene or are too wrapped up in their personal lives to stop. It's just as well since I must decide the best action to take right now. "Hello, Mama Jane."

"Yes, hello, Lucy! I sense you're about to come over."

"That's why I'm calling, um, but there is something else. I need your advice on what to do. I'm in a parking garage and a very strange sort approached me like they wanted something, but they were asking for Zeke."

"What were any of their names, honey?"

"The only name told to me was Lamar. Who is this? They really scared me, Mama Jane, and they were not the ordinary humans!"

She pauses and says, "They are Vampires, the Order of Draco. You didn't look directly into their eyes, did you, Lucy?"

*What an odd thing to ask.*

"Yes, I did look into their eyes. Why?"

"Their stare hypnotizes their prey just like a cobra. Thank heavens it didn't work on you. How's the girl?"

As always astonished at her psychic ability to know this, I respond, "She's drugged or something and looks sallow. I need to take her to the hospital and call the police. This is why I've called you, to ask what to do?"

"No, keep the lass with you and bring her out to the farm. We can find out where she's from and try to reconnect her to family. She's been hypnotized and not drugged."

*In fact, she appears to be under a spell.*

"Why don't we just call the police?"

"Under these circumstances, the safest place for this girl is within your protective shield. Remember, there are members within the Dark Brotherhood serving in all kinds of areas, including the police, and they protect beasts like these for dollar rewards. I will call Officer Garrett and have him come out at the same time you bring this gal. He's someone we can trust to get her home safely. Also, we both need to ask her some questions."

"I'll be right there."

I close the door and help Sarah place her seat belt on. She looks weak. What kind of monster can do this to a young girl? There are puncture wounds to her neck and wrists. Only a soul-less creature is capable of such callous evil; a Vampire! How does this fit into the schooling of invisible worlds? Several weeks ago I never would have believed there were real monsters, but today I have confronted them.

*Holy shit! I actually stood face-to-face with one of my greatest fears and scared them away by shining my Light force!*

Officer Garrett arrived before me at Mama Jane's. Another female officer stands next to him and Mama Jane. They advance toward me as I rush from the car.

"Hello, Lucy, what do we have here?" Officer Garratt asks, a fatherly air about him.

"This is Sarah. I don't have the words to actually explain what happened, Officer. All I can tell you is that this girl was at risk with these," I pause wondering if it's the right thing to say "Vampires."

"Its okay, Lucy, we know what they are. You can call them Vampires. They go by many names, but Vampire is a lot easier title."

I instantly feel comfortable in Officer Garrett's presence and can trust that Mama Jane was correct in contacting him. I walk over to Mama Jane as the two Officers attend to Sarah.

Mama Jane hugs me and says, "You did good."

"What's going to happen to Sarah? Will they come after her?" I ask.

"No, I don't think she'll be in any more danger. Why don't you go inside and kick off your shoes for a bit. You've been through an ordeal, hon."

I don't argue with her. Upon opening the door, I get a whiff of fresh baking, a scent I am familiar with. It reminds me of home. I grab a throw blanket and cover myself, closing my eyes for a bit. Mama Jane is right. This ordeal has been emotionally exhausting. The base of my skull throbs as if my head will explode. I wonder if this has anything to do with my developing sight and abilities.

Mama Jane returns from outside and I hear the crunch of the gravel as the police cruiser leaves. I ask, "Did you get any information from Sarah?"

"She knew little, but enough to call her parents. They're relieved to know that Sarah's alive and returning home. It's comforting to know she'll be back with her family."

"But won't she be traumatized the rest of her life from this experience? Just having been a few minutes in their presence is enough to terrorize anyone, let alone what it may have been like for her. By the way, did you find out how long she'd been with them?"

"For a week as they came from Portland. This subset of the Order found Sarah alone while walking home from school. They are not local and have been hunting, moving from place to place, looking for a candidate to gratify their blood thirst. The legends about Vampires are true. They do not like a bright source of Light, but can exist in diffused light from the sun."

"That explains why they left like cockroaches when I was finally able to develop the Light shield. Mama Jane, I was attacked psychically at the mall by some old lady who touched me, taking my energy! It's too strange to even talk about. When it happened, I couldn't believe it myself."

"These Vampires were able to get closer to you because it sounds like your energy was depleted some. They can only get close to subtle Light and when they do, they take advantage of the victim by extracting the higher Light fields released through the bloodstream. They are Light eaters through flesh and blood. They cannot exist or attempt to get close to those who hold elevated amounts within them. In addition, the Vampires cannot survive without it. No being can exist without the Light, but their source comes from secretions released within blood. In order to get access to this source, they must induce extreme fear in their victim. The pineal gland is a Light receptor having the ability to activate their liquid remedy. It's the most powerful source of ethereal energy available to humans in order to initiate supernatural abilities. The blood drinkers call it the 'nectar' of the gods."

"Where is their point of origin? They appear so unnatural."

"Like all beings on this planet, we came from various Star races. They are descendents of the Draco from Orion mixed with the human gene. They cannot be in this world currently without some sort of human form because they would be exterminated by the governing Naki if they appear too out of the ordinary.

"Our folklore says that these gods originally wanted the resources of the yellow gold, or ambrosia, from the mines as it could be turned into a powder and ingested as food for the gods. When the planet became almost depleted of ambrosia, the lower ranking Dark Brotherhood was left to drink the nectar in blood from preying on humans and became addicted to this practice. Like all species we need Light to exist, but the darkness within these creatures requires another form and it's through this process. Both ambrosia and blood provide the sustenance for these creatures to continue living, giving them supernatural abilities. These Vampires prefer living within the deep, hidden subterranean tunnels and chambers beneath many large cities. They can only survive on the surface as long as they drink their vital life force; blood. Like any other race on the planet, they produce offspring and continue their species, but remain exclusive. If the masses of people on this planet were to become aware of their existence, an all-out blood bath would occur."

"It's already a bloodbath isn't it? But only a few sadistic psychopaths are actually caught. How often do they have to feed?"

Mama Jane continues, "Not often. They eat food just like every human, but they must feed on blood four times a year in sequence to the seasonal equinoxes."

"This is unreal! I still can't believe we're talking about real life Vampires!"

"Think of them as any other creature, honey. They do not have to exist in this state of darkness."

"Huh, what do you mean by that?"

"Every creature on the planet has a choice to embrace the higher Light fields, these star codes."

"Wouldn't that make them die?"

"No, this Source can make them crazily insane and even painful to take on, just like when a heroin addict stops pumping poison into their veins. If they are not ready to embrace it, then they will succumb to death. It's like this. We cannot live on Antarctica without proper gear to protect us from the elements. They cannot survive once the Light cranks up on the planet unless they become transformed by it or have the right gear to live in these conditions. The Dark Brotherhood does their best to create an environment that will continue their way of life on the planet. The Keepers of the Light are doing their part to bring star codes to assist in guaranteeing that the next Cosmic Year is blessed and will restore the planet back to its original design.

"What about the Naki? I thought they were the worst as Eli said."

"Both the Naki and Order of Draco are in the same predicament. These Star races are closely related, but currently the Naki are on the higher echelon in their pyramid of power.

"Do you know of any Dracos who have embraced the light?"

She smiles at me proudly and says, "Yes, his name is Zeke."

Flabbergasted I now know why Lamar was looking for Zeke and called him his brother and comrade.

"How did Zeke accomplish this transformation and how long has he been well, clean?"

"Zeke tired of the life style and bits and pieces of the star codes over many many years gently struck him until he was ready to be released of this burden. You must know that he once was a Light eater and this power gave him longevity and his supernatural abilities. He's much older than we are physically."

"Like how old?" I ask.

"He was born of nobility at the rise of the United States."

"That means he's like over two hundred years old?"

"Yes."

I find Zeke likeable and he makes me laugh. I chuckle to myself.

*Maybe he can help me in my American History class.*

"Why has Lamar been looking for Zeke? Does this have something to do with leaving this gang?"

"Everything to do with it! Never is it okay for one of their own to cross over to the other side. It's a slap in the face and the Order becomes threatened as Zeke knows too much about their secrets. Once Zeke was able to reach the point to take on even more of this Source at the ancient site, the Order couldn't come close to him but only watch his every move from a distance. Zeke has become more powerful than they are. But like a wild predator, they wait to find a weakness in their victim so they can go in for the kill."

"Can I stay here tonight, Mama Jane? I'm a little crept out by this new disclosure. The farm feels more safe than home right now. Mother will be away most of the evening."

*Plus, it gives me a reason to stay nearer to Eli, wherever he disappeared to.*

"By the way, where did Eli go?" I ask.

Mama Jane replies, "He left to meet with a few members of the GC who requested a private conference."

"You mean he's not even on the planet right now?"

She snickers, "Not even in our time because leaving morphs space-time."

"You're implying Eli's at a meeting somewhere in the future?"

"Yep, sure is. He's getting a better picture as to how to help you."

"He said he'd be gone for a few days."

"He'll arrive back soon as our few days are actually more like a few hours for his frame-of-reference."

*That's a relief. I feel as if I can't breathe without him near.*

"Let's have some dinner. I have a full meal waiting. Please let Marcus know its suppertime. He's down in his lair in the barn."

Walking outside to fetch Marcus, I feel warm like someone is staring at me. I look around, but don't see anyone. Squinting further and looking with my new sight, a shape forms into Isadora.

Instantly I yell out, "Where the hell have you been?"

# Chapter 16
# Riding the Cosmic Wave

"Isn't your job description, "Watching?" Those Vampires came too close! What kind of help are you?" Posturing with my hands on my hips, I question Isadora's role behind her claim to be my personal guardian and protector.

"Lucy I was keeping my watch on you from Alcyone. I can observe what's happening from multiple locations. There's no distance keeping me from my duty. Didn't you notice how well you gathered that energy to make those sickos shake in their boots? My insight cautioned me that if I arrived as the rescuer, you'd never learn how to protect yourself."

Isadora claps her hands and shimmies, showing her praise. "You also saved the girl and if I had come to your rescue, the girl would still be in their clutches. It had to be you, Lucy! Not only did you help Sarah, you also discovered your ability to serve yourself well in the upcoming events about to be embarked on."

I grasp Isadora's reasoning and dismiss my original frustration at what seemed to be a lack of support during my most terrifying confrontation. She's right as it's invigorating to experience directly the capability of my shield and ability to control it.

"Where was the protection for Sarah that could have prevented her abduction in the first place?" I'm really bothered by this. "Doesn't Sarah have a personal Watcher protecting her as well?"

Isadora clarifies, "Of course she does! Not everyone pays attention to the caution signs. You know, that gut feeling humans are meant to experience in the pit of their stomach."

"That seems too simplistic."

"There are more reasons why things happen the way they do. For instance, energy attracts alike energy, which causes your protective shield to lower just like a draw bridge when you feel fearful or miserable and hateful. That's why it's very important to stay wise and not fall into a gloomy attitude. If you unknowingly open that bridge, then be prepared to fight off shady creatures. We cannot interfere if the individual doesn't want it. It's not like we don't try either as it can be immensely exasperating on this side when a forewarning gets muddled and disregarded. Sovereign beings have free will and aware of it or not, the connection becomes murky and the message doesn't transmit. Even you, Lucy, have been hard to communicate with prior to your activation at the ancient stone. It's not fun being ignored as it would've been easier talking to the rock!"

"Wait! It was you that day messing with my radio, moving the curtain sheers, the door handle, my car not starting? And, oh my God, flashing a warning sign inside my head! You prodded me with cautionary signs throughout that day, the very day I met Eli. But why?"

Isadora solemnly says, "It's convoluted and it wasn't me. Leave it for another time." She turns around and floats toward the barn.

*She really cannot expect me to hold out for answers that I need now.*

"No, I want to know now! Is it because you're biased against Eli?"

She turns around saying, "I like Eli."

"Well I don't perceive Eli as being a wrong decision." I huff up.

"Ghats! Lucy, it's not wrong. Just a more problematic route. I'm not passing on any more information so change the subject."

"You're aware of much more then I am. Why can't you tell me?" I plead.

"I'm committed to an oath to not interfere, well, typically."

"So, there are times you interfere, right?" I attempt to be facetious.

"I'm only here to lend a hand."

"Whose hand then?"

"You have to know everything! There's a time and place for every perfectly constructed plan. This is not the right moment to lay it all out as your emotions have a huge impact on how well you can control your Shield and if, Oh! Let's just focus on training for Peru.

I finally concede to leaving some items alone, but only for a short while. "Fine, I'll change the subject. Tell me more about these Vampires. I'm more freaked out than ever after personally meeting these creatures! Not to mention how scared Marcus looks when chatting about the jungles in El Salvador."

She responds, "Vampires flock to places more suited to their needs."

"But there's a lot of sun down south."

"That doesn't matter because they travel through tunnel systems connected to every location they choose to go. Wherever war and turmoil exist, they are responsible, and, of course, their local stargate in Peru doesn't emit direct Light either. Virtually, it's a haven for Vampires. Legends go far back on bloodletting and sacrifices to their god Camazotz. This god wasn't a deity, but a dark entity who entered this realm after the catastrophic events that took place on Atlantis. Camazotz demanded the Mayan and Aztec people to provide victims or he would destroy their lands and all their people. So regrettably, they did what they were told as they were frozen with fear. Camazotz was killed by one of the local tribes after they'd found their courage and had endured all they could. Unfortunately, Camazotz produced offspring and these anthropomorphic creatures are the Vampires of the present time."

Disgusted, I react, "It all makes sense why the Mayan people were peaceful and intelligent and then stories of gruesome blood sacrifices scorched their reputation."

Isadora continues elaborating, "When a new Vampire king took the throne, a child's still beating heart was given to him to eat."

"Yuck, all of this talk about blood makes me feel queasy and wobbly."

"Lucy, we need to toughen you up before any more confrontations with Vampires. The Lucy I know is a thrill seeker, just waiting to ride the biggest wave in the cosmos, but you still have to overcome more fear. The capabilities you hold can either manifest something good or your worst nightmare, which won't be controllable once it's created."

*I'm unsettled at her remark that she wants me to toughen up for more nose-to-nose confrontation with Vampires.*

"Are you implying that I could think up a monster and it would materialize right before me?"

"Something like that."

"Well, I want to know what I am and where I come from." Instantly an outpouring of submerged memories from somewhere faraway; perhaps prior to or in a future space-time, flow through my mind. Her words, "riding a big wave" also cracked open buried data. I feel as if my sub-conscious is splitting open and now it's becoming clearer as I dig into hidden crevices.

Like a movie, extremely vivid images slip into view. I see myself waving goodbye to family and friends and entering a white room inside some structure on Alcyone. Upon closing the door to this room, which is a complete mystery to me, I recognize that I've prepared myself for this moment. I stand in the middle of the room completely alone and wait for something to occur. Five minutes pass. My curiosity builds and my patience wanes until a male's reverberating voice asks, "Are you ready?"

*Ready for what?*

Then I can see myself along with others waiting for an important mission to commence. While anticipating this event to occur, impressive depictions of the most pivotal moments in my life fill me: the choices to be made, pain and sadness, love and hate, family, friends, strengths, weaknesses, desires and on and on. To my astonishment I see my life unfolding, but only to the moment I met Eli and his family as I am prevented from viewing more. Where I stand on the floor is a highly technological device increasing my vibratory fields. I now come to believe this event consists of cosmic proportions. Individually we all rapidly shapeshift into spheres of Light. I'm aware that I am one of eleven beings separated by white walls who are about to descend on an important mission.

Moving incredibly fast back through space and time, my awareness hovers above my mother in the throes of labor, pushing and straining while doctors and nurses attend to her. My father, sensitive to sharing this emotional moment, stands next to her bed waiting for the baby to appear. I know this child is me for I now view this sphere of Light give life to this infant at the same moment that my mother's womb ejects me. This alien environment shocks and elicits my initial cry.

The remote viewing clicks off. The gravel crunching under my flip-flops and the big white barn causes me to slam back into my body and I am once again conscious.

*I'm back! I just witnessed something other-worldly and how I came to be Lucinda Marie Hayes.*

Spiritedly Isadora speaks, "You have your answer where you came from. Well, most recently that is."

"I'm struggling to assimilate what I witnessed. Is that how we really come to be here on Earth? There must be some advanced information explaining what I just viewed and how it occurred. I mean, it seems so magical and I felt like I was flying through the cosmos."

"Life is magical everywhere in the Universe. This is one way the Light beings achieve presence on Earth," she answers.

"I'm going to ride out this big wave coming from the Galactic center! Like Eli shared earlier, there's no way I'm going to miss this!" I exclaim.

*Beyond a doubt, I truly am a thrill seeker and love challenges. I've come to Earth at this specific time for something most important.*

I express my impressions from the vision. "It's not the darkness that most frightens humanity. It's the not knowing what to do with our hopes. Confusion causes so many to simply give up trying. It serves no one to play alone while together unified, we can influence a critical mass awakening to stop the Dark agenda." I look directly at Isadora as I clarify my whole purpose behind my mission. "We can't let them lock Earth into an imprisoned planet, isolated from the rest of the natural cosmos. That's a miserable, hellish existence, to be isolated and deliberately restricted."

"It's most important to remain calm and walk inside the eye of the hurricane as magnified fears surface, all the while with an unwavering fearless confidence stare down these dragons," she says.

I try recapping. "Eli elaborated on the fact that this entire planet is under the domination of malicious lower entities that want to enslave and control, thriving on human fear.

Isadora explains, "The Naki and Draco both want to rule as a repressive dictatorship. They are attempting to finalize their intentions before the shift completes. They are infighting as the Naki want to return to a less populated Earth as this fits their need to take over and gain the super power, a one world government under their control. With less population, less strife, the more power they acquire. Whereas, the Draco are in conflict with the Naki because they need human blood for nourishment. The Draco have already helped certain less informed members of the Dark Brotherhood by building the underground facilities and safe places for select humans to survive any catastrophe. They are protecting their self-interest; the food supply."

Clutching onto my stone pendent reminds me of Mama Jane's story about the Land of Mu and the state of harmonious living on the planet. Some of the fog has lifted as I now recognize that hope happens to be an activated seed deeply rooted inside my heart.

"Oh crap! I almost forgot about following Mama Jane's instructions to alert Marcus to come inside," I state.

I'll resume my nagging questions to Isadora later after I fetch Marcus for dinner. I see that he's already walking up the stairway from his hideout. Since he can't see Isadora, I bet he thinks I'm insane speaking into thin air.

Marcus nonchalantly brushes by me, saying, "Hi Lucy. Hello Isadora." Seriously, I really don't know why anything ever surprises me, but, of course, he too would see Isadora and whoever else pops in from the Overworld.

*I'd like to meet more Light beings as well.*

After dinner I follow Marcus out to the safe room under the barn. He said that he has something to show me. I toddle down the stairs while listening to him rattle off in scientific terms about a specific room in which to control time travel. Marcus catches my attention as soon as he states time travel. Instantly my heart gravitates to Eli and my missing him again.

Marcus walks toward the back of the room and behind a white board is a door. He leads the way into a larger room where mirrors encircle a raised platform. The surface of the base glows in a ring of white light. Glass separates the platform from a desk with computers lined along the right side of the room.

*He's introducing me to Maggie.*

I see a shabby worn-out couch positioned next to this workstation. I had imagined the focal point of the time machine to consist of a specialized chair and robotic gear.

Marcus still shares his knowledge about how this works. I walk closer to the platform attempting to come nearer to Eli as this is where he disappeared into the future to help me. I daydream for a moment remembering his affectionate embrace.

*I wonder what he's doing and what interesting facts he might bring back, hopefully nothing disconcerting.*

I quickly turn around so that Marcus doesn't think I'm ignoring him. Attempting to make a good impression, I ask, "Can you track the exact location and time where Eli can be? I mean, is there a way to communicate with him?"

Marcus points to a computer monitor and what appears to be a map of some sort with a flashing red light. "This flash here is Eli. He has monitors attached to him that send data if his vitals are under duress. When he needs to communicate, Eli sends a script through his hand held instrument."

"Eli told me little about a hand held device."

"It's similar to a PDA, but looks closely like a mirror. He and I can communicate by sending messages back and forth, but we've agreed to only send messages if they relate to the mission."

"Bummer, I kinda thought it would be nice to send a hello."

"Everything looks good for Eli right now. It's a wait and see when he returns and it depends on the composition of time waves he's carried back on. We have a general idea that he'll arrive any time between three in the morning and by late tomorrow night. I stay down here during this expected return time. Okay, I pretty much live down here, most of my time anyway!"

Marcus has a couple of nice computer chairs next to the main frame. He sits down and I take the other chair and relax. I ask, "So what kind of exciting adventures have you guided Eli through?"

"There are so many to choose from. Um, let's see. I think the most harrowing was when Eli went back during World War II in the middle of the actual conflict in Germany. The Nazi's had a collection of many artifacts they had stolen, two of which were the works of Fulcanelli and an ancient Sumerian tablet explaining the last four ages. Eli bit off more than he could chew as he had to charm the daughter of a Nazi general to steal the book."

Jealousy arises within me and I want to squash this negative emotion as I know that giving into it will make me feel worse. If Isadora is correct that I can create outcomes with my thoughts and emotions, then it would be unspeakable to manifest a reason to be jealous.

Marcus continues sharing bits and pieces of more stories. "Another time was when Eli wanted to get his hands on an oversized statue. He was persistent and said it was a family heirloom. I took his word, even though I'd never seen it before as it would have been at the manor, but I suppose that's how it works. The statue at that time only existed in Eli's memory."

"What do you mean?"

"The statue never appeared while I was growing up and I've been to the Manor many times. I never saw it because it disappeared shortly after being carved."

I assume he's speaking about the large statue of the half man-snake in the loft. "Is this how Eli retrieved all of his antiquities that I saw displayed upstairs?"

"Yes, most of them. It was a busy year collecting all that stuff."

"Can't you use the same time control technology to fix the blockage of the stargate?"

"I wish it were that easy."

I sense his fear when I mention the stargate and ask, "What scares you the most, Marcus?"

"Um, well, Vampires. Hoards of them and personally, they scare the crap out of me! Wherever there are mass slayings, blood, death, carnage, gang fighting and massive amounts of drug smuggling, Vampires are the root cause."

"How about Peru? Are there many Vampires?"

"Many Peruvian shamans in the area drive them away. That's what I've heard at least, but I've never been to Peru. Eli doesn't always tell me everything as he knows I shudder in their presence. That's why he goes on these time quests while I sit behind the controls. I like it better this way."

"Aren't you gonna go to Peru with us?"

He stares at me; his lip curled, raises his eyebrow and asks, "Do I have to? I didn't think it was a requirement for me to go."

"But you have to. I want you to be there! We can give each other courage." I strive to persuade him to feel a little better about journeying into the unknown with me.

"We'll see."

I think I've convinced him a bit by charming him with my eyes.

A beeping noise sounds from the computer tracking Eli and I see the flashing red light race faster than it originally had. "What's the signal?"

"It's Eli's vitals. They're increasing above normal range." He stares intently at the numbers and graphs, which I know not how to read. I wait for an explanation while Marcus computes what is occurring, but I can't stop the urge to ask.

"What is it? How's Eli? What do you know?"

Marcus, tensely engaged with the statistics, quietly says, "I don't know yet."

He starts typing and sends an instant message: "Provide data." We stand frozen, tense, over the monitor, waiting for what seems hours. Probably only minutes have passed. Then a message pops up on the screen: "I'm good. Back soon. On schedule."

Thankfully Eli is all right, but I'll feel much better once he returns. I probe Marcus, "What would be the reason for his vitals to go crazy like that?"

"Beats me. Usually, the monitoring system doesn't respond like it just did, but who knows? He answered and we know he's still alive and on his way back soon."

"Yeah, not soon enough though. I still need answers and I need to know what to do to ground myself to the gravitational field." I start to laugh as I remember hovering above the pavement while kissing Eli.

Marcus pipes up, "Hey, why don't you try some magnets? I have some in the other room. Just keep them in your pockets and the bracelets on your wrists."

"Really? You think it's as easy as that?"

"We can at least try. Right?"

"Sure, thank you for the idea." I head back upstairs to check in with Mama Jane, thank her for letting me stay the night, then head to bed. I'm extremely tired, but I instructed Marcus to wake me if any other alarms sound. While lying in bed, I think of ways to justify skipping school tomorrow, yet, knowing that I can't unless there's an emergency. I'll just have to wish that time speeds up and tonight turns into the next day.

I'm worried about Eli and before falling asleep I try to mentally locate him in the ethers of time and space. Heartache fills me. I see Eli sad. Hopefully, my gut is wrong. Now that we've crossed paths in this world, there's no doubt that I want to be with him through eternity.

# Chapter 17
# The Initiate

He's back. I received the news after Marcus fulfilled his promise to announce Eli's arrival. The solitary text message didn't provide any details. I'm beginning to worry. It's been three days after his return and Eli hasn't called or sent a personal message as he promised to do. Whatever the reason, I know he's particularly concerned about why after standing on the stone, hovering in midair isn't the norm. I cannot become too discouraged because his thoughts have been focused on me.

The waiting around drives me mad! My judgment tells me to stop waiting for a phone call and barge right over there to get answers. I am left uninformed and still wondering what he may have discovered at this privileged, off-world, special meeting. For the moment I'll tame my frustration as he might misunderstand my temperamental behavior.

*I wouldn't want to push him away.*

My emotions race when remembering our kiss. Incredible proof of his affection for me during that passionate embrace changes to a tinge of fear that he might have changed and not like me that way anymore. His lack of contact causes me to doubt that meaningful kiss as nothing more than just that, a kiss.

*I cannot take the waiting! I must rush into his arms right this minute!*

My impatience stops my wavering. I'm impelled to drive over to the farm following my last class to gain answers from Eli.

I get to my car and abruptly stop unlocking the door when a thought enters my head, "Lucy, restrain yourself! Don't overload with a ton of emotions."

I wonder if this little voice is my own or Isadora's? Before appearing irrational in front of passing students, I slip inside my car and state out loud, "Isadora! Are these your remarks?"

Big success as I pin down her presence sitting in the passenger seat when she manifests from a sphere and shifts into her more human appearance. "You really shouldn't mope so much, Lucy, as it's distracting."

"Mope?"

"Worrying about Eli not liking you is gibberish right now, a waste of focus. You shouldn't get too lovesick, but despite my advice, this guy has deeply and madly fallen for you too. You're only going to hurt him, not the other way around."

I stare at Isadora, pondering how to respond as I couldn't possibly cause any pain toward Eli. He is my everything! She must know more than I do since she has a different point of view, but I quickly push that idea to the side as an unlikely possibility. Like a giddy youngster, I squeeze the steering wheel and squeal, "Really! Madly fallen?"

Isadora raises her eyebrows at me like she can't believe how unaware I've been to Eli's attraction for me. "Okay, but why does it feel like he's snubbing me? I know it's only been a few days after his trip, but I thought he'd show more zeal and want to see me right after he got back."

"It's always complicated on this planet, isn't it? Having to guess what the other is thinking or feeling, it's rather grueling. Ugh!"

"So how different is it in the Pleiades? Is there such a thing as a passionate love on your world?"

"Of course! What would the Universe be like if there wasn't love and romance? Just because we come from another realm and shapeshift into Light bodies doesn't mean we don't have what you term 'tangible and touchable intimacy.' Actually, the closeness in our relationships is much more powerful because everything is straight forward and upfront. We don't get jumbled into mixed messages as humans do. I suppose there are still those who do like melodrama and dive right into the middle of the theatrics of your world, such as yourself."

I acknowledge her depiction, "I kind of like the excitement of emotional highs."

"Be careful. You have the emotional ability to manipulate and create situations, but if you let them out of the cage and run amuck, then we're all in trouble. You don't realize your power yet!"

"Well, if I have this creative power, then it hasn't presented the very thing I desire the most, now has it?"

Isadora gives me a little assurance when she says, "Your phone is about to ring in five, four, three, two, one."

Within seconds I grab the cell phone from my sweater pocket. Anxious and on edge from expecting Eli's call, I flinch as the phone vibrates in my hand, even though Isadora gave me a heads up. I wait until the third ring to answer so I won't appear too eager.

"Hello."

"Hi, Lucy. Sorry for not calling sooner. I had to take some time to pull myself together. This kind of voyage knocks me out for days."

His previous surliness doesn't matter now that he's on the phone with me. I had never considered that such a journey would be taxing on the body. Uneasiness tugs at me while I patiently wait for an invitation to meet face-to-face again.

"I'm feeling more like myself today and I need to fill you in on the specifics. Are you doing anything right now? How about coming over?"

I don't want to appear over-zealous so I pause for a second before giving my answer. "Sure, I can come over. How about in an hour?"

*What am I thinking?*

I don't know what I'll do for an entire hour since I'm actually dying to zip right over. Isadora gestures as if she's amused at the double meaning behind my words. Just a moment ago, she basically said not to play mind games.

I change my stance and say, "Actually, I can be there in about twenty minutes. Is that alright?"

"Good. See you soon!" he replies.

I end the phone call, exuberant.

"One suggestion, Lucy. Just be yourself and honest about how you feel. I'm saving you from awkward moments like this. Just be straightforward."

Sarcastically, I say, "Thanks." I know she's right, but it's still hard to purge old patterns of rejection. I harbor memories of Sonny Magee, my fifth grade crush. It's difficult to realize how the impact of a boy at age ten can continue to hurt my pride at eighteen. Sonny was a few grades ahead of me and never took a second to give me a fair chance. I felt deeply defeated. Today I revert to protecting my ego by safeguarding my heart with Eli.

I confess to Isadora, "You're right. We do play too many games and squander opportunities by not being more direct and to the point. I promise to practice this." I start the engine and Isadora shapeshifts back to her sphere and disappears.

Eli and Marcus are sitting outside under the tree in the yard when I arrive at the farm. I'm completely captivated when

I spot Eli. I walk faster until I reach him, ignoring all of my previous fears of what his reaction may be. It's like a magnet drawing me to him, even though it's out of character to be so incredibly brave while foolishly following my heart. Opening my arms while at the same moment he reaches out feels like the sun ignites my very dim world. He holds me tightly and I sense he equally shares my affection. I gasp, breathing in his essence, but he soon loosens his grip and moves off to the side.

"Want some lemonade?" Eli asks as if he's circumventing the obvious emotional electricity we just exchanged. I tip my head to the side, considering the cause of this obvious distraction, but then decide to let the last few minutes slide away after detecting his confused reactions.

"No, thanks. I just had a large quantity of water. Lately, I've been thirstier than ever. Does this have anything to do with my Ascension?

"More than likely, since water acts as a conduit for energy." He gives me a reassuring smile. "Marcus said he gave you some magnets to wear."

"Yeah, I haven't had any more episodes of floating away." My new idea of bravery has failed me because I'd like to ask if we can test the magnets by sharing a kiss, but I don't. I consider it's the least that could be done for research if his previous assumption might be correct.

Marcus pipes up, "Catcha later guys, I'm running a few tests on a lithium battery." He walks into the barn and now Eli and I stand alone together, awkward and silent.

"Hum, so any word from your sister?" I ask.

"No, thankfully. I did find out more about the anomalies in your DNA. When I came back I checked Mama Jane's, Marcus and my own as well."

"What were the results?"

"Every one of us carries dormant abilities waiting to be activated. Our genetic codes are getting upgraded. What this means is that the force coming in from the center of the galaxy quickens our acceleration and we all get some of that inner technology the Lemurians once had long ago. No living creature is totally limited by the laws of biology and physics and it will quicken at different intervals.

"Um, you mean speed up, then slow down and then pick up again?" I ask, seeking clarification.

Eli continues, "Understood. However, quickening is usually an arduous process as evidenced by what once was accomplished in a year can actually be now accomplished in a week, then soon within an hour."

"Like time is speeding up?" I ask.

"More like what can actually be done within a certain amount of time as it's more about perception of speed. This quickening compares to the labor and birthing process of babies. Also, think of this accelerating pressure during this cyclical alignment like a pot of boiling water. The faster the atoms move because of increasing energy, the more bubbles and splashes are created inside the pot. When off the hot burner, the water settles down. When a baby is born or a new world, the pressure alleviates."

"Sounds like we need to be careful not to lose our minds in the process." I sense a bit of disappointment from him for joshing at his explanations.

"Seriously, we know that patterns repeat, correct?" Eli asks.
"Yes."

"The Fibonacci sequence is a mathematical key of the Universe where nature exists as a fractal building upon higher rates, and then, more complex life forms. The evidence of this symmetric journey of patterns is found by looking at the spiral arms in daisies, pinecones, sunflowers or the sequence in leaf patterns twisting around a branch. Even family trees in how they branch out. The growth curve in which the previous two numbers are added to create the third," he reaches down and with a stick to scratch in the dirt *0,1,1,2,3,5,8,13,21.*

"Let me get this straight. The pattern expands from zero outward?"

"Simplistically well said. I could go on, but I believe you get my point now." That crooked smile that I so dearly love lights up his face.

"But how does this relate to anomalies in my genetic makeup?" I'm still a little perplexed how he's using math to try to explain biology. I do admit that I like the comparison to patterns I can see in nature.

He answers, "Right before the pattern of elements shape-shift, they undergo extreme pressure from the tightening atomic mass spinning, then fluttering into a more complex design or a more dynamic life form. This would account for your hovering having been activated by a positive emotion."

"So I'm becoming a more complex life form?"

"A whole bunch of us are, but you're at the front of the line for an upgrade."

"I don't like being at the front of the line. I like the back," I protest.

"I was informed at this meeting that you feel emotions a great deal more strongly than you let on or even realize. This is how you have managed to understand and communicate when irony and sarcasm run amuck in society. Your ability to interpret others through your intuition has strengthened your survival mechanism. Like you grew invisible tentacles and became like a blind octopus."

"Great. I'm being compared to a bottom sea creature."

Eli laughs at my comeback, which forces me to smile and I join in his laughter. "But, when you love, rays of Light flash outwardly, drawing others to share the same. Heart-based emotions create the precise conditions to rapidly elevate the body's defenses inside this pressure cooker and activate sleeping codes. Mainstream scientists have only been able to release data that maps out the human genome seen within our realm, which consists of only ten percent. The other ninety percent is invisible quantum energy. Within this DNA contains the record of all you have ever been, accomplished and learned. It is similar to software programming. This ninety percent carries a tremendous amount of unseen information and energy, the all of who you are in the grand cosmic scale."

"That makes sense because I had a surreal vision the other day when I asked a basic question. Flashes of memories from some other life and location in the cosmos resurfaced, but it was me as a Light being. I don't understand why I can't remember." My antenna twitches for I sense a distressing feeling emanating from Eli. I know he's purposely blocking information that he discovered while at his off-world secret meeting.

"Eli, what is it?" I ask bluntly, practicing saying "what's on my mind." I stare deeply into his eyes, discerning something uncomfortable. I'm frightened what he might say since moments ago Isadora revealed that I will be the cause of his pain.

*That's ridiculous! I haven't had a chance and I wouldn't.*

Bravely he begins to speak and I discern that he's deciding what or how to say it. Tension arises between us while I wait for his response. Then, Isadora shifts into form on his left side. He obviously is aware of her presence since he looks in that precise direction.

Isadora addresses Eli, "You can't tell Lucy yet. She's still not prepared and needs more training before..."

Eli cuts her off, irritated. "Members said it would be perfectly fine to start instructing her."

I find myself left out of a debate regarding my life. I listen intently hoping to learn more from this mysterious squabbling.

Isadora puffs up, "No, absolutely not! I've been here this whole time helping Lucy and I know what she needs more than you do. We wait a tad bit longer."

I hate being left out of a discussion. I assert myself. "Hey, Isadora! I want to know and if Eli was given permission by members of the GC to share, then let him."

"Permission?" she huffs. "This covert operation didn't counsel me until the eleventh-hour in any of their plans to use you in such a way."

I cut in. "Use me in what way?"

She responds directly to me. "Their planted initiate." Swiftly she begins bellowing at Eli again, "It's too risky placing her in this situation. I'm not taking the chance of Lucy getting stuck in your realm! I will credit their instructions, but I don't like their haste." I get the impression she's riled for not being included on the finer details to this as-yet unrevealed plan. This explains her previous annoyance at the lack of candor in my world, although I too am bewildered as to why the secrecy.

Isadora turns and faces me. She softens her aggravated tone. "You have the capability to do it, but I just believe you need a little more time to practice shielding and controlling your fear."

"Capable of what? I think I've done a pretty good job so far, wouldn't you think? I'm not afraid of the dark anymore or things that go bump in the night while I sleep, and the Vampires and saving Sarah." I declare.

"Precisely. Good job. Stand your ground," Eli aggressively asserts.

Isadora hesitantly concedes, "Okay. I'll step aside as the high orders have been communicated, but I will be the one to tell her."

"Well, I'm all ears, guys? What's up?" I impatiently demand.

Isadora softly explains, "You will carry the four disks once we get to the stargate."

"That's it?" I ask, feeling a bit concerted as it seems too simple.

"You will insert them into the bedrock underpinning the keystones," she continues.

"Wait. Why do I have to do this? Where will you be?" I don't know whether to be excited or angry to be chosen for such an important job.

Eli replies, "Above, on the surface. Don't fret. It has to play out this way."

"I'm getting the idea that you've already been shown what will happen in Peru."

Looking solemn, Eli avoids eye contact. "Yes."

I loudly exclaim, "Come on, you have to tell me what happens!"

"I am obligated to honor some rules that not all things should be revealed before they are to occur," he replies.

"That's bogus. Come on. Just a little something!"

"The probability for a good outcome leans on our side. Isadora only desires to keep you safe, but we are working against time in this realm as this quickening accelerates and we have to prepare you to confront more Vampires."

My eyes widen. I gulp the second he mentions the blood-suckers, but this time I intuitively know it will be much worse than my recent encounter. All I can do from flipping out is to stare into his eyes as they comfort me.

Eli divulges more ground-breaking secrets. "Many things have been hidden on purpose and for good reason as you've been a main target hunted by the Dark Brotherhood."

Tension begins to mount within me until Isadora calms me with her essence of magical coolness and says, "Kept safe and incognito for all these years as no one knew of your great quest; protecting and guiding you while I hadn't been privy to this scheme."

Eli continues, "You've been hidden away, covertly working for a division inside the GC. Until this point, you basically had to stay secreted with nothing betraying you. Previous attempts have rendered other initiates as inoperative because of discovery by the Dark Brotherhood. They have hunted them down using technology to zone in on their energy waves, timelines and potential threat, then killing them. The GC only has a few initiates that are still alive on the surface of Earth with the abilities you currently possess. One particular initiate, having acquired a special ability, has been imprisoned in the jungle of El Salvador.

"Why is this initiate locked up?"

Isadora answers, "He doesn't look like any human on the face of this planet and as you can imagine, that would thwart the plans of the Dark agenda as they only have power so long as they can keep it secret and hidden. If humankind fully understood its potential and latent abilities to overthrow this bondage, then the struggle would be over. Most folks brush off this great news as something fictional, believing it to be untrue and too simple. In ignorance, they continue going about their daily routines."

"You want to know the greatest hidden secret?" Eli offers.
"Yes! Who doesn't?"

"The visitors in the crash at Roswell were us, humans from an alternate future timeline. They were time travelers trying to warn the public to not allow the Dark agenda to succeed. These visitors arrived during the war with the Nazi's, hoping that their message would get out, but the Dark Brotherhood gained control and hushed the entire event up, blaming it on a weather balloon. Hitler was a puppet for the Naki as he was told what to do and given technology and occult secrets, but he became obsessed with these underground beings. Hitler's scientists became skilled and advanced. Anyone can correlate the rise in technology and science at the time of the Roswell crash and the end of the Nazi regime.

"Except there never was an end as Nazi scientists were brought over to the states as Project Paperclip and an infestation arose from the ashes into a new form: slowly installing a manufactured global reconstruction of the fascist dictatorship, all the while calling it a free democratic system.

"The Roswell visitors wanted to stop a creation of another human slave race on the planet and a resultant downgrade in the genetic DNA of their bodies. They risked everything to send out this warning and, in the end, their message has been suppressed, but not completely lost. They did not want to crash, but were shot down by a Dark Brotherhood weapon. The information could not be squashed as it came out by a Light Keeper within the US military who heard the message and, as a whistleblower, held onto the data until the time was safe for him to share this story."

Isadora adds, "As you can see, this information along with the boy locked away in a secret facility in El Salvador, could blow the whole game the Dark agenda have been plotting."

The light turns on and I ask, "Is this the big reason why Thurston's working in the jungles?"

"Yes. Thurston and his crew are trying to free this young man, but it's also heavily guarded. So they spy and wait for an opportunity," Eli replies.

I gulp at the thought that I could still be in physical danger. "What if they locate and harm me?"

"Never allow fear to enter your emotions. It will lower your protective shield. This is why you need more training. Emotions influence your defense, whether of a negative or positive nature and when distressed or worried, your protection is weakened. You'll have to learn to overcome every last ounce of fear before heading off to Peru. You must learn how to control your intense reactions as it could potentially harm not only the mission, but end your life and you would remain stuck in the lower realms," Isadora says more directly, leaving nothing to my misunderstanding.

Eli shouts, his anger rising, "Nothing more important exists right now then to have you carry those four disks to open this stargate; a grand potential to end the terrible sicknesses that plague Earth: wars, poverty, conflicts, hierarchical thinking, aggression, ritual demonstrations, fear, educational dumbing down, deprivation of freedom and sovereign rights of individuals. Plus heavy toxins being released into our environment until our bodies become so bombarded that the star codes struggle to merge with the humans who are evolving on this planet!"

While Eli paces back and forth fuming, Isadora enlightens me, "Anger acts as a motivator if used correctly in the midst of heart-centered beliefs."

"Lucy, knowing this drives me to fight harder for the greater good and prohibit their defecating on our divine right to the entire planet and Universe. If they succeed any further, my God, I cannot even contemplate the outcome," Eli mutters.

I want to reach out and comfort him as he appears agonized over what he learned during his off-world meeting. I look at Isadora and she shakes her head "no." Eli stops pacing and subtly glances in my direction. I can tell he's worried about my reaction to his outburst.

"Lucy, I apologize for my bad mood. I wouldn't want to affect your frame of mind."

I step up and openly practice my straightforwardness with a bit of cynicism, "I've been initiated at the ancient stone to launch an off-world mission that I apparently agreed to execute, but have no memory about. All the while I'm to prepare controlling my emotions that are linked to manifesting abilities that can wreck havoc if I don't keep myself cool in order to face Vampires and carry keystones to open an ancient stargate all by myself. Is this all I have to do?"

"Um, we'll save the rest for later," Isadora wisely says.

"I can't fathom there being anything more to this disclosure," I state.

"We have a lot to prepare getting you geared up, Lucy." Eli, suddenly changing his mood, optimistically cheers me on with that incredible smile and I melt in response. But I can still continue to feel his heart-felt agony and wonder what invisible dagger stabbed him there. His sad blue eyes pierce me and I know now isn't the time to pry. It will have to wait for another day.

# Chapter 18
# The Mystery Man

The last three weeks has been arduous to say the least, not to mention the undertone of agitation Isadora and Eli have for one another. They certainly share obvious personality differences and tutoring styles, as Isadora's more sassy and blunt while Eli's sophisticated and debonair. I know they both have my best interests at heart, but I get the picture it's now all about the mission at the stargate.

I've become much more familiar with the landscape at the farm. Many hours of preparation and training have become a customary daily routine prior to leaving for Peru, which has become the main focus, competing with my schooling at Willamette. The magnets seem to be doing their job as I haven't had another episode of hovering, but I'm sure it has more to do with the preventive training to avert any extreme moods.

The night when Eli kissed me has slipped by unnoticed as the spotlight tends to center around my escalating Ascension. I'm despondent about his sidestepping any sign of affection whenever the opportunity presents itself. Eli seems to focus solely on agendas. Apparently I'm his prime mission to opening the stargate after having recently gained this insight. I admit to sharing his same heartfelt oath to do whatever it takes to blow the whistle on such deceitfulness, though I'd like to be holding his hand in the process.

The grueling schedule after my college course work begins everyday with a two-mile jog on dirt roads through connecting farmlands. Eli says it's the best way to prepare for possible spur of the moment roadblocks or detours. In these few weeks, I can now see small differences in my stamina plus my shapely curves are beginning to shrink. Isadora says the extra oxygen in my bloodstream clears out the pollution of this world. Whatever the benefits, I do feel stronger and mentally clearer, but I still hate to run. I tend to lag behind Eli as his jogging shorts expose a clearer view of his eye-catching, strapping build.

After jogging, we enter the barn where I sit on a yoga mat while Isadora guides me into a dreamlike meditation. Eli joins, but he sits vertically straight with his legs crossed, resting his palms upward. I often try to sneak a peak at him while he appears completely blissful. Isadora's talents shine through her method and techniques. I've been able to push out the energy Light shield by willpower with little help. It's incredible how releasing the imagination within the mind's eye creates a useful ability to open one's manifesting power.

Isadora repeats every day, "Now breathe very s-l-o-w-l-y. Perceive time slipping away. Find your center. Visualize the energy sphere expanding outward from this midpoint."

Whenever I get stuck, she says I panic and fear prevents me from functioning properly. If I'm to reach the depths of my mental strength, then I must come back to my center and start once again to exercise better self-control. There's definitely much to be fearful about in this world. However, Isadora and Eli have taught me how to develop self-control when alarmed. Everyday Isadora repeats the words, "Don't feed the dragon. Become the dragon slayer." I assume she's referring to not giving into my personal anxieties and doubts.

I do my best to redirect worries and sharpen my defense shield. It's a challenge as my thoughts often drift toward Eli as his presence distracts me.

*Can anyone ever prepare for such an enchantment? Not even my childhood fantasies of falling in love can compare.*

I cannot stir up an emotional storm. These intense reactions are kept tightly contained as restraint cannot cage them much longer. These indelible feelings need to be explored despite his holding back any sentiments for me. Certainly he's either protecting the mission in Peru or his heart because he knows something that he won't let on. I'm going to question Isadora to help me understand this crazy madness. Perhaps I can discover why he makes me feel like no more than just an assignment.

At the end of this long and tiring day, night has arrived and I gather my personal items, preparing to leave for home. Eli's busy talking to Marcus in the corner of the barn.

"Goodnight, Eli, Marcus," I say, walking to my car unaccompanied.

"See you tomorrow, Lucy," Eli casually replies, waving farewell and I think about another day spent pretending only to be friends.

I arrive home, parking my car on the street as Mother's boyfriend has taken my familiar spot with his Mercedes. She spends a lot of time with William. I can't blame her as he's quite a catch. They burn up a lot of mornings fishing on his Bayliner as Mother reports details of her new and exciting sport on the water. Her evenings are spent dining out and dancing. I'm completely happy for her as it provides a distraction so she doesn't question my habitual absence from home. I have a lot to endure already: the rapidly changing Ascension and personal coaching to confront Vampires at this stargate. Furthermore, I don't have a clue what will happen when I ascend.

Perhaps I need to inform her soon about this trip. If she doesn't approve, then I'll strive to convince her that it's a life or death matter and hope she doesn't get too angry at my insistence. Obviously, it's in the cards, but I just have to make sure to take the appropriate actions so all will come to pass.

Walking toward the family room, I hear chatting and laughter while the stereo plays *Antonio Vivaldi*. Approaching this noisy playfulness, I know that Mother and her boyfriend have been sipping wine as an empty bottle sits on the kitchen island. Neither of them has noticed my entrance into the house and I stand, waiting for a reaction. I clear my throat and say, "Hello. I'm home, Mother."

She cackles and turns abruptly in response to my announcement, "Oh look. Lucy's home. Let me introduce you two."

She continues with her introduction, "Lucy, this is William."

I respond rather gruffly, "Hello."

"Come here, honey. We have something to ask you."

I approach closer, wondering what she has to say.

"Well, you know William and I have been seeing each other for longer than a month now and he just invited me to accompany him on a business trip. Would you be alright staying home alone if I were to be absent for about four weeks?"

I'm a little stunned as she has never left me alone longer than a day or two.

"Where are you going to be for that length of time?"

"France!" Mother exclaims.

Obviously she's overly excited and I think I'm happy about it too. Mentally I review the calendar of upcoming events as I coordinate my plans with hers.

"When are you leaving?"

She shrugs her shoulders, at the same time looking worried, she replies, "The week of Thanksgiving. I hope this doesn't upset you, honey."

I know it should sting at least a little for choosing a trip to France with a boyfriend during the holiday season, but actually this works perfectly; great timing to have this excellent advantage to share with her my vacation plans.

"I don't mind. I can have Thanksgiving dinner with Mama Jane and the boys." I clear my throat, preparing to beg the question. "I haven't told you something either. Eli and his brothers have invited me to travel with them to Peru. We haven't bought the tickets yet, but, Mom, I really want to go!"

Her eyes widen and William jumps in saying, "Peru's a splendid place to travel. I took a trip there two years ago."

Mother stutters, "Peru? Isn't it dangerous down there?"

"Not at all, Anna. It's plenty safe as long as you don't enter the mountainous regions," William interjects.

"I don't know, Lucy."

"Anna, she's eighteen now and in college and it sounds as if she'll have good friends accompanying her."

"When is this trip?" she asks, unable to hide the trepidation in her voice.

"As soon as finals are over the second week of December. Please Mom. This is really important to me."

"Give me more of the details of the trip: where you're staying, the map, phone numbers and there is no way you can go with out a cell phone on you at all times!"

"Yeess!" I squeal, knowing that the tension of asking her permission is now over and she has agreed to let me go without a huge argument.

I say goodnight to both William and Mother, excitement streaming through my body. Gleeful, I run upstairs and flop onto my bed. The soft bedding and pillows hug and comfort my worn-out body. As I kick off my running shoes, I sigh, relaxing my tense muscles caused by the stress that I'd been holding. Within moments I fall asleep.

It's four in the morning and I try to slip off my running shorts, thinking the elastic fits too tightly around my stomach, but I can't get a grip on the fabric. When rolling over, I am startled to discover myself hovering above my body. I'm shocked and I can only watch while this part of me floats horizontally above my sleeping body.

*Can this be a dream?*

I can't compare anything to this out-of-body experience. It appears more real than my waking life. My arm has the same smoothness as I run my fingers up and down my skin. Oddly enough, my hair flows as if I'm in a pool of water. However, the substance is not liquefied, but more ethereal and airy. Isadora becomes visible as I remain transfixed, examining my sleeping body, attempting to discover how this odd circumstance came to be. I'm not sure if my lips are moving in this strange state when I say, "What's happening to me?"

"Come with me, Lucy." She signals to come closer and I gain a vertical position. Isadora takes my hand and the sensation surprisingly processes naturally with a new energy surging through me. This state of reality parallels my current understanding of what it means to be alive, but this space has more vitality and the heaviness of gravity no longer exists. I wonder how it's even possible for my physical body to remain operational when I'm absent.

She encloses me inside her luminous halo and I feel her warmth. Like a flash of lightening, she takes me on a flight through space. I can see the outer field of the Earth's ionosphere flickering a short moment as we bear our course toward the intense light of the sun. We suddenly find ourselves inside a massive starship.

*This seems almost unreal like being inside a blockbuster movie.*

It's absolutely invigorating how she has freed me from the confines of the gravitational field, giving me a chance to understand this otherworldly excursion. I get it now: that it would be too hard to show me everything all at once, as my old paradigm of what I thought was real, could have easily forced me to lose my mind, even as I desperately crave to have answers to my eternal questioning. Down deep I've always known that I came from the stars.

I follow as she joyfully skips making it known that Light beings can move just like Earth humans, except it feels so effortless. Slowly a few deeply embedded memories rise to my consciousness, revealing that I've been on this starship before.

Isadora explains, "The Light beings have evolved over the course of many millions of your Earth years through the process of Ascension. We've traveled to this point in space and time within the Universal cosmos to give assistance. This ship contains the central meeting point for all members of the Galactic Council to gather and devise plans to assist at this pivotal point on your planet. Many millions of Light beings have become lost and trapped inside a deceptive matrix at the hands of the Dark agenda. It's not enough to merely possess good intentions. Our allies who are stuck and unable to complete their missions on Earth need much assistance to insure the outcome in favor of the higher order during this next round of the Cosmic Year."

My attention is drawn to varied beings and other star races, both human and humanoid, walking around us. I hadn't seen their presence before, having been so immersed in Isadora's words. We walk onto a deck after entering several passages. I watch the crew members busily moving about on shiny steel-like stairways leading to various zones within a giant landing space. This section has embellished natural elements where some species of trees and shrubs are familiar and others are foreign. The ships vary in sizes and some look like stealth versions of our planetary fighter aircraft, except these are a much more superior and highly developed alien spacecraft.

An important appearing human suited in an unfamiliar fabric greets both of us as we approach a control center. Isadora continues taking me on a personal tour, but diverts herself when answering to this commanding officer. He's extremely tall with large almond eyes like Isadora and his skin shines multiple hues of unidentifiable opalescent colors. His perceptive skills appear to be sharp as he looks me over, then smiles as though accepting whatever data received from his examination.

I try to avoid getting in the way of the busy activities, but my attention fastens on the incredible technology behind me. The Officer continues to speak with Isadora and I walk a few steps away. The various parts of these enhanced spacecraft captivate me. This giant starship I am standing inside seems to be critical to the mission on Earth.

Then my attention lures me closer to focus on a specific spot on the platform leading to three smaller craft. While staring upward, I see boots of three separate individuals walking up the ramp on the other side.

I shift from side-to-side, attempting to catch a better look when one pilot draws my attention like a moth to a flame. I observe the three men ritually shaking hands before they enter these customized fighter craft. They appear as friendly colleagues.

Extreme confusion overpowers me as crushing sensations surface. If stars could be seen in my eyes, this would be the moment as I wait to identify this mystery man. I cannot stop staring at his quintessential form. His dark black hair braided along the sides of his face, pulled back and gathered in a leather band. Slightly bronzed skin enhances his already arresting, masculine features.

*He's absolutely beyond belief.*

Unbeknown as to why piercing vibrations swirl within me, I refuse to look away. I can only see his backside, dressed in a uniform like the Officer. I strain to see his face and then exacerbating my confusion, I instantly recognize this soul, but cannot understand how or from where? Or why this mystery man arouses indescribable intimacy? He's like a dream within a dream.

At last he notices my piercing stare when he turns his head into my direction, finally making eye contact. My beating heart escalates faster when he smiles, acknowledging my presence. He enters his craft, which then takes off through an opening on the starship's deck and soars out into deep space. He must be on an assignment of his own.

I stand motionless, overcome with a variety of emotions and unable to identify why I feel so restless and panic-stricken.

*How can I know him?*

His name pops into my mind; Aaron. Timeless lost memories begin to engulf me, but I hesitate to complete this transmission in my mind. I can't see anymore as thoughts of Eli resurface.

*This can't be.*

It feels absolutely unacceptable and wrong to have the same passionate feelings for Aaron as I do for Eli, but undoubtedly I have known this mystery man for eons. At the same time, I am additionally confused since he hasn't been inside any part of my reality until this incredible reaction at the sight of him. I am strangely attached to both of these two men as foggy, unexplainable bits of Aaron flood me. His image now haunts me. It's like hitting a brick wall every time I deny his importance in my life.

As if it isn't difficult enough to understand my unexplainable passion for Eli, I now have the enigma of resolving the mysterious identity of Aaron and his sudden introduction into my psyche.

Building tension and the swirling circus of my affections mushroom into a loud ringing in my ears and I cry out, "Isadora." Instantly I bolt back into my bodily presence, gasping for air and sit straight up. Tears are streaming down my cheeks as I must have been crying from the confusing dream. But it wasn't a dream as the reality of it doesn't fade. Tears well in my eyes and my breathing, becomes erratic as I panic from knowing so very little about this other life of mine.

My convulsive trembling causes my bed to shake and I feel an intense cold. A shadowy creature appears in a dark cloud in the corner of my bedroom. My emotions must have discharged a negative energy, creating a channel for this apparition to lurk inside my bedroom.

*Where is she?*

Isadora is the only one who can help me and fast! Mentally I call for her, hoping she'll receive the message. Within seconds, softness enters my bedroom and the shadow vanishes. She has come to my assistance and sits at the foot of my bed. My body temperature rises again, but this spasm in my heart won't stop quivering.

"I know what you're going to say, and yes, its time to reveal more to you."

I'm more scared of the pain of love than the dark shadow that was gaining shape in front of me. I raise my voice. "Is this your way to break it to me, ripping my heart to shreds by showing me someone that I cannot possibly have such depth for?"

"Strange, I thought you'd react differently. Aaron is not a momentary passing encounter. You two have a long, long story together. This is a less destructive way by letting you see Aaron. Besides, you would not have believed me," she explains.

I whimper, "The authenticity of the space travel I just encountered is understandable. The facts that I carry codes of an initiate to open a stargate and that Vampires and aliens actually exist in this world, as well as the fact that the Naki want the majority of the human population destroyed, are actually comprehensible. But the most important issue baffles me. You're implying that Aaron means something to me? Why?"

"You cannot deny Aaron. He dwells within you. It's called "soul amnesia." Crossing the Great Divide between realms initiates forgetfulness. Snippets containing your absolute individuality have become densely compressed into the quantum memory fields of your genetic DNA. This is why crossing back to our side can never be taken lightly as it's difficult to adjust to both realms at the same time. Different forms of love at different points in time and space exist throughout the entire Universe. This fixation with Eli was never foreseen to cause so much distress on you."

"I don't see Eli as just a crush," I argue.

"Despite your youthful age and hormones, you have a committed task to attend too. Your recent awakened abilities can shield you from harm and get you physically close enough to this heavily guarded stargate."

"When will it happen? Me leaving? Ascension?" She sends me peaceful waves, preparing me for something alarming, which she is about to reveal.

"It will happen in Peru."

A small tear trickles down my cheek as I know drastic changes approach, all of which I must fearlessly face.

She continues sharing, as if trying to cheer me up, "You may consider Aaron as an eternal counterpart of yourself, who never dies and always exists whenever you venture out into the vast universe of experiences. Likewise, so are you for him."

"But I felt that way about Eli and now?" I pause.

"The collective on Earth believes that only one romantic soulmate can exist, even though so much divorce on your planet invalidates any reasoning of such belief. Partnering unions are forever and forthright as no one can deny affection for the energy that becomes polarized between those in love. But there are many realms in this Universe. It is endless. Unending and timeless opportunities to explore different situations at diverse phases and points of reality are the greatest highlights of eternity. Nothing can alter this bond as it's impenetrably strong and constant, once recognized.

"At this point in time, Eli and you have crossed each other's path as you walk between these two realms, thus igniting a passionate spark. On the other hand, Aaron anxiously awaits a reunion once your Ascension occurs."

My eyes widen, "Oh my," Isadora has just affirmed what I discovered, "It was Aaron that day I met Eli. He was attempting to interfere somehow, wasn't he? That's why you said Eli's a problematic route because I'll be shapeshifting into a Light being!"

"Bravo, yes, it's now more complicated though. You have things to accomplish and it has nothing to do with creating a great love experience at the present moment. It was just fine having a superficial interest, but your ability to manifest has created something most powerful, which has caused your emotions to be even more uncontrollable!" Isadora moans.

"That's why Eli stepped back, withholding his affections for me, so I don't lose control and deter the mission somehow. But I wouldn't." I wonder if this could be the reason for Eli's reservation? That I ascend permanently, never coming back and happy to restore my existence with Aaron. My heart can feel the same jab as Eli must have felt when he arrived for his secret off-world meeting, having learned of this undertaking that I have come here to do. The very idea of leaving Eli and everyone I love is difficult to swallow.

Isadora explains, "You're just now learning how to better control your reactions. Human emotions are tied directly into manifesting situations. This planet's been in utter chaos because so many humans allow their emotions to run wild. Furthermore, you cannot be distracted from this most important mission. You have come too far to turn back now. I am sorry. The capability to control this massive energy that you carry can only be done by you and time is running out. There will not be another chance for the next 26,000 years, and lordy who knows what this planet will look like by then!"

I react, "But, if I open this stargate, won't it allow more Star races and Light beings to enter this realm?"

"In time it will shift the vibrational gravity fields. Once you ascend, your memories will be restored and, to be honest, you will have a change of heart about the definition of Love. Aaron joined the command ship closest to Earth because he couldn't keep away from the action. Just like you, he also has a mission to battle the dark forces by serving the GC as a Light Warrior. He resists the Order of Draco and the Naki. Furthermore, he chooses to be closer to your location when you return very soon."

"So, I've been dreaming, but part of me has been coming to this ship astrally?"

She nods in agreement. "Since your blueprint for Ascension launched, you've been wandering around more and more often during the dreamtime, checking matters out by using your Light body. Astral projection or dreaming, as it's been labeled, allows one to move about more freely when asleep. The memories of these journeys disappear and fade upon slipping back as this world becomes too cumbersome to understand this other reality. Most humans in your realm can only perceive a two-dimensional piece of paper and, of course, three dimensions and this understanding go beyond into higher dimensions of time and space.

"I am aware that you've been seen coming and going and Aaron eagerly awaits your Ascension back home."

*This is crazy!*

Once the wall of forgetfulness fades away completely, then there is no doubt a vital and hard decision lingers in my current life on Earth against the fast approaching Ascension into something otherworldly. I'm more scared of the extreme pain I will surely cause for either one. It gnaws at my gut. I can't imagine Eli disappearing as my northern star, but one look initiated a frenzy of passion for Aaron and remembering his face tears me apart even further. Even if I only did see Aaron briefly, he is unbelievably real.

I stubbornly deny the undeniable by refusing to untie my affection for Eli. "What did Eli see or hear at his off-world meeting? He's been holding back something. I can feel it. Eli doesn't seem the 'player' type and he did kiss me before that meeting took place, exhibiting signs of desiring more and now it's like I'm just a friend or his student. I don't like it, despite whether Aaron is real or not!"

"This isn't something that should come from me. You'll have to be straightforward and talk to him, but I warn you not to do it."

"But why?" I ask.

"Eli's trying to keep you from creating a mess that could trigger an uncontrollable storm of very dark shadows. This ability will accelerate and if you cannot control your emotions then wala! It will manifest just like that shadow you conjured from the lower realm that began to manifest in your bedroom. It feeds on your fear so be courageous!"

"That's what it was, a shadow from the Underworld?"

"You can create beauty or incredible horror with this ability. It takes one of pure heart to walk this path and self-sacrifice for the greater good."

"But Eli, why is he denying his affections for me? I am certain he holds the same feelings as I do for him." I sense Isadora becoming impatient with my dramatic emotions as I fixate on my love life.

"You can have such tunnel vision, Lucy! He's following direct orders from the GC and focused on getting you to the stargate as nothing else matters right now. His intense desire to rid this planet of darkness is more powerful than any amorous need for love at this time. Eli has seen unsightly things that have caused a rift in his memory, which motivates him to complete this mission."

I wonder about the horrible things he may have or possibly experienced first hand. Unwisely I conclude that I'm going to see Eli first thing in morning and force him to talk, regardless of his instructions from this off-world meeting. I'm not just a mission to be completed. I am a human Light being with ordinary desires.

# Chapter 19

# For the Greater Good

Eli stands on the porch holding coffee mugs in each hand. It appears he had prior knowledge of my arrival at Mama Jane's this morning. The closer I get to him, the more I remember how much he means to me. I stifle my recent awareness of Aaron as he disrupts any certainty of having something more with Eli. How can this be my fate right now? To leave this beautiful world never having a chance to discover our intense connection. I need him intimately now. I've suppressed my passion too long.

He sets the mugs down on the porch railing and we wrap our arms around each other. There's no need for words as our intense affection silently communicates itself. One of his hands embraces the curve of my back while the other cradles the base of my neck. He teases me by breathing closely, as he seems to be tempted, but I sense that he's conflicted not to give in to his sensual appetite. He rests his forehead on mine. I cannot be kept at bay any longer.

*I need him like air, water and food.*

I move myself closer to kiss him, but he pulls me aside like the other day. I cringe from his rejection, yet, I feel that he suffers from some sort of torment.

"What, Eli? Is there something wrong that you can't kiss me again?" I wait.

"No, no, nothing is wrong with you."

"Then kiss me!" I demand, irritated.

Suddenly dizziness and a rush of emotions inundate me and I grab the railing to prevent falling. He reaches out to support me and leads me over to Mama Jane's porch swing. He just stands there staring. I become even more frustrated as I look up at him waiting for a reaction. I feel like screaming so he'll say something, anything to provide insight into why he won't kiss me.

He kneels down, intimately making eye contact. He chooses his words carefully. "These are extraordinary times we are living in. An accurate report on how best to proceed had not been exactly clear until I met with members of this Division. They presented to me a much bigger undisclosed agenda. It is incredibly promising, if you can keep from creating a dilemma before we can reach the stargate."

"But, Eli, you make me feel good. How can I create a crisis if I feel absolutely wonderful with you?"

"You are incredible, Lucy. I have no options but to follow this plan. They brought you to me, not for love, but to awaken star codes and to get you to Peru." His voice softens. "I am here to teach you how to control your emotions, which will focus on your ability to shield and protect yourself. I was foolish trying to map your heart to mine. I did not have an accurate understanding of your role in this endeavor to take down the Dark Brotherhood until I was asked to meet with this Division inside the GC."

"I feel like a chess piece being played. What if I changed my mind and I don't go to Peru. How about that?"

"No! You have to make this happen. Abandoning this mission will surely plummet the Earth into a state of atrophy. The planet and all of the fallen need you before our solar system moves away from the great rift. We only have a narrow window of opportunity."

"But I'm going to change forever and I won't be the same. This is my life and all I want to do is live it out, right here with you by my side. I'm scared, Eli. Of losing my mind, losing you, and everything I love in this world," I cry.

"Your playing small doesn't serve anyone, least of all, yourself. The authority with which you command your inherently powerful emotions will make or break this endeavor. This is bigger than you and me. It has to happen!"

I ask the very question I presume Eli already knows, "Who's Aaron?"

His voice quivers, "You are not supposed to be focused on me. Do you not understand that this is killing me inside? Falling for a girl that is vanishing right before my eyes."

"But I can come back. I will figure out a way to endure any discomfort and it might not be for long if the gates all become unblocked, bringing in this crystalline energy for this next age."

"He will be right next to you, regardless."

"Aaron doesn't mean anything to me!" I shout, trying to squash my doubt that Eli could be right. He gives me a cynical look. "What are you holding from me?"

He stares directly into my eyes. "He is someone whom I cannot compete with and when you fully ascend, that is when all your memories will unlock as to what Aaron means to you."

"Well, it doesn't count because I," pausing I ponder whether I should say it or not. My confusion puzzles me. I fear that I may lose this intimate closeness with Eli and I might scare him away, but I have to show how much I deeply care for him, not Aaron. Tears stream down my face, "I love you and I know that you also feel something for me."

His lack of response confirms that he's shocked by what I said. I panic and begin to shake from that same coldness I felt last night when that shadow formed in my bedroom. "Please look at me, Eli." I can see from his facial expressions of surprise, love and pain that he's fighting emotional torment caused by my blunt announcement. Finally he raises his eyes to meet mine. Afraid that he has misunderstood me, I clarify myself. "Regardless of my amnesia or Aaron lingering somewhere between the ethers of this world and the next, I can't deny my feelings. Don't push me away. It will only draw me closer to you."

Eli states, guardedly, "I was led to bring you to the ancient stone at the grove. I am your guide to help harness the skills you will need in Peru. I have committed to an oath not to interfere in this mission. I cannot."

"At this GC meeting? Who was in charge?" I impulsively conclude that Aaron may have something to do with Eli's oath.

"No one specifically is in charge as everyone at this meeting lead equally."

"He was there at this meeting, wasn't he?"

"It will be my fault for not being strong enough to keep you focused on your mission rather than me. I cannot stop your Ascension, nor will I. You are the biggest hope for all of us right now."

Tears are streaming down his cheeks and I sense he doesn't want me to see this side of himself. This is completely and utterly unfair. I don't even remember Aaron and the continual reference to him is getting on my nerves. I feel defeated as Eli appears to be slipping away from me. I know there isn't anything I can do to change the circumstances. It's incredibly hard as he stands there, tangible and in my life right now, whereas Aaron is just a mystical dream. I finally lose control and yell, "Holy God Almighty, how freakish is this situation!" My entire body vibrates and shakes and I sob harder, unable to control myself. I'm not angry at Eli, but I feel so out of control that I feel like I have a fever. My shaking becomes more intense. Just as I think Eli's about to comfort me, he stares out toward something in the tree line. I look in his direction and see a large shadow amassing.

"Oh, no!" reacting to my creation of some kind of monster that Isadora warned that I could attract if I didn't always remain controlled.

"Eli, how did I create that?" I hope to hear that I am not responsible.

"That shadow located you. I suggest that you start amplifying your shield right now."

Concluding that I am completely at fault for causing such a breach, "What can we do?"

Right then Marcus comes out of the barn and Mama Jane walks out to the porch where we stand. This dark thing must have sounded the alarm system.

"How did this happen?" Mama Jane asks.

I speak up, "I don't know. I was stressed and lost control. I think I did this."

The dark mass has not come any closer. I stare at it trying to understand what this thing might be. It pulsates and two glowing red eyes peer from the center as it is now forming into a shadowy human figure. Eli instructs, "Lucy, think of something good and use your shield to force it from here."

I stagger as I realize I must not be responsible for causing any harm to my family. The only good stands right next to me so I do what he says. Reaching out for his hand, I gaze up to him at the same time and faintly say, "I don't know if I can do this." He smiles to reinforce the confidence I need. I close my eyes, attempting to gather in the goodness needed to protect those that I love. I intuit the energy pulling up from the earth and providing the fuel to overpower this dark force. The moment I sense the shield thrust out, intense optimism empowers me and I shoot out these rays toward this shady apparition.

Marcus, standing behind me says, "Badass!"

The form scatters until completely disintegrated. This energy field within me is now more powerful. I hold this radiating shield a bit longer to make sure all negativity has been cleared from the farm. I smile and look at Mama Jane. Isadora floats beside her, showing her approval. Thankfully I found the willpower in the midst of my emotional breakdown with Eli to dismantle this shadow. Isadora did warn me to be careful, but at least I could fix it, this time.

"Let's see. Who wants breakfast?" Mama Jane asks. The confrontation with Eli has ended and it's back to our regular routine.

*In the future I have to be more careful, like Isadora said, as my abilities are pretty intense and if left uncontrolled, I might unintentionally create a messy circumstance.*

Still holding Eli's hand, he squeezes it to assure me that we will be alright. At least I know now that he isn't trying to push me away on purpose. He worries about me and the mission. He protects himself from getting too close, shielding his own heart from possible heartbreak.

Isadora doesn't stay long. She greets Mama Jane and Marcus and then disappears into deep space. After breakfast, Eli arises from the table and says, "Come with me to the barn."

Gleefully, I leave my comfortable chair and follow him. We walk downstairs to the safe room where Maggie, the time instrument, is located. He punches numbers into a safe encased in the wall and once the door opens, he pulls out a tray with four disks, well protected on top of black velvet. He sets the tray on the table behind us.

"This is quite remarkable, Eli." I enthusiastically exclaim as I have a good look at each disk, yet keeping myself from touching them. The fine raw material sparkles a clear message as each disk has engraved identical markings. Three of these disks are made of solid gold, silver and bronze and now, the missing one, iron, is reunited with its counterparts. I ask, "How did you locate these disks?"

"I had the help of time traveling."

"Of course, why'd I ask?" That was a dumb question.

"It would not have been so easy discovering them in the first place if I had not read an article about a man in Germany who dug them up after taking his metal detector out to a field, when a crop circle had appeared with the same symbol seen on each of these four disks."

"Really! That's a strange coincidence."

"Not when you realize that the GC has left many messages using crop circles. The GC began creating symbols in the fields as a nonthreatening approach for onlookers to spot an obvious sign, but of course, the Dark Brotherhood countered with their scheme to make it appear as a hoax. Thus a few clowns with a rope and a board flattened grain in small circles, determined to destroy the validity of these colossal patterns."

"I never really bought into that theory as it didn't add up that these schemers were responsible. Then I saw documentaries on how it could be done," I add.

"Yes, well explain hundreds of crop circles appearing in grain fields all over the world in a few days' time with no sign of footprints, appearing as intricate designs, even to replicating certain mathematical mysteries and scientific symbols!

"The GC wanted the disks to be found and they were. This man originally sold the gold disk. Then the Dark Brotherhood found out about them and all four were mysteriously stolen; vanished into thin air as the museums were about to lay claim to them. The only recourse available was to make certain that they remained safe by traveling back in time to a location where I would not be observed digging them out of the ground."

He leans over and opens an envelope, pulling out a printed image. "Take a look at this crop circle."

I look closely at it. It's a picture taken of a crop design by someone above it in a helicopter. It's the typical outline of an alien being with a round compact disk next to it. Eli's handwriting scribbled below says, "We dispute with these false prophets. Great deception and broken order. Have faith that good is near."

Eli explains, "This crop symbol appeared with a decipherable code and these words are the encryption. Here is a mug shot of a notorious Naki."

I gaze into Eli's face to detect any resemblance, but find none. Then I remember Mama Jane's description of how the human looking Naki bloodline has a slight difference once off planet and away from the gravitational grid force. "Eli, I don't see a family likeness."

"I still look more human than Naki, even off-planet."

*Whew! Am I ever relieved as this entity isn't attractive in the least.*

"I'm to carry these four disks and for how long? Are they heavy?"

"We will place them in a backpack and you have only a few miles to walk."

"Looks like I'm gonna to need more weight training."

"Staying in the right frame of mind is more important than gaining additional physical strength, but yes, it could help these feeble muscles," he jokes.

I friendly punch him on his upper arm.

My thoughts return to the Order of Draco and I wonder how much worse it will become and what can possibly be worse than Vampires guarding the stargate. "Is there a particular reason why gates to interdimensional realms are hidden and difficult to access?"

"If it were easy, someone would have already accomplished it."

"Isadora said that you have good reason for bringing down the Dark Brotherhood. What happened to you, Eli?" Instantly his eyes glaze over as if my question has alarmed him.

"That is a hard one to answer. I have trouble sharing sometimes as it is almost unspeakable what they do. I mean what terrible horrors they inflict on young children."

"Children?" I repeat, shocked. "What kinds of things have they done to kids?"

"In order for them to have the level of control they desire: psychological abuse, deprivation, pain infliction, you name it, is employed at a very young age in order to split the mind and use these multiple personalities as their personal soldiers."

I'm floored by his claim and become enraged. "How can this be tolerated?"

"Most people don't realize it is happening. It is too awful to believe so most people choose to ignore it and allow them to continue committing horrendous crimes against these innocents. You have to remember, these members of the Dark Brotherhood do not feel like we do toward others. They have disconnected themselves from Source by their actions and are extremely narcissistic."

It finally hits me. I ask, "Were you one of these children?"

"Yes. This is how I learned to time travel. At first, I was just a guinea pig and then having realized that they owned a great gift, I was used as one of their time traveling soldiers to manipulate people and situations to benefit their agendas. At the time, the split personality only holds the memory of what has been done to them, while the core personality remains living a normal lifestyle just like everyone else. I struggle to overcome my hatred for what they did to me and to all those children that died for the sake of their agendas. The ancient stone helped me greatly to reintegrate the multiple personalities that had been divided inside me."

My emotions have flipped on and off all day. It's almost impossible to deny the bottomless, nightmarish fears I am being asked to confront. But I must keep them under control. I'm almost afraid to learn more of Eli's nightmares from his childhood. I, too, hold the same constructive anger that Eli carries within him, even though I could never imagine the terror he must have endured as a child growing up. I desire real change that benefits all for the highest and greatest good. My courage anchors within me, but I question whether I'm capable of releasing it again to face more Vampires. I fully realize that there is no backing out as I am too deep inside the mission to turn around now.

# Chapter 20
# In Love with an Alien

"Okay, Isadora I haven't asked this *very* important question yet? I mean, my father isn't dead. I know this with all my heart and so with all the power you have, please tell me where he is?"

I've spent another day out at the farm, training, meditating, watching Eli in his jogging shorts, kicking back after a fantastic dinner and now I sit at home relaxing for a bit before hitting the sack. I reflect on how completely and utterly happy my life seems to be going.

I grill Isadora for answers to the hidden mysteries, but she tells me little about how I should proceed with this dilemma of falling in love with Eli while Aaron remains yet to be seen. Of all the questions, I can't believe I haven't thought to ask the most important question. Where I can find my Dad?

"Yes, your father isn't dead and he also works as a Keeper of Light within the U.S. military. Right now, he's a prisoner of war in the mountains of Afghanistan," Isadora answers.

"I knew it! He's alive! Is he okay? I mean, will he return home soon? How?" I'm consumed with questions as this knowledge is like a buoy thrown to a drowning person. "Oh, please, tell me what I can do to have him sent home again?" I plead with Isadora and then think of how much time has passed for Mother and her new boyfriend. This is too awful to rationalize as they are in two separate places completely detached from each other's realities and, yet, I know in their memories they continue loving each other. It strikes me how their situation compares to my own alternate realities with Eli and this faded memory of Aaron.

"Unbelievable! Why haven't you told me that my father is still alive?"

"You never asked and you already knew the answer that he's alive and still on this planet," Isadora replies.

"If only I could have prevented it from happening in the first place." I outwardly express my thoughts as I detested that my father left on another tour that left him stuck in a war zone.

"Your father is safe, but held captive. He's been given good treatment in exchange for teaching English to the young Afghani boys and even some girls too. The people there are also awakening in their own way, although poverty and lack of education have slowed the process. The stargate off the coast of Pakistan is also highly guarded as the Dark Brotherhood remotely directs negative technologies to inhibit the star codes from unleashing.

"You must stay focused on your trip to Peru as this very action will reverberate throughout every stargate on the planet. When this one opens, it will also help your father and his operations on the other side of the world. It's an ancient power grid that gets a kick-start when the Great year shifts into the Golden age. Remember, we all have our time and place where we are needed. Where we want to be as no one does anything unwanted.

*Is she implying that I inherently wanted to be right where I'm at; on a mission to open a stargate and face some of the worst criminals this planet has ever seen?*

"Keep up the good work, Lucy. You've come a long way in a short amount of time. The members of the GC are amazed at your progress and are looking at you as the crucial key." She winks at me, smiles and vanishes.

My eyes tire. I mentally run down my busy schedule for early tomorrow. I really don't see the point of attending my classes when it looks like I'll be consumed with this Ascension sooner than later anyway. In the manner in which both Isadora and Eli express it, I don't have much time.

I'm aware that I still have a choice to make on the subject of Love, but it is like I walk blindfolded regardless of my opening sight. The unknowns of my future cause me to have swirling bouts of dizziness. The idea that my father is actually alive and well animates me. I drift off thinking of ways to find him.


Clammy and restless, I realize upon waking that I just had a lurid nightmare. My skin is cold and my throat dry. I might have been screaming during my sleep. I panic as I look around to see if I conjured up any dark shadows.

*Could I have unknowingly created something here while knocked out and not in control of my emotions?*

It seems like I'm in the clear as my room looks perfectly serene. Lying still in the middle of my bed, I reflect on the profound message that coursed through my dreaming mind. I close my eyes to conjure up the symbols and images:

The dream sequence began when I saw myself asleep and then I woke up from darkness and all of my friends and family surrounded me at the largest occasion of all time. All of the people enjoyed the excitement of the party and chatter permeated the atmosphere. I was remotely distant from this gathering and swam off into the dark, unforgiving ocean. I saw a faceless, beloved soul drowning and I felt that I must risk my own life to save this person. The stars twinkled in the sky like tiny flickering diamonds. I watched his body drift slowly out to sea, towed along by the currents and finally he cruelly sank below the surface of the sea.

I searched down into the water; bursts of color suffused my vision. Lighter colors of white, yellow and orange merged into a jewel tone of green-blue-purple, all bordering an angry red center. This soul drifted into the deeper regions of water until he was sucked into the deep red center and the chance to rescue him was lost.

I escaped the depths of the deep by looking up into the heavens. Death ate at my soul and bled from my eyes in the form of salty tears. The dark blue sky turned black and the bright stars faded out until I became sightless.

The struggle to get back to shore awakened me while I still remained inside this dream. The darkness faded and I returned to the party. All of my friends and family encircled me and to my surprise, I relived the same events of the waves on the dark sand and the animation of the partiers as it all repeated again like a broken record. I stabilized myself and realized that while still inside my dream, the redundancy signified my return to the beginning of a dream within a dream.

I had gone back in time and been given the opportunity to start over again to save this cherished beloved one. The second time I returned to the same spot where he drowned, but there were tears of joy, enlightenment and the burden released as I warn him of the eternal ocean and to receive life from this new choice to avoid his death.

I jump up out of my stupor, excited. I now understand the message. Convince Eli to let me see my father. If Eli will take me back in time before my father leaves on his tour of duty, maybe, just maybe, I can say something to make him stay. The dream signifies that I have a second chance by time traveling back before any of this happens.

I'm optimistic that I might be able to plead him into taking me on a quick trip into the past. It's the least he can do before I sacrifice my entire life, friends and leave my mother!

I didn't take in the consideration what this might do to her if I can't return. If my father was by her side again, she might not be so sad once I leave. What if I do find a way and I'm just a fluttering ball of Light. That will really flip Mother's lid. I can't allow that to happen. Not to mention, letting her know that I'm in love with an alien. Better yet, my boyfriend's fighting a nasty alien race that desires world domination, which he shares a family lineage with. And, Mother, be careful of Vampires! Ugh, I can't think about this. It's too late anyway. I can't stop the star codes activating this mission. Drastically my way of life is spinning out of control and I can't seem to find a railing to catch.

*Crap!*

I want to skip school today, but I have an important exam to take. I've already missed yesterday. I am so conflicted between the world I've been born into and this other, most extraordinary supernatural realm.

I sigh, intensely brooding while performing my daily morning routines and making myself presentable. I stand in front of my bathroom mirror, brushing my teeth when I sense something peculiar, which alerts me that I'm not alone. Looking around, I squint to see if Isadora might be lingering about. There isn't any sign to confirm my gut instinct. But when I look back at my steamy mirror, I witness a ghostly heart being drawn. I just stand there, speechless although I instantly understand the message of this supernatural heart. I can't see him, but I know instinctively that he's here. Aaron has left a symbol representing his affection. This shy Light being wants to make contact between our two realms, but I shrug it off today. I can't waver from my feelings for Eli and I surely won't change my mind because of a coy ghost in my home.

The exam has been trouble-free as it seems effortless when not concerned. I have bigger issues to contend with like devising the best way to approach Eli about taking me back to see my Father. Driving past the big white barn at the farm, the right words finally come to me about how to show my desperation to rescue my father.

I walk up to Mama Jane's house and nobody seems to be home. Turning around, I walk into the barn hoping to find Eli or anyone.

"Hello!" I yell loudly.

"Up here, in the loft." Eli's voice sounds muffled and stressed. I run up the stairs swiftly. Upon my entering, I see Marcus in a headlock, wrestling with Eli. They laugh and jab at each other in a friendly way. I suppose they're showing brotherly love in a rather competitively, combative way. I stand there waiting for them to stop, hoping that neither makes fools of themselves. While watching the struggle, I scrutinize Eli's strength. It's kind of nice observing him flexing his muscles.

"You give up?" Eli asks.

"No." Marcus strains.

"Time is up. Lucy is here," Eli declares, while considerately releasing Marcus from the hold he had on his brother.

Eli amiably greets me, "Hi, Lucy."

Marcus, out of breath, adds, "Hey"

"Hope you did not mind as Marcus challenged me to wrestle as we were competing for Mama Jane's last piece of apple pie." Eli pants, also out of breath.

"Where is she? I went to the house first, but no one answered."

"She's at the grocery store. I'll catch you later, Eli. Enjoy that last piece. I'm going to ask Mama Jane to make another just for me and you won't get a single slice," Marcus jokes, while walking back down the stairs.

"I see you act just like any other human boy," I snicker.

"I'm just as human as most on this planet," he replies, nudging me.

"I'm really curious. What do you look like? I mean when the gravitation or whatever force keeps me from witnessing your alien-like appearance."

"You really want to see? You are that inquisitive?" He asks, smiling in that quaint delectable way.

"Yeah, of course!" I am excited that he's about to show me what he really looks like.

"Then have a seat on the couch and I will be right back."

I sit down, astonished that he's going to show me something.

*I wonder how he will do it.*

Only a few minutes pass and he runs back up the stairs to the loft. He holds a small device similar to a lapel pin in the palm of his hand, which he attaches to his shirt collar. "When I push this button, you will see me as I truly am, without any illusions. It's not entirely the gravitational field that affects the masses of people on the planet from viewing unfamiliar features. Gravity produces different levels of magnetism and the Earth has been held inside a dense magnetic field for a long time. Synthetic manufactured EM pulses are causing the global trickery. When the alignment occurs and the stargates activate, a shift of the magnetic fields will become less dense and more that has not been seen by the human naked eye will be revealed. That's why the Dark agenda wants to keep the magnetics of the planet at a low hertz because it threatens their lifestyle.

"This piece of technology actually morphs the magnetic fields around me so that you can see me looking less than human. Also, another mechanism spins oppositely for those beings that look even less humanlike than me and to provide a stronger illusion as they have to wear this device continuously while present on the planet."

"You told me about a boy who looks alien and that Thurston and his comrades are trying to release him from imprisonment. Why does this boy appear in this way while your appearance remains obscure?"

"This boy was born with a crystallized, vibratory cell structure that permits him to lessen and warp the magnetic fields within and around him. He is what the shamans of Peru are calling a homo-luminous and some of these newly evolved species reflect outwardly the naturally inborn star race genetics that are not always human attributes."

"If this boy's locked away, unable to prove himself to the world, then why don't you use this device to show yourself to the public?"

"I wish it was that easy because the minute I reveal myself, the agents of the Dark Brotherhood will know I have such a device and take it. Then I would be left in my human form and all they would have to say to the public is, 'It's a parlor trick from a street magician.' Then I would become an easy target to be drugged and placed in an asylum or even killed.

"We need this stargate opened to aid in the release of this boy and bring in vast star codes to help overcome the remnants of this ancient invasion. The dominant timeline is the one chosen by the majority. Once a sizeable amount of the hypnotized population of the planet can shake off the controlled delusion that aliens do not exist, then the great revelation will transfer the timeline to the betterment of Earth. There will be much work to do even after the stargates open as countless people will probably think they are losing their minds. It will take many Light Warriors and Keepers to help stabilize and rebuild the communities and prevent them from being frozen in fear. That will be my role when the time comes."

The insignia on the small device has a black background with a large white X positioned in the middle. I'm a little afraid of what I'm about to see.

*What if Eli repulses me?*

I'm about to tell him to stop. I can wait a little longer to see his appearance through this device or even when I ascend, but he turns it on before I speak. I hear a rippling hum and then it stops. The same Eli stands before me except that his skin is more luminescent, the pupils in his blue eyes are no longer round but slitted like a cat's eyes and I didn't notice until he pushes back his shaggy hair that his ears are smaller and pointed like an elf. Everything else about him resembles Eli until he opens his mouth by smiling and revealing his human-looking tongue, which has a slight split at the tip like a snake. Gawking at him, to me he still continues to be most attractive, but perhaps now with a mystical twist to his appearance. I wonder if he's part of the Elfin race spoken of in mythical tales of old.

"Do I frighten you?" he asks.

"No, not at all."

*What is it that creates my fantastic attraction to him?*

It's a complete mystery to me, but it must be his spirit. I watch him take off the pin and his more striking human features return.

"Eli, I have another favor to ask of you. Please hear me out before you say 'No.'"

"Go ahead," he replies, waiting.

"Last night I woke up from a nightmare. I interpreted the meaning that the time traveling ability you have might actually help. At least I think so, um, I want to see my father again. I mean, I think I could stop him from leaving for his last tour of duty before being captured. I can't bear the idea of him imprisoned in a remote country in the middle of a war. Isadora says he's safe, but it makes me ill thinking about him there when I could do something to maybe at least warn him."

He pauses for a long time, resting his chin on his fist. "I validate your concern and, yes, the time control device could take us back to warn your father, but what does that do? Would you be the same as you are now? How does imparting this warning to your father have an impact on everything around you, him, your mother. Maybe your father decides to sell the house in Silverton and you move away to another state? Then we would never meet and everything that you are experiencing now shifts into an alternate reality. The only way I can move in and out of timelines is to not make changes. Most importantly, one cannot infringe on the free will of the souls residing in the past, at least not without heavy karma."

I don't want to admit that Eli's correct as it hurts tremendously to have been without my father for so many years, let alone, aware that he's alive as a prisoner of war. Another option exists; to continue on my path to Peru and open that darn stargate. However I'm to do this. "Alright, I get it, but please take me back to a point in time where I can at least see him physically again." Tears well up in my eyes and I sense Eli will succumb to my request.

"The only way I will consider this is if you don't disclose your identity and we go to a point in time where your parents or anyone else will not recognize you. Let's say, anywhere before the age of nine."

"Oh! I'm so excited. How about age eight? I remember a July 4th party my parents gave. Actually the entire block celebrated with us and it was one of my best memories. I'd love to see it again, as a semi-adult, that is. When can we go?"

"Let me talk to Marcus and mull over some of the details as journeys like this take some planning. I don't want to rush into this and risk putting you in any danger, let alone affecting devastatingly shifting time waves." I watch him walk down the stairs and I'm about to burst from the anticipation. I know he wants to make me happy and do this for me.

I follow Eli while asking, very genuinely, "How long will it take for you to come to any conclusion?"

"Give me a call by noon tomorrow. I should have the finer details worked out." I jump up and down from the excitement and can see that Eli's pleased that I am so exuberant. I have much to look forward to as my time traveling alien, sort-of-boyfriend is taking me on a trip to see my Dad!

# Chapter 21
# Lucy the Time Traveler

"It's noon, Eli, so I'm calling as you instructed." I leave the message and hang up my cell phone, frustrated, as I'd hope to hear good news that he will take me back in time to see my father.

Eli drives me crazy when he doesn't answer his phone. I send a text informing him my last class ends in an hour and I'll be over to talk to him in person. I decide that Eli's not one to communicate willingly unless in person, and then he's much more sociable.

I get to the farm and he greets me with a genuinely welcome smile. I can't restrain my impatience and ask, "Well, what's the verdict? Can you take me?"

Immediately thereafter, Marcus yells from the barn door. "Hey, Eli I need you to check something out."

"Lucy, I have to help Marcus. Why don't you go upstairs in the loft and I'll be up shortly to give you my answer."

"Alright." I head up to the loft, trying to distract myself. I want to give into the urge to eavesdrop on Marcus and him, but I restrain myself and check out his book collection. It's not very polite to be nosy as much as I'd like to.

After some time passes, I'm about to go on downstairs anyway and intrude. I have organized his cluttered book shelf and folded all the clean towels the boys left in a laundry basket. Soon the entire loft will have my feminine touch added to this masculine space.

At last I hear footsteps coming up the stairway. I leap up off the couch to hear the final decision. Eli appears cheerful so it must be a good outcome.

"I want you to know that I had to give up the last piece of pie to Marcus yesterday to help us do this," Eli says.

"Sorry, I'll make you one myself if that will make it better."

"I am holding you to it," he says, a flirty smile flitting across his face.

"Well, I always follow through with my word. Thank you." Sparks ignite in me and I fight off an impulse to grab and ecstatically kiss him. To do so might cause undue emotional strain in case it goes bad. I know he's holding back the same impulse. Isadora's correct regarding the crazy way humans on Earth hold back feelings by not being straightforward.

I follow Eli downstairs to the location of the time machine. Marcus is already gearing up the instrument and inputting some sort of data into a computer. I radiate with happiness since I don't have to wait a day to go on this journey through time. I'm not quite sure if my excitement is more for my father or the actual chance to move backwards through time, using this fantastic tool.

Marcus stares intently into the screen and directs, "Okay, guys, I think we're locked into the specific date. You did say the Fourth of July when Lucy was eight years old, right?"

"Yes, that would be, um, the year 2000."

"Oh! I almost forgot! I'll be right back." I run to my car to retrieve the book of Inanna that Eli gave me on that momentous day. My instincts told me to bring it with me just in case Eli said, "yes." Fumbling around in my bag, I find it and quickly grab a pen, writing something important on the back page to make sure the book is found on that high shelf in the library. Mulling over something to write, I realize I must hurry before the boys change their minds. Quickly I scribble a heart with Eli's name in the middle of it, just like the mark when I found it in the library.

Winded from running back so fast, I show Eli the reason for my brief departure. "I have to place this on the shelf in my parents' library. I already found it there a few days before meeting you. It's really important that I find it."

"Let's take it then. Slip it inside the back of your jeans." I do as he says and it slides up against my skin easily because of the sweat on my backside.

"Where should your location be when crossing into the entry position?" Marcus asks.

Eli looks at me, assuming that I would have the answer to the question. "Probably not in the house or yard as it will be full of people. I think the best spot would most likely be in the park near Salamander Island. Do you know where that is, Marcus?"

"No. Can you show me on this map?" He points to a diagram on the computer screen.

I scan it until I find the location. "Right here."

"Okay, got it," Marcus replies, rubbing his hands together, demonstrating his confidence to follow through.

"Here, Lucy, you need to put this belt on. It is a tracking locator and it will record important data for Marcus as he monitors us from his side," Eli instructs.

I quickly put on the leather strap and I see some kind of small GPS chip positioned on the inside of the belt.

Eli squares himself toward me, directing my attention, "There are a few vital rules you must follow and stay by my side at all times. Don't act on any sudden impulse and if you have the urge, just look at me for a cue. It's most important that we get in and out without disturbing the natural flow of the time waves. Most important! It's like having respect for the ecological elements. The worse karma can result from altering something that should not be changed for it harms the free will of the souls involved. The book is fine, as it only affects you and obviously, it already occurred."

"I promise, but can I hug him, my father?"

Concern shows on his face. "That is tricky. Can you do it without displaying your emotions or making it look out of place?"

"Yes."

"Just remember, self control," he adds.

He guides me up on the platform, passing through the mirrors and now we stand together in the center. He takes my hand and says, "You can either close your eyes or look at me while it transports us."

"I'll look at you, but does it hurt?"

"Not at all. Be optimistic and control your fear. It is always easier when you think of a pleasant memory."

Marcus must have pushed the start button or something because I hear a buzz and now vibrations hum through my entire body. It feels like I'm on a gyrator. I continue gazing into Eli's eyes of encouragement. Flashes of light enfold both of us and within seconds, I see trees in the background as I continue looking at Eli. It takes me another second to shake off the gyrations still rumbling to the core of my bones. I peek around and it looks like any other summer day in my home town.

"We made it," Eli declares.

"Pretty cool!" My eyes widen as I realize that implausibility just became a reality.

"Continue holding my hand, Lucy. It makes me feel better knowing you are safe and nearby in case something unusual transpires."

I don't argue. "My house isn't far from here. We only need to cross the bridge and walk down Water Street."

The close contact with Eli stirs up my love for him, but right now I keep my focus directed to my goal of seeing my father in the flesh once more. Convertibles drive down the road as we walk and kids are lighting fireworks on the sidewalks. Once in a while we hear a loud pop signifying that today is, indeed, the Fourth of July. Turning the corner to my house, I find many cars parked on the street. I'm happy Marcus took us back to the year I requested.

It never occurred to me what it would be like to run into myself at age eight as I now see "little me" playing with the neighbor kids, Jackie, Johnnie and little Olive. Watching the play proves to be nostalgic and I recall my innocence and lack of worry about the real world. It's quiet between Eli and me and I'm incredibly nervous, yet seriously following his rules. As we walk toward the front door, I realize that this party provides the best opportunity to infiltrate my own home since it's swarming with lively guests.

We walk around nonchalantly like we'd been invited. Surprisingly, few guests notice us as they're busy chatting. I steer Eli towards the house library entrance to accomplish my first task. While many people are walking around and socializing, I slip into the library as if I'm interested in the collection. Glancing over my shoulder, I see Eli standing guard. I grab the desk chair and stand on it, reaching up and sliding the book back to the identical spot where I found it. I'm satisfied now as the book waits until I find it in years to come. I jump down and move on to my next agenda.

We both explore while pursuing Father, but I'm the only one who can identify him. Ten minutes must have passed while we stand quietly in the back yard under the trees awaiting his appearance. I know he must show up soon as the back yard is his favorite spot, along with the barbecue. Finally I see him coming outside from the kitchen with a plate full of meat to grill. I whisper to Eli, "That's him over there with the funny hat."

Eli responds, "Wait for the opportunity and don't forget, self control."

We silently watch as more time elapses, but I enjoy resting my head on Eli's shoulder while we observe Father from a distance. My mind races as I consider the best approach to getting a hug. At the same time, I'm worried about making a mess of things. My father's busy cooking while talking with his buddies.

I can see more clearly that my dream about rescuing my father represents this date at the Fourth of July party. I've been able to turn back time with the help of Eli and Marcus, but I can't change his actions. My selfish desire to save him to avoid my own pain could alter my mission to open the stargate. I now have a higher obligation even though it seems upside down and mixed up. Besides, everything happens for a reason, I suppose. If I infringe on what has already occurred, I might not be where I am today or never come across Eli for that matter. Or what changes would it make in Father's life? There are too many unknowns and probabilities that I hadn't considered before.

*Time traveling really does require responsible ethics.*

This happens to be a sad moment, but I'm okay with how my life has turned out. It's true. We cannot understand the reasons for every choice we make as the possibilities are infinite.

"We need to get back," Eli says.

Ugh, I could stay here a little while longer, but I know he's right. We walk by the gathering around the barbecue while I hastily think about what to articulate and then approach Father. "Thank you, Robert, for the invite, but we have other plans. We love your home. It's beautiful." I can tell my father wonders who we are.

*Maybe deep down he has an eerie feeling that I am someone important to him.*

Cocking his head, but with a blank face, politely he responds, "Thanks."

Walking away from that moment in time, I hide my disappointment that the fatherly hug I needed so badly couldn't take place. But it's okay when I remember he's not the touchy, feely kind of guy. At least, I've gained a fresh new memory by having him near me again. Tears flood my eyes. Eli notices and taking his thumb, tenderly wipes them away.

The stroll back to Salamander Island allows me time to process the loss I feel in my heart for my father.

*Was it cruel to put myself in this position for I remember him more deeply in my memories? The experience revives lost details of Robert. He's been gone for too long.*

Standing near the same spot, but further back in the trees as a few kids play along the riverbank, Eli holds my hand again while I rest my head on his chest, wrapping my arms around him with closed eyes.

"Here goes." He alerts Marcus through his PDA and in a flash, light enfolds us and we are back on the platform. I'm a little exhausted and dizzy. Eli did say it takes a few days to regain one's balance while recovering.

"Lucy, I want you to stay here tonight. Let your Mother know. Okay? We need to monitor you since this was your first trip. Nothing to worry about as it is quite normal."

"Alright, but can you text her? I'm too tired to even lift my arm." My eyes feel heavy and before I know it, I'm asleep on that worn-out, battered couch.

Two days have passed and I'm feeling like myself again luckily, since I dislike feeling out of it. Time traveling causes me to feel sluggish. I realize why Eli didn't get back to me after his last trip since I practically slept an entire two days.

I'm feeling sentimental this afternoon so I pull out the photo albums Mother has stored in her library. I reminisce, flipping the pages remembering the good times with Father in our lives. It's interesting how memories are stored like film strips replaying inside my mind. Now I have a new memory to be stored, but from an *older* me having a different perspective and fresh point of view.

I'm intrigued how I placed the book about Inanna on the shelf that I found years later, the beginning of my awakening journey. I consider checking out the two books and see if I can detect any discrepancies, if they are indeed the same book, but manifesting in different time lines. My obvious marking of the heart and Eli's scribbled name would not have appeared when he gave me the book so I rush to find both books. I distinctly remember placing the book I had found in the library inside my nightstand drawer. I can't find it. Where has it gone?

I gallop downstairs where Mother sits quietly reading a romance novel, "Have you seen that book I've been reading about Inanna?"

"No, sweetie. Where was the last place you saw it?" Mother's typical response.

"Inside my nightstand in the top drawer. You didn't do any cleaning or something and maybe moved it?"

"No. I don't step foot in that cluttered room and it's your job to clean anyway. Not mine and, by the way, you should pick up a little."

I'm sorry I asked her about it since I've been instructed to clean and attempt to organize myself. My bedroom isn't too messy. Mother's just a clean freak.

I pick up the other mysterious time traveling book. I hold it in my hands staring at it while I sit on the edge of my bed. This book has become such a strange enigma. I'm the one who placed it on the shelf back in time when I was eight years old, but this concept is a hard one to think through.

*Where's the other book?*

Oh my God! I figured it out. In my hands exists the only single, actual bona fide book. Once I took the action to place this book in time and arrived back, then it became one instead of two separate books. I smile since I solved the mystery.

*Nice.*

The door bell rings. I run downstairs to get it, but Mother's already opening the door. To my great surprise it's Eli.

"Good afternoon, Anna. Nice to see you again."

"You too, Eli," she replies, exuding friendliness.

I'm standing at the bottom of the staircase when Eli says, "Hi, Lucy."

"Hey." I wonder why he's at my doorstep. It's become the standard that I go out to the farm. Something isn't right. "What's going on? Why did you come by instead of calling? Oh yeah, you really don't like conversing on the phone." I kindheartedly make fun.

"You want to take a walk?"

"Sure, let me get my coat." I'm feeling nervous.

We stroll slowly down my sidewalk. Eli says, "It looks a lot different now, doesn't it?"

I ponder what he's implying and then I get it, "Oh yeah, the bushes and trees are a lot bigger and the house color is now green. Mother had it painted two summers ago."

"I want to tell you in person that we received some information that Zeke might be in trouble. We do not have any facts yet, but I am assuming the negative energies and being back in his old stomping grounds have beaten him down."

"So, you don't know anything else?" I'm concerned.

"No, not yet. Mama Jane said they'll be arriving back any day now. This means we need to start packing and preparing for Peru."

Reality hits me that my life will be transforming soon as we are about to kick into high gear, creating more tumultuous waves of change on the horizon.

We take our chatting inside as the whether has turned cold and windy. Today I will play my cello once more. I might not have another chance, and I want to honor Father as I know he won't return from the Middle East before my trip to Peru. Eli's my audience as he waits for me to play while sitting on my bed in my messy room. I tune the strings and before I know it, I become lost in the sonata, expressing my passion and memories through the melody.

# Chapter 22
# Return to the Grove

"Get the water canteen on the kitchen counter!" Eli commands in an unsettling manner. He's particularly edgy today, having received a personal phone call from Zeke stating they'll arrive at Mama Jane's by mid-morning. The strain in Zeke's voice was most disturbing to Eli as he knows he'll require another trip to the grove to restore the star codes. The way it sounded, his Draconian genetics must have taken a toll on him. Eli believes that Zeke was strongly affected by his return back to where he once fed off of humans. I'm sure the cause for his physical strain relates to his refusing alternative sources in lieu of the nectar of human blood also. He's a strong soul. Zeke wouldn't reveal how severe the side effects are on him, but he did agree that Eli and Marcus should get the gear ready for a trip to the grove as soon as he arrives.

"I got it, Eli!" I yell, assisting however I can in preparation for the hike. Eli refuses to let me stand on the stone again as he believes it could accelerate my Ascension faster. Everyone besides me gets a spell of the Light spring gushing from the ancient portal as it boosts good vibes for us before the big trip to Peru.

The gear must be ready to go when Zeke and Ki show up as we're taking off up the canyon at the moment of their arrival and Eli doesn't want to take any risk seeing that Zeke is weaker than normal. The greatest threat appears to be Lamar and his crew skulking in the neighborhood. They seek a breach to physically execute Zeke, thereby removing him from this realm. Vampires have huge egos and tend to despise exposure of their secrets.

Eli's nervousness intensifies the seriousness of the situation. If Lamar can get close enough while Zeke's fading, then a lot's at risk. It's making me jumpy as well. The good news is that I finally get to meet Thurston as he's arriving with Zeke and Ki. I have little information about Thurston and it seems he's bringing a few of his own friends too.

Marcus enters the front door of Mama Jane's and says, "Bad news. Officer Garrett recently spotted Lamar downtown and believes his gang inhabits an abandoned crack house somewhere in the vicinity. Apparently, he's hanging out with a few street kids who are oblivious that he's a prowling Vamp. They see him like some kind of Gothic god. He has some sort of sick charm that fascinates these senseless youth. Yuck! If only they knew."

"Great! That means they're passing time to locate Zeke, aren't they, Eli?" I am concerned. Having knowledge of so many legends and stories about existing Vampires continue to terrify me, except for Zeke. He's different, having embraced the star codes and I'm at ease with his friendly, humorous personality.

"Yes, we will have to be smarter than a Vampire. Marcus, text Zeke and Ki to head directly to the entrance of the trailhead where we will meet. No need to forewarn these Vampires as to their arrival when Zeke is not presently strong. It will be a run up the mountain unfortunately and much cooler with possibly the soil being iced up. Lucy, make sure to dress warm and bring extra clothes in your pack."

"Have you thought about opening the safe, Eli?" Is Marcus hinting about something unknown to me? I watch Eli's body language, attempting to understand the meaning behind the question.

"Sadly, I think you are correct, Marcus. It is better to be prepared and have the advantage than to be ill-equipped," Eli replies.

Piping up, I ask, "What does opening the safe mean?"

"Weapons." Mama Jane answers, entering the living room where we stand together, now preparing for a possible battle within my own county. I look at Eli, then at Mama Jane, speculating about a possible confrontation with these Vampires.

Curious, I ask, "If the legends are correct, then do stakes and garlic help fend them off?"

"No, some stories are elaborations, sweetheart. Their bodies die just like any other human being on this planet when shot with a regular bullet. It's just that they know how to enhance their longevity in a single lifetime," Mama Jane explains.

Eli adds, "And nobody will turn into a Vampire by a bite either unless the victim carries traces of the Draco's genetic bloodline and begins to become addicted to the pineal secretions they extract from their victims. Remember, they are just another species here. Let's hope tomorrow is a sunny day outside."

"No matter how much light they secrete from the blood of their victims, they can never tolerate the sun. Down south where the sun shines more, often they travel underground in tunnels between cities they've built below the surface of the Earth. There's a whole other world going on beneath our feet!" Marcus fervently asserts.

Mama Jane says, "I'm sorry, Eli. I checked the weather this morning and it's predicted to be overcast tomorrow. Remember, its Oregon in November we're talking about? We'll be lucky if it doesn't downpour."

"Oh, yes, do not forget to pack the rain gear, Marcus," Eli adds.

I'm looking forward to the warm sun in Peru. I only wish there were more time to laze around. The boys' homecoming from El Salvador cuts close to the exodus target date. Only a few weeks remain until our flight departs. Mother left a few days ago and it's unbelievable that tomorrow is Thanksgiving. I feel really bad about leaving Mama Jane here alone at the farm while we trample up to the grove, but she insists as she knows we'll return hungry.

With all of the training Isadora and Eli have given me regarding self-control over fear and raising my protective shields, I wonder why weapons are needed. Eli taught me to believe if an enemy is out there, then an enemy will appear. I suppose that doesn't make complete sense as the free will of these Vamps has actually overpowered our awareness of them and they continue to pursue Zeke regardless. Like Eli says, it's better to be prepared then caught off guard as many variables still exist.

"So, about these weapons, what kind are you talking about?" I ask.

Marcus excited, blurts out, "Silenced 45-auto's and AR-15's."

My stomach starts to churn into knots as guns are not my forte' even after growing up with them around as my father, being a military man, had a large collection. Mother never liked them much either.

"What kind of force are we going to be up against?" I ask, wearily.

Eli directs me, "Lucy, we need you to embody this energetic Light field like a sanctified amulet. This is your weapon as your presence will repel them, but only if you can remain fearless and dominate your emotions."

Mama Jane adds, "It will be good practice before reaching the stargate, plus Zeke needs to be close to your protective shield while reaching the ancient stone."

Instinctively I know that today is the beginning of something profound. I sense the dawn of a whole new set of abilities about to emerge within me. Another hidden side awakens from a buried power about to become unleashed. I won't be able to hold Eli's hand nor be able to rely on anyone else to get me through it. Mama Jane confirms her confidence in me. Instead of being afraid, unexpectedly I'm now overcome with excitement about the upcoming events.

"Can you tell me more about the abilities these Vamps possess?" I ask, out of a sense of caution as well as being inquisitive.

Mama Jane speaks up, "They are very strong, can move extremely fast, their keen senses are like a hawk and make sure to never stare at them because they can hypnotize you like a cobra, which can weaken even the most physically powerful. They can hover if they fed recently and they also release venom from their sharp teeth to render you frozen and unable to move while completely cognizant."

Marcus adds, "They'll possess weapons including guns and, of course, blades, although they'd prefer to take their victim's blood and flesh by causing terror rather than a quick kill with a bullet. Nothing is more frightening to a human than a freakish predator staring you down."

"It is enormously imperative to control your inner responses when carrying the amount of higher Light that you possess, Lucy. Do not let them weaken you because their power is all show. If they create enough horror and panic within you, then they can break through your energetic defense," Eli instructs.

Mama Jane delivers another facet of information. "We process Light through solar-powered cells by bathing in the rays. As children of the Great Sun, we metabolize this Light through photosynthesis by using the Light energy trapped by chlorophyll from plants and the animals that eat the vegetation. We consume these life forms in order to extract the photons of Light and, most importantly, we harness the star codes through the pineal gland. On the opposite spectrum, these Vampires cannot process direct Light like the rest of us. All creatures require some Light to survive, but the Vamp's dark energy fields keep them trapped within the lower realms and so to remain in our realm, they must extract it by producing fear. Unless they can transform their negative forces, they'll be consumed by this purifying Light storm about to hit this planet as we drift into the center of the Great Cosmic Sun."

"Very true," Eli interjects. "Whether they like it or not, the bursting out of the magnetic rays allows the Keepers of the Light to have the upper hand, but their last iron grip is this stargate. We have to do what we can to stop the creation of a dim world and from being cut off from the Keepers within the Universe. Tomorrow, Lucy, you will be our accessible cosmic sun shining this cosmic Light for us."

Marcus voices, "Yeah, they don't belong on this planet. That's why they can't handle the heat!"

Mama Jane adds, "Now, I don't want any one of you boys and Lucy getting hurt tomorrow so I made contact with Officer Malachi."

Eli is being cagey about something. "I am glad you are concerned, Mama Jane, and thank you, but do we really need the GC to stand guard? I mean no disrespect and I am pleased for the extra support."

Marcus speaks out directly, "I think what Eli's trying to ask without appearing rude is, well, does it mean Aaron will be fighting with us? It's his position of responsibility with the GC, isn't it?"

Anguish sweeps over Eli's face at the mention of Aaron's name. This happens to be the last issue I thought I'd have to confront. I've been under the impression that I still had more time before seeing Aaron again. Up to now, I've been cautious to avoid even a hint of his name verbally or mentally, attempting to squash any residual memory of him. The hairs on my skin prickle as I might see him sooner than expected and with Eli by my side. I can't stand the idea of causing any more tension. Somehow I feel responsible for hurting Eli even though I know it isn't my fault. It's just this crazy situation.

"What kind of assistance does the GC provide in times like these?" I speak up, but I'm still caught up in a mental image of my recent contact with Aaron. He almost frightens me more than Vampires.

Mama Jane remonstrates, "Boys, don't get in a bunch now. They're willing to step in only if the Vampires gain control and target Lucy as she has to stay alive. It's just insurance."

"What about the rest of us? I'm not willing to put myself out there for Vamp bait!" Marcus shouts.

Mama Jane appears a little perturbed. "Marcus settle down. They'll be there for the entire team, but if you remember correctly, the GC are sticklers about interfering in human affairs as that would also affect their fate. They have to be very careful to not get sucked into human dramas and cannot descend without proper grounding or they'll fall victim to this lower realm. That's why we're here to do it, this is our undertaking, and don't forget the potential force we carry within, Marcus."

"Glad I'll be heavily armed in that case!" Marcus roars.

Mama Jane speaks directly to Eli, "The GC are brothers and sisters of the Keepers of Light. While Lucy acts as a beacon, warding off these beasts, there will be four sent to protect her as she walks the trail. Isadora will be one of them and, yes, Aaron's another."

Eli interjects, "We must focus on Zeke and get him to the grove. I'm afraid we are all obligated to bring him there before the trip to Peru. We need him. I am also sorry that none of this was revealed in the timelines as Lamar's gang was never in the picture. I guess it correlates to Lamar making contact with Lucy for I never considered him as a potential problem. Something changed slightly and I do not have a moment to check it out either."

I assume Eli speaks about his ability to read probabilities in future timelines.

Compassionately Mama Jane says to Eli, "Don't fret, honey. It'll be all good. There's a lot of staying power behind this team."

I try to get a telepathic read on Eli, but I feel him block me mentally as he intuits my invasiveness. I know he's thinking about Aaron and my imminent Ascension. Before dispersing, Eli makes eye contact with me and I attempt to visually show him that I'm not bothered in the least about the Vampires hunting us or the fact that Aaron will be one of my guardian Watchers while we climb to the ancient stone. He disrupts the silent dialog between us and says, "Marcus, help me get the ammo for the guns."

"Sure," he replies and both of them leave the house.

"Lucy, I could use an extra hand in the kitchen with the pies," Mama Jane says.

"Alright," I respond, even though my attention remains with Eli, struggling to understand this confused link between the two of us. It hurts knowing there's a revolutionizing change about to transpire; that I'm undergoing a sort of metamorphosis and nothing can hinder it, no matter how much we desire to cultivate our love craze.

Doing something normal among all this strangeness actually comforts me. I feel totally fatigued from the extra focus to keep myself in the right frame of mind. Helping Mama Jane is a great distraction and I think she knew this when she asked me to help. I scoop the last bowl of filling into the pie shell and decide it's about time to call it a night.

When I yawn, Mama Jane says, "Go to bed, honey. I can finish cleaning up this mess. Another big day awaits you tomorrow."

"I can't argue with that," and I head to the guest bedroom down the hallway. If only I could hover above the ground, this would be a good time since my legs feel heavy from being so tired.

Upon opening the door and entering, I get a gut reaction that I'm not alone. I have an overwhelming feeling like someone is watching me, but I'm too tired to investigate. It can't be Isadora as she arrives and announces herself at full volume. The energetic imprint can be likened to another Light being. The presence doesn't scare me as it feels warm and comforting. I take off my shoes and socks and barely hit the sack before I'm out for the count.

Waking up to a black swirling, I feel as if I'm about to fall off my bed. I wonder if I'm out of body again.

*Nope.*

I pat the comfort of my quilt. Hours seem to have passed after drifting off to sleep, but when I look at the clock only twenty minutes have slipped away. "What the?" I mutter, outwardly astonished and faint-hearted at the same time. I see him hovering straight above me.

*This can't be happening.*

I recognize this Light being as Aaron. How long has he been watching me or what if I can't remember engaging him in the astral realm while I slept? Ugh! How many times have I done this to myself? Split my personality by refusing to remember while I pine over Eli?

This is only the second encounter with Aaron, at least within my awakened cognizance. Although, somehow I believe he's been following me around unobtrusively like the ghostwriting of that heart on my mirror. I don't move and allow myself to stare back at his translucent ghostlike appearance. I need to confront my fear of knowing this mystery man for he currently haunts my soul even as I've denied this part of myself in order to remain devoted to Eli.

Confusion surmounts because his eyes glow like he passionately adores me, but yet, he imparts a level of angst. We look intently at each other while he forces me to recognize him. Without forethought, I reach my hand out to his vaporous face and he moves his hand to touch mine. We remain entangled in the moment. I struggle with his telepathic suggestions, which seem to make him despondent. I'm dazed by the sudden knowledge that a Light being can feel heartache and emptiness for he projects these images to me while I resist. I cannot deny that he's absolutely beautiful and perfect beyond anything I can ever remember.

He vanishes like smoke, dissipating into thin air. My bewilderment deepens now that he has left for the core of me wants to wail out his name, but I don't as I'm afraid that I would be heard. I believe I've hurt this mystery man somehow, which causes me anguish. How much pain has my situation caused those whom I love? I know there is no one to blame since I have been walking blindly into this arrangement.

I must focus entirely on Zeke and make sure that I can protect him, while getting us all safely to the ancient stone in the grove where all this started for me in the first place. The foreseeable spiritual journey launches me tomorrow. I've got to find my inner strength and overcome these fears of the unknown by morning as so many are relying on me. I rest in bed, seeking an empty space inside me to avoid feeling intense emotions for both Eli and Aaron.

# Chapter 23
# The Battle of Forces

I hang onto the seat belt tightly as Eli speeds around the last corner before reaching the entrance at the trail head. Eli's certainly hassled this morning, expressing a hasty demeanor. He'd been hard-pressed to get Marcus and me out to the car and arrive an hour earlier than Eli previously told Zeke.

"It's okay, you can slow down now. Look. No one has arrived yet," I softly say, hoping to calm his nerves.

Eli gears down and the wheels slide to a sharp halt in the gravel, at the same time smiling brashly. "No problem." Eli's confident self and steady persona reappears reassuring me of his stability.

Getting out of the car, Marcus adjusts his undergarments. He's testing a new specially made bullet proof vest as it covers his entire midsection and neck. Not only did he say it could repel bullets and shards, but it covers his main arteries, as this material cannot be penetrated by blades, more specifically Vampire teeth.

I assist the boys to unload the prepared supplies from the cram-packed hatchback. I'm ecstatic to return to the grove as my first trip had been a breathtaking experience. My adoration for Eli revealed itself at this extraordinary place.

Helping me to lift the pack over my shoulders, Eli accidently slides his fingers over mine, initiating electric sparks to course through me. These static charges pulse between us while we linger closely for a few seconds. I can almost feel the heat radiating from his body and it takes everything within me to keep from intimately grabbing his face to kiss him.

Marcus distracts us from our intense moment when he says, "Let's take a look around, Eli." He holds two pairs of binoculars and gives a set to Eli as they both walk up the tree line of the forest. I relax, leaning against the car and bask in the natural beauty of the woodlands. I close my eyes and focus my thoughts on conjuring good vibes for the day as I power myself up with the natural energy flowing from the magnificent trees.

Upon opening my eyes, I catch sight of three orbs descending from above the misty woodlands. Straightening, I discern Isadora shifting into her human form. Two other Light beings stand at her side, but neither happens to be Aaron. Just as I begin to wonder if he decided to skip out today, another Light orb arrives from the same direction. By now I can detect its Aaron even as he delays shapeshifting. I assume he's intentionally maintaining his luminescence.

Isadora introduces me, "Lucy, I want you to meet, um, you already know them so it seems silly, but this is Dagan, Lara and well, Aaron."

The orb continues to remain motionless and I consider how to reply to this formal re-introduction in every practical sense, given that I have soul amnesia. I sense he doesn't want to alter my peaceful frame of mind so he stalls to avoid making me feel uncomfortable.

I squint to catch sight of the twinkling diamond-like outline of the bright energy field surrounding me. I need to make sure it's fully operational. Its glimmer intensifies when I swing from emotions of fright to peace and the field fluctuates and becomes visibly protective.

Isadora reports, "We've already searched the trails looking for any signs. That's where we just came from, but rest assured if

Vampires have a thirst for revenge, they will find a way into these woods undetected."

"We'll be by your side," Dagan adds, confident.

Isadora dramatically informs us, "Zeke's vulnerable as he's very frail at the present, but we're to be unsurpassed!" Hearing this disturbing news from Isadora somehow makes the situation seem more dire and desperate, regardless of her buoyant spirit.

In response, I whisper, "Oh no! How soon will they arrive?"

Lara speaks up and says, "Only moments from now as they're driving up the last ridge, about to reach us."

I try hard to hear the vehicle revving up the mountainside. At last I make out faint sounds of the motor. Eli and Marcus run down the hill, returning from their scouting in a hurry as they must have heard the same motor noise.

"That's them," I say to Eli, noticing that he's relaxed, probably in anticipation of their arrival. It's like reuniting tribal brothers, obviously in high spirits and lively for they shout and holler when they view us. Eli runs up to the approaching Jeep Cruiser and when the vehicle slows to a stop, he grabs a hand hanging out of the window. Five passengers step out while Eli anxiously paces to the back hatch when it pops open. I take a closer look. Lying in the bed of the trunk, a blanket covers a pale and critically ailing Zeke. Eli must have whispered something funny in Zeke's ear for I see a semi-grin faintly lighting up his once jovial face. Marcus comes over to help Eli lift Zeke to a sitting position. I cannot help but know his physical status as his pasty and gaunt skin disfigures his youthfulness. His nails are blackened and he seems lethargic. Without any thought, an impulse moves me closer to Zeke and I touch his cheeks with both of my hands, tipping my forehead onto his while directing a bit of my Light field. I know without a doubt that we cannot make the journey without providing Zeke some healing and strength.

"That's enough, Lucy. Anymore and you won't be able to protect him or yourself," Isadora cautions.

Stepping back, I see that my action has energized him somewhat. I'm astonished at this positive result as I had no idea I possessed such ability. I'm confident now of having the ability to protect Zeke today.

I'd almost forgotten about the rest of the group as they stand around waiting for a formal introduction. I refocus myself, scrutinizing our new allies. Elated to see Ki again, I reach out and give him a big hug. Eli introduces me to his old friends. "Lucy, this is Thurston, Ballard, Arrack and Brit."

"Hey, I've heard a lot about you," Thurston says.

"Likewise," I respectfully reply, observing that Thurston and Ballard are powerfully built; likely the result of participating in many battles inside the jungles. Visible scarring on Ballard's arms reflects his many conflicts and the reason for the many medals bestowed upon him. Arrack is slightly smaller, but I'm sure he comes with great expertise. Brit is a beautiful young lady outfitted as a warrior. I suppose her name might be short for Britney, but the abbreviation is most apt for her calling.

Isadora reminds us, "We need to get moving." Her eagerness shows.

The friendly gathering quickly turns serious now as we turn to the purpose of why we're all here. It's advantageous having Thurston and his comrades as additional physical protection. Eli takes out the rest of the supplies and the team members each select a weapon of choice. Thurston reaching under Zeke's arm, lifts him to his feet. He looks better, but is still comparatively weak.

"Ready, Lucy?" Thurston asks.

Understanding my task, I state, "Let's stick together. We'll walk in sync keeping Zeke close to me."

"Let's bounce," Thurston announces to everyone.

Eli and Ki head up the trail and I'm guessing by their gestures, it's secure to rest a bit. Several hours pass before reaching our destination as we've paced ourselves for the sake of Zeke. Wildlife screeches and bushes tremble along the way, arousing my protective instincts, but now I'm a little nervous as to whether the hard work may have worn me out. I'm relieved to find my fully functional shield perfectly polished, a favorable confirmation. We're almost there, as I recognize the trickling stream just ahead, indicating the meadow before reaching the downward slope where the ancient stone lies inside the encircling pine trees.

Thurston attentive, with his deep voice inquires of Zeke, "How you holding up?"

Taking turns with Thurston to support Zeke walk, Marcus jokingly complains while lowering him to the ground, "Dude, you weigh a ton."

If I didn't know better, I might think Zeke suffers from a horrible virus. I say to him, "Here's some water. Drink up."

I extract another water bottle and gulp it down to quench my own thirst. It's wintry, but the extra exertion keeps me warm. A vaporous haze conceals most of the sky, along with the dense covering of trees and a gentle breeze casts a shadow over our location. Suddenly my instincts kick into gear and I observe the lack of sounds as another bout of time begins to slow to a creep. My senses alert, I seek answers to this slip. Without delay, Isadora and the other Light beings shift into large radiating spheres like suns in four directions. I realize that we're in big trouble.

This instinctive sense of alarm must have triggered a slowing point in time as I can see everyone, except for the Light beings in slow motion. The lack of motion grants enough time to position myself while preparing to encounter a mêlée of Vampires as they have found their chance to target Zeke. I stand directly over him and place one hand on his backside. Fearfully I search for Eli because I can't physically locate him. Instead of remaining disempowered, I say a little prayer, seeking solace before entering such an encounter since this very action demands a good deal of courage.

Upon opening my eyes after this brief request, the unimaginable unfolds before us as sizeable boulders cast spiraling shadows that sway and shapeshift into Lamar and six others. The cold blooded creatures veiled themselves by becoming shrouded with the cold rocks as they literally appeared to glide directly from them. Not even the highly developed eyes of Isadora and the others identified this kind of cloaking. No matter how sharp we are, the Vampires always come ready. Surveying our positions, I see that we are fully operational and set to take action.

All at once, their muscles protrude the translucent layer of waxy skin, elongating and remolding their forms like beastly disfigured humans. The intruding Vampires gain speed and without a single word, bullets stream through the air. Because of my own fear, my heart beats incredibly fast, but I strain to extinguish it. For a moment the intense reality of this situation shakes me and instead of being alarmed at maybe being hit by a bullet, I center on maintaining the Light shield, envisioning invisibility. The Light beings hold steady, providing extra encouragement.

I count slowly to three, and at last, my heart rate decreases to a normal rhythm.

I turn my attention to the fight outside of the barrier that I, with the help of my other worldly guardians, created. Ballard makes progress as he forcefully pushes a Vampire against a tree, breaking its limbs. I become nauseated at the blood bursting out as Ballard drives his shiny blade directly into the heart of this alien creature. I hear a frenzied blood-curdling last scream as this male Vampire's eyes bulge in terror at the moment of its last breath, afraid of losing its position on the surface of this planet as he dies. The body remains lifeless on the ground while remnants of a black shadow zip through the trees, rushing away.

Turning my attention to the other skirmishes, Eli and Thurston are confronting another Vampire. Thurston advances with his fists, jabbing Lamar in the gut and then the jaw, but it barely interrupts the Vamp's momentum as the bloodsucker forces Thurston back, baring his teeth. Lamar's altered muscular form demonstrates his powerful control. Thurston holds him back while Eli, clutching a long blade, thrusts it into the backside of another Vampire that collapses. I don't see his gun and wonder what happened to our fire power. Two other Vampires creep up on Eli and Thurston as their battle with the parasites intensifies.

Since my attention has been distracted watching Eli, without forewarning, a Vampire stands ten feet away snarling and showing his elongated teeth. He holds a jagged knife in one of his hands. He looks as if he's trying to intimidate me enough to step aside so he can reach Zeke. Just then, I notice another behind me draw near. Because of my terror of these creatures, my heart accelerates. Yet, I know they cannot come any closer as the higher Light shields us from their violent assaults. I deeply exhale and say to myself, "Remember stay calm, they are less powerful, do not fear."

I discover that I've become the next target for these creatures as they attempt to get at Zeke. Thankfully, Isadora and the other Light beings are holding another impenetrable force field surrounding us. To my horror, Lamar approaches, clutching Eli with a blade at his throat while exposing his sharp teeth, hoping to torment and distress me. Lamar acts as if he's a wild animal ready to go in for the kill. I know that Lamar's venomous bite can render Eli helpless as he flashes his fangs like a snake about to strike.

He shouts, "I've captured your beloved, have I not, Lucy?"

Lamar taunts me as he has recognized my deep attachment to Eli. I don't flinch, but anger boils within me as my protective instinct to defend Eli makes me want to gash out Lamar's eyes. I remain silent while ideas rapidly flash through my mind about what to do next. I can't do nothing and watch while Lamar harms Eli or even possibly kills him. I couldn't bear the emotional pain and I'd die myself. He's attempting to terrorize me and disengage my shield, using fear as his weapon, thus luring me away from the other defenders.

Considering the possible threats, I see Thurston continuing to fight another Vampire in the near distance and Brit and Ki back him up. I'm concerned for them too.

Just then I see Arrack running through the trees unloading and reloading his weapon and then flinging himself through the air in one leap. He surprises me at his sheer force and agility to leap higher than most humans. Soaring toward the other two Vampires, Arrack releases the fire power as he carries weapons in both hands. His skill and ability is exceptionally heroic while he takes out both of these parasites. How can we not win this battle with all of this incredible herculean expertise? With confidence that the Light beings will now protect Zeke, I begin to step forward, but I'm stopped by Isadora. "No, Lucy, stay in position."

This frustrates me because I'm certain I can force Lamar to back off by getting closer to him. I check to see if my shield's strong enough to push him off of Eli, but to my dismay, I've allowed my anger and fear to weaken it. I become aware that the Light beings are not only protecting Zeke, but also me. I try envisioning and returning to peaceful sensations, but Lamar continues to taunt me.

I hear Isadora, "Easy now. Don't let him distract you."

I scream inside my head at her, "I have to stop Lamar!"

She responds to my desperation, "Wait a second."

What does she mean, "Wait a second?" There's no time. Then I remember to force my thoughts to slow time. Everything creeps at a snail's pace, allowing me ample pause to decide our best manner of defense.

Isadora continues, "Stand closer to Zeke as we are about to change positions." I follow her directions, wondering what plan they're devising. Time resumes normal speed and within a nanosecond, the four spheres shift from a pattern of a square into a triangle, leaving one outside the alignment. Not understanding the purpose of this action, I realize this sphere is Aaron.

*What is he about to do?*

I brace my feet solidly on the ground waiting for something, but I have no idea what. I watch the lone sphere become larger and more brilliant as gathering more energy from the atomic spaces between this world and the higher realms. A large pulsation blasts outward from this effervescent Light being. Sharp sounds hurt and puncture my ears as the throbbing quake vibrates through everything in proximity. The sphere disappears and, at the same time, I see the remaining Vampires disintegrate into fragments of ashes and bones. Staring directly at Eli, I relax, seeing that he's safe from Lamar's clutches. I run to him, grasping him tightly.

"You're alright!" I exclaim.

I sense that this explosion radiated higher Light fields, thereby destroying the Vampires. I'm electrified in joy as the battle has been won!

While I examine Zeke to confirm that he's fine, Isadora, Lara and Dagan shapeshift into human forms. "Thanks, Lucy." Zeke articulates slowly. I reach down and hug him, knowing that the conflict is over. Our destination to the ancient stone isn't far away. There's no sign of Aaron. I inquire, "Where's Aaron?"

I find Isadora and the others circling a small area of tall grass. Stepping closer, I see a nude body of a man lying on the ground. "Strange. Where did he come from?" I ask.

Then Isadora attempts to answer, "Lucy."

As she begins to speak, the motionless body stirs and his head turns in my direction. My knees buckle and my breathing becomes erratic as I suffer a sinking feeling. Unable to restrain myself, I say out loud for all to hear. "No. It can't be, but how?"

Ki brings over a jacket and an extra pair of sweats and shoes packed away inside his bag for Aaron to dress himself against the cold and harsh environment. I'm rendered speechless that Aaron has sacrificed his non-physical Light embodiment to save Eli from these Vampires. The blast of energy has left him imprisoned in this Earthly realm. This beautiful Light being has rapidly descended from the higher realms, shapeshifting into an actual, physical human form.

Leaping forward into the circle, I ask, "Why did you do this?" For a moment I lose my train of thought because of Aaron's nudity while he adjusts to his new surroundings like a newborn. Eli closely stands near me and the reality that both Aaron and Eli are now physically together in the same world with me is insane. I feel bound to embrace Aaron as somewhere deep within the recesses of my amnesia, I miss him, but I can't. Eli's radiating presence also captivates me. I'm trapped between two equally intoxicating magnetic poles, stuck in the middle of these powerful forces.

Candidly, Isadora speaks, "There was no talking Aaron out of this as he knew the consequences and did it anyway. We need to get him to the ancient stone as he also needs the boost."

I ask, "What are the consequences?"

Marcus explains, "To be trapped here with us in all of the earthly drama until the entire planet ascends."

"Not unless we can get the ancient gates opened before it is too late," Eli sardonically states. His tone betrays him.

"That's not too far off, right? But, why can't he go back sooner?"

"It's going to take some adjusting to this environment and learning how to harness the human experience before he can gather enough Light energy to ascend," Isadora interjects.

Eli announces, "It's getting colder, everyone. We need to get to the stone. Especially before any more Vamps come after us in revenge for killing members of their gang."

Both Eli and I help Zeke walk the last kilometers to the masterful ancient stone. Ki and Thurston assist Aaron as his legs are weak from the change in densities of these different realms. Upon reaching our destination, Eli guides Zeke onto the stone. Unable to stand on the site again, I watch the incredible transformation of healing restore Zeke back to his old self. It only took twenty minutes before he felt invigorated and enthusiastically performed a back flip off the rock. Delighted, we all laugh at his restored strength and good-humor.

Thurston and Brit guide Aaron onto the stone as I silently sit by myself, observing. I try not to look directly at Aaron, fearing that I might see something that could cause me to fall madly for him. I attempt to ignore this deeply seeded attraction. I divert myself by pulling grass between my fingers until it becomes uninteresting. I look up, hoping to see Light beings emanate from the stone portal. Dismayed, I find my eyes locked onto Aaron as he sits crossed legged and then opens his eyes.

*Oh, Crap!*

I feel magnetically drawn to him. He pulls at my soul. I cannot love two men in this world. Contemplating the possibilities only complicates matters.

Eli sits down next to me. "I thought you would be more excited having Aaron present on this side."

I know he's testing me to see where I stand as he struggles with this new shock. Eli had been prepared for me to stay on the other side with Aaron after my personal Ascension into that realm. Now everything has shifted and right now I don't know which way is up or down. I reply, "I won't be here for long. Looks like you're stuck with him?" I jab him in his ribs. "I suppose not even a genius can read future probabilities, huh?"

"Yes, I think I'll give it up as it is too problematic."

"Does that mean I might not ascend sooner than expected?"

Passionately, he stares at me. "I don't know. Anything can happen."

"I saw what Aaron did as raw evidence that I can return, just like him."

"Lucy, do you know why Aaron took on this very action?"

I shake my head "no" while waiting for Eli's perspective.

He continues, "He wanted to protect me for you."

"You're telling me he made a completely selfless act? I don't think that's the entire story, Eli? Last night in the middle of my sleep, he appeared to me and I could sense his distress. He did it purposely to be closer to me."

"While you were sleeping," he sneers.

"Have you ever loved someone so much that your heart felt like it would explode if you can't be near them?"

He raises an eyebrow, signaling that I hit a nerve.

I continue explaining, "Well, I think that's how he feels about me. I'm sorry. I don't have the same reaction for Aaron as everyone assumes I should have. I don't remember him. I just don't understand why you've been denying your feelings toward me."

He pauses, playing with my fingers, "We will see what transpires after the mission to the stargate. Who knows what will happen? This has to be our main focus for now."

"Fine, I'll agree to that, but afterwards there's no more holding back your feelings. Got it?"

Composed, he nods in agreement and smiles. "Yes."

I return to focusing on the ancient stone and I see Aaron intently watching Eli and me sitting together closely. I sense a sliver of jealousy arise in Aaron. Encouraged by having Eli next to me, I glance back at Aaron. He locks into me with an etheric grip, as if he's trying to influence my affections toward him. Quickly I look away as our mutual gaze becomes unbearable.

"So, where's Aaron gonna stay as he obviously has no where to go?"

"With us at Mama Jane's farm."

I appreciate Eli's kind-heartedness as this is why I adore him, but the entire situation seems crazy and mixed up. I won't be able to avoid Aaron in the flesh when he'll be all over the place within my range and I don't know if I can endure it. I have very few moments to play out this love game with Eli on this planet. To divert myself, I remember the Thanksgiving feast Mama Jane cooked for us and I can't wait to get back as I assume all of us are ravenously famished from our accomplishments today. I'm ready to get out of here anyway as the stares from Aaron are uncomfortable.

Aaron appears to have gained a scope of favorable energy from the ancient stone and he walks robustly toward me. I arise from my sitting position, defensive, aware that I'm his prime target. Before I realize it, Aaron has me locked into a clinched embrace, passionately kissing me. Unable to think clearly, the shock of his aggression overwhelms me until the name Eli echoes in my heart. Pushing him away, I say to Aaron, "What the hell do you think you're doing?"

In a soft masculine tone, he replies, "Forcing you to re-member."

I seek to read Eli's reaction from this hot mess. He's sulk-ing in the same spot on the grass and his peaceful expression has changed to a tightlipped, fixed stare at the ground. One look at Eli and I can see his hurt. It now forces me to defend my self interest. "Aaron, I don't remember and just because we've had something doesn't mean it continues to exist right now!"

I walk away from both Aaron and Eli, unable to cope with hurting either of them, most of all Eli. This jumbled assortment will cause some interesting drama at Mama Jane's farm. I can only hope to keep myself together. Most frightening are the re-pressed emotions that boiled to the surface when Aaron kissed me. He was right as his kiss did provoke a memory of a sacred ecstasy between us.

I reach down, grab my backpack and rush back onto the path in the woods by myself. Sensing the others are right behind me, I grit my teeth, hoping Eli and Aaron are sophisticated enough to not trade punches.

Zeke sprints to catch up with me. He's fast now as his reserves are at full strength. Putting his arm around my shoulder in a friendly manner, he says, "I know your agony, girl. No need to get all tense."

"Zeke, can I speak to you about this privately without it getting back to Eli?"

"Of course, I'm all ears," he replies.

"I can't deny that I don't remember Aaron, but I won't betray my hope to have something with Eli, regardless of whether I can find a way to return."

Zeke suspends my rambling. "I know Eli's protecting himself from getting hurt. If it's meant to be, it'll happen. I will say this much: Aaron deserves credit for saving all of us and especially averting harm to Eli as I know he'll honor him for this. He's won't start a conflict with Aaron. That's not Eli's style. Aaron does have tenacity. I'll give him that."

# Chapter 24
# Sacrifices

"The table looks fantastic, Mama Jane," I comment as I walk into the kitchen to see if she needs help for this feast. The table had an extra dinner plate as Mama Jane somehow intuitively knew to prepare for one more.

Aaron's newfound brothers have taken him to the barn, most likely to clean up and outfit him suitable for his current environment.

"Oh dear, come with me, Brit. We'll have you stay in the guest room with Lucy. I have an extra roll-out bed." Mama Jane directs Brit to the back of the house, leaving me alone in the kitchen. I suppose I'll have a new roommate for awhile as I've been staying on the farm while Mother's on her long Parisian holiday. I look forward to learning more about Brit and the other welcome warriors. She is quiet and reserved so it might take some prying to gain beneficial information.

"Awe, Crimany!" Alerted by something behind me, I swing around and see Isadora. "I didn't see you coming. Please give me some forewarning," I complain, sighing in relief.

She ignores my statement and vehemently rants, "Lucy, you're walking into deep water right now; overcome with all of this commotion with Aaron descending to be with you! And, of course your having the hots for Eli. I can see from my vantage point that your emotions are potent right now, blitzing you out of your mind. Don't drag yourself into a mess and become inordinately upset again!"

"What mess? I'm going to avoid Aaron."

Isadora laughs. "Yeah, right! You're not going to be able to pretend you don't know who Aaron is for much longer. I saw the sparks burst between the two of you at the stone. Plus, very soon your memory will be restored."

"What? When he kissed me without my permission? By the way, what if I don't want to remember Aaron?" I remain obstinate.

"Ugh, it's been laborious getting you to wake up and at this point in time, there is nothing more important than controlling your abilities and that means your emotions. Ghats! How many more times must I remind you to keep a lid on it?"

"Why did Aaron make this sacrifice? I'm indebted that he saved Eli and bailed us all out of this conflict, but didn't he have a sense that this situation could cause additional problems like instigating a storm of confusion for me? Didn't he have any other options?"

"You were ready and willing to be filleted by Vampires to save Eli. Of course, we couldn't allow that to happen. Aaron couldn't endure your pain or watch you die horribly and keeping you alive right now overrides everything else. Aaron's rash decision to relinquish his higher Light fields to destroy the Vampires became the only solution. That, of course, dimmed his Light body into a more physical one."

*She's right. I was about to make a foolish mistake.*

Isadora continues lecturing, "Before I forget, there's nothing wrong with love. It's the glue that holds this Universe together, but this extra fuss can simply make or break your undertaking at the stargate. We need you to be absolutely focused and not become Vampire bait! So, please, try and keep your romantic cravings to a minimum." Laughing, I salute. "Affirmative! Got it!"

Composed now, she says, "Regulate your emotions in order to direct and hold your Light shield. This method will be the root of our success at the stargate. After today, you clearly need better self-control. We can't let these dark ones dominate the outcome, regardless of their tactics."

She disappears before I can say another word as she means business. I'm fortunate not to be in her shoes. I don't think I'd have enough patience. That's probably why I'm here while she remains the ascended Light being.

Everyone gathers inside the farm house, eager to select seats at the dinner table and eat. I sit down and, uncomfortably, Aaron and Eli sit on each side of me.

By clanging her spoon on her crystal glass, Mama Jane signals that she wants our undivided attention. "Welcome, Thurston and your friends, and thank you for bringing Zeke back to us. All of you deserve a medal for your dedication and courage. It's not everyday that a Light being sacrifices his divine position in the higher realms for such a noble cause. We deeply thank you, Aaron."

Zeke initiates our appreciation by more clanging on his crystal glass and we all shout our approval. Eli stands up and clears his throat, preparing for his own speech. "I applaud you, Aaron. I am in your debt for such heroic action to stop the Vampires from slaying me. We are all here at this table because of you. There is not a better day than Thanksgiving dinner to share such gratitude."

More hoots and hollers rise from the table. I react a little more civilly and modestly than the crew when I clang my crystal glass. I'm withdrawn for the moment as I haven't reached any conclusion as to how I feel about Aaron's heroic actions or his loutish kiss at the ancient stone.

*Was Aaron just waiting for his opportunity to descend or did he truly save Eli for me? I know he's been lingering around like a ghost ever since I met Eli. Regardless of his intentions, it all seems to revolve around me. Sort of like a stalker? Aaron hasn't said much and I wonder why?*

"I'm waiting to decide what to say, Lucy." A male voice reverberates in my head and I almost jump out of my seat, looking around for the culprit.

"You all right?" Eli reacts to my alarm, unaware of what I just heard.

This voice wasn't the female tone of Isadora and I know it wasn't my own thoughts. I lock eyes with Aaron and realize it was him. He then leans toward me and whispers in my ear, "Stalker?"

My mouth opens and my eyebrows rise from the shock, realizing that Aaron can communicate with me by thought transference like the Lemurians once did.

*Are we the only ones able to hear each other's thoughts?*

"Yes," he mentally responds.

*Well get out of my head!*

Mama Jane ends saying grace just in time so that I can now devote myself to eating and bar Aaron from invading my private thoughts. I'm thrown off balance. Can my secrets be revealed by Aaron reading my mind? This is outrageous! Now I have to concern myself with what I think!

"Heavens to Betsy, look at you eat, Aaron!" Mama Jane exclaims.

"He's starving," Marcus remarks.

"No, he hasn't had human food for, how long has it been, Aaron?" Thurston inquires.

Aaron's fiercely gobbling down his dinner like a wild animal. I hear his answer in my head that nobody else at the table can detect, "at least a couple millenniums ago."

I debate whether to answer for him or not and reveal that we can communicate by thought. Impulsively I blurt it out, "He says quite a long time ago."

"How do you know that, Lucy?" Eli questions.

I pick at my food, answering softly, "Because we can hear each other's thoughts."

Eli's obviously upset as he drops his fork on his plate. He stares at his dinner while clenching his teeth. I think he's jealous, not angry.

Mama Jane speaks out, having observed Eli's edgy reaction. "Isn't that remarkable? Has anyone else been able to communicate with Aaron telepathically?"

Everyone responds all at once "no" and shakes their heads, just as perplexed as I am.

Barely uttering the words through his tightened jaw, Eli asks Mama Jane, "Do you have an answer for this glitch?"

"I do and it's actually an ability not a glitch," she clearly answers and I sense that she's trying to change his opinion as his prickly demeanor shows.

She continues, "Let's keep this simple. Cell phones emit microwaves whereas human mental telepathy uses brainwaves to connect. Not everyone can make this connection unless they have a matching frequency. You see, these two are rising and falling as Aaron descends and Lucy ascends. Their telepathic wires have crossed and that's why they can communicate as they're on the same channel, you might say."

Aaron speaks again inside my head, "That's true, a united surge in energy."

"Get out of my head, now, Aaron!"

"You can't ignore me indefinitely. We've been connecting telepathically since we became attuned to one another on Lyra, forever ago."

"That's not fair since I don't have a clue as to what you're talking about."

"Can't fight it. We're mates in this grand Universe." He's annoyed at my aggravation. He wants me to acknowledge an eternal bond of some nature.

Thankfully the silent dialogue stops. Maybe there's some kind of otherworldly rule where he has to do what I say. Like a genie, maybe I can wish him back inside the bottle for a while. It's hard to fathom that he has been transposed from this beautiful airy ethereal Light being into a barbaric, food-gobbling animal with no manners.

*I think we're more like polar opposites instead.*

I notice Aaron still wolfing down his food and chuckling in response to my bitter private deliberations. Unfortunately, I feel he's enjoying this spirited circumstance as his presence jars my affection for Eli. I can't admit it and I won't think it, but I feel that I kind of like Aaron. He's different, more robust and rough around the edges, a strong personality and, at the same time, has a cool laid-back air about him. He's extremely attractive. If he can sense my feelings too, then he's not paying attention. At least I hope not. I'll just have to make it clear that we're leaving the past in the past.

Eli's posturing signals that he's uncomfortable with this situation. I have one more problem. Eli can strongly sense what I'm feeling. I have to purposely block both of them out of my personal bubble and create some boundaries.

Despite everything, the evening is quite intimate with my bigger family and great entertainment, especially from Arrack and Ballard as they are just as playful and comical as Zeke. Thurston and Ballard are musical and have talent freestyling rhythms and beats so much that it's difficult to not groove with the flow of their raps. The amusement deflects the uncomfortable vibes sizzling between the members of this triangle: Eli, Aaron and myself.

The noise level dwindles. Aaron has fallen asleep in his chair, resting his chin on his fist. A full stomach and releasing his celestial position have finally drained him. Zeke has initiated a lively game of "Texas Hold 'Em" in the living room. I skip the card playing. Too much lingers in my mind.

While Aaron's passed out asleep at the table, I can freely think without any intrusion. I'm determined to draw a boundary between what I will allow Aaron to overhear and what he's forbidden to access.

*Could there be an ancient rule book written by the Lemurians on the principle of ethics and code of conduct when gifted with this sort of ability?*

Thurston rises from his seat at the dinner table after having a long debate with Eli about how to solve the world's problems. Mama Jane refuses to let me help her clean up in the kitchen so that I may rest and enjoy myself while observing the conversations. Eli stands and stretches before he takes Thurston to the barn. He wants to plan the logistics and strategies in Peru, in addition to reviewing several maps of our target location.

Thurston observes Aaron asleep and says, "I think we need to help this guy to bed."

Eli attempts to awaken him, but with no results. He's like dead weight and sleeping like a baby as we attempt to wrestle him up. I decide to try something different. I mentally yell, "Wake up, Aaron!" He jolts backwards in his seat, startled.

Aaron's cheek has a dent and his hair messy from resting his head on the table. He yawns and stretches, barely awake. I watch from the front door as Eli and Thurston steer him to the barn.

*I hope they didn't arrange a place for him to sleep inside one of the old horse stalls. No, Eli wouldn't be that unkind.*

I remain at the house and decide to find my coat and walk outside by myself. There are many extra bodies in this space and I need some fresh wintry air. The full moon shines brightly, lighting the trail along the stream and I find myself further away from the farmhouse. I like the time alone and the night sounds of owls and critters squeaking from the trees. The isolation allows me to reflect on my heavy heart.

I can't disappoint Isadora as she has often cautioned me. I don't need to hear an, "I told you so," comment about creating a rollercoaster of emotions and fail on my mission. It is what it is and the best approach is to endure the high winds by accepting the circumstances that already exist. What transpired in the past theoretically cannot be changed. I have to keep moving forward instead of giving into my fears.

There are two incredibly attractive and mystical guys in my present reality and it appears that neither of them will be a problem once this approaching Ascension occurs. I'm leaving while they stay. I don't really want to arrive like an apparition and I haven't a clue as to what it feels like to be a Light being. I want nothing more than to learn instantly the greatest secrets of the Universe. It must be an intense rush, returning to a place so magically dreamed about my entire life. It burns me to know that I have to leave this world to access all of the lost mysteries stored already inside me. If only I can find a way to live in both realms at the same time.

I've been walking for a while and lost track of the time. The cold air has kept me awake. I turn and start heading back when I see him. Not only do I detect the size and shape, but I also feel Eli's presence coming nearer. My insides flutter, stimulating that crazy love feeling again. I can't wait to reach him and I stride quickly in his direction. I impulsively rush to see what nature may reveal from our close contact and while standing alone in the middle of these several acres, I sense he feels the same way.

Nothing stands between us as he gently holds my face with his hands and pulls me into a most incredible kiss, more breathtaking than the last time. Intense frequencies shift inside me. I briefly open my eyes to see a glowing Light sphere absorb both of us. His warmth and scent erase my last ounce of composure. And then it had to happen, but this time it doesn't scare me. It electrifies me that I'm hovering above the ground.

*This obviously is a symptom of kissing Eli.*

We hilariously giggle together about the situation as it doesn't matter and we continue touching each other's lips softly. I know that Aaron waits in the back of my mind and I don't care right now. I'm in the moment, giving into my desire to kiss Eli again. I have made it clear inside my own heart and mind that all I need is this moment once more. I can deal with the puzzling reality of Aaron in my present world later.

"It's getting late. We need to get back before Mama Jane sends out a rescue team for us," he says.

I don't want to leave. For it seems like eons that this is the moment I've hungered for, but I give in, "Okay."

We hold hands, walking back slower than usual, stalling to reach the house. "What's on your mind?" I ask, seeking a clue into his thoughts. I wish he and I were telepathically linked because I don't want Aaron inside my head.

"Aaron's sacrifice came as a complete surprise. I am still in shock about it. I had no idea that a Light being could extinguish their higher Light fields and descend like he did. At least, it never entered my mind that this could be done.

"So that means something very different could transpire after I open the stargate?"

"I simply do not know. There is something unknown about you, Lucy. It mystifies me. Maybe it's your willingness to jump in blindly and accept this mission the way you have done as it only magnifies the powerful role that you play in all of this. But, just because you feel like sticking around, doesn't mean that next week you will want the same outcome. Do not make promises you cannot keep. It is not healthy for you or anyone else."

I assume he still guards himself from the possible outcome after the trip to Peru. He believes I won't come back after the GC informed him that I wouldn't be returning to Earth. "Fine, we'll just see what happens."

He cannot hide the few tears. He's fighting to maintain his composure, but his voice cracks as he says, "I cannot endure putting you in danger. Every night I am haunted by images of you becoming one of their cruelly tortured victims. I want to be your protector, not lead you into the lion's den. If I could do this myself, I would, but these Vampires can devour me before I walk twenty feet. I am forced to trust this insane plan the GC have designed: to use you as the sacrificial infiltrator of great hope and, yet, I cannot face this world without you in it."

We're back at the house and Eli kisses me goodnight, slightly briefer than in the woods. I'm moved by his words and remain silent, not able to respond. He stands there holding me on the porch and I am aware of his erratic breathing. I know he wants nothing more than to save me from my mission. He rests his forehead on mine and we don't share words, only a tender hold. I cannot let go the wonder of what tomorrow will be like having Eli closer to me and barring Aaron from invading my thoughts.

# Chapter 25
# The Radiant One

"Lucy, get out your passport. You need it stamped," Zeke says as we head to the customs gate at the airport in Lima. I open it and see blank pages. This will be my first international stamp. Might possibly be my only stamp?

Eli trails behind, hauling both of our carry-on bags as he persists to express being a gentleman. His wise suggestion to travel light lessens our load so we won't have to mess with burdensome luggage. We all split up into separate groups taking different flights. Thurston said we could invite unwanted attention by having our entire crew arrive simultaneously. My flying partners are Eli, Zeke and Marcus. I couldn't ask for any better companions and protectors, besides Isadora, of course.

The telepathic conversations with Aaron have been causing me to feel shaky. I deem myself untrue to my heart by keeping Eli unaware of how frequently he communicates with me. Aaron's loyal to his cause of releasing my repressed memories, but I'm stubborn and will keep squashing his lovesick, fallen angel plea. Thankfully, a few days ago Arrack and Brit volunteered to take Aaron in their group.

Brit's quiet, but she does share common girl insight. I think she stepped up to take Aaron so I'd have a break and some alone time with Eli. After all, I am about to shift my entire life soon to complete this mission. Regardless of how scary it seems, I'm driven to face my biggest fear of things that go bump in the dark. I get the impression that I won't be coming back from this journey as the same Lucy.

It's mid-morning and the long wait to begin our trip to Peru has finally come. We flew during the night. Sleeping on the plane hurts my back, but Eli's shoulder eases the pain. A larger airplane would have been more comfortable. I haven't traveled too many places despite Father's military deployments as Mother insisted on staying home in Silverton. In my opinion, I believe she wanted to shield me from the rest of the world by living in a small town. She had many fears of her own and has done what she could to keep me from becoming a military brat. It did cause stress between my parents.

The trip to Peru could be much better if Mama Jane hadn't stayed back at the farm. I wish she were here to share this moment, but for some unknown reason, she insisted to remain back there. I think she doesn't like leaving our home base vulnerable.

All of us will meet in a small town called Sayan. Apparently Thurston knows some locals in this area and the site nears the opening crack in the ground leading to the stargate. I follow their lead given that I have no idea what Peru's even like. Any foreign country away from my hometown appears alien to me, comparable to entering a whole other realm.

We hire a taxi to drive us toward our destination. "Porfavor, dirijase` Norte` hacia Huacho," Eli tells the driver. Luckily I know a little Spanish. Enough to understand that we are heading north to a town called Huacho.

I gaze out the window at the streets and plazas crowded with taxis and motorcyclists almost running into each other, people crossing the street against the traffic, a loud cacophony of sound. The metropolitan area looks modern, having large buildings and streets like any ordinary city in America.

Zeke makes small talk with the driver as we cruise up the highway. "Han haumentado los temblores poraqui?"

"What did he ask him, Eli?" My Spanish isn't good enough to keep up with his accent.

"He wants to know about the earthquakes and if the driver has felt many lately. The driver says there has been a rapid increase within the last year."

"That's linked to the blocked stargate, isn't it?"

"Correct."

Marcus turns from the front seat and says, "You're not the only one who can't understand. I received a standing 'D' in Spanish class. Languages are not my specialty."

Eli holds my hand while we sit close on the sticky seat. Its summer in Peru during the month of December and the humidity is high. His palm sweats in my hand and I feel overly clammy already, but I don't care since he's finally comfortable outwardly expressing his affection since Aaron's descent.

Now that I know that Eli struggles with some personal demons, I can now see by the pain on his face that he wants to be my rescuer, while at the same time he fulfills his mission of devising ways to save the world. That's a lot to wrestle with.

"How long will it take us to get to Sayan?" I ask.

"Once we reach Huacho, we will pick up a jeep and head east down another motorway. We should get to Sayan in a few hours," Zeke answers.

I sigh because I'm not comfortable in tight spaces, sticky hot weather and the lack of air conditioning. The car slows down, turning onto a side street. Eli's arm is completely saturated because of my using it as a pillow. The boys climb out and grab our bags.

"Muchas gracias," Eli says to the driver and hands him several soles.

"How much did you give him?" I wonder how the currency works in this country.

"Not to worry. He's pleased with the tip."

The ocean waves crash in the distance and I can see partial views of the southern Pacific while following the boys to a white Jeep. Zeke gets into the driver's seat, reaches under the floor mat and pulls out a set of car keys.

"Let's get this rig on the road," he says.

The engine's roar deafens me so I concentrate on the landscape. The hills are rocky with sparse vegetation. Large dump trucks pass us on the road carrying loads of rock. Cows' wandering on the lane tries Zeke's impatience and seem oblivious to his continual honking. He speeds up again and the wind provides some relief from the heat as I hang my head out the open window.

Before I know it, Eli announces, "We're here."

Vibrant colors decorate the buildings as we pass through this charming old-world town. Zeke drives further, passing the rim of Sayan and slowing to a small structure. Signs of the Peruvian culture and the local Indians are more apparent in this rural location. I'm thrilled to find telephone and power lines, indicating that the back country isn't totally deprived of modern technology.

When I climb out of the jeep, Aaron and Thurston greet us with big smiles. I'm disappointed in myself for my heart skips a beat when I look directly at Aaron.

"It's about time. You guys are the last to arrive," Thurston announces.

Aaron's sparkling eyes concentrate on me. I try to ignore his stare, but still feel the intensity of it.

*Why can't I have another day free from fighting this intense at-traction for Aaron and, yet, withholding these private conversations from Eli?*

I know Aaron received that thought because he snickered.

"Hope you guys are hungry. Our host has prepared anti-chuchos," Thurston says, which leads me to wonder what kind of cuisine is on the menu tonight.

Aaron pops into my head, "Marinated grilled beef heart."

Ugh! Silently between the two of us I share my disgust at the thought of eating a cow' heart.

"It's food. Don't think about it," he telepathically responds.

I privately answer, "Well coming from a wild beast."

I cut myself off before I say anything else, revealing my passing judgment on his carnivorous habits. I don't need a long sub-conversation with Aaron right now when I've just arrived.

It's completely uncanny how Eli and Aaron react to each other, definitely all for show. Aaron struggles to hold back his arrogance and not piss me off and Eli's afraid of losing his sophis-ticated composure by giving way to jealous rage. I really can't stand the idea of being the center of this uncalled for tug-of-war, although I can admit that I do like the extra attention as it fas-cinates me.

A small native man, face deeply wrinkled, approaches me from a rectangular building. He speaks rapidly and I don't know what he's saying. I know he's trying to greet me. When he opens his mouth broadly smiling, it displays holes of missing teeth. His broad grin and cheer brightens his face. I sense that he's wise beyond his years.

Leaving the boys outside, he takes my hand, pulling me along with him and sits me down on a wooden chair in a humble room in his home. He opens his fist to reveal a bone and then gestures to several scattered on the dirt floor. All the while, he never stops speaking rapidly in his native tongue.

"I don't understand," I say.

A young lady of the house enters the room and translates. "He knows who you are and our people have been waiting for you. I'm Liliana, the granddaughter of El Curandero."

I'm astonished by her statement and explain, "But I'm not anyone extraordinary; just a silly girl crazy enough to take on Vampires and aliens to open a stargate."

"No, he see's your inner Light and recognizes this force you carry. Not a silly girl."

He keeps saying the word, "luminescencia." I speculate as to what that might mean. I sit with El Curandero completely spellbound. My lack of verbal understanding moves me to listen with my heart. He's absolutely beautiful as I can see the Light within him. He takes his hand and points to my heart, then to my head as he continues repeating this same word over and over.

"He's calling Lucy the radiant one," Eli translates as he and Thurston enter the small room.

Thurston says to me, "Our host is a wizard of the natural living world and can see the shining Light radiating and stored inside your body. He has this insight that you walk between the worlds of iron and gold, carrying the codes of the newly evolving human species. The shamans have been calling such beings the 'luminous ones.'"

I examine his Light field more deeply. "His Light also holds a shade of green."

"This great, living master is a healer of natural organisms and energy for the planet, which accounts for the green ray of Light," Eli elaborates.

I wonder, "Do you see if I have a color tint to mine?"

Eli answers softly, bending his knees to speak to me at eye level, "I have noticed every day that your energy fields become brighter and much larger, never shifting color from the brilliant crystal luminescence. If I did not know better, I would describe your Light field as angel wings."

Aaron stands aside off in the corner. I would not have noticed him if it weren't for him grumbling something about me, although it felt like he was sneering at Eli. Still sitting on the chair, I turn and look him squarely in the face, intending to telepathically tell him that I don't belong to anyone and ultimately, it's my choice who I choose to give my attention to. Instead, I feel sad for him as he looks incredibly bewildered. His pain becomes mine in this second even as Eli kneels down near me. It must be hard for him to endure all these human emotions and to watch Eli and me outwardly flirting and displaying our mutual adoration.

Motionless, he gazes at me and my thoughts whiz around uncontrollably. I question if I truly have what it takes to become this radiant one and open the seal of the stargate when I've been so cold and heartless toward Aaron. As it stands, I'm hurting Aaron as he longs to reunite, but I cannot waste a minute without Eli. Even after my Ascension from this realm, my unbearable love-stricken grief cannot be relieved because my heart will be empty without either of them. I almost forget about the others in the room as I hold back tears caused by my own emotional torment.

El Curandero rises from his seat and shuffles toward me, his fingers wrapped around a vibrant orb of energy. Instinctively I absorb this energy and I know he has given me something fiercely powerful to carry within me on this journey.

*He performed some kind of magic as I feel a shifting towards bliss.*

"Hey!" Zeke bellows from the open door as he spots Brit, Ki and Ballard walking around the hillside like they were exploring.

Ballard yells "Hella' good news, my Zeke man. We just found the hole to hell's gate!"

"Nice, man, but no need to frighten the little lady before her big day tomorrow," Zeke cautions.

"That's okay, Zeke. I already understand what crawls beneath the crust."

Zeke explains. "Isadora has instructed that you be kept in a tightly closed jar so you don't flip your lid before tomorrow. Mama Jane also gave us all an ear full before we left."

"I guess Ballard missed that lecture then," I joke.

Almost out of breath, as they get closer, Ballard says, "Glad you guys made it. There's been a lotta activity moving up the road. We need to snake it to remain out of sight."

"What kind of activity?" Eli asks.

Aaron says, "Armed military forces. So far I've only seen them on the roads and not up in the territory where Ballard located the concealed alternate entrance."

"Let's hide this jeep behind that shed." Thurston points behind the rectangular home of our Peruvian hosts. A fenced garden surrounds the shed while goats and chickens meander around.

"Do you think they sense we're here?" I ask, concerned.

"Hopefully not yet and that's how we need to keep it," Ballard responds.

Thurston commands, "I want to leave early before sunup. We must sneak through those hills without making a single sound. It'll be best if Zeke, Brit, Arrack and Ki patrol the side lines with Ballard leading on the trail. Marcus, can you manage following the backside?"

I sense his reluctance, but he winks and smiles at me, saying, "Anything to demolish these bloodsuckers and tear down their net."

"Eli, Aaron and I will follow along with Lucy and guide her as long as we can," Thurston adds.

A small sliver of fright streaks through my body as I know there will be a point when I'll be alone and by myself. "I know Isadora will be communicating with me like a two-way radio as I descend deeper, but I want to have some kind of idea where I'm headed."

Thurston shares his expertise, "To be honest with you, Lucy, I've never been down in those caverns. Only those who serve the Dark agenda or haven't returned would be able to describe their adventure."

"When you see snakes crawling all over the damn place and smell a stench, then you're about to walk into the Vampires' den," Ballard bluntly states.

"Could you tone down the fear a little?" Eli says, his question masking a command.

"The girl has gotta know what to expect," Ballard replies.

"Don't worry guys. I'm not a scared little girl. This happens to be my mission to complete and I've accepted it. I only need to know where I'm heading." My declaration of bravery masks my nervousness.

"Proceed downward. We'll have to rely on Isadora as our radio signal. Oh yeah, and Aaron too," Thurston says.

Eli slips closer to me and softly says, "Just shine your light and don't let the darkness break you." He then kisses my forehead and cradles me for a moment.

I can't stop myself from glancing over at Aaron to see his reaction to Eli's affection. He stares off into the hills like he wants to keep from watching.

These incredible Peruvian people have been so gracious and warm. I challenge myself to eat a portion of a cow's heart as I want to appear appreciative. Our thick blankets are spread on the dirt floor, which causes me to be thankful for my own comfy bed at home. This two-room residence is such a different environment. I do feel safer from the lingering dark forces when all of my favorite people are nearby in these tight confines.

I close my eyes, but can't sleep, and so concentrate on lying next to Eli, fantasizing and running my fingers through his hair while he sleeps.

"I'm forgetting, Lucy." His voice quivers inside my head. Across the moonlit room, Aaron's sitting up against the wall. We're virtually alone, even with the sprawled sleeping bodies of our friends.

"What are you forgetting?" I ask, curious and wonder what he's implying.

"The longer I remain here, the more this planet inhibits me from remembering when you and I were once together. Its dense magnetic waves cloud my memory. I'm afraid I'll forget you entirely and who I am or where we come from."

I telepathically say, "You're asking the wrong person. The answers I have are from everyone else. I'm still trying to put the pieces together. I don't even know who I am except for small flashes of memory and images. For the last eighteen years, I've identified myself as Lucy Hayes, but who am I really? I have a past, but now I've become aware of a much longer history and infinite future, which confuses me greatly!

"Where does anyone ever start to comprehend that all beings are infinitely capable of creating a harmonious world in which all benefit? It's a fact of life and yet, a fake system has convinced the masses that we are separate and detached from each other. This only destroys our compassion and empathy for one another."

"That's what I've always loved about you, your bursting passion to light the way for others," he says. There's honesty in his words that I cannot ignore.

"What do you still remember about me, before I came here to be Lucy, the crafty stargate liberator?"

"Beautiful, powerful, an ambassador serving many benevolent star races. Not only do you passionately desire to save this planet from plummeting into eternal darkness, you want to save our entire Multiverse from these intruders' destructive actions on other perfectly ideal planets"

"Sounds like a big job."

"Yes, a well respected undertaking."

"Do I ever take a vacation?"

He snickers, struggling to be quiet. "You're an addict to blind human emotions, but you've already figured that out, haven't you?"

"I reasonably agree to that assumption."

"I love you and what we have can never die or be undone."

"What? You're just going to wait for me to come around. That's pretty sad from a human point-of-view, Aaron." I snap, responding to his tenderness.

"We're not human in the sense that you're describing." He changes the direction of our private thoughts.

"You're a fallen Light being and I'm an ascending, um, well, a Light being too, I guess. We would carry similar coding for the new human species that El Curandero called as the luminous ones," I say.

"I've also discovered that I have some kind of unique ability besides our telepathic communication," he says.

"What is it?" He doesn't answer me right away. "You're not gonna tell me?"

"I don't want you to take it the wrong way and I wouldn't misuse it either," he answers.

"But what is it?"

"Thought travel," he discloses.

"Any where? I nervously question.

When he doesn't answer right away, I begin to wonder if he could surface as a big surprise. This disclosure makes me feel a little vulnerable. "Have you and can you just show up without a warning?" I ask.

*What if he just shows up when I'm having a private moment with Eli?*

He hears my thoughts and says, "I wouldn't do that to you. I'm not that callous." I can feel that my thought hurts him deeply. "I haven't been able to travel more then a few miles from my location and it's still not exactly accurate where I arrive. When this mission's over, I'm going to experiment near the ancient stone away from people. I already scared a family by manifesting in their home. I don't want to do that again."

I laugh thinking about what this family must have thought seeing Aaron appearing out from nowhere. I affirm, "Yeah, probably a good idea."

He redirects the topic, "I don't know how much longer I'll be able to keep my memories from becoming fuzzier. It's difficult keeping it all straight and I get this sick feeling that I'm being cut off, severed from Source."

"You won't forget everything. There will still be a stirring restlessness and you'll recognize people and places regardless of whether the details are clear or not. I recognized you despite the fuzzy cloudiness."

"Yet, you want Eli as your boyfriend right now!"

"A great passionate love is all I've ever wanted since being a little girl. I want a normal Earth life. Once I ascend, there will be too many life experiences missed that I hold precious, like marriage and wild romantic lovemaking, bringing into this world new children of the Light and watching them growing up, through their different life stages, and even go-cart racing or eating cotton candy at a county fair."

"Go-cart racing? What's cotton candy?" He looks confused. I had assumed he already knew.

My eyes become heavy and groggy, I'm barely able to think, and "Perhaps I will have a chance sometime, maybe, to show you."

Aaron doesn't hold back and says, "Goodnight, my love."

I don't flinch.


Eli's stands above shaking me awake from my brief slumber. Instantly I jump up, realizing that today's the day. I wash up outside in a water basin. Everyone's ready and geared up. Isadora becomes visible walking beside me. We take the positions Thurston instructed as we walk silently into the hills.

The further we walk, the quieter it becomes. The stillness gets to me so I ask Isadora, "Why aren't there any animal or bird sounds?"

She responds, "The disharmonic resonance that blocks the stargate causes the living creatures to naturally move away if harmonics are at a dangerously low vibration."

"What about El Curandero and his family, including all the domesticated animals?"

"He and his family, along with other Light Warriors, anchor vortexes of Light within their bodies so living creatures flourish near their homesteads."

"It doesn't really feel that bad here."

"Animals are much more sensitive to these subtle vibrations as they are instinctively tuned in," she responds.

"That makes sense."

"You're very calm, Lucy."

"Yeah, I know. I have a whole Universe to save. There's no room for a catastrophic disaster to happen on this day."

# Chapter 26
# Reclamation

I'm the maiden about to be lowered into the mouth of the beast. I have no one to save me. How can anyone ever prepare for such a life altering moment like today?

Eli cradles me in his arms, holding tightly, unwilling to release me. I can see Aaron fighting back his irritation over Eli's shoulder. I want to hug Aaron, but I fight myself from reaching out to him. In the last seconds before the chase, I've decided to focus inflexible adoration only for Eli.

The loaded backpack isn't as heavy as I'd thought it would be. I have my instructions and at least I know Isadora will be remotely communicating with me if I need any counsel. I really hate entering dark places.

And now, the test.

Eli helps me put the harness around my waist and attaches the rope. Thurston lends a hand to lower me through the crack opening into the cavern. I watch their faces become smaller as I'm lowered to the ground. My foot searches for the bottom as the rope twists me around. The dirt feels sandy and rocky. Careful to not be too loud and announce my entrance, I pull hard on the rope signaling I've reached the bottom.

Isadora transmits directions, "Don't be afraid."

She's right as I notice my nerves are sucking up my energy. I take a deep breath to calm myself. She reminds me again, "Remember the power of the mind and heart."

I follow her observations and test the Light shield. I have to remain centered and in control of my emotions during this entire journey down the passageway of this dark cave. However, I want to irresponsibly throw in the towel and allow doubt to swallow me whole.

*I admit defeat!*

I'm ready to run far away from this place, but I can't. I'm the only option capable of holding the star codes suitable to maintain this shield and open the stargate. I know the task over-rules any degree of fear as I'm eager to get this done.

Sarcastically I think to myself, *what's the worst that could happen anyway? Probably become dinner for hungry Vampires who want only to consume my Light through blood and flesh. No problem!*

Isadora speaks again, "Expand this shield now, Lucy, and lock it in place."

"Lock it?" She never explained how to do this before.

"Seal it by attaching a pleasant thought or memory," she responds as my cranium reacts to her vibrating words. I move my jaw back and forth as the sensation feels weirder this time.

*I guess I'll just have to conjure faith that I can reach this stargate on my own.*

"It's time to get moving, Lucy," Isadora transmits.

This time I can't deviate from any trickery that might arise when I face a Vampire. I gaze at the Light shield to make sure it's working and I lock it by recalling the night when Eli's kiss felt like a collision of galaxies merging between us. I look up and blow a kiss towards the surface before I leave the fissure. I can see Eli, Thurston and Aaron peering down at me and I walk into the darkness with my Light shining brightly as I tread onward.

*I feel like a lightening bug.*

Roughly estimating the distance inside this cavernous abyss, I've advanced about a mile. I'm making good progress, but it's jarringly chilly the further the elevation drops deeper into the body of the Earth. I'm thirsty, but I don't stop. I stride as fast as I can, relying only on the Light radiating within me. It creates a bright beam to guide my steps. I stop when I come to a rope bridge. The shabby twine appears flimsy. I don't think the structure will hold me. Examining my location, I find that I'm standing inside a massive opening and can hear the chirping of bats and other strange noises. I mentally transmit a message to Isadora about the bridge. The same vibrating quiver resonates causing my teeth to throb.

*The distance underneath the bedrock must be the cause of this annoyance.*

Instead of giving me advice, she inquires, "Lucy, how are you doing?"

"Good so far. I haven't come across anything unusual other than this bridge. So what should I do about it?"

"Don't go on it!" she exclaims. "It's a trap."

"Then how do I get to the other side?"

"Just a sec," she says and I remain paused.

I talk to myself, "What's she doing? Thurston has an EM device that maps the subterranean earth formations. They're the lucky ones hanging out on the surface. I wish I could be with them right now instead of stuck layers beneath."

Minutes pass and I hear pebbles of rock beginning to fall from the overhang. It's not coming from me and a shot of panic lessens my shield. I notice the declining glow and concentrate on reliving that night again with Eli. Another sound echoes off the cave walls to signal that I'm not alone. I close my eyes, preparing for contact with whatever it might be while focusing only on the Light shield.

*I'm in control.*

Upon opening my eyes, I see that the Light adequately illuminates the cave. To my horror, I see slithery snakes beneath my feet and can now smell a putrid stench. Gathering my courage, I slowly lift my head and see pale creatures surrounding the edges of this hollow space.

*Vampires!*

I transmit this to Isadora while taking in a deep breath, thereby mustering my focus to not give into any splinter of fear.

Quickly I get a response back from the surface. Isadora says, "Keep your cool. You've already confronted Vampires before. Your Light will shield you, thus keeping them at a safe distance. They don't want to come any closer than they are now. They've been following this entire time, so don't let them intimidate you now that they're observable. It's time to initiate everything you've got, but first you have to walk around this ridge to your right."

"That's where these Vampires are positioned, Isadora!"

"They'll have to move as you approach them. Have confidence. Stare them down as if they're the intruders."

*Ugh, I'm just going to bear down and move quickly. They can get out of my way.*

I approach them, but cannot keep from staring. These Vampires are grossly disfigured creatures compared to Lamar's gang: their pasty, barely clothed bodies, fluorescent red glowing eyes, sharp claws and long protruding tongues, which wet their lips. Hissing sounds ricochet off the rocks and I see their tense bodies hurdle to avoid the Light coming too close as if this force would cause unbearable pain to their shadowy carcasses.

I cautiously arrive at the other side and come across another passageway. I glance carefully behind me and see thirty or so Vampires at least twenty feet behind me, still hissing and acting as if I'm their remedy for a quick fix like a drug. I'm not sure how much longer before I reach the stargate so I distract my fearful thoughts by musing over favorable moments with Eli as I increase my speed.

In between the reflections, the image of Aaron persistently pops into my view. Instead of invoking unidentifiable softness for him that I cannot nurture, I try remembering the actions he took to descend back into this realm, releasing his higher Light fields. He's now stuck here while I'm about to increase mine and enter the realm he just fell from. I already know that if Eli isn't in the same realm as me, I won't want to stay, regardless of how perfectly divine and wonderful it might be.

There seems to be more excitement in this realm anyway: Eli, Aaron, my family and friends, not to mention the upcoming big cosmic wave. I'd rather be in the middle of the greatest show in the Universe! There's a lot of adventure in my life after all and I can continue to help Light Warriors sufficiently tip the scale of power. I have a mission to fulfill, but free will and choice reign only after I'm released from my devout promise to open this stargate.

*I'll figure out the details later and hope I'll know what to do.*

I'm walking into some invisible pressure that painfully grinds and unnerves me. The unreal pulsation attempts to hinder my progress through the passageway. It's like walking into a web, but instead, a synthetic spinning net of energy must be the cause of this discomfort. The air suffocates me and my heart feels like someone is squeezing it. The energy becomes heavy and thick like walking through deep, rapidly flowing water, causing my ears to ring. Despite these grating hindrances, I force myself to move forward. My shield remains in tack regardless of the deceptive snare obstructing this stargate.

Slithery movements from behind me reaffirm that the Vampires steadily continue to follow. The cave walls narrow and I eerily feel enclosed like I'm trapped inside a coffin. I come upon a turning point intersecting left and to the right of me.

*Why do I feel cut off from Isadora and the rest?*

I can't get an answer from her.

*Okay, fine! I'm disconnected by this synthetic force field and with no guidance.*

I have to get a look so I close my eyes to trigger some kind of remote control device inside my mind. A part of me leaves as I envision an orb swirling through the right side of the passageway. I see an opening and find that both routes lead through to the other side into a grand hollow space. Confidently I take the right passage and walk until I come to this enormous surreal cavern.

Twelve massive statues carved from the cave walls encircle the room. I attentively examine the stone icons and realize differences in each. They seem to represent Star races that long ago openly walked on the surface of Earth. I identify six males and six females alternating around this circle and a giant, cloudy crystal centered on top of a stone column. Symbols decorate the circling stones and I become awestruck by the unfamiliar engravings.

*I feel like a vanguard pioneer uncovering a lost city.*

The thick atmosphere continues to pull at me as if I'm holding a ton of bricks. I don't dare take my backpack off as I must protect and guard the disks. I'm on my own down here and there's nobody to rescue me if I get into a mess.

One statue particularly captures my attention so I walk closer to study the monument. She is a beautiful nude female with wings, standing empty handed, unlike the other statues holding items and wearing clothes. The statue's feet form into lion's paws, signifying the Lioness in battle.

I whisper to myself, "This statue represents the goddess Inanna!" When walking deeper into the underground, I sense a likeness to the journey Inanna had once taken.

The Vampire shadows form on the walls behind the statues as they continue to wait for their lucky break to strike.

Quickly I jerk back as I hear the sound of footsteps behind me. A figure wearing a robe walks toward me. I can't see the features of this stranger as a hood covers the face. It stops at the rim of my sphere of Light. I wait for a response or possibly a horrible confrontation. More figures masked in the same garb step toward me now. I gather the strength and hold myself together. I tightly grip the straps on my shoulders, holding the backpack in place. There are at least five robed shapes, all standing in a semi-circle at a distance in front of me. Then a much taller, strangely cloaked figure approaches, close enough to break my shield. I take a step backwards. I'm scared, but feel strong. I'm furious at myself. I shouldn't have allowed myself to become distracted and I must locate the inlays for the disks right away.

I stand even closer to this figure as it pulls back its hood. This creature alarms me. I can't wrap my mind around what I'm seeing except for possibly a Naki? The others behind this creature remain cloaked. Amazingly, it speaks, but guttural and strident, first in a dialect I'm not versed in and then fluently in English. I'm completely amazed how this creature resembles a human looking dragon because of its scaly granular covering, the nodes on the forehead and its slivery, yellowish retinas. I assume he's male. Most likely, these creatures are the source of dragon stories as well as snake legends. Witnessing this exotic alien being unlocks any lingering illusions as my diminishing sense of reality has fallen to the wayside. More than anything in this moment, deception of what 'isn't' supposed to exist cannot gain victory over me.

Instead of being intimidated, I influence the Light shield to expand. This humanoid dragon moves backwards and I speculate as to whether these creatures might be the last remaining Naki watching over this stargate after the others left for Phobos.

*Did they stay to confront me?*

I've literally become the Dragon Slayer as Isadora continuously hammered into me almost everyday while in training. The reflection makes me amply brave. I clasp the stone pendant Mama Jane gave me as it stimulates my wisdom as to why I'm doing this in the first place: to widely release the iron restraints blocking this stargate before moving away from the great cosmic rift, which star codes, will help restore this lost planet back to a paradise.

This larger dragon, demon or Naki, all resembling the same likeness, roars while speaking in my language, "Do you really believe I will allow such a pathetic and weak child to open this gate?!" Arrogantly, he bellows out in laughter.

I don't allow myself to cower and shrink from the insult. Instead my heart-centered anger focuses on expanding the Light shield, impelling the creatures back once again. I confidently step toward the crystal stargate, surprised that by willpower alone, I have gained control over the situation. But I'm stopped! I can't move! Something has cut off the air flow in my windpipe and I'm suspended off the ground by an unseen force. I can't stop it and pain crushes my chest. The dragon beast has broken through my protective shield.

*How can that be?*

I'm a mouse about to be swallowed by a snake and I'm barely able to make a faint sound as pain ravages my body.

*How can this hateful and malicious creature triumph as the successor to a dark timeline? This cannot come to pass!*

My last remaining pieces of inspiration surge through me as I strain against the heavy force. Fearing what might occur if the stargate remains sealed, my heart aches. Laborious breathing diminishes my strength to resist and my reasoning mind wanders.

Too many people don't understand the power of our own spirit. Life is truly mystical. Having lost ourselves, humanity has become apathetic. If the worst can happen, then it's absolutely possible for the best to occur, which means we can reclaim our right to live freely and return the knowledge that has been deliberately veiled from our sight.

I hear shuffling and a clash of some kind of conflict. Struggling to discover the source of the noise and dangling above, I see two of the shrouded figures clasping reflective swords. Their hoods have been pushed back during the attack and one of the mysterious figures thrusts a sword into this beastly dragon. It nearly takes my last breath away. I drop hard to the smooth limestone ground, comforted by the cold temperature and relieved to be free of the pain. Vigorously coughing, I try to stand upright. I jerk away from the hand of one of the figures who just rescued me. She's speaking to me, but my mind's running in all directions from the shock and I can't understand her.

"Are you okay?" a soft feminine voice inquires.

I struggle to understand what just happened. "Yeah, who are you?"

"We are from the Naga race. We've been operating undetected by the Naki while secretly helping the Galactic Council of Light. We knew you were coming as we couldn't open the stargate ourselves since these disks in your satchel are the only keys not under the control by the Naki. Yes, we knew about this mission. Too much was at chance calculating the power that Lord Enu possessed.

"Who's Lord Enu?" I inquire.

"The Naki commander about to kill you until Elil stopped him. Our purpose has remained concealed until the given opportunity as Lord Enu had a crass fixation and planned to destroy you."

The other Naga that I presume to be Elil says, "We are sorry if you are hurt."

"No, I'm okay," I respectfully reply as I appreciate their help.

"There are many who have a hand in shifting the balance," he continues. Elil looks like a smaller, less aggressive version of Lord Enu. My attention is drawn to the female releasing some kind of powdery substance over each carcass, igniting it into flames and the evidence of their existence disappears.

"I am Ninna and this is Elil. Let's get this done. There isn't much time before the Vampires close in on us," She urges.

We walk up to the crystal stargate. Ninna, just about to speak, suddenly stops. Shadows bleed from the cavern walls, soaring at us. Panicked, I look to Ninna and Elil, seeking answers for our next best actions.

"Quickly, Lucy, take out the disks and place them each inside the keystone indentations! They fit like a puzzle."

Elil takes his sword and lifts it above his head in defense. I instantly thrust out my Light shield, but it's faintly dimmer after my contact with that dragon beast.

"Hurry, Lucy!" Ninna shrieks as she fights off these shadowy ghouls and now I can see the Vampires approaching.

I open the bag and grab the bronze disk.

"Where does it go?" I cry.

It doesn't fit inside this one. I fumble about like I have no fingers. Once I clear the dust inside, I can see an iron casing inside the keystone.

*The iron disk goes here!*

I run around matching the disks to the correct keystones while Ninna and Elil hold off these shadows and creatures. I'm about to insert the last disk, the gold one. I hear a cry from Ninna, "Lucy, tell everyone, not all of us want to live this way, hidden from sight!" The appalling shadows consume her until she vanishes. I don't see Elil. He must have come to the same end.

*Oh no!*

I have to act fast. I hastily shove the last disk inside the keystone and step back as something activates. Swirling blue colors start moving within the crystal until glowing flames spark, radiating and pulsing. I hear chilling shrieks coming from the Vampires as they run away and then shatter into fine dust. The energy is strong, very hot and sparks strike my face. This voltage pushes me off the ground. My body rises and my feet lift. There's no escaping and I come to terms that this is it.

*My grand Ascension!*

The waves pulse harder and I feel heat inside every cell within me. I choose to relax as it isn't painful, only an unfamiliar sensation. The stargate finally builds enough pressure to release a magnificent force. It's quiet and I only see Light with greater intense vibrant colors.

*Where am I?*

It's like I'm suspended out in a void. Only my thoughts are familiar as nothing else exists. There's no sense of space and I've lost all sense of direction. I see an orb off in the distance coming towards me. I'm thankfully happy that it's Isadora. A beautiful radiance illuminates her face. I've never seen her like this before.

"Isadora, have I ascended? What now?"

Her beauty shimmers and answers my questioning, "You're in the astral between the two realms. You've been inhibited from completing the full Ascension, assuming that this isn't what you want, at least not presently. Every sovereign being has a choice and you've already found the answer. The ascended goddess Inanna once stole the "me" from god Enki. The "me" represents *order out of chaos* and she was able to defeat Enki and bring back the knowledge to her sacred city on Earth. You have been given this knowledge as you carry it within your template.

"If you choose to continue the Ascension, the Earth remains blessed with the unsealed stargate as the released pressure now flows through the ley lines, and forcing the others to open. If you choose to descend back to Earth, you will carry this new template that holds more of your spirit within your body. Pieces of heaven will shine and it will show for all to experience. And, you can continue to reveal that which has been hidden, thereby defeating the darkness."

"And what should I do about Aaron? Eli?" I ask, perhaps expecting a magical potion.

She responds, "That is up to you to decide."

Disappointed from the lack of clarity, I already know what to do. There's no other choice, but to return.

Sarcastically making fun of the unusual circumstances I ask, "How do I get back home? Is there a special button I need to push or something?"

Isadora raises her hand and presses two fingers upon my forehead. Subsequently, I'm not sure if I fell asleep as my sense of time is twisted within this space, but I finally become aware of Isadora's voice again. Not only do I hear Isadora, I also can hear Eli's voice in the chatter. Then I detect Aaron's also.

"Ugh," I moan as I become aware of stiff, listless muscles.

*This isn't how a half-ascended being should feel.*

I try opening my eyes, but my vision's unfocused and I can't see with all the bright lights flashing around.

I hear Isadora's soft voice whispering inside my ear, "Reflect this piece of heaven for all to see. Be the shining light for others to find their way out of the darkness. Be the light, reflect the light."

Instantly I gain awareness and details of everything that has transpired: the journey to Peru, the stargate, being attacked and my brief visit to the astral realm. I pat my body to make sure I'm really physically back. The result thrills me as I've crossed back from the great divide. My eyesight returns, but the once gifted sight I received at the ancient stone is now enhanced.

*I'll have to get accustomed to this.*

Not only has my vision been given a boost, all of my senses have been amplified.

Aaron mentally transfers a private message to me, "You'll have new abilities and skills as the days progress. There will be more like us and they will need coaches."

*Wonder what special talent I've acquired? Can't wait to find out what it is!*

"I can't wait to find out too!" Aaron expresses.

*I can't get accustomed to the idea that he can hear my thoughts.*

I see Eli standing off to the side, patiently waiting, but cautious. I can see more visibly his faint alien like traits. Without hesitation, I excitedly whisk myself into his arms, kissing him. I'm delighted as he has openly accepted my charm, madly kissing me back without any hesitation. My impulse causes me to forget that we have company and I stop and awkwardly turn around. I finally realize that I'm not inside the cavern where the stargate resides and definitely not in Peru.

Confused, I ask, "What, how did I get back to Mama Jane's farm?"

Mama Jane approaches me, "Honey, it's because this is your home."

I'm still confused until Isadora explains, "It's been three days since the incident at the stargate."

"But how?" I ask.

Isadora clarifies, "You wished yourself back to the place you consider home."

Happy tears fill my eyes as I'm elated to be back and ready to continue contributing assistance as a Light Warrior in the biggest disclosure agenda that Earth is about to embark on.

# Chapter 27
# The Light Storm

It's cold outside, but the temperature doesn't bother me in the least as I gaze at the first light. The morning sun rises differently today as beams seem to dance across the sky. This recent change in appearance has sparked debate globally as to why the hues are so brilliantly displayed. Although, some of us already understand that the opened stargate has something to do with it.

The diminishing magnetic field and solar intensity has created more vibrant auroras lighting up the skies, indicating that now the biggest Earth changes are about to begin. I sit on Mama Jane's porch swing, valuing the treasure of the new colors the sky reflects. Its splendor cannot be verbally expressed.

I walk back inside the house to help Mama Jane with breakfast. We're all about to sit down and eat when Marcus forcefully throws the front door open and he stumbles over his feet like he can't get to the breakfast table fast enough.

"Look! The newspaper says 'Alien Boy Found in the Jungles of El Salvador' and right here it shows a picture."

I lean over his shoulder to look at the paper, thinking it to be a tabloid. I'm shocked as it's a reputable news source. It's weird and wonderful how bold it appears on the front page. The picture depicts a young-looking teen with less than human features! Similar to Eli's traits.

"This cannot be a coincidence. It must be the same boy locked away who Thurston and his crew have been trying to free," I shout, spiritedly.

"Read the article below this one!" Eli says, expressing his excitement.

I focus where he points at the paper. The article headlines, "Across the World: Mass Gatherings at Ancient Ruins." I quickly scan the words. It reads that masses of people are gravitating to these sites, publicly stating their demand to banish corruption worldwide, most importantly calling on all those with information regarding cover-ups to come forward. This mounting, assembled group offers security to protect all whistleblowers who speak out publicly and also to speak at these sites, revealing what they know.

Several pictures show men and women holding signs and it looks like they are chanting. Some wave peace flags while others hold hands in a long line encircling the ruins. One sign reads, "Truth cannot be denied."

"Madness!" Marcus yells, enthusiasm in his voice.

Eli lurches for the television set in the living room and turns it on. He finds a news channel. These public gatherings have reached the world news as the news anchors report the same details as the newspapers. I see thousands, maybe tens of thousands of people crowded together. They all look happy and cheerful as the cameras scan the crowds, but no threat of violence has taken place, although military police walk nearby in the event of any civil unrest.

One news anchor announces, "This recent movement outwardly demonstrates a nonviolent protest, a different approach to the riots breaking out near the crashed site."

Just as I'm about to yell out the question, the bottom screen flashes the headline of breaking news: "Crashed UFO Causes Riots at the Metropolitan Oakland International Airport." Then the news anchor switches to this breaking news. "It has been reported that the crash is, indeed, a genuine Unidentified Flying Object. People are rioting, demanding the truth from our world leaders and a US flag has been etched on the side of this alien spacecraft, causing many people to question the connection."

Another news anchor asks, "Now why would an unknown advanced technology display English inscription?"

"George, this is a good question. Unfortunately, the rioters have taken it upon themselves to find out before the officials perform their investigation."

The news anchor replies, "Roy, this event will not be easily covered up. It now re-opens the investigation as to if the crash at Roswell in 1947 was really true."

"Indeed, it does open the door for questions that now must be answered."

I turn to Marcus and ask, "How do you think it crashed?"

"Someone decided to shoot it down. Not just anyone has this kind of equipment and I don't believe the Dark Brotherhood would do this purposely. Someone got inside and wanted this level of exposure."

I ask, "But, what's happening here? Peaceful demonstrators and then angry riots?"

"More people have turned their focus from the negative to the positive timeline as evidenced at these ancient sites. I believe the real cause for this demonstration has not been encapsulated in the news yet," Eli explains.

Mama Jane wisely shares, "Where we place our focus is where the great shifting begins. This is just the beginning as the day has finally come for disclosure."

"Agreed. We are seeing the first developments and the masses of people are feeling the effects from the activated stargates across the globe," Eli agreeably acknowledges.

"Many voices can be heard when they truly are united. Real change will only be accomplished at the grassroots level," Mama Jane adds.

"Their sheer numbers are phenomenal, but it's going to take a lot more effort," Marcus says.

Zeke pipes in, "This is so awesome! The fact that the mainstream media has even published this information about the boy is a good sign and now it's snowballing; the boy, mass gatherings and now this crashed UFO."

"When did the masses begin congregating?" I ask.

"Looks like about two weeks ago, the same time we all got back from Peru," Marcus replies.

"I wonder if any of them know why they're gravitating to these ancient sites," I ask.

"If they don't know, then they must feel it stirring restlessly inside them, sort of like how birds can fly south always to the same location," Eli surmises.

Mama Jane elaborates, "The star codes flowing out from these ancient sites began this exodus. Down deep, they know a mystery waits to be revealed. Insistent actions will force the truth out."

"They need to know: who we are, why we're here and our history in order to know where we're going," I passionately state.

"Especially, before they start regaining their innate abilities lost since the invasion. It could cause mass confusion," Eli shares.

"The veins of the ley lines have been reawakened throughout the planet. Now it's up to us to start taking down the wall brick by brick; letting the people know about the star races and everything else that has been hidden. We, the Keepers, need to get louder. I believe it will be safer at this time, but we should still proceed with caution as we need a clever plan," Mama Jane advises.

"This movement must be causing extreme desperation among those who'll undoubtedly interpret it as a threat to their status quo, especially once they realize the game's up," Zeke adds.

"Almost all of the Naki are off the planet now and the Order of Draco are leaving too, but I suspect that the remainder of the Vamps are struggling with the activated grid system; trying to escape and move far away from it," Mama Jane says.

I ask, "Where do you think they're running to?"

Just then Isadora manifests and answers, "The mountain caves, as far away as they can get from the star codes pulsating from the activated ley lines. Some of them have literally lost it mentally and been captured by servicemen, fangs and all. This information hasn't been released to the public yet, but rumors are spreading.

"Why haven't they left? Don't they have the technology to return to wherever they came from?" I seek clarity as to why they just don't leave.

"No, they don't have the tech like the Naki or wouldn't know where to return to as they're abandoned descendents of their own Star race," Marcus states.

"Members of the Dark Brotherhood have to make a choice now. Either run and hide or tell the truth. They only have until we reach the edge of the great rift," Eli says.

"How do we proceed in the first place? I mean, how do we make things right on this planet once and for all?" I ask.

Eli answers, "Believing in humankind and the natural wisdom we carry in any crisis. We could start by speaking up at these gatherings as whistleblowers."

"We've been waiting for this moment!" I say excitedly.

But, won't they laugh at us? Who are we to show the world?" Marcus interjects.

"Who are you not to be, Marcus? Every one of us has to come forward now. These folks will know the truth when they hear it, but we have to speak out soon before the message becomes twisted by the remaining Dark Brotherhood," Mama Jane asserts.

Isadora shares, "Thurston and the rest of his crew are attempting to rescue this boy before the media coverage dies out and the Dark Brotherhood generates an alternate story to claim he's nothing more than a hoax and right now, their desperation poses more danger to the boy. They will kill him if given an opportunity."

"Thank God that hasn't happened yet! This boy must have some mad skills to keep himself alive under so much threat," Zeke states.

I wonder, "Why didn't they just kill him a long time ago if he was such a risk to expose their secrets?"

"They're afraid so they took grafts and studied him. He's one of many homo-luminous, one of the new humanoid species on this planet," Mama Jane says.

"Where is the boy right now, Isadora?" Eli asks.

"In a village outside San Salvador with a family that found him wandering in the jungle when the Peruvian stargate was activated. Thurston and his crew are detecting much escalating violence as the locals are showing signs of fright because of his disclosure," Isadora answers.

"The villagers are very superstitious people," Mama Jane adds.

"Thurston has asked me to report to you that this situation is getting worse. He doesn't know how to get out of the area safely yet. They need help," Isadora says.

"Why doesn't the GC interfere in such an important case?" I ask, bewildered.

"It would make things so much easier, wouldn't it?" Zeke scoffs.

"They won't interfere if they don't have to. We have to do the work ourselves or our species will never learn," Mama Jane clarifies.

"Well, looks like we need to help Thurston get the boy to a safe place and bring him to these gatherings while we still have the chance to tell our story," Eli announces.

"It's a first step," Mama Jane says.

"More whistleblowers will certainly surface and start talking once the masses of people show their support," Eli says.

"And, that it's safe to speak out openly too," I add.

"Hum, it might just work," Isadora confirms, a smile crossing her face.


After a quick breakfast, everyone disperses to formulate a great plan of action. I head to the bathroom next to my borrowed bedroom while sketching ideas in my mind. The more people who see the alien boy in person, the better for the disclosure and we must act fast.

I'm also distracted since I just found out yesterday from Mama Jane that they all want me to move in permanently. It's a great solution to my new life living on the farm. I'll be much closer to Eli and my extended family. I plan to break the news to Mother when she gets back in a few weeks from her trip. I suppose living close to Aaron makes it more difficult, but I cannot refuse the invitation to move in.

*Interesting how I haven't seen Aaron all morning. Wonder where he disappeared to?*

School starts up again soon. I'm not looking forward to it, but will endure the customary daily grind to still earn that college document, even if I might not have time to actually complete it. I have no idea what tomorrow will bring as we move forward with this disclosure agenda. We're all in this together. It's rather exciting, but nerve-racking at the same time since too many unknowns exist as to how it will all play out.

I grab my towel and tie it around myself as I get out of the shower. I hum a blissful tune, deeply immersed in the moment, when Eli enters my thoughts as I reach out for my hairbrush.

*I wonder what he's doing right now.*

I'm about to set the brush down when I suddenly notice the counter isn't there.

*Where am I?*

I'm not in my bathroom when I loosen my grip and the brush drops on the hard wooden barn floor. All I see are shoes belonging to Eli. After a long purposeful gulp, I look at him, humiliated at having only a towel around me with absolutely no makeup. I look up, wondering how I arrived from my bathroom to be standing almost naked in front of Eli. I see Aaron coming down the stairway from the loft, his face masked from betraying any emotion, but he snickers.

Eli says, "Lucy! Did you see what you just did? I mean, you instantly materialized right before me!"

I ponder this enigma and slowly try to understand what just occurred.

Aaron says mentally to me, "I see you've discovered your new ability."

I think it's rude to keep Eli from my private discussion with Aaron, so I openly state, "And what's that?"

"By the looks of things, you were in the bathroom. Now you're here," Aaron explains.

I must be slow or shock has stalled my brain from making the connection quicker. "It can't be," I softly say.

I've always wanted that ability to travel by thought. "I was just thinking about Eli and that's when I transported myself here in the barn standing right in front of him."

"Why couldn't you've thought about me while in the shower?" Aaron telepathically says. I scowl at him. I'm glad Eli didn't hear that comment.

"So I can read emotions, telepathically communicate, slow time, hover above the ground, fight off Vamps with a force shield and now mentally transport myself," I formulate the most incredible in my bizarre new world. "Aaron, you can do this too. Show me how it works." I demand.

"Of course, and by the way, I was out this morning practicing in the woods and I think I transported myself somewhere much farther away. I think in Africa because I know elephants and giraffes don't roam wild near here," Aaron says.

"That's amazing! Do you know what that means? We might be able to thought travel all the way down to where Thurston needs our help in El Salvador. Eli, Aaron, I really have to try this out to see if I can reach Thurston, but first I'll get some clothes on."

I shout enthusiastically, "Bye, boys." Then I think of my bathroom, feeling utterly blissful and in a snap, I'm back standing in front of the mirror. I am a little shaken, knowing that I now have such a talent. No need for my car. Then I realize I've forgotten my hairbrush on the barn floor so I imagine myself standing in the same spot, feeling happy at the same time. I arrive and grab it where it remains on the planks, while holding tightly onto my towel still wrapped around me. I wave goodbye to the boys who are now talking to each other and then I return in the same way to finish my morning rituals.

I hurry and, without thinking, I use my legs and run to the barn to find Eli and Aaron. I'm buzzing with excitement when I find the two of them standing together. But once again, my surging emotions incite my attraction for both of them at the same time. I cannot resist their incredibly powerful forces as they stand side-by-side.

*My emotions can stir up a storm of trouble if not regulated correctly.*

I haven't the willpower to deal with this right now, so I blow it off by diverting my thoughts to more important things, such as this new ability.

"Aaron, how did you get to Africa? I mean, how do we locate Thurston and the boy."

"You want to know my secrets, huh?" he says, sending me a flirty look. I glance at Eli and he frowns, probably from knowing that Aaron will be my teacher for the day instead of him. I wish that Eli could thought travel with us.

"How do we do this?" I impatiently ask again.

He begins to instruct me, "Envision the image to where you want to go. Then feel the place inside here." Aaron takes his tightened fist and positions it exactly in front of his heart, signaling his intention that thought and emotion must work together in order to thought travel. "Most importantly, believe in its power to work," he adds.

Eli asks Aaron, "Can you take any equipment with you while traveling this way?"

"I don't know. Let's try," Aaron replies.

"Take this phone. I need to talk with Thurston," Eli says to me. He hands me a bulky military cell phone and I slip it inside my front jean pocket, which stretches the fabric as it's a tight fit. He then hands me something else. "Here's a tazer just in case you need it. Who knows where you might show up?"

I hand the tazer to Aaron, not wanting to carry it as it intimidates me since I don't know how to use it.

"Okay, so should you go first?" I ask Aaron.

"Take my hand and let's see if we can go together." I look at Eli after Aaron says this and he motions that he agrees with his idea. I grab his hand and it feels warm against mine.

"Think about the location. See Thurston and this boy and only focus on their energy signatures," Aaron instructs.

Before I know it, we are sent somewhere. Not sure where, but it's a jungle. The massive tropical trees shade the incoming sun. I'm still holding onto Aaron's hand when I scream, "Aaron, Look out!" I see a machete being thrown at us. Luckily it misses.

"Quick, let's try this again," Aaron states.

This time I close my eyes while focusing solely on Thurston and all the details of what he looks like, his facial features, the clothes he wore the last time I saw him and even his scent. I begin to hear talking, and Thurston's voice bellowing out. I open my tightly closed eyes to regain my focus again and witness Thurston standing before us. I'm still holding onto Aaron's hand with an iron grip because having a machete thrown at us scared me.

"Lucy, Aaron!" Thurston shouts, delirious with joy at seeing us. I look around and it appears that we're in a basement. Several others are in the room with us, including Ballard and Brit.

"Where's Arrack?" I ask.

"Upstairs in the kitchen," Ballard responds.

I'm elated to see all of them, even though it hasn't been that long since our jaunt to Peru. I grab the cell phone from my pocket, relieved that it made it with us. I dial the number to see if it works, then quickly hand it to Thurston while saying, "Here, Eli wants to talk to you."

I scan the room searching for the boy, but I see nobody that looks alien. Then across the barely lit room, he turns around. To my amazement, he's absolutely radiant. He appears extraordinarily different. His ears are pointy and his eyes are almond shaped just like Isadora, with irises that shimmer rainbow hues. His delicate features soften his fair skin and a slender body. His head is shaven closely or he doesn't have any hair. I see his back cranium is elongated. Similar to the images I have seen of the ancient royal class of Egypt and Peru.

He looks benevolent when he genuinely smiles as we make eye contact. I feel his words dancing toward me as he telepathically says, "Lucy, I knew you were on your way to us." I'm awestruck as this teenage boy emits extreme compassion, wrapping me in a psychic cocoon as we speak.

"Nice to meet you, um, I don't know your name," I say to him.

"My name is Jeffrey. You can call me Jeff if you'd like."

*What a common name.*

Telepathically he responds, "My parents gave me a standard earth name. What did you expect? Zorto or Jay-12?" He's quite humorous.

"Are your parents from here?" I ask, curious about his background.

"From Earth, yes. Human? Not entirely. As you already know, we live amongst you and consider ourselves part of the family tree, just a different variety of fruit. I, on the other hand cannot be controlled by the mandatory cloaking devices. I'm not going to hide. I like the way I look, I think I'm quite handsome," he says, wittily.

I find Jeff to be impressively headstrong.

He continues, "I've been placed inside a circus, been caged for too long and I'm tired of the big lie." He leans closer to me, telepathically saying, "You do know they aren't that smart. Clever, but blind from seeing the bigger picture."

"Are you referring to the Naki and Draco?"

He replies, "Anyone who claims to be proud members of their secret Brotherhood. They think like robots, collecting data, but can't see how it all fits together."

From his statement, he must have learned a great deal about them. "You've been locked up in that facility for how long?"

"Almost my entire life," he responds.

Thurston gets off the phone with Eli and shares, "They reduced Jeffrey's defenses by piercing him with disharmonic technologies. The same kind of gadget used to block the stargates, but directly centered on him."

"That sounds torturous and painful. Were you scared?" I ask.

"Only their fear scared me," he says.

Admiring him, I respond, "You're very strong. I've heard about their tactics and mind-programming."

His eyes light up, "Reversing the disinformation and propaganda by exposing the big lie to millions of people will erase all those years locked away in that facility."

Aaron looks at me, and then toward Jeffrey. He asks, "Do we know what we're going to say once we arrive?"

"We come in peace?" I laughingly blurt out.

"The majority of people already believe that we're not alone in this Universe. It won't be too tough," Thurston adds.

Suddenly, an overwhelming feeling hits me that we need to rush before the opportunity closes. I impatiently demand, "Let's hurry!"

I reach out for Jeffrey and grip his arm. Aaron repeats the same gesture. I look at Aaron and ask, "Wait, which gathering are we showing up at?"

"I thought you'd know?" he replies.

"Giza. I've always wanted to see the Sphinx in person." I announce, hoping we can rematerialize with Jeffrey in the right spot. I'm confident that I can envision the Sphinx in my mind. But I don't know if Aaron can? "Do you know what our target location looks like?"

"Of course, the Sphinx has been a long standing relic that dates all the way back to the last Golden age. I was here during that time, although it looks a lot different today. It was tropical and lush back then. Now it's all sand."

I'm very interested in learning more about the olden days as Aaron still possesses clear memories, hoping that listening to his stories may perhaps awaken my own memories.

Together we close our eyes, at the same time, holding onto Jeffrey. I picture us standing on top of the Sphinx, thinking about what that might look like. I begin to imagine what senses can be felt.

I notice that the air feels different and hot. We've reached our destination and I hear what sounds like thousands of people gasping and yelling. When I open my eyes, I see their shocked faces as I look down at them. We may have startled the crowds by appearing out of nowhere.

I'm relieved that Jeffrey has arrived with us. Now we have to think on our feet. There's no time for stage fright. Its dark outside, but the flood lights make it bright. I step a few feet in front of me and confirm that we literally are standing on top of the Sphinx. Helicopters are flying above shining lights everywhere and the security guards look agitated for some reason.

Isadora shows up, "They are about to start firing rubber bullets into the crowds."

"But why?" I ask.

"To break up the unity and cause confusion. The high orders have come from the Dark Brotherhood, spreading fear in the ears of uninformed leaders. It's not just happening here, but at all the gatherings. They don't want the truth out."

I see many people with camera phones and know that we will hit the airwaves soon, which is about to go viral. I take this desperate moment to speak out.

I yell as loud as I can, speaking from my heart, "Humanity has been lied to! We have been led astray to believe that magic is nothing more then folklore. Humanity is capable of great things! We are the ones we've been waiting for. Change cannot occur unless we understand our true history. We share ancestry with the star races! And we have the power within us to improve our existence on the planet for all of us, not just the few!"

I wait to see what kind of response I'm about to get, while looking out for flying rocks or arrows of fire to come barreling at me. Instead, the crowds are quiet. I'm not sure if they heard what I said or if their silence has to do with being shocked by Jeffrey's form. I conclude that it must have something to do with the combination of Jeffrey's appearance, materializing in front of them, the crashed UFO and the message I've just announced. Even the security guards have stopped to listen.

At this precise second, the ambassador within me is born; the emissary that Aaron and Isadora said they know me as in their realm. In this moment, I thread the pieces together to see that timelines and dimensional planes are one and the same. Aaron isn't from my past, but my future. I have arrived here as a time traveler, piercing the veil between the physical and non-physical realities. Everything that I am exists in my mind: compartmentalized in timelines, dimensions and separated by walls of attained knowledge. Somehow, what we do right now for Earth, will have a huge impact on the future of all dimensional realms. This is why I'm here at this precise moment in time. As I stand at this moment atop the Sphinx, I know that we as a planet are about to create the next renaissance of empowerment. Do we take the higher road or the lower one? I know we've stepped out into a different world as I look out and see smiling faces expressing optimistic liberation. I have complete faith in the people.

"I think they got the message. It's time to get moving," Aaron telepathically communicates to me.

He's implying that we should thought travel to the rest of the gatherings: sharing the same message to others that it's okay to believe in aliens and the mystical world.

# Chapter 28

# A New Day

The President of the United States, appearing on television before the entire world, begins, "My Fellow citizens, it is important that we remember that humanity has not changed. We are still the grocer working at the corner market; the mother dropping off her kids at daycare on the way to her job; or perhaps a preacher delivering a sermon. But what has changed is our viewpoint of what it means to be a human from Earth. Only moments ago, I was briefed on matters concerning authentic extraterrestrial life.

"You may wonder who is telling the truth. Anything of which I am about to say can be denied, except that staying hidden under a rock does nothing to support the challenges that may lie ahead for us. There is a choice here to be made. We can choose to be afraid or we can light a new path for all citizens around the globe.

"It will take many months and different solutions to redeem all the wrongdoings and reset the rules in order to improve the standard of living in every nation. Games have been played and many rules broken in order to support only a few. Pointing fingers will not solve our problems. The acts of evil can only be redeemed by shining light on secrecy and denial and then making improvements. Instead of focusing on anger, we must focus on rebuilding and shaping our future. Only we can decide what that will look like.

"Earth has been at ground zero because of insidious programming. I recently have been informed by those in charge of this propaganda that it is time for the United States to instigate a world war as a distraction from the recent events. I will state here that I have not been aligned nor involved with this private group causing so much trouble globally. Just like you, I have recently been handed information concerning and exposing these aggressors. This secret group has lost its power and is disintegrating as I speak. We cannot allow room for any more lies and must reveal the truth to all those who choose to listen.

"We have been looking for alien life through our satellites and technology when, in fact, all we need to do is look next door. Not only in our neighborhoods, but throughout the entire Galaxy. Intelligent life exists on Earth, but on other planets as well. It has come to my attention that elite groups more influential than the presidency have funded black projects supporting off-world secret space programs. Advanced technology does exist and will reshape the way we live our lives on this planet, including providing more green living and sustainable products.

"A great mystery has been revealed this momentous day: that we are not alone in this vast Universe. Earth has been visited and inhabited by our space brothers and sisters for a long time. The only cost to acknowledging this information is that we must rewrite our history books. We also now realize that Earth was first visited and inhabited thousands of years ago rather than first occurring with the recently crashed UFO.

Most of us now presently alive know nothing about this. Some may ask, how could the President of the United States be unaware of this? I have been under the same disillusionment as most people on this planet. Now is not the time to point fingers. We must focus on how we choose to view and manage this situation. Nothing will be accomplished by reactionary hostility. We must move into this new evolution of our world with courage and I pray that you join me in our new quest.

"At this time, our scientists have discovered a cosmic wave, soon to bombard our planet. It confirms from ancient writings that this is a reoccurring event. We must remain calm and un-afraid for the sky is not falling. I guarantee you that it is not. There will be confusion and possible fear, but this does not mark the end of life on the planet, but only a shifting in our conscious-ness about the concept of time and what we choose to create in the next procession of the Ages. Our planet is moving into a pristine age where dreams do become a reality. Do not focus on despair, but on ways in which to bless Earth. Many people lack foresight, but we together must become visionaries to explore new concepts and vistas. Out of every great ending arises a new beginning. We have the power to rise to great heights on what has been learned today.

"I will now open for questions."

Eli turns the television off.

With tears welling in her eyes, Mama Jane says, "It's really happening. I'd thought this day would never come."

I sit quietly, mulling over the President's statements. We had all gathered around in the living room to hear the speech, except for Jeffrey as we had taken him to his friend Dan's place in Ecuador, a better environment for his needs, he said.

"I had hoped to hear more, as it still lacks much more information, but at least it is a start in the right direction," Eli states.

Zeke is skeptic. "I seriously doubt the Presidents' claim that he's just now been briefed on all this."

"Truly we don't know the answer, Zeke. Everyone should be outraged, but the President is right. We need to rebuild. To do so, we all must unite to determine how to fix this damn mess the Dark Brotherhood left for us to clean up," Mama Jane says.

"The world hasn't stopped. New wars haven't launched and the backlash of people everywhere seems to be pretty hopeful, despite some of the riots," Aaron says.

"It's not like it's a big shock to find out officially that they exist or that sinister aliens have masqueraded as some of our leaders. When it comes right down to it, we all have a little alien inside us," Marcus adds.

"I'm still trying to determine how the bigger Universe works. Someday I know I'll have all the answers, but for now it's fun trying to figure it all out," I say.

Eli directly states to me, while he smirks, "There is so much to uncover and you have an important role to play as a promising, new, apprentice ambassador."

Aaron and Eli both tell me what budding new abilities I possess, but I still struggle with lack of confidence. I know in time it won't be an issue and for now my life is full of adventure, and love.

I sum it all up, "There are no endings, only new beginnings. Everything happens for a reason. None of us are meant to flounder around waiting for someone else to fix the problems. The hope and results that we all seek cannot happen by just one of us alone. It will not be one man or woman to save the world, but an entire storm of Light Warriors willing to blow the whistle and raise the roof. Now more than ever is the time to shine the Light."